ALSO BY MICHAL GOVRIN

The Name

 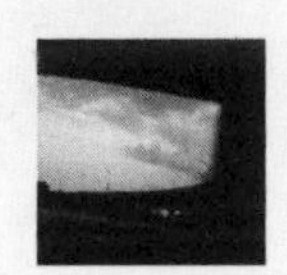  

RIVERHEAD BOOKS

a member of Penguin Group (USA) Inc.

New York 2007

SNAPSHOTS

Michal Govrin

Translated from the Hebrew
by Barbara Harshav

RIVERHEAD BOOKS
Published by the Penguin Group
Penguin Group (USA) Inc., 375 Hudson Street, New York, New York 10014, USA • Penguin Group (Canada), 90 Eglinton Avenue East, Suite 700, Toronto, Ontario M4P 2Y3, Canada (a division of Pearson Penguin Canada Inc.) • Penguin Books Ltd, 80 Strand, London WC2R 0RL, England • Penguin Ireland, 25 St Stephen's Green, Dublin 2, Ireland (a division of Penguin Books Ltd) • Penguin Group (Australia), 250 Camberwell Road, Camberwell, Victoria 3124, Australia (a division of Pearson Australia Group Pty Ltd) • Penguin Books India Pvt Ltd, 11 Community Centre, Panchsheel Park, New Delhi–110 017, India • Penguin Group (NZ), 67 Apollo Drive, Rosedale, North Shore 0632, New Zealand (a division of Pearson New Zealand Ltd) • Penguin Books (South Africa) (Pty) Ltd, 24 Sturdee Avenue, Rosebank, Johannesburg 2196, South Africa

Penguin Books Ltd, Registered Offices: 80 Strand, London WC2R 0RL, England

First published as *Hevzekim* in Israel in 2002 by Am Oved

Published simultaneously in Canada

Lines from Marina Tsvetayeva, "Yesterday He Still Looked in My Eyes," translated by Elaine Feinstein, are quoted from *Selected Poems of Marina Tsvetayeva* (Dutton, 1981).

Library of Congress Cataloging-in-Publication Data
Govrin, Michal, date.
[Hevzekim. English]
Snapshots / Michal Govrin; translated from the Hebrew by Barbara Harshav.
p. cm.
ISBN 978-1-59448-959-4
I. Harshav, Barbara, date. II. Title.
PJ5054.G665H4813 2007 2007028036
892.4'36—dc22

Printed in the United States of America
1 3 5 7 9 10 8 6 4 2

BOOK DESIGN BY MEIGHAN CAVANAUGH

The unicity of the poem depends on this condition. You must celebrate, you have to commemorate amnesia, savagery, even the stupidity of the "by heart": the hérisson.

It blinds itself. Rolled up in a ball, prickly with spines, vulnerable and dangerous, calculating and ill-adapted (because it rolls itself up into a ball, sensing the danger on the highway, it exposes itself to the accident).

JACQUES DERRIDA

R. Joseph learnt: "If thou lend money to any of my people that is poor by thee" [this teaches, if the choice lies between] my people and a heathen, "my people" has preference; the poor or the rich—the "poor" takes precedence; thy poor and the [general] poor of the town—thy poor come first; the poor of thy city and the poor of another town—the poor of thine own town have prior rights.

TALMUD BABA METZIA 71A

The writings of Aaron Tzuriel are based on *We Were as Dreamers,* by Pinchas Govrin (the author's father).

SNAPSHOTS

When the call came from Alain, it took me a while to make out who was talking. The strained voice (as if he hadn't stopped running since that night) obscured the reserve I remembered.

"Ilana was killed in an accident on the Strasbourg–Munich autobahn. Yes, she was driving alone, at night, to lecture at an architects' convention . . . I went with the boys to the funeral in Haifa . . ." he managed to say before his voice cracked.

I didn't really understand what he was talking about, through the screen of shock. He had called me. The first one he thought of. Because of the language, of course.

"Personal notes . . . were in her handbag . . . everything in Hebrew. It will take me years to decipher. You know, our personal abyss . . . Yes, the sooner the better, Tir-sa . . . Tomorrow, if you can . . ."

And then, the next afternoon: the apartment at the top of the tower, among the other buildings of the construction site on the Seine. And the distant gleam of Pont Mirabeau capering at the bottom of the glass wall, behind Alain's back, outlined in the armchair. He practically didn't budge the whole time. Becoming a black negative etched on my pupils.

Alain Greenenberg. Ilana's husband. Historian. Scholar of the Holocaust. As I remembered him from our single, fleeting encounter. Fair hair slewed to the side, his look pensive. Coming out of the café as I came in to meet Ilana. Apologizing politely, departing with a quick handshake.

He greeted me at the door with the same tweed jacket and the same remote courtesy. Drops his hands, doesn't seem to know what to add beyond the few bits of information. (Less than half an hour. Almost no word of the accident, or the sons, or their plans now. And I, facing him, imprisoned in the inanity of routine words.) "About one in the morning, according to the police. In the Black Forest. Killed instantly. The ambulance took her to Paris. We buried her, as she would surely have wanted, in Haifa."

Then he placed a bundle in my hands. "Here, Tir-sa."

The only time he looked straight at me, and for a moment pain gaped from his pallid face.

"Lana's notes. You'll know what to do with them."

May 21, 1991. Sitting across the living room table. And only the scrunch of Alain's eyebrows hints at what wasn't said explicitly.

Then we stood up, Lana's file of notes in my hands, the gleam darting from the bend of the river erasing the dusk of Alain's face. Next to the stereo was the CD of *Don Giovanni*. Alain dropped the *Frankfurter Allgemeine* on top of it, pointing to the door. We passed the open door of his study. Cartons of documents, piles of paper, photographs I couldn't identify upside down. We walked in silence, first mine, then his mute steps.

The little I knew of him came from Ilana. "Born in Czernovitz. A child in the war . . ." That's how she summed up the components of his life, the story of their complicated marriage (the presence of absence, all that was silenced), his double life in that international group of historians, attorneys, prosecutors—mostly Jews, taciturn, survivors like him, always on the move, tracking down aging war criminals with fake identities, budding neo-Nazi organizations. Fascist cells, assemblies, publications, websites. Revisionism, denial, obliteration of history. Money laundering, cooperation with the international terror network, the disease fomenting under the roots of Europe, spreading to America, the Third World. They gather evidence, catalogue.

And then we were standing at the door. He held his hand out to me and said, "I'm not sure if I'll be able to help, Tir-sa . . . but if you have any questions, you can get in touch, of course. . . ." His look still gaping, as if he were about to add something.

Then he quickly lowered his eyes. "Goodbye, Tir-sa," he said and brushed aside the hair that had dropped, and retreated to the door with an embarrassed bow, before I turned to the elevator.

In the sinking elevator Ilana's profile hovered before me, flickering through the mane of black curls, looking into the distance. As then, the last time we met, when she landed in Paris in late December, before the Gulf War, on her way back from America, before she went with her sons to Jerusalem. We sat on the glass terrace of the café near the Centre Pompidou. Her hair caught the winter light, surrounding her with a halo that enhanced the sculpted beauty of her face. The full lower lip, the wide, doe-like, almost haunted look that lent her a new softness. She said a few words about her parting from Alain, "I think this time it's the end," and fell silent. Gazing at something with empty eyes.

As the elevator door opened, it occurred to me that in fact this was the first time I had been in her apartment. And all trace of her seemed already obliterated. As if somebody had seen to that.

Outside, in the shrill light on the marble plaza between the towers, the note that had gone on buzzing since Alain called died down a little. I meandered back to the Métro between the pits and cranes of the construction site, over Pont Mirabeau and the gray rippling rustle of the Seine, gripping her papers, Ilana's—Lana's—the object of my pounding heart all these years, under the casual disguise of our relationship. The two adolescent girlfriends from Haifa, brought together again, by fate, in Paris.

I never really dared to hope for any sort of relationship with her. Not even during the twenty years we both spent in the City of Light. She certainly didn't know that I had emigrated, and I kept my distance, keeping track of her through rumors—outstanding student of architecture at the Technion in Haifa ("That's an inheritance, to build and be rebuilt by it . . ."), leaving Israel because of her radical leftist involvement, studies at the Beaux-Arts. Then opening an office in Paris, the innovative plans, communes in Marseille,

"Lodgings of Life," "Feminine Architecture," international renown, and a trail of gossip about her stormy life before and after her marriage to Alain. And her two sons, six-year-old David, and Jonathan, born after we reconnected three summers ago. For a whole hour I hesitated in a store in Montparnasse about what gift to buy, standing intoxicated among the baby clothes and the toys: I, a skinny, childless woman whose only structure in life was a position as professor of narratology in the literature department of the Sorbonne, the appointment I paid for with many hours hunched over manuscripts, and honing the sting of my style.

All those years in Paris, I didn't try to wipe out the distance between us. I hid behind the embarrassment left over from the camaraderie we believed existed once—"in the Youth Movement." Now and then I'd come across a picture of a field trip to Mount Arbel: Lana at the top of the cliff, against a backdrop of the valley of the Sea of Galilee and the mountains of Bashan, legs slightly splayed, with her bold beauty, laughing, hugged in the arms of the counselor, her boyfriend for the last two days, who looks at her, confused by the realization of his dream of hugging her. And on the bottom step of the rock, smiling, with eyeglasses, me, a backward little girl, on my first field trip with the Movement, not really understanding my role in the relationship above me, just grateful to Ilana for inviting me to be in the picture. I'm completely lost in the dry landscape I was thrown into from the "Gomulka Aliyah" from Poland in the sixties—the temporary apartment downtown, the unpacked cartons, Father trying to fit in as an engineer at the shipyards at the port, talking about Gdansk, and Mother, who went to the market in the lower city, and fled home from the "Levantine coarseness" to the fine china from Poland.

And then our meeting by chance five years ago at the opening of an exhibition in the Musée Galiera. Her dazzling beauty that had deepened with the years, sailing toward me through the crowd of guests: "Tirtsa? Tirtsa Weintraub? I don't believe it!" She wound her arms around me, holding me to her tiny, perfect body, flooding me with the ring of her laughter.

And the bursts of joy ever since. Something of that distant youthful intoxication, or the nameless joy after we got back in touch, the tremor at hearing Ilana's voice declaring in the receiver, once or twice a year, at the end of one of her trips—

"Tirtsa! My second phone call in Paris!"

Summoning me, "I'm dying to see you, Tirtsa . . ."

And I become addicted to waiting. Gulping the days, the hours until we meet. And the meetings, ending not long after the joy of hugging and shouting—in Hebrew—and the taste of family she seemed to need enough to keep making dates. And after a little quick chatter, she'd jump up from her chair, cascades of black hair and a dazzling smile, and announce she had to run. Gathers up her handbag (the one she had with her on her last journey), hugs me, then leaves me alone facing the cup imprinted with her lipstick.

Ilana's father, Aaron Tsuriel, I remembered from my few visits to their apartment back in high school, when he'd linger next to me and declare with a soft smile: "Tirtsa, the dreamer, Tirtsa, you know what Herzl says: If you want it, it is no dream." In my eyes he became the exemplar of the "Pioneers"—those tough old people, with burned faces, bony gestures, hewn Hebrew. The generation of Titans.

Her mother I almost didn't remember, except for a later meeting in the Carmel post office. I was on leave from the army, surviving with foggy senses the months of complete obliteration at the base in the Negev. And suddenly, Ilana's mother, in a flowery summer dress and a cloth hat—

"Where in Poland does your family come from?"

"Gdansk. Originally Warsaw. During the war my parents escaped to the Urals. My brother and I were born there . . ." The words burst out of me through a crust of silence.

"I'm from Warsaw, too," she said excitedly. "I left home at twenty-one. With the Youth Movement. Father and Mother were ultra-Orthodox. They wept, but they gave me their blessing . . . Father had a butcher shop, in the market of Warsaw. Katz. The Katz family. All of them were killed . . ." She thrusts out her face, covered with age spots and freckles. And then it was her turn at the counter.

How could I imagine what would burst out of Lana's pages. The little bit about her mother. And all that had been hidden, all the years, between her and her father.

I found out about Sayyid only from reading. I should have guessed. Her great excitement this past year about the binational performance at the cornerstone-laying ceremony on the site of "Mount Sabbatical."

I probably refused to listen. As when she'd casually mention others, in one sequence with her stories about the trips, and the projects, and the prizes, and mischievous descriptions of her sons. I protected myself, apparently. Kept my own Ilana, one who didn't disturb the sediment of my yearning too much.

Now a few words about the notes: the fragmentary nature of Lana's legacy ("snapshots," as she put it) made it very hard to decipher (even though that's clearly not the only reason for my continued long involvement with the material). With the limited means of my old Hebrew computer program, I tried to find a fragmentary layout, smiling at myself for the tension between form and content—"my professional expertise."

I have also prepared for publication, as an appendix, some preliminary drafts for "The Settlement of Huts" and "Mount Sabbatical," the last monument (or "anti-monument," as she put it) that she worked on. Everything that was in the file of "snapshots."

A CD of *Don Giovanni* plays. "Lana's music." I'm switching back and forth between acts of the opera. And someday I'll have to talk about my life, too. But not here.

The expression that comes to mind—"sincere charity"—may fit. Only Lana's "snapshots" here, as she herself prepared them for delivering. She still had time for that.

New Jersey

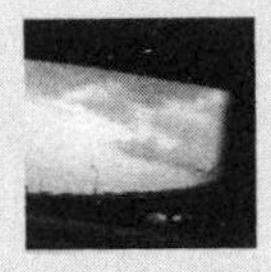

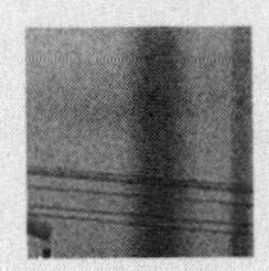

[From the suburban bus. Summer. Hazy, gray. Afternoon. New tablet.]

[New Jersey Turnpike Exit 10.]

Light rain skids across the window. Entrance ramp to the turnpike. Traffic islands. Grass, chrysanthemums. Opposite a strip mall in the fields. Sports equipment, household goods. Work on the shoulders of the road. Piles of asphalt, gray as the sky.

(Only in movement does the tremor subside. A kind of identity is fixed.)

Sitting in the tenth row back from the driver. The seat next to me is empty. The handbag is on it. The anonymous rushing on one of the twelve lanes. Cars all around, sliding, sealed crates touching in silence.

[Between Edison and Elizabeth.]

Bridges on the horizon, steel tracks. Freight trains. Empty cars, blue, black, rusty red. Even a silvery lake with reed nests on its banks trembles a reflection of the sky.

(As if the journey isn't already prescribed, dictated in advance.)

[Between Exits 12 and 12A.]

A tower cuts the horizon. Profile of power-plant chimneys in Newark. Pistons of an inferno throb next to the highway.

Labyrinth of pipes. Steel joints darting. A tongue of fire spirals up.

Opposite, in the marshes, round white oil tanks. North White, Sunoco, Getty. Going off in the mist, to the docks of the port and the warehouses.

And everything now is swallowed up under the overpasses.

Black puddles, heaps of asphalt, an overpass under construction.

On the horizon, at the top of the lanes, at the edge of the greenery and the water, a pale negative of the towers of Manhattan suddenly sallies forth from the mist. A tiny vision of a blurred future cuts the heart off from its walls.

Dear father. Once again with you, in the traffic to the city hovering in the distance. No longer able to resist the silence ever since I left you in the crumbling, damp winter ground, among the pines on the Carmel, burying with you our whisper of speech, a niche of closeness, a sense of place in our wandering lives.

> The call from Sayyid came, at last, in the afternoon. And right afterward I ran, without thinking, to catch the four o'clock bus—with the pretext of getting to the MoMA store before it closed, to buy Aldo Rossi's *Scientific Autobiography* for the seminar. His soft voice from the distant night in Amsterdam. "It'll be fine, Lana." Avoiding the news from Iraq—"American exaggeration," he laughs in a whisper.
>
> Alain won't come back from the archive in Washington until the day after tomorrow. And the boys are invited to friends after soccer practice (to think of Jonathan kicking, excited, his fair curls bouncing).
>
> And the paralysis all morning, facing the sketches. As if everything is rushing toward some inevitable disaster.

Writing fast (to you?) in the stolen space between Sayyid's phone call and Alain's return. The two of them only an excuse for impelling me from the house to the bus, out of a yearning to rip something. Six months after the members of the Burial Society ripped my shirt as a sign of mourning, standing paralyzed in the mud at the open grave. Wearing throughout the seven days of mourning the same shirt with the torn lapel, feeling nothing. Leaving for Paris, and then here. According to plan. Renting the house in the insipid suburb next to the turnpike. Façade painted blue, backyard seen from the kitchen window, the boys kicking a ball until evening. Settling between the archive in Washington, with the invitation to Alain, and New York, the seminar at Cooper Union, the conference on "Monuments of Memory" planned for late fall. Dragging here the final stage of the project in Jerusalem (picking up the pace after the fall of the Berlin Wall and the "end of the Cold War" with budgets from the Dag Hammarskjöld Fund and UNESCO. The whole focus shifted to Jerusalem with resounding headlines of peace and pan-nationalism.)

Working in the faceless suburb, such a contrast to the views of Jerusalem, the utopian dimensions of the project.

[Exit 12A.]

Lanes to the airport. Blue, red tails of airplanes on the asphalt runways. A plane with lights on descends over the highway. Frontal dive, cuts the streetlamps.

The words cover the notebook. Whispering to you, still turned as Jews in prayer to Jerusalem . . . clinging to the window, flooding the look with the industrial landscape. Begging for alms, chance coins of views—the meager wages of the wanderer.

Like the moment before getting off a train, when a spark leaps up from the pillars of the track filthy with grease and paper wrappings, a momentary flood of warmth. Like then, in that unexpected sitting together in the railroad-station buffet in Haifa, waiting for the bus to the airport. We had already said goodbye that morning, at the taxi. On the way, I passed by the Technion to take something from the secretary of the architecture department, and the move back to Paris already separated me from the concrete setting of the station. And then, suddenly, your figure approaching in the light summer shirt, cutting the square, concentrated in your trajectory to me. Melting again the softness, all at once, "I came to see you off." Leading us to the plastic tables of the buffet, buying us orange juice and sugared waffles, tasting slowly, attentively. Raising to me the smile of your blue eyes, and saying, all illuminated, "Look, Ilanka, we make lots of things now in Israel. We've come a long way."

[Exit 14, Hoboken.]

The black bridge of the Skyway.

Freight trains and trucks move slowly between the tongues of water, plowing the thicket of access roads and railroad tracks.

Crouching wood posts bear cables for the local electric supply. Swallowed up among the wooden working-class houses on the slope of Hoboken.

A billboard hung high, over the interchange.

SMILE—YOU'RE ON PANASONIC

Curled up in the lap of the bus. Gripping for a moment what's passing outside, cutting the trip, the pupils, heartbeats released in movement.

Collecting "snapshots" for you, Father, whispered breaths from the river of roads.

Otherwise, how to tell? How to hold the fragments of our torn story?

[Lincoln Tunnel.]

The road twines over the football field. The Manhattan skyline withdraws a moment from the other side of the river.

The bus slides into the tunnel, is swallowed up in the dark. Rocked by a kind of underground sleep, smeared with the milky lighting, the red streams of brake lights.

The bus climbs the access ramp of Port Authority. Gasps to a stop.

Continuing to write, Father. Stealing a last minute together. Before the movement that will slam into the gloom of the platforms.

■ ■ ■ ■

[Local cab. Old red upholstery. On the way to the Transportation Center.]

How much guilt has to be fended off to leave home, to mumble an excuse to Alain about meeting students. (Couldn't say I'm running away to be with you on the New Jersey Turnpike . . . There's no more room for such sentimentality in our careful life.) He looks at me anxiously, asking again if I left Graciella instructions for the boys' dinner.

Two nights ago, when he came back from Washington, I lay in bed, stony. Watching him undressing, putting his clothes on the chair, self-absorbed, silent, and yet seeing immediately what had changed in me.

I got up, compelled to shatter the delicate balance that still holds us, stifling my passion to make love, claiming I had to fax something to Paris before morning. I lay down on the sofa in the study among the rolls of paper and the sketches, and covered up with the wool blanket.

The attempt to reach Sayyid at three in the morning, my heart pounding. Muffling the receiver, the long rings, no answer, a silent wave of jealousy that broke for his morning across the ocean.

[Highway 364.]

The taxi driver's thick neck. She and the seat are welded into one mass. The steering wheel responds to her fingertips.

On the radio, a smooth tenor, "I really want to be great with them, but I just can't make it . . ." High-pitched female giggles, "How many girls want to go out with you? . . ."

[Route 103.]

Fields. Some flowers. A gas station.

At the edge of the road a crippled girl leaning on her mother. The two walking close to the side of the road, shrinking from the traffic.

". . . You've got to be independent in life, that's the thing! . . ."

On the road again, Father. Apparently need the conglomeration of New Jersey roads, the "nowhere" of the "American dream," to tell you what I never dared. (Once when I tried to start, you immediately melted the fervor of my plea with a joke you translated for me from Yiddish.)

> The worried faxes from Colette and Fernand from the office in Paris. They don't understand why I persist in planting myself in this depressing suburb. Yes, they know my craziness. "Lana's Don Juan outbursts." But there, in New Jersey, there isn't even "anybody on the horizon" . . . they laugh when I admit that I really did drag along the Walkman with the *Don Giovanni* CD. "That's what holds me together here . . ."

I owe you an explanation, Father, a belated one, of my leaving, "Ilana's desertion"—what finished you. You didn't understand why I didn't come back to build in Israel. I, your pride and joy, "the second generation of builders." (In this rattletrap of a taxi.) I've got to try to explain to you the need to leave everything you held dear, the "love of the Land of Israel." And the constraints of Alain's work, or of mine (what you called "Ilana's wanderings"), and all the ideology, they were only excuses (as you always knew).

That's why I turned down the position at the Technion and settled in Paris, joined the radical cells, and the building projects for immigrants, refugees, homeless. Culminating in the "Lodgings of Life" in Marseille, "the organic, feminine building," in the commune of architecture students and immigrant workers, who build what will be their home. What became known as "Tsuriel's project," dragging me into struggles with the authorities for permits, with the local population. And the sense of brotherhood created there, in the stormy months in southern France, with my trio with Charles and André, "the Trinity," and the joy that infected the tenants and the café owners in the suburb that came to life. And then, the relationship with Alain, who's obsessively devoted to squaring accounts with Europe, completely cut off from "the Zionist enterprise." The hasty marriage. And our life together (with all the lovers), which can be summed up in one of those jokes about the two Jews on a train from Warsaw to Lublin. And your grandchildren, born in "Exile" (fighting over whose turn it was to ride on your lap, on the last visit, before you got sick). Everything just to get as far away as possible from your story, Father. To live on the other side of the century, the story of our own wanderings.

[Route 17.]

A long line of traffic lights. Signs. Strip malls. Long warehouses.

Next to the steering wheel, clasped in the driver's hand, a photo of a little girl with a ball, in the doorway of the house.

Ever since we came, I've been mechanically tending to the house, the boys. Only for isolated hours am I really with them, when Graciella, the babysitter who holds us all together, is away. They examine me, assess me with a look, like small animals. "You're not mad, Mommy?" "No, no, kids." Try to hug them, but they already slip away, burst out to the lawn and the ball that fill their world.

I sink into some destruction gaping open around me. Sinking in between me and Alain, penetrating the sketches of Mount Sabbatical and the Settlement of Huts, the plan for the performance of the al-Kuds troupe, Sayyid's phone calls. Addicted only to this yearning to assimilate, to be obliterated in the anonymity of the suburban silence, the somnolent rhythm of the once-a-week attack of the guys mowing the lawn with their spaceman headphones; the twice-a-week burst of the garbage truck with a rumble of screeching, dragging, tossing; and the once-every-ten-days recycle truck and black overalls tossing plastic bottles, torn vinyl chairs, hair. Leaving a crushed stream next to the lawns.

(A scene from two weeks ago that won't go away. By mistake I left the extra freezer open in the garage with four frozen chickens wrapped in plastic. By the time I discovered it, the rotting mass was reeking. Trembling, I threw the chickens into the garbage can and immediately dragged it to the street. Then an unexpected holiday ruined the rhythm of the garbage collection. And meanwhile the heat and humidity, the stink spreading like a dead body, creeping in a pale jet to the lawn.

When the garbage truck finally came, I watched from behind the shutter as the workers thrust the trash into the truck. And only when they disappeared around the corner did I dare come out and pick up the tossed can with my fingertips. And the dizziness at the maggots gasping in plump whiteness on the sides, swarming, thick, gushing out, to the sidewalk, shouting publicly what was hidden.)

And in the background the invasion of Kuwait. A surrealist nightmare taking place every evening on the screen.

The charges fired back and forth, of rehashed American contempt and Arabic rhetoric. Saddam Hussein, a kind of mustachioed asshole, facing the erect Bush with a golf club.

Words changing to reality before your eyes. Caught in the iron rules of the war machinery, of rising oil prices, of stock market jitters.

And last night battleships with Marine units sailed.

How fast meanings turn over. How once again "history" writes its perverse story in us, makes the "hut of peace" I'm planning on the Hill of Evil Counsel—my Mount Sabbatical—obsolete even before it is put up.

And maybe our conversation, Father, is already crushed, too.

Access road to the Transportation Center. Traffic lights.

A few trees on the banks of the puny river.

The driver's clasping hand squeezing the steering wheel.

■ ■ ■ ■

[The waiting room. Another ten minutes for the bus to Manhattan.]

On the opposite bench a young man in sneakers and a kippah reads a paperback. Next to him a young man reads a Chinese newspaper.

Next to the snack and drink machines bursts of laughter from three young black men.

In a line at the gate businessmen in suits with James Bond briefcases. One seems to be from Pakistan or India.

Two aging housewives, apparently on a shopping trip to Manhattan. A girl with a big purse, maybe from Puerto Rico.

That calming mixture, Father. "The melting pot" of the world. No pretense. Yet one society, melding the sharpness of shades, tastes, with one economic glue, the faceless force of dollars. Beyond all ideology, all belief. The religion of profit, the nation of consumption. The distorted, perhaps most piercing, mirror of the dream you raised me on.

So why our persistence not to assimilate, to remain "a nation that dwells solitary"? Why, at the end of our tormented century, still to brandish the obsolete formulation of "You have chosen us"? Why go on being separated, "for He has not made us like the nations of the lands and has not implaced us like the families of the earth; for He has not assigned our portion like theirs nor our lot like all their multitudes." Why go on provoking in spite of, or because of, weakness? Why not throw away all attachments to the nation, the people, concepts that immediately smell of nationalism and fascism? Why not cast off, once and for all, all the "separations" that will be buried anyway beneath the planes, the freeways, the Western race to get rich, sending its troops to the Arabian desert?

At the end of the station, next to the bathrooms, a peroxide blonde in a red mini leans into the public phone. Her muscular thighs, her shabby sneakers, her thin hair poking out of a red rubber band. She holds a newspaper open to the want ads.

"What?" she shouts into the phone. "Yes, yes? What? So when should I call back?"

I clutched my bag, to go on writing. Straighten up conspicuously, attempting to convey belonging to the proper world, though in fact I've already been expelled from it, like the blond girl over there. I'm already one of them, the homeless people in Port Authority. Lying on the platforms, blocking the sidewalk on Forty-second Street and Eighth Avenue with their flattened cardboard boxes. Those with no hold. Refuse of the world.

Standing in the straggly line for the bus. On the platform. Continuing to write.

Behind the glass wall is the waiting room. The entrance to the bathrooms. The ticket windows. The blond girl shouting into the phone. Still.

■ ■ ■ ■

[In the bus, on the road to the freeway.]

Miles of strip malls. Bradlees, Innovation Luggage, Party City, Foodtown, Kids-R-Us. Treasure Island—Garden Furniture.

The artificial sights flood the eye, calming.

[The turnpike from the height of the window.]

A negative of a gray landscape trembling behind the windowpane.

The side of a tanker. Steel boards sliding faster in the oncoming lane.

Profile of chimneys on the horizon, beyond the marshes and the screen of hot haze.

Fenced marshes. Reeds. High-tension wires. Plaits of cables.

Bulldozers biting a strip of forest. Preparing another brown surface of naked land for "development."

Lines of inclined wooden crosses of electric poles receding in the haze.

And playing in my head is the sixties song by Simon and Garfunkel: "They've all come to look for America . . ."

They've all come . . . All of them, all the seekers, the immigrants, *Homo errans,* the Wandering Jew, dreams huddling on the deck facing the shores of Ellis Island, soaking with sweat the sewing shops of the Lower East Side, in the land of unlimited possibilities. And in the background, on the reddening horizon, gallops the cowboy next to black cutouts of cactus plants. Comes and goes, loyal to the roads and the distance, in the name of all utopias, in the name of all dreams of redemption.

And suddenly, from the rocking of the bus, from the silence, once again your soft melodious voice washes over me. As when you'd carefully put on your reading glasses, pick up one of the forty-page notebooks filled with your dense handwriting, and shyly ask if you could read me something. You begin in a hushed voice that grows stronger, immediately sweeping me from the present—away from Palestinian Land Day demonstrations, political activities at the Technion, or projects in Paris: "Yes, Ilanka, nineteen hundred twenty-one. We departed from the Ukraine after the Petlura pogroms. We crossed over the border to Bessarabia, and from there we arrived in Istanbul. And there we waited for a ship to transport us to the shores of the homeland. And meanwhile came news of riots in the Land of Israel. The murder of Brenner, the battle of Tel Hai, the fall of Trumpeldor, which horrified us all. And then came the day, the great hour, and the signal was given: "You're sailing!" You raise your eyes from the pages a moment, all absorbed there, "I board the bridge of the ship. The anchor is raised, we're off! All of us crowding on the deck, and a song bursts from hundreds of throats. We sing devotedly, excitedly, prayerfully, gratefully:

We rise up to the Land and sing
We rise up to the Land and sing . . ."

You hum in a bass voice. And something in your erect body, in the song, shows through the wrinkles of your face the excited, curly-haired boy looking from the deck with a salt-soaked face.

"As we approach the shores of our Land, the air grows hotter and hotter. The lights of the ship burst out of the dark, on the way to the desired shore, Haifa. All of us gathered on the deck in holiday clothes, watching the city and the bay slowly approaching, and we start singing, 'There in the delightsome land . . .' Many times we had sung the song, but this time it was different, exalting. And all because of one letter. And what a great and profound change. We left 'there' behind us, and instead we sang 'here':

Here *in our fathers' delightsome land,*
We shall do all that we have planned.
Here *we'll live and here create*
A life of freedom, free of hate.
Here *the* Shekhina *will ring,*
Here *the Holy Tongue will sing.*
Sing song song song
Ring long long long
Furrow wide, wide, wide
Buds are bright bright bright . . .

Yes, Ilanka, buds will come. And the road is so long. A new life opened before us, a life of mission, of building. And now it's your turn, you and your generation, you, the young people."

You lift your look that sails far off, carries me to the great adventure of your youth, which always was, after all, my youth, too. As if there couldn't be any other Hebrew youth. Even when I tried to flee from it to the flower children's dream of international peace on nights on the beaches of Sinai, in the alliance of bodies laden with sun, salt, sex, singing to the beat of the guitars, "Counting the cars on the New Jersey Turnpike. They've all come to look for America . . ." The lines echoing in me now, on the 1981 recording in Central Park, with the bustling crowd, steeped in nostalgia, and that's why I also bought the record on boulevard Saint-Michel. And how amazed I was to find the same record at Sayyid's place in Amsterdam, between Umm Kulthum, Adonis, and Mahmoud Darwish reading his poetry, to discover that he, too, was affected by the same nostalgia. Then, at the hallucinated night between trains, when time flowed transparent in the attic studio, between the words and the smoke, and bodies sloughed off. In the heart of that night, before dawn would rise on the canals and illuminate the northern sky pinched by gray, you returned to me. Walking behind my back, bending down to your writings and reading—

"We came out of the quarantine gates and the order was given to 'line up.' Rows and rows were formed, flags were hoisted, and a moment later we paraded solemnly through the streets of Haifa. The director of the immigrant house, Dostrovski, ran from one person to another. Uttered all his pleas, 'Don't bunch up,' 'No demonstrations,' and nobody listened to him. The only compromise that was achieved, 'No drums or trumpets.' We silenced the trumpets that were polished and buffed for that great hour and they didn't make a sound. We didn't know that only a few days before, on the anniversary of the Balfour Declaration, there had been a lot of tension in the city. Incitement in the mosques, shops closing, a procession after prayers. The convoy moved. We crossed the narrow streets of Haifa. Arabs in red tarbooshes gathered in the doorways of the shops and on the sidewalks. Their eyes shot darts of hatred, and a lot of talk poured from their mouth, and we didn't understand any of it, except for one word: 'Moskubi,' 'Moskubi,' Muscovites.

"In straight lines at the same pace, we marched to the immigrants' house, and a mighty song burst from hundreds of throats. A marching song, an ancient song. The song of the exiles in Babylon, the song Grandfather, the pious Hasid, sang every Sabbath meal before the blessing over the food. He sang it in a sad and sighing and heavy heartbreaking melody, 'ay, ay, when the Lord turned again the captivity of Zion,' and he would hide the knife under the tablecloth, lest he thrust it in his heart out of grief and pain for the destruction of the Temple, for the disgrace of exile. Thus he sang the song of the exiles in Babylon. And for us it turned into a song of return to Zion, an anthem to all the Pioneers entering the gates of the Land of Israel. The song of the immigrants, the song of ascent.

When the Lord turned again the captivity of Zion,
We were like them that dream.
Then was our mouth filled with laugher,
And our tongue with singing."

A labyrinth of tubes among the refinery pools. Jets of smoke blackening the horizon. Branching off interchanges. Freight cars. Marshes.

A gray airplane is cast into the sky from the runway.
Erect with outstretched wings, like Superman, like a crucifix against the sky.

While sitting shiva, as the old-timers went in and out of the apartment, I was afraid to search in the study for your forty-page notebooks. Scared they were lost. That, at the last moment, you decided not to leave them. I was even afraid to mention your writings to Ella. I just decided with her that, for the time being, we'd leave the apartment as it was. And when I come, as planned, to lay the cornerstone of the site next winter, I'll help her empty it.

Another plane, white and red, takes off. Its white belly darkens the freeway a moment.
Graffiti on the granite rocks.

"They've all come to look for America"—you walk with me among the cars on the expanses of death and promise of the New Jersey Turnpike. Always beyond the borders, outside the camp of the gold diggers. You return me to the tatters of your voice, rolling through the underground tunnels of the dead for resurrection in the Holy Land. You stubbornly reset the compass of my heart to the east.

[Exit 16E, Lincoln Tunnel.]
Signs in green and white:
LINCOLN TUNNEL, SECAUCUS
STAY IN LEFT LANE
US 1 & 9
STAY IN RIGHT LANE
YOU ARE LEAVING NJ TURNPIKE
OBEY LOCAL TRAFFIC LAWS

■ ■ ■ ■

[Café on Forty-second Street.]

I went in for a quick espresso before getting the bus back to New Jersey at Port Authority.

A whole day of work with the students. Passing from one drafting table to another, with the whole group in the beehive of the studio, looking at their variations of the Huts, engaging in a long discussion of "place," "holding or letting go of it." Trying out on them my fresh versions of Sabbatical. The students' excited reactions, their personal comments.

Bar next to a window. Silhouettes pass from the other side of the air conditioner.

The flooding crowd in Times Square, the square of time. Belly of the city. Our stolen meeting place, Father. Close to you. With no distance. In the heart of shame, disgust, and open commerce. The big supermarket of all stories. Our story will also have to pass through it.

A large black woman in torn jeans passes along the window, mouth gaping with laughter.

Businessmen with ties, neat haircuts, and leather briefcases, cutting the crowded sidewalk of Broadway, probably analyzing profit and loss from the tension on the Iraqi border. Passing the can collector bent over the dumpster.

A Hasid (maybe a diamond dealer) skittering to a glatt-kosher pizzeria. A sign in the colors of Italy, in English, but in faux-Hebrew lettering.

Father, how to tell you that what you bequeathed me, in a genetic mutation of generations—beyond the Zionist interim, beyond the thin layer of connection to the Land of Israel—is that passion for wandering. A passion no structure I built could stop. No architectural plan, in spite of all the prizes. Not even David's Falling Hut I'm putting up now, in the shadow of the rocket launchers going up in Iraq.

The curse of wandering. The "stigmata," Father. That madness to escape, to uproot. Cain can't hide, is vomited up again and again to Nineveh from the belly of Leviathan. Isaac turning into Jonah, a dove flying off the altar and the wood and the fire, before its soul would fly away.

The constant wanderings with Alain, years now. Out of choice? Or need? Plucked up at night with the few suitcases and the soft hands of David and Jonathan uprooted from sleep, groping for the bottle in the cab slicing the streets of the sleeping city, the nighttime freeways. Walking in the hushed corridors of airports. The same shops, bathrooms smelling of perfume steeped in the mists of feces, and the cleaning woman stooped over the bucket and the rag. Swallowed up in the weak lighting on the moving sidewalks, beside passengers hovering with their bags from air to air, discharged from the end of a glass tube into the sky.

Genes infected with waste pass on the disease to the third, the tenth generation. Our ancient legacy we shall leave, shall sing, shall shed. (If any heir remains at all, somebody who will continue our terminal story, who'll collect the tatters.)

> And the Lord shall scatter thee among all people, from the one end of the earth even unto the other; and there thou shalt serve other gods which neither thou nor thy fathers have known, even wood and stone. And among these nations shalt thou find no ease, neither shall the sole of thy foot have rest; but the Lord shall give thee there a trembling heart and falling of eyes, and sorrow of mind: And thy life shall hang in doubt before thee; and thou shalt fear day and night, and shalt have none assurance of thy life. In the morning thou shalt say, Would God it were even! And at even thou shalt say, Would God it were morning! For the fear of thine heart wherewith thou shalt fear, and for the sight of thine eyes which thou shalt see.

(The obsession with "sources" lately. Ever since the project of "the Yeshiva" in Strasbourg, and then the lectures in Munich and Tokyo, and now "the Hut," "the Sukkah," "the Sabbatical." The fingers reach for pages of the Bible, of Mishnah, of Gemarah. Sink into the forgotten tongue. Formulating a kind of "Laws of Sukkah" rather than an architectural sketch . . .)

Neon lights sharpen as evening deepens.

Another end of a hot New York day.

In the doorway of a sex shop a vendor follows the pair of cops on the beat with the indifference of a panther.

Selling incense, perfume, healing oil.

Islands of sparse and shabby hair scattered on the sidewalks at the feet of the pedestrians. Delineating areas of the homeless.

In a little while I'll go out into the reddening evening, Father, to the human medley of Manhattan. I'll take you with me on my way back to Port Authority.

■ ■ ■ ■

[Late at night. My study.]

The boys are finally asleep now.

When I returned home, Alain was standing in the garage door, not waiting for me to get out of the car, scolding, "It's good you came, the boys can't fall asleep! Even Graciella couldn't calm them down." He followed me into the corridor, the two of us entrenching ourselves in silence, until he turned to his study and closed the door behind him.

Yesterday, in the kitchen, he blurted out casually, "So what about the Palestinian troupe?" Disguising with irony his tension about Sayyid's coming. "Still planning to come to New York, despite the invasion of Kuwait? . . ."

"As far as I know, that's still their plan," I answered drily.

Alain turned his head aside sharply. "With their director?" he asked my back.

"Yes, with Sayyid Ashabi. I arranged to work with him and the troupe on the performance for the laying of the cornerstone," I uttered with an effort.

Alain continued leaving. At the door he stopped.

"Lana . . . this time you've gone too far . . ." Seeking the expression that would hit the mark. "Think about your father."

"Alain, shut up! You hear!" I shrieked, out of control.

Graciella greeted me at the door of the children's room, surrounding me immediately with her pleasantness. "It's good you came, they've been waiting for you," she said.

"Here's Mommy," she whispered into the perfumed dark and the sound of breathing and weeping, "now everything will be fine. Goodnight." And she went off, already swaying to the bossa nova she'd soon play in her room.

David pounced on me first. Clasped me with all his weight.

"Wait, let me sit down . . ."

I landed with him amid the twisted sheets. Jonathan climbed out of his crib and pressed into my lap, too. The three of us sat like that, together, embracing, until they went back to bed, and I read them a story. David held my hand, and Jonathan held his three pacifiers, "one for the mouth, one for the nose, and one for the hand," sucking one rhythmically, rubbing his nose with the second one, and pulling the third with his thumb.

"Mommy, stay a little more," whispered David, after I kissed them again and again, running my hands over his thin, fair hair, caressing Jonathan's thicket of warm curls.

"Stay a little . . ." he pleaded.

I turned out the light. We looked at the Day-Glo star stickers David had spent a whole day pasting on the walls of their room of wandering, covering them with a private galaxy. Jonathan pointed, as always, to the stars of Ursa Major over his bed. But that didn't help either.

"I can't fall asleep . . . can't . . ." complained David.

"Mommy, sing to us . . ." he said suddenly, as if he understood or recalled. "Mommy, sing, sing," he clutched my hand in his sweaty palm.

"Sing . . . sing . . ." repeated Jonathan.

"What shall I sing?"

"You pick . . ."

So, in the dark of the children's room, in the smell of quilts and bodies, your Pioneer songs from the turn of the century burst out, Father. Tatters of words I remembered from your humming bass voice, "Blue is the water of the sea," "Fields in the Jezreel Valley," flooding from me with that Slavic breadth, "darkened, darkened the face of the sky," echoing from my lips into your starry nights, "torn are we, worn are we . . ."

David calmed down at once. Pulled the blanket to him. Looked long at me with the very blue look he inherited from you, noticing before he fell asleep the choking tears rising in me, like a screen of dampness that would tremble on your eyes. At last Jonathan's heavy eyelids also dropped. David's breathing evened the sucking of the pacifier. And for a moment, beneath the Day-Glo stars, your heavy breathing seemed to rise from the bed next to me. As on the last nights when I stayed with you in the hospital, listening to the throbbing of the intravenous, to your breathing.

■ ■ ■ ■

[Diner on the corner of Thirty-sixth Street and Sixth Avenue.]

On the way back from the seminar at Cooper Union. Leaving the bubble of light, the sketching thinking fingers of the students, and stifling longings for you leads me from street to street. Flooding me with the movement of your elbow, the tilt of your head, your eyes raised in wonder.

Maybe those are the real "monuments of memory" for the conference in the fall . . . Sights, smells, whispers of love, shouts in all tongues—the mental structures carried over the heads of the throng in the streets of Manhattan.

Swept up in the flood of people in the canyons of skyscrapers. Glass-and-steel constructivism. Adolf Loos, Paul Scheerbart, Walter Benjamin, Mies van der Rohe. The groan of romanticism in the giant skyline with Lexington Tower, the Empire State Building, and the cliffs of the Twin Towers at the prow of the stone ship crossing the Hudson.

A red Formica table, at the window.

Back with you, Father. Sitting alone, the only woman in the empty diner, to live fully the yearnings for you, the betrayal of all your dreams.

After all, that's the love story of the father and daughter hidden in the dark notes of *Don Giovanni.* The fire that will consume them all in the end.

And the soprano voice of Donna Anna, the daughter, melting in me the guilt, the pain, Padre amato.

Gulping the stories of the old-timers. During the week of mourning, they come in with their wrinkled faces, sit a while with Ella and me, tell tatters of things. And the sentence that recurred, "How your father loved . . ." Even after almost seventy years, what burned was your forbidden love, in the Valley. The silenced name that wasn't mentioned in the house echoes again in the emptied apartment. "And your father's great love for the 'idea,' for the Land . . ." I imagine you in the fields of the Valley, opening a virgin furrow, tearing the sacks of seed, waving in a slow march a handful of golden flow, and a mist rising from the earth, you yearned so much to forget everything in its warmth, to give birth to yourself from its furrows, a New Hebrew Man.

(Among the photos we found in a carton in the drawer were nude photos of you from then. Standing on a rock, maybe the peak of Mount Gilboa, the light flooding the shining skin of your erect, muscular body. About to clasp your friend with twined fists, leaning with bent knee and raised chin as in a stamping dance.)

And what of all those expanses ended up in the apartment in Haifa, through the public functions, the decline? I remember you devotedly tending the plants on the balcony. Hurrying to the street with tin buckets, in the wake of a horse-drawn cart, returning with a treasure of droppings—"Organic waste, the best!" And when I was six or seven, you sowed wheat with me in the flower pots. "An urban fellah . . ." you declared. Every single day, we checked the sprouting "produce," saw a dozen stems grow erect, ripen. Finally, we "harvested" the tiny "plot," gathered the few seeds, ground them between two flat stones, mixed the precious flour and kneaded a tiny challah from it. I remember you, in later visits, still laboring to carry the old kettle from the kitchen to the porch, watering the pots of the plants one by one.

For years I'd watch you, unseen, from the end of the street on the slope of the Carmel. I'd see you leaning over the ledge of the balcony, looking at a budding flower, following a honeybee leaping between spots of light and shade. I'd stand in the street, looking at you, amazed at the beating of my heart, at my bursting joy. As when you'd squeeze orange juice and give it to me, during all my years of study at the Technion. Bringing me the thick liquid with your blue, loving eyes. You also saw all my loves, Father. Looking at me slowly, as at the passage of the full moon from your desk, and approving. Silently.

And the dreams of making love with you. The one I dreamed in the recruits' barracks, among the girls curled up on their cots, my soul shriveled from the "socialization" of the whole noisy rabble. When the remnant of privacy was shaken out every morning with the order to fold the khaki-colored blankets. There, suddenly, you're suspended above me, slowly descending to me, with a heavenly crane. Mouth to mouth and groin to groin. And the smell of cigarettes wafts from your approaching lips. And all around full goblets of red wine, in honor of the marvelous ceremony. Red wine that will be poured, soon, when your lips cling to mine. Your lips whispering something.

Meanwhile three men sat down at tables behind me. The Asian waitress serves them french fries and beer.

Humming fans.

Vortices of juice softly stir colorful waves.

And everything you yourself betrayed to live the love in the Old-New Land. "We threw everything away behind us, we were drunk, Ilanka . . ." you tried to explain to me after Mother's death. Still amazed, as if with the years the guilt had only grown . . . "Until '41, letters still came. We hoped we could get papers. For Tiomka, my little brother." Talking more to yourself than to me, "Ida would run around whole days. Trying to get signatures, approvals. For her family in Warsaw, too. Me, you could say . . ." you uttered with an effort, "I cut myself off emotionally." Raising your eyes to the window overlooking the bay. "The thought of my parents doesn't let go of me. They fill my dreams at night."

The waitress puts the change down in front of me.

I pick up the handbag, the notebook.

Clearing away the remnants of our conversation, Father.

[Study. Writing next to the site sketches.]

From the corridor comes the sound of Alain's footsteps. One of our rare mornings together. The common breathing of our life.

Sounds from his office. Opening of drawers, dragging of files. His voice in a long phone conversation.

(And the countdown to the arrival of Sayyid and the troupe.)

Last night working until late. Alain on the other side of the house, beyond the children's room, full of sleep. Hearing him turn on the desk lamp, taking out files, seeing who'd blink first. And as always it's me, I get into bed with a glass of vodka. And at two, he comes. Gathers up my body from the depths of sleep. Tames it through the murmur of refusal, draws it to the dark primal animal beneath our married life.

Alain's door opens again. He passes my study, his hair mussed at the end of a phone call.

Goes to the kitchen for a drink of water.

His voice in French. German. Russian. Not reporting.

I'm very familiar with this screen of silence. And yet. Fragments of Alain's excitement filter through, like archives that burst open all at once in Prague,

Bucharest, Vilna, Stasi headquarters. And recently the remarks he muttered on "the Jewish card file" that was discovered in Paris. Hidden since Vichy in the police archive.

Yes, it's time to talk about Alain, Father. What you refrained from asking. (Out of discretion? Decision? Persisting in not visiting us in Paris, refusing "to leave the Land of Israel," "to return to Europe," all sixty-nine years since you came to the port of Haifa.) "Alain, the historian." What you knew. And the restrained friendship between you, beyond the barrier of language, in the few meetings in Haifa. Alain in broken Yiddish and you in the English of the British Mandate period. You make do with "facts." Childhood in Czernowitz, four years old when the war broke out. Ten years old when he came to the orphanage in Montmorency in the jeep of some American soldiers who picked him up in the forest. A withdrawn child, escaping from place to place, surviving alone.

On the Sunday before registering our marriage in City Hall, he said to me out of the blue, "Lana, I'd like you to meet Madame Heller." He took me on a suburban train to Montmorency, silent most of the way, his hand holding mine. Telling me in his laconic way the few details that prepared me for the firm handshake of the tiny woman, with a smile that lit up her bold face. She looked like one of your group in the Jezreel Valley, but in a cashmere suit with a gold lapel pin. That same Eastern European look, leaving in her rich French the youthful trace of Czernowitz, of a member of Hashomer Ha-Tsa'ir, the leftist socialist Zionist youth movement, who went at the age of twenty to complete her education in Strasbourg. And the youthful laughter of this woman who never married, never had children, devoted her life to the orphanage she established, to the progressive system of education she developed.

Sitting in the apartment packed with books. Looking at the green, lighted valley out of the wide windows. Drinking tea with Viennese torte, as Madame Heller tells about the war years, the flight to the south with the children of the institution, the activities in the group of Jewish partisans of Clermont-Ferrand, smuggling children to Switzerland and Spain when the free zone was occupied. And how as soon as Paris was liberated she gathered the children across the border, and returned with them to Montmorency, to reopen the suburban house that filled up with the children of transports from the east, and became a center for the illegal immigration to Palestine, a meeting place for the uprooted, for Jewish officers in the Allied armies.

And then, while pouring us another cup of tea, she told with her thin smile how, one day, the wild child came to the institution, in a jeep of American soldiers, who left him along with their monthly provisions. And how she communicated with the suspicious, mute child, an orphan from her own hometown. Gets close to him, instills trust in him gradually. Invites him to her private apartment to hear music, to look at photos from her youth. So she starts weaving scraps of memory with him. A city park going down to the river, steep streets, a market square, cafés he was taken to on his outings with the Romanian nursemaid from the apartment of his doctor parents where he grew up. The young parents, the big sister. The little bit that returned to him with an effort. "As Rosh Hashanah approached, I told him to help me prepare the holiday table," she tells me beyond Alain's bent head. "I gave up the atheism of a member of the Communist Party, and decided to follow the calendar of Jewish holidays to give the children a sense of home. I assigned that wild boy to cut the apples and fill the bowls with honey, and it worked . . ." She smiles with a blend of mischief and affection, and Alain nods with downcast eyes.

And later, too, always with that pensive smile on the long face, always in the tweed jacket. As when we met. As you knew him, Father. Only the hair became thinner with the years, and the slim body lost its youthfulness. Never did I deceive myself that I could "understand." I make do with isolated words. Father, mother. The sister, Bella, whose hair was black, sleek. When they took them from the apartment, he was six years old. His mother urged him to run. ("Run, she shouted," the only sentence in which his voice shook.) For a whole day, he hid behind the garbage bins. A neighbor woman discovered him. She took him out of town. She left him in a field with a loaf of bread. He was afraid to run after her when she went back. And later, "peasants. Forests." And beyond that, silence. He didn't tell anymore, and I didn't ask. I honor the silence, afraid to break something in Alain that always remains a withdrawn child, even in the struggle to excel in high school, in preparation classes for the école normale, in the department of history and law, even in the photo from his university days with an unruly pompadour and a shaded look, and despite the degrees, the appointments, the position.

Never is he really with me. Not even after the boys were born. (As you understood without asking, with your sensitivity.) He immediately answers every phone call. Goes out day and night. With the tape recorder and camera in the old leather case. Bends over in the door, hugs the boys, who hang on him, sweeps back his hair and whispers, "I'll come back in a few days, Lana, okay?" and disappears. For two days, ten days. "Nothing's ended, it's only buried. Goes on below in the meantime, Lana. Under the bulldozers, in the safes, in the archives, in the international terror network. Everything is only waiting to burst out again. And you and your naïve utopias, what do you know, Lana?"

And in truth, what do I know, with all the political involvement from the days of "The Compass," the radical anti-Zionist group, and the revolutionary groups in Paris, to membership in the organization of radical architects. What do I know about Alain, or about his comrades in arms who wait in railroad stations. Every one of his colleagues has his own reasons for the double life, for silence. Men, women. Resolute like him.

In all the years, only once did a call come by mistake to me (somebody inexperienced, apparently). A female voice, worried, in French with a heavy Walloon accent. After one in the morning. She hung up immediately. And ever since the fantasy about Alain getting off a night train on the platform of an empty station in a northern town. Walking in the nighttime streets of an industrial suburb, in the eternal tweed jacket and the old case. Going down circular stairs to the entrance of a tavern. Standing a moment, and then pushing the door, going through the screen of smoke, among the full tables, to the bar. Exchanging a word with the bartender, and led immediately through a side door to a back room. A modestly furnished room with lace curtains. He takes off his coat, sits down at a table, and the arms of a young woman put potato pancakes and cheese pastry before him.

What do I know, after all the years, about that restrained man who came to me at the end of the lecture on "Building and Immigration" in Munich?

"Thank you for the lecture," he examined me with his eyes. "I'm interested also in the question of refugees. In certain circumstances, can they lose their identity as refugees . . . ?" He gave me a long pensive look from the straight lines of his face beneath the drooping pompadour. "Alain Greenenberg, historian," he said his name, decisively, and held out his hand.

"Yes, the settlement of the refugees . . ." I was drawn into a conversation that went on as I exchanged words with the last of the colleagues and students who came up to thank me, and as the audience left the auditorium, and the projectionist returned my slides, and the organizer of the conference stood waiting to escort me.

"I'm going back to Paris in two weeks. We seem to live in the same city . . . I'd be glad eventually to hear more details about your work."

He went on surveying me with a polite smile, put in my hand the address he had scribbled in a square handwriting, "Boulevard Grenelle 125, 15th Arrondissement."

And then, while preparing for the Marseille Project, and the telephones ringing nonstop, in what later became the joint office of Fernand, Colette, and me, I found myself counting the days until the date that introverted historian mentioned, controlling myself a few more days until I finally picked up the phone, with the excuse that if he were still interested . . . the question of the refugees . . . the projects . . . and heart pounding, with absolutely no preparation.

I arrived in the afternoon at his scholar's apartment, the Métro bridge cutting the window, and the smell of tobacco, and heaps of files along the walls. Alain listened to me explain my thesis at the Technion, "The Settlement of Displaced Persons in the First Years of the State of Israel"—research on

Jewish refugee camps in Cyprus, the transit camps for new immigrants, the mass building of the housing projects, and, on the other hand, the establishment of Palestinian refugee camps. I went on telling about my advanced study at the Beaux-Arts, on mass building for those left homeless by World War II. Sucking on his pipe, inhaling the smoke deep, Alain followed my explanations of the waves of immigration of foreign workers to Europe, life in housing projects for the slaves of the economic machinery, of migration from the villages to the slums of the Third World, to the ghettoes of the megalopolises in South America, to the cities exploding in the Middle East, in Asia—he listens to my words as his long fingers knock the ashes of his pipe into the ashtray, fill it with new tobacco, tamp it, light it. Now and then he comments on "the century of refugees," the "scars of ruins," without explaining what's going through his head, and only slowly, devotedly inhaling the smoke and blowing it out in a soft jet between his lips. Finally I came to the establishment of our association to restore honor to the enslaved body of the workers, to fight megalomaniac architecture, which imposes on the tenants the architect's ego, the economic considerations. "That's what I'm trying to do in planning the neighborhood in Marseille, that the foreign workers, the future tenants, will build for themselves," I conclude and spread some plans on the table. And Alain leans over, surveys them under the sheaf of light, nods in concentration shrouded in smoke. Heads come together. Body odor. And the choking, immediately. As if everything was decided long ago. At some primal encounter. Beyond everything that separates, and that will remain silent forever between me and Alain. And later, in the elegant brasserie, the knees touching all through the meal, the body flowing under the table.

Alain's steps in the kitchen. Making coffee for himself, carrying it back. Doesn't slow down at my makeshift study, as he used to do in the (not-so-distant) days when he'd come in, after knocking on the door, stop in back of me, glance at what was spread out in front of me on the table, ask in an elegant hum, "Anything new?" putting his hand on my shoulder, moving it to the base of my neck, knowing how he immediately inflamed me, and then putting me down, still without a word, in the bedroom or on the sofa in the study. Afterward, with a last glide of arms disengaged, we'd go back to our desks, buttoning up, him lighting his pipe at the end of the hall and me picking up the pencil at the same time.

Yes, the body always conducted its own story, Father. From the start. I can reconstruct our first two days together, our visit to the exhibition of pre-Columbian urns, and the bodies inflamed, burning at night and the morning after. Returning to my studio with my body inundated and sketching until dawn, with a force I hadn't known before. At first only urns, as we saw at the exhibition, and on them statuettes of a man and woman with two heads burgeoning from under a clay blanket, surrounded by clusters of children. And afterward, elaborations of images of the urn, the womb, the bed: a series of sketches that led to the breakthrough in the plan of the "Lodgings of Life." The spaces defined from the bed, coming out of it in expanding circles of gestures of life. The hand bringing the infant to the breast, walking from the bed to cooking, to reading, filling out this kernel that nourishes the space. What turned into my personal style, called "neo-humane architecture," "the female, organic architecture of Tsuriel." And in their wake, the prizes, the bids, the lectures.

The longing for Alain, bursting into the planning, in the middle of penciling lines over the white page. The groundwater of my creation, that keeps gushing despite all my wanderings and lovers, catalogued in Alain's thin smile. That homeland in whose name I betrayed our story, Father. Alain refused to learn Hebrew, claiming he was too old. He didn't visit Israel, except for the courtesy meetings with Mother and you. And even then, he didn't leave the apartment in Haifa, and flew back to Paris after two or three days with the excuse of work. Belonging wasn't part of it, not for him, a citizen of places wiped out. Responding with growing dread whenever tension rose in the Middle East. Hissing with a pale face, "The Zionist lunacy of gathering all the Jews in one place, preparing the conditions for an easy final extermination! What blindness! That madness of destroying the Diaspora. That's the only reason the Jews survive, because they could move, find temporary shelter in another place every time!" Then spitting out between his trips, "How come you leftists don't understand that everything is part of a long-range plan to destroy the Jewish people. The ancient disease of the Christian, Muslim world. Fear and hatred of the Jews is an incurable disease . . . And you characters just fall into the trap . . ." And only the tremor in his thin lips indicates the suppressed internal turmoil.

The desire for Alain, that always laps the shores of death when he gathers me into him. The shadow that accompanied me even when I joined him at Rosh Hashanah in the synagogue in the second-floor apartment behind the St.-Lazare railroad station. Alain returned from Moscow the day before. When I called you on the eve of the holiday, you admitted, "I am a little weak, Ilanka, yes . . ." As if you knew you wouldn't last the year.

I sat with the boys among the women who smelled of Eastern Europe under the Parisian splendor. Clutching the boys to my body throughout the prayers, Jonathan on my lap and David clinging to my hand. And ever since, the blind impulse that's tearing me away from Alain.

Next week he goes to Washington again. Then on to Berlin. I'm already waiting for him to leave.

(Who knows where Alain and I are going, Father.)

■ ■ ■ ■

The study. A dreary summer day. Late at night the rain started. Traces of last night's storm on the wet plastic table in the yard. From the window of the study a green-black maze of wet plants. Three days ago, Alain flew to Europe for two weeks. We didn't look at one another when he closed the files, the valises.

Your closeness saws through the dreary weather this morning. I reach for our notebook. Work on the drawings of the circular path surrounding the Settlement of Huts, and leading down the slope to the structures of Mount Sabbatical. A trail of six hundred seventy meters, crossing borders of ethnic, national, political territories, all in only one square kilometer in Jerusalem. And the fan of light and the vista revolving around the summit. In the north, the Governor's Palace and the UN Camp, and beyond the grove of pines and cypresses the giant opening from Mount Moriah and the Old City, the Kidron Valley, the Mount of Olives with the ancient Jewish cemetery, the steeples of the churches and the minarets of the mosques, all the way to the ridge gaping to the east, above the houses of Arab-a-Sohra and Jabal Mukhbar far off toward the Judean Desert, to the Jordan Valley and the mountains of Moab suspended in the distance. In the south the trail faces East Talpiot, with the lawns and trees between its buildings, and burgeoning through them the truncated summit with the Herodion and Herod's Palace, the peaks flanking Bethlehem, and the aqueduct rising from the springs near Hebron. And in the west, it overlooks the fields of Kibbutz Ramat Rachel that lap old Talpiot, immersed in green. And the blue-red mist spreads over the neighborhoods of the New City.

Yes, I'm still busy with the Sabbatical year. As in our conversations last winter, until your final days in the hospital. Coming back to those verses that always open onto a new meaning: "When ye come into the land which I give you, then shall the land keep a Sabbath unto the Lord, six years thou shalt sow thy field, and six years thou shalt prune thy vineyard, and gather in the fruit therof; but in the seventh year shall be a Sabbath of rest unto the land, a Sabbath for the Lord: thou shalt neither sow thy field, nor prune thy vineyard. That which groweth of its own accord of thy harvest thou shalt not reap, neither gather the grapes of thy vine undressed: for it is a year of rest unto the land. And the Sabbath of the land shall be meat for you; for thee, and for thy servant, and for thy maid, and for thy hired servant, and for thy stranger that sojourneth with thee. And for thy cattle, and for the beast that are in thy land, shall all the increase thereof be meat."

The Sabbatical Year and Jerusalem. The female, utopian place, as I explained to you. Like the Gihon Spring bursting beneath the Temple Mount. A female tank, emptied and flooded. Bursting with gushing throbs, with rolling tremors of passion. The source of life of Jerusalem.

In the last plans I lead the ancient aqueduct arriving from the south, and crossing the site all the way to the Gihon Spring. I connected the mountain sources to the gushing of Jerusalem, articulating a dimension of Sabbatical, by the flow between the basins, the canals, and the waterfalls all around the site.

In the meantime, last night Saddam Hussein rejected the West's call to remove his army from Kuwait, declares "Jihad to expel the forces of the Western Crusaders from the ground of Islam."

His face framed on the screen, in the flow of the clattering rhetoric. And Bush looking harsh, in a speech taped especially to be broadcast in Iraq:

"Iraq will not be permitted to annex Kuwait, and that's not a threat, and that's not a boast. It's just the way it's going to be."

And then shots of the "human shield": Saddam Hussein "invites" the Western hostages to "be guests" in Iraqi army bases. Holds in his arms the shaking English boy who says to the cameras: "We're grateful for the hospitality . . ."

The effort to concentrate this morning. Trying to calm down, the eyes linger on the photos I've pinned up to the sketchboard without thinking, in a kind of attempt to indicate a personal area of four cubits, a Sukkah in the heart of the soul's wanderings . . .

Like the memorial candle I swept off the shelf of the local Foodtown, I immediately tell myself to take it out of the shopping cart, put it back on the shelf, the first anniversary of your death will be only after we leave here, and anyway, I never lit a memorial candle on the anniversary of Mother's death—but I keep following the candle advancing along the check-out conveyor belt, among the containers of yogurt and cheese.

The photo of you from our trip to the Jezreel Valley, to "the Hill," to celebrate together the sixtieth anniversary of your "ascent to the land." Standing, leaning on the cane, pointing at the horizon and explaining to the lens, "There, at the foot of Mount Gilboa, there. The small mound." A study in brown, furrows of the mown field where I parked, in the heart of a dark green valley of citrus groves, and behind them the perfect blue of the sky, mirrored in the damp exciting blue of your eyes. "After the split in the Labor Brigade, those who stayed in Kibbutz Tel Yosef moved to the northern part of the valley, and the Hill was deserted."

Next to it is a photo of the boys, from late spring. David with the baseball cap he insisted we buy him at Macy's, and Jonathan stooped over, trying to execute a somersault. Preparing, concentrated, before he gives himself over to colliding with the grass. You see only his legs and his curls spilling over the hands planted on the lawn. I went out to photograph them in the yard, two weeks after we moved in. They pose for the first picture. And some uneasiness of framing exposes our joint effort to believe in reality's illusion here.

The photo with Alain in Prague, two years ago. At the sunken entrance of the Alt-Neu Shul. A slightly blurred photo, taken by a young man who came out of the Jewish community organization's offices. Yet it conveys something soft, from that trip full of screaming silence. Alain takes me, halfheartedly, to "his" regions, and in fact there, too, he slips away from me. Only at the entrance to the synagogue did something come unraveled in his position. As if we had arrived. Not really, but to some address. I in the black leather jacket, my face peeping out of the red scarf, wound around a few times, thrusting into its edges the disheveled curls, lighting up the face. A moment of softening, beyond my official function as consultant on repairs of the historical quarter, and my secret meetings with dissident architects, members of our organization. Giving myself a moment to be with Alain, with his "other" story.

He hasn't yet called since he arrived in Europe. Being alone with the boys and Graciella has already gelled into its own routine. The house is full of Brazilian music, and I put the boys to bed every night. Yet the distance brings Alain closer, this professional wandering Jew, and the body, meanwhile, with its own laws, is open now, indulging.

The last picture came from Paris with the blueprints. All of us in Jerusalem on the Hill of Evil Counsel next to the UN radar tower, at a site we already called "Mount Sabbatical and Settlement of Huts." The Paris trio, Colette and Fernand (who went from there to the airport) and I, with Yaron Matus (who's hugging me possessively) and Erella Hernik, from the office in Jerusalem. Two of Yaron's students from the new department of architecture at Bezalel are kneeling on the ground. All of us are huddled together, and last winter's cold wind blows the spiky, varied styles of hair. My face is completely covered by the mane, a kind of curly-haired Gorgon, without a head, above tight jeans. And in the background, behind (what now interests me much more), the slopes to the Judean Desert, on the eastern flank of the ridge, with the villages on top.

In the corner the prow of an Arab truck bursts out toward the New City, a moment before its passing split up the group photographed in the middle of the Intifada, despite the mute wave of the UN man on the other side of the road. Two days later I met Sayyid in the foyer of the al-Kuds Theater in the Old City. But maybe then, in a flash of fear, the need to break through some border had ripened, in the heart of the paralysis of the first days after the seven days of mourning.

> The incandescence of that affair in the Jerusalem winter. Me, coming with the Swedish cultural attaché and the UNESCO representative of the Dag Hammarskjöld Fund, the sponsors of the binational event of "laying the cornerstone for the site of Peace in Jerusalem." We emerge from the tumult of Salah-a-Din Street into the foyer of the al-Kuds Theater. And the tall figure advancing toward us from the gloom of the entrance. Introductions, handshakes, and the flash of the look lingering on me beyond courtesy, descending from face to body, and only then cut off. The rest of the conversation, with mugs of coffee among posters of performances and the actors passing by, carried on now in the whirlpool that swept me away, and goes on through the next day, spent until dark and again in the sunrise in the room with the narrow bed in the Scottish Hospice, until my panicky departure in a cab for the

airport. And the body that didn't calm down even on the flight back to Paris.

Sayyid is supposed to return to Amsterdam from Tunis. I'm afraid to call. Still haunted by echoes of our last conversation, before he left, "Yes, the plans haven't changed, we'll come to New York. The show must go on, right . . . ?" he confirmed tensely. And then he mumbled in a voice that was suddenly hoarse, that there was a certain change in the play *The Clown,* which terrified me immediately. "Don't worry, nothing the Public Theater and the Jewish mafia that runs it won't like," he burst out in his broad laugh. And even after gasps of parting, and a series of dizzying whispers, "Lanaaah," the evasive words and the dread kept echoing.

And what will happen now with the performance of the al-Kuds troupe in the cornerstone-laying ceremony in the Jerusalem winter—that event sold out in advance, formulated in the safest politically correct terms about wandering, refugees uprooted, and Orientalism. Even before the members of the troupe had confirmed their participation. And on the background of the tension in the Gulf (despite Sayyid's and my effort to pretend it was "business as usual"), what will be the position of the troupe?

Telephone. "Mrs. Greenenberg . . ."

I know the singsong voice that starts out like that and goes on in an impervious flood about conditions for subscribing to the local paper, the special offer for exterminating insects, or some such thing.

Unable to hang up immediately, despite the rage at the violent invasion. Lying in wait for the human crack in the voice needing that monstrous livelihood, to blurt out, "No thanks, I'm not interested."

■ ■ ■ ■

On the bus to Manhattan. Relieved to talk with you again.

Alain called before I left. From Berlin. Said he's staying on. "I have to, Lana!" he burst out. "No, I'm not sure I'll be able to come back by Rosh Hashanah to be with you and the boys . . . I know that's important to you, but everything's happening fast here. There's now a rare access to the archives. You don't read the papers? There's a real world out there, beyond your dreams!" And then, after one of Alain's charged silences, indicating the censored words, he struck again. "By the way, did you see the list of Western companies sending raw material to Iraq to develop chemical and biological weapons? You read about the cooperation between the West and extremist Islam? Tell me, you really don't see?"

I was silent, as always after Alain's remarks. Even when he went on in a flood of sarcasm and pain, "Maybe you read at least what happened to the Israeli officer who made a wrong turn and wound up in a refugee camp near Gaza? How the mob stoned him? When his car turned over, they set fire to it and burned him to death. Maybe you'll suggest to your Palestinian director to add that scene to your joint performance . . ."

I was silent, I knew how I swooped down every time the phone rang, thinking it was Sayyid. My body shaking, I gathered up the material for the seminar and hurried out to catch the bus. And then I recalled how, for the first time, Alain and Sayyid changed in me, got mixed up in one another within the voice of Sayyid lying next to me in the Scottish Hospice, his feet twined between my legs.

"Understand, whenever I sit on the bus to Tel Aviv, in my head there's a map that's erased. I pass Lod, Ramle, Beit Lid, and my heart is cut with pain. I hear my father describing the aunt who'd bring lemons from the tree. The yard, the chickens . . ."

And at some point through the words Alain's voice started echoing from when we first met, when I teased him in front of the maps hanging in his study on the boulevard Grenelle.

"What's this, you've turned into an architect? Maybe under the influence of some female architect?"

"It's not exactly a map of future plans . . ." With a slow look, he checked whether he could talk candidly with me. "You know, I deal with the architecture of the past. Places buried in fields, forests. Here . . ." He moved his hand from one point to another, poking names that had previously been in the fog of names of rabbis or yeshivas for me, "Zunz, Poniewiecz, Belz, Bratslav, Berdichev, Tulchin . . ."

"Where are you," Sayyid cut in, moving a finger around my nipple. "Nowhere . . ." I run my hand mechanically over his skin. "I'm a little blurry, you understand . . ." I camouflaged my distraction.

The whirlpool swept me away ever since the beginning of the official meeting in the theater. At the end of it, Jorgenson suggested that the director of the troupe, Sayyid Ashabi, tour the site with Madame Tsuriel. I felt the floor of the foyer begin to move, along with the rock stratum of Jerusalem.

"Excellent idea!" said Sayyid. "I can take you in the car." And the whirlpool increased, practically an earthquake.

"I'll wait at the Khan Theater," the words burst out of my mouth.

"Tomorrow at eleven?"

I only nodded.

"Fantastic," his voice was cutting my back now, along with his hand smoothing, with delicate courtesy, when we got out of the car at the foot of the site. He climbs behind me, a model of European restraint. Looking in turn at the landmarks and at me, with the maps blowing in the wind, through the smile kindled in the lines of his eyes, slightly twisting his well-shaped lips. Mumbling a few ideas about scattering the members of the troupe among the pods of the Settlements of the Huts, about music and singing from the top of the ridge and along the path, and "of course, a mixture of texts from the Koran and the Torah . . . That's what they expect from us, right? . . ." Knowing he had already captured me among the ruins of earthquakes.

[Jersey City Exit.]

The bus gets off the Turnpike. The driver speaks over the intercom. Traffic jams. Have to detour. Industrial area. Warehouses. Broken sidewalks.

On the way back in the car parked in the sun outside the UN camp, the incandescent air. Sayyid put his hand on the key, without starting the car, examining me in the increasingly charged air. Only then did he put his hand on my face. Knowingly. And how, with ravaging lips, I'll gulp the finger he left on my lips, waiting for me to take it between the tongue, the lips. The bitter taste of sweat and earth, in the floods of hair and skin and sucking. Only then did he start the car with one hand, while the other went on sailing inside me. That's how he drove along the St. Clair Monastery that blurred, along the entrance road to the Scottish Hospice. I remember the sway of his hips as he slammed the car door, leaving me gaping open on the seat, and climbed the gravel path, was swallowed up in the blue of the ceramic gate of the Mandatory enclave, to find out if there was a room. Then he returned, took the bag from the car, and me, leaning on him. We went up the stone slope, and as soon as the mother superior closed the door, he took the gas burner out of his backpack along with the pot, the coffee and pitas he had smuggled in, preparing everything in advance, even how he'd put the mattress of the narrow bed on the floor, gently take hold of my waist, press his tongue on my scared laugh, lead us to the wintry rectangle of sun that would set and rise again on us and would withdraw, inundating the cypresses on Mount Zion, the flow of cars at the foot of the wall. We left the room only after a whole day of black coffee cooked on the gas burner, and pitas dipped in hyssop and shared saliva.

And the speech that burst out of Sayyid. Wave on wave. Not really to me. Like a chance conversation on a trip. To a stranger to whom he could entrust his story, for free. And the tatters of his voice have wound around me since then. Even now, on the highway, galloping to Manhattan.

"Let's start with childhood. In Silwan," he lit a cigarette sometime in the heart of the night. "Yes, not far from here. Mother from near Bethlehem. Father taught English in a mission school. A Jordanian position. 'Study and work hard,' that was his lesson. My career begins in school. A choirboy, helping in the holiday preparation, decorating for celebrations. Sneaking near the border in the afternoons with my friends. Running on the roofs up to no-man's-land, provoking the Israeli soldiers in the distance. Completely innocent. Everything changed at the end of high school, in '64, when I went on vacation to Father's sister. She married a UN soldier from Indonesia and moved to Amsterdam with him. My brother-in-law took me to work with him in a garage. For me, a boy from southern Jerusalem under Jordanian rule, everything was new. Even the discovery that my singing made an impression, and getting to know a group of musicians from South America, performing in the squares on Sunday. And the first rumors about those who were forming cells." The cigarette smoke rose from his dark profile, illuminated only by the table lamp, and from his armpit I watched the skin of his face stretched in talking, dragging on the cigarette.

"I don't have much left from the university in Amman. I studied engineering, hard to believe, and I was head of the dramatic activities of the student union. And then, in the summer of '67, I returned to Jerusalem. To another world. The defeat. The Israeli army. The shame. The Jewish girls walking around in the alleys of the market, half naked in miniskirts and tank tops. The worshippers. The destruction, the building. And the West that burst in all at once. The tourists, the commerce. And the paralysis of friends, family. And then, with friends from Haifa, we started going out to cafés. Telling Palestinian stories, that had to be written from the beginning. We toured a little in Nablus and Ramallah, and then in the Arab villages of the Triangle near Haifa and the Galilee. In Taiba, in '69, when we performed after the Communist Party demonstration, the Israeli police put me in jail for two days. So I had a record. I decided that wasn't for me. The smell of Amsterdam pursued me along with everything that came from Europe, from America, from the student uprisings. I hung around Kuwait and Cairo awhile, I flirted with the volatile beginning of the PLO. But in my head I had only Amsterdam and theater. I come with my suitcase. Put all the rage into working with Grotowski's students. Work days on the body, the voice. Start a kernel of a troupe.

Take in friends who escape from Iran. Some of them went back in '79, after the revolution and Khoumeini's rise to power, and later, after the exile of Shapour Bakhtiar, they escaped back to the West. Yusuf Mahdi also returned then. A genius designer. We worked together on all the plays. He died two years ago of blood cancer . . ." Sayyid took a drag, moved his hand mechanically over my body, went on in English heavy with the smell and taste of coffee and cigarettes. "Victor Garcia came at the beginning to work with us. He was the one who named the troupe Gilgamesh, when we didn't really believe we'd last. He urged us to work on a mythic, epic repertoire, and to go toward the great theatrical style of the popular storyteller al-Qussas, the clown al-Muqallid. And after the famous tour in Europe, I came with those ideas to Jerusalem. That was also with Victor's help. He was directing at Ha-Bimah National Theater in Tel Aviv then, and he brought me on as an assistant. His letter of recommendation appeased the border police. He wrote about the importance of establishing a Palestinian theater, and that worked. A few tired theater people even came from Tel Aviv to help us . . . We called the troupe Al-Muqallid-Al-Kuds. A repertoire of farces with acrobatics and clowning. That didn't bother the Israeli censor. And that's how the clown was born, a hybrid, symbol of the troupe, the Palestinian who pretends innocence, to cover his pranks. The street was so humiliated by the occupation that just a word of Arabic from the stage was amazing. I'd come for a few weeks, work with the actors, and go back to Amsterdam.

"One of those times the family arranged for me to meet Kayyina, the daughter of a pharmacist on Salah-a-Din Street. Twelve years old, a schoolgirl in a striped dress and a pinafore, looking at me with dark almond-shaped eyes. We decided the wedding would take place when Kayyina finished school, and then I went right back to Amsterdam. I forgot her," he went on in the dark before sunrise, his voice penetrating me through the blanket we were wrapped in to preserve the warmth of bodies covered with bruises from hitting the floor through the thin mattress. "And then, Mirabel. Mirabel Mansour. Her first performance was in the club of exiles from Lebanon. Most of them were rich, the first ones who escaped at the beginning of the civil war. Like her father, who later moved with his new wife to Detroit. A frenzied hall. We'd all heard about her. This legendary actress from Beirut. I sit there on fire. An evening of erotic poetry in Arabic. Couldn't take in the dazzling beauty, the voice of velvet and embers. I begged her to come work with us, on whatever she wanted. I directed her in enormous roles, whenever she was free between all her performances with Peter Brook or Ronconi. And of course, all those years I was mad about her. The only one who didn't put out. Only saying with her regal smile, 'We'll see, Saaayyiid,' and 'Not noooooow.' Until she escaped in '81, in disguise. Back to Beirut."

The red glow at the end of the cigarette kept time with his breathing. "I left everything and followed her. I arrived two weeks before the Israeli invasion, I put down my suitcase and went out to look for her, knowing they'd kill me if they discovered a Palestinian in the Christian Quarter. I found the street, but at the number of her house, there was nothing but ruins. Later, when we were together again, in an apartment in her hotel, the Israeli air raids started. Only then did she give herself to me. I was drunk on her body. I adored her. In the collapse of everything all around. The buildings, the water. And for me a celebration. And then the expulsion of the leadership, the exodus to Tunis."

He stopped a moment, red roses blooming in the bushes of smoke, and went on in a thick voice. "Kayyina waited six years for me. Not the same little girl anymore. Her almond-shaped eyes grew deep. Her parents arranged everything. The cakes dipped in honey, and the furnished apartment above their apartment and pharmacy. My parents stayed away. Coming up only seldom from Silwan to the splendid house in Sheikh Jarrah. Every night, I'd make love to Mirabel with Kayyina. After two months I couldn't do it anymore, I went to Beirut, via Amsterdam. Mirabel wasn't there anymore. She had escaped to Tunis, taking my heart with her. Kayyina, in her patient way, slowly returned my body to me. But not my soul. She, in her quiet way, decided to continue studying. English literature and education at Birzeit University. To forget the shame of an unloved wife. Later, she also insisted on going to work, an English teacher in a high school in the Maronite Quarter. You know, on the street above the Protestant church. It's not that she needs to work. Her parents' pharmacy is well-established, and even now, in the Intifada, business is off but it's still doing fine. And the summer house in Jericho . . . The bourgeoisie is holding fast . . . And the children. Five-year-old Slima, and Adnan, who's a year old. That keeps her busy. And she gives me space. I can go on directing the troupe. We also do youth groups, festivals, plays, even with the support of the Jewish city government. But, before the Intifada, everything was running down, and when it became too smothering here, I escaped back to the theater in Amsterdam."

He lit another cigarette, and only then did he seem to discover me wrapped up in the blanket on the narrow mattress next to him. "A month after Adnan was born, the Intifada started. And then things started moving. The theater turned into an auditorium for symposia, for press conferences to update foreign correspondents. The troupe changed, too. And the repertoire. As soon as the photo of the boy running with the stone at the tank appeared at the beginning of the Intifada, I knew that was it, a symbol, David and Goliath, something that can electrify the masses, the world. Ever since then I've worked on the play *The Clown,* with the whole story of the Nakkbah, the Palestinian catastrophe. Postponing everything, even work on *The Binding of Ishmael,* which I started with the troupe in Amsterdam. Harnessed to what's happening here, with everything around it. The fall of the Berlin Wall, the release of Mandela, and now it's our story's turn. We also decided that in the near future, we'd try to win as much as possible through negotiation. To play along with the offers to cooperate, even in the middle of the Intifada. There was a poetry festival here in Jerusalem. My friend Assad el Assad agreed to participate. And I also agreed to suggest to the troupe to work on a performance for the opening of that monument to "Peace," built by Madame Ilana Tsuriel . . ."

He looked at me with his ravenous smile and burst out laughing, taking my head in his hands, "And then, with those two Scandinavians, some gorgeous little dame from Paris enters the theater, with a black Afro and a red scarf, walking like that against the light of the entrance, letting in behind her a river of cool water on a hot day, and her head full of ideas about a performance. Something about a Hut, about letting go, excuse me, Sabbatical, I wasn't exactly concentrating, I was peeling off her clothes with my eyes . . ." And again he drew me up in a wild gallop, banging the floor, finally burying his head in my hair, not feeling the tremor still rocking me, without a sound, liberating the weeping inside me that hadn't burst out since your death. Drenched with tears, sweat, sperm, swept away in a whirlpool until the next afternoon, when I caught a cab back to the hotel. I informed Alain that the flight was arriving in Paris on time, and then left almost late for the airport.

The road twists around through marshes and power stations, over train tracks. The skyline of lower Manhattan hoisted on the upraised arm of the Statue of Liberty, sailing off to America's expanses of freedom.

■ ■ ■ ■

You walked through my dream last night. We were sitting together at a bus stop in Haifa. In the lower city. Sabbath afternoon. Shutters closed on workshops and stores. The neglect is clearer in the empty streets. Men's voices burst out of isolated gambling clubs. Playing backgammon in undershirts. The noise of a mob penetrates the street from the distance. Wave after wave sweeps over rooftops, between buildings. Apparently from a stadium beyond the refineries and the port.

We sit on the bench at the bus stop. Not clear how we got there. Waiting for traffic to start after that demonstration, or soccer game. Listening paralyzed to the echoed shouts.

Opposite, on a high first floor, a window flies open. A thin little girl with black hair leans out, seven or eight years old. Very dark, wearing a simple cloth dress. Looking into the distance. Stretching over the sill and thrusting out her lips painted with a woman's bold lipstick. As if she felt our look, she preens with a kind of caustic innocence. And then, all at once, she withdraws. Leaving a dark, empty space, as if she were hinting at something.

You slowly turn your head to me. The blue glows from your eyes, rips the dream like a laser beam, clears your wrinkles, your white forehead. Your lips move, utter something.

Then (or a minute before, and only because of the gleam I didn't notice), the noise of the mob breaks into sounds landing in the dusty street, immediately covered by the rumble of the bus. The mob bursts out of the stadium to the sidewalk, the bus emits hot exhaust. They immediately rustle in its windows, twitching hands and heads.

You get up from the bench, clasp the pole of the bus, tug yourself up the steps. And I'm behind, trying to protect you, not knowing exactly from what—from stumbling? From the enmity of the faces staring from the windows? From the driver urging, "Well, you gonna move, man?" Choking with the insult, helplessly following your supreme effort.

The realism of the dream. Bringing back the painful illuminated hours together at the end. Lying a long time before the dream went away.

Last night. Fifteen minutes after I came in, a phone call from Sayyid. As soon as he returned from Tunis to Amsterdam, at least that's what he said. "You're my second phone call, Lana, after Kayyina in Jerusalem . . .

"Stop believing the newspapers . . . if the Americans don't show some colonialist muscle, nothing will happen . . . It's not Saddam . . . Sooner or later they'll have to accept the Third World, the Muslim world, yes, the invasion of Kuwait may have been hasty, but it was justified. To return the lands of the Iraqi nation. That's nothing compared to their haste in mobilizing an army in the West to defend the prices of oil and some rotten sheikhs . . ."

He spits out the syllables choked with wrath, in a voice drenched with a sarcasm I hadn't known before. "Is anybody in America talking about the suffering of the population in Baghdad? A friend of mine saw a woman in the street in Baghdad leave her crying baby on the sidewalk and run away. Absolutely crazy. Shouting, 'I can't listen to it crying anymore! I don't have the milk, I don't have the milk!' It all takes me back to Beirut, Lana, to that awful summer of '82, a month without water . . . everything repeats itself . . ."

Covers everything with his pained laugh, the clown of history. Laughs as if it were all just one more of the violent farces he directs, "What is really happening with us, Lana, is the mass migration of Jews from the Soviet Union to Palestine. A Zionist plot. A base exploitation of 'the crisis' by the Jewish lobby in Washington. Every month tens of thousands arrive. Russians again, like your father . . ." In a panic, I found myself asking, "What about the performance?" as if building the falling Hut of David is what will protect us now. "Haven't yet made a final decision in the troupe. You've got to understand . . ." he answered quickly. "We'll talk in New York . . . No, the theater tour hasn't changed. Everything is as planned. Also our meeting in the New World . . . although it's impossible to know, Arafat's support of Saddam Hussein doesn't increase our market value. They don't even let us tell about the pain . . ." He burst into a long, teasing, wounded laugh. "The expelled sons of Abraham, eh?"

And then he broke off, whispering sweetly, without any embarrassment, "I want you, Lana, I want you, now . . . Lana, Lana . . ." whispering in a blend of pain and mockery, almost like a phone-sex operator. "Give me your body, swarthy as you are, I want to climb with kisses on the palm tree of your Jewish neck, give me, give me, Lana . . ." He didn't really wait for me to answer when he hung up.

His whispers stay with me all morning, at odds with the dream about you, Father. As in Amsterdam, when I stole a night changing trains from Copenhagen to Paris, a few days before the trip here with the boys and Alain.

Maybe our softest meeting. Sayyid waits for me on the platform, wrapped in the black leather jacket and white scarf. Looks different in the northern light. Takes me to the car that smells of tobacco and old upholstery, and piles of journals in Arabic, English, German, Dutch, on the backseat, the floor. And the hours sipped slowly in the director's studio of the Gilgamesh Theater, in the garret over Prinzengracht. With traces of other lovers. The lipstick in the drawer of the bathroom, a pair of women's sunglasses among the coins and the key rings in the copper bowl on the cabinet. And the rustle of the canal, the Dutch light descending slowly on the wooden beams of the ceiling, and the silence that wrapped the two of us, as if that were possible.

And sometime in the middle of that night, the two of us wrapped in white jalabiyas Sayyid took out of the closet, we opened the folder of Rembrandt engravings he had collected for his work on the play *The Binding of Ishmael.* Intently going over the various versions of the expulsion of Hagar, amazing in the depth of their commentary. The etching of Sarah and Isaac at the dark lintel of the window, in the center. Watching Hagar and Ishmael going off, with Abraham's back still visible between them. He is accompanying them for only a short stretch, not leaving Sarah's sight. And the etching of Sarah raising her hand, ordering Hagar into exile, and Hagar turning her head aside. Abraham doesn't appear at all. Only the lady and her maid, the passionate hatred between the two women, the two nations. And the softest etching of all, Abraham following Hagar and Ishmael, refusing to part from his loved ones. Bending over them, caressing the boy's head, the woman's arm, one last time, torn away from them at the crossroads. We passed the etchings one by one under the lamp, with Sayyid's quotations from the Koran, with my interpretations from the Midrash, shrouded in the pleasure of thinking together.

And then, the etchings of the Binding of Isaac. Rembrandt's long peeling of the enigma, layer after layer. Until his last etching, the most human of them all.

"Look, Sayyid," I grabbed his arm, stunned. "Look how the angel comes right out of Abraham's forehead. That's not an angel! That's Abraham's thought. It's over Abraham's forehead that the angel spreads his wings! Look, the center of the etching is the illuminated forehead. The drama takes place here, in the new understanding forming in Abraham. See how he looks into himself, concentrating on what's becoming clear in him. This is the moment when he understands the test God has set for him! Yes, now, at the last moment, he understands in a flash, that the test of faith is precisely in disobedience, in refraining from the selfish yearning to demonstrate his faith, in not sacrificing his son, but saving him! Abraham understands he has to struggle against the madness to kill out of faith. Because instead of a son you can sacrifice a ram, a substitute, an expiation . . . See, Sayyid," I whisper to him. "See, only now does Abraham understand, and the new idea shocks him. It moves the angel's wings. See how he lets the knife go from his fingers. See how his hand is completely flaccid. And how softly he covers Isaac's eyes with his right hand, as in the Shema prayer, as in the wonderful engraving of old Abraham and little Isaac playing between his legs. And see how the boy puts his head in the lap of the old man, who looks like Rembrandt. And the old man strokes him like a mother, like a father. As in the chapter in Jeremiah," I'm carried away and quote to Sayyid fragments of biblical verses I translate into English with an effort and a lot of gestures, "'Is Ephraim my dear son? Is he a pleasant child? . . . for since I spake against him, I do earnestly remember him still: therefore my bowels are troubled for him; I will surely have mercy upon him . . .' You understand, Sayyid, in that chapter, God talks about his troubled bowels, God with a womb . . ."

And then, in one of the moments that night, you walked there between us, Father. In your white robe. Echoing the verses I quote from your writings, you joining your breathing with my breathing drenched with the taste of Sayyid's tobacco. Then, in those few hours, when it seemed possible to let everything go, everything between us. "You understand, Sayyid, that's my plan for the Hill of Evil Counsel, there to let go of the knife, to let go, there, dwelling in the Settlement of Huts, with the study groups at Mount Sabbatical . . ." ("This is the place where, according to tradition, Abraham stopped on his way to Mount Moriah," your voice echoes in my ears explaining on the family outing, and the wind blows Mother's hat, the lapel of Aunt Rachel's shirt.) And the smell of Dutch cheeses blended with the steam of the black coffee Sayyid made at dawn, and the ride to the train, I'm wrapped all the way in his leather jacket, and then his image receding on the platform. Standing alone with his white scarf, until he was swallowed up. I'm carried south in the heated railroad car. Through the distances swathed in the mist of northern Europe, plains dotted with electric lights, running along the tracks. Blocks of graying dawn sally forth from the dark. The somber flicker of canals, hills of coal, factories, long, blind buildings. All of me torn between the smell of Sayyid and longings for you. Carried south in the swaying railroad car, a few days before the trip here, in an effort to save the relationship with Alain. And the light rises on an alien, northern spring.

■ ■ ■ ■

[Eve of Rosh Hashanah.]

A few more hours before the holiday. Quickly moving the students' sketches of the Huts, the drawings, to clear a place for our notebook. Scared, yes, just scared to cross the threshold of the year without the traditional phone call to you, wherever I was in the world, to wish you a good year, my heart always pounding in my throat, that maybe this time was the last time. Ever since morning, my hand reached out for the phone and withdrew. As if when the phone rang with no answer in the apartment overlooking the bay, I would lose you again. And Mother already left us fourteen years before. And Aunt Rachel passed away at the end of April, a little more than two months after you. Fingers disconnected, one by one, from the hand. This cluster of threatened blood relations, me and the children and Alain, who returned at the last minute, to be with us. Maybe that's why I insist on celebrating Rosh Hashanah. Sending the boys with Graciella to wash. Ironing white shirts for them. And in the kitchen, my hesitant cooking efforts send out to the rented house on the freeway the smells of the kitchen from Haifa, where they wandered from abandoned kitchens in the Jewish Pale of Settlement in Volhyn.

And maybe it's all about conjuring up the smells of early autumn with the bitterness of mothballs wafting from the sweater I wore for the first time that season in the evening falling on Mount Carmel, as we walk together to the small synagogue. On Rosh Hashanah, on the eve of Yom Kippur, and on Simkhat Torah with a paper flag and the picture of the Ark of the Covenant covered with crumbs of gold, and the apple and the candle you carefully made for me, or for you.

As we walk together in the quiet streets filling with your voice, and the round challahs and the bowl of honey ready in your childhood kitchen. In the yard, your grandfather's atonement rooster already running around, your companion for two weeks. Every year, you'd hide under the bed so as not to hear his cries when he was slaughtered, and wouldn't come out until Rachel, your older sister, coaxed you. We walk together along the well-tended gardens and the pine tree trunks, to the synagogue. And then you'd add, in a whisper, like a prayer before the prayer, "In '43 they destroyed the town. Grandmother had died before that. Grandfather, Father, and Mother were murdered at that time. And Tiomka, too, my little brother, with his bride, Bath-Sheba. They dug a mass grave at the edge of the Jewish cemetery of Tulcin, shot them, and they fell into it."

And in the men's section, where I would sneak in because I was short, I'd look at you, in the small tallith, and the satin kippah, which you'd take out of your pocket in embarrassment a moment before we entered. Only later did I understand that only with me, the daughter of your old age, did you start the custom of going to the synagogue a few times a year.

This morning, after calling Ella in Kibbutz Nahal-Oz in the Negev, and congratulating her and Hezi on their third grandchild, in an attempt to break my anxiety, I finally called Uncle Yehiel in the moshav. Never had there been a direct connection between us. Differences of age, his taciturn nature. He remained Aunt Rachel's son, or David's father. Yet, ever since the Yom Kippur War, I've called him for a brief talk once a year.

"Nice you called, Ilanka! A good year to you, too."

I hear the surprise through Uncle Yehiel's heavy speech.

". . . Right, Mother passed away so close to Uncle Aaron . . . I know, you had a special relationship with her. She talked about you with great admiration, Ilanka."

I didn't dare mention David.

"What, Iraq?" echoed Uncle Yehiel's voice. "Yes, there's a little tension. People are buying rolls of plastic."

"Buying what?"

"Yes, they issued instructions to the population to get hold of plastic, to seal the windows. In case there's a chemical attack."

And finally, ". . . You, too, a good year, Ilanka, and to Alain and the darling David and Jonathan. A good and blessed year. Thanks for mentioning Mother. Thanks, Ilanka."

And from the international line, capering on the ocean floor, "the story" of Aunt Rachel burst here, into the house at the other end of the world, from the kibbutz overlooking the Valley of the Kinneret and the Golan. That story, immutable down to the last tones of your voice, the pauses, the emphases, I would proudly imitate at the youth movement meetings, appropriating the story of Aunt Rachel, the short woman with the masculine haircut and the cheap cigarette drooping from the corner of her mouth, standing erect, her hand in the pocket of her cloth trousers, with her hoarse voice and her humor. "David's grandmother," the cousin "named after him," who looks at me with his blue eyes, on our visits to Uncle Yehiel at the moshav.

"That was in the second year after the kibbutz was founded," the story opens solemnly. "Hostility reigned in the Galilee, even under the British Mandate, after the Turks left. Palestinian tenant farmers who had worked the land of the Damascus effendis for years were incited against the Jewish settlers. David, who came at the turn of the century with the Second Aliyah, had worked the land ever since his youth in Kherson. He was one of those Jewish farmers from the Ukraine. Tall, curly-haired, with soft eyes. The Arabs called him Dawud. He was popular among them, as one who knew their tongue, who went in and out of their villages on his purebred mare, Ruhamka. It was at the workers' movement conference soon after Rachel came to the Land of Israel that she met David. She was one of the advocates of the women's training farm, and David, an old-timer in the Land, shy, a man of open expanses, came to hear the voices of the young generation, and there he saw Rachel." Here you'd stop and a flicker of laughter capers over the lines around your eyes, anticipating the punch line, "There was great love between them. They were a special couple.

"The evening before, shots were heard. Arab gangs crossed the Jordan and inflamed local elements. The kibbutz members who were clearing stones or planting the prepared fields returned to the settlement lying in their carts, hiding from gunfire. The next day, David went to the mukhtars of the nearby villages, riding on Ruhamka, to ask them to intervene to calm things down. He relied on their respect for him, on his good connections. Afterward, he planned to continue south, to the settlements in the Jezreel Valley, to alert them to the approaching gangs.

"Before he left he went by the infants' house to kiss two-year-old Yehiel." Here the voice grows stronger, and the eyes are raised. "Yehiel was one of the first children in the kibbutz. That day, like every morning, David left next to the bed a smooth stone he found during his night guard duty. They had a joint collection of stones, the collection now in the moshav at Uncle Yehiel's, do you know it?" The story never omits the detour to that rather wretched heap of stones at the edge of the lawn. And I also include the detour in my imitation for my friends in the youth movement. "In the moshav, at my uncle's, you can see the stones David brought him from riding the mare Ruhamka. Stones from all over the Land of Israel. Even from the Golan, and from his secret riding to Syria and Iraq . . ." I would exaggerate to add a halo of Orientalism to the heroic feats I appropriated.

"Aunt Rachel went out to say goodbye to David. That was one of their customs, and nobody dared disturb them, even though their married life deviated from the rules of behavior of the kibbutz. She would accompany him to the top of the hill, and from there she'd watch him gallop across the fields, until he and the mare disappeared into a small cloud in the distance."

Here, the silence gapes. And then, the voice is cracked, weary. "David was hit by a sniper's bullet from an ambush of the gangs from El Bira and Arab-el-Bashwa. Ruhamka continued with David hanging on to her, bleeding. She galloped to Merhavia. From there the settlers took him in a wagon. On the way to the hospital in Afula, he passed away. The mare accompanied him all the way to the gates of the hospital." And again, after marveling at the horse's loyalty, the voice grows hard in consternation, even anger, never expressed explicitly. "The news circulated all day. But it got to Rachel only in the evening . . . When she finished putting Yehiel to bed in the children's house, Reuben Berger and Zelig Schwartz waited for her to come out. She understood immediately."

I heard several versions of the hours she stayed on their hill and shouted. The story always gets to Rachel's shouting, and there it's torn off, anarchic. Like her shouting, all night long. Keeping the kibbutz awake, and nobody dared approach. Until morning. Then she fell silent, wiped her face, and went to the children's house, to be with Yehiel when he woke up.

The story of the shouting is what accompanied me throughout the night flight from Marseille, in the summer of '74, and afterward, when I changed three buses from the airport to go straight to the kibbutz, for the ceremony of moving David's body from the military plot to the kibbutz cemetery, "to be buried next to his grandfather." I was the first one of the family to get to Aunt Rachel's quarters, and I went out with her up the climbing path facing the mountains of Bashan, above the palm groves of the Valley of the Kinneret, listening to what she told me in her smoke-drenched voice, as if she were obliged to deposit those words in my ear. "When David was gone, I had thoughts of the end, Ilanka," she said abruptly.

For a moment, I didn't know which of the two Davids she meant, and only the sight of the black earth and the straw stalks in the fissures of dryness streamed in front of my eyes.

"I had to make a decision whether to go on or to follow David," she continued with the same directness. "Yes, there was the ideal, there was communal life in the kibbutz," she pondered a moment. "But private life existed only in secret. You didn't talk about it. It had no place. We didn't know how to live it, Ilanka," she concluded with a phrase she had surely been ripening for a long time.

"I decided to go on only for Yehiel," she said, and straightened her head with the masculine haircut, the cheap cigarette in the corner of her mouth. The shadow of the cypresses in the cemetery loomed over the gleaming path. And then we reached the square.

The family poured out of the vehicles. Ella and Hezi went through Haifa to pick up you and Mother, who was sick by then. Uncle Yehiel and a few other members of the moshav were milling around, along with David's army buddies and officers in uniform. Aunt Rachel was receiving them there, shaking hands, and next to her was Uncle Yehiel, a broad-shouldered man, a bit stooped, and now the last chapter of the family story passed to him. Right after Tsilla and he got the announcement from the soldier who knocked on their door, he got into the pickup truck and drove north from the moshav, to the kibbutz. He arrived after midnight. Aunt Rachel had already gone to sleep. When he came into her room, she sat up in bed and looked at him. He didn't have to say a word. He just sat down next to her. She put her hand on his head, and he burst out crying. "The only time he ever cried," the story concludes.

You were afraid to tell me the news directly on the phone to Paris, or in a letter. Maybe you guessed something. Claude went to Israel at the end of the Yom Kippur War, and he also paid you a visit. You told him then about David's death and asked him to tell me in person. He hurried to Paris, called me out of the meeting of our association, and there, in the corridor, hugging, supporting as always, he very slowly said the few words. When I didn't respond, he repeated what he had said, thinking I hadn't picked it up, reciting what you had told him:

"Your cousin, David, yes, your aunt's grandson. Killed. On the last day of the war. By a sniper at the Suez Canal." Only later did he admit how much my response scared him. I returned to the meeting and stayed there until it ended. I didn't let him come with me.

I walked in a daze to the Métro, sitting stonily all the way, with a look that erased the billboards, the façades of the rue de Rivoli at the Métro station exit. And for some reason, a gleam of the wintry sea kept flickering over and over in me, on the Sabbath when David came unexpectedly to Haifa. He stands in the door of the apartment with his bright smile, a fifteen-year-old boy. Both of us embarrassed by the boldness, we went out for a long walk, from the Carmel to the port, sneaking through a breach in the fence to the jetty, standing at the end of the pier to feel the wind on our faces. He with a laugh of blue splinters and I with a burst of curls that struck my face, his face, not even daring to hold hands. Only later, in the apartment, did the crying burst. Hours, Father. For what I never had time to tell you. When I finally came from Paris to be with you, I understood that it was too late now, that you could no longer stand that chapter of the family story. I silenced it in Sayyid's chest. Wiped the tears on his skin covered with salt and the bitterness of cigarettes. Weeping, too, because I'll never be able to tell him, because he'll never be able to hear.

The boys are washed, wearing white shirts. I sent David to pick some branches to decorate the table, and Jonathan ran after him. "Watch out for your white shirts," I called to them, knowing that was the extent of our ritual here.

Soon the holiday begins. And two generations of Jews will sit at the decorated table, in a kind of postmodern station, beyond the Sambatyon River of planes and airports. And the arms of the boys that will twine around my neck, Father. Lifting your eyes to me through their look.

The words of the Mahzor, the holiday prayer book, suddenly echo: "Who will live and who will die; who will die at his predestined time and who before his time." And the yearning to clutch your white head to me now, to wait for your blessing, "Yes, a good year, Ilanka."

[Holiday Inn. Broadway. The bar on the second floor.]

Another fifteen minutes until the meeting with Claude.

Electric-blue sofas. On the glass table a shot of vodka. The alcohol rush dulls the searing sights on the highway, on the sidewalks of Manhattan.

Snatching a minute before I ask the desk clerk to tell Claude I'm here.

He called from Brussels, coming to New York for two days. To arrange final details for the conference, "Monuments of Memory," "and to see you."

"I've reserved a room at the Holiday Inn. Yes, in the middle of Broadway . . . What, I want to feel the big city, with all the junkies and with you," the Flemish way he chews up French. "When does your Palestinian director arrive? In another week? Good, by then there won't be a trace of me left."

"Lana," passionate about his work, he becomes serious, "I need more for the interview with you in the catalogue. A few more questions about, the Hut, your 'anti-monument,' this 'temporariness' and 'letting go.' How you connect those two radical notions of space in a monument to peace. The material goes to the printer next week." . . . "Good, Thursday, after you finish at Cooper, I'll start the countdown . . ."

Claude Campens. Our fleeting love affair. "The ruins of time," as he hummed at the fixed, ceremonial end of our first kiss (and everything that was sewn together and unraveled in that long dive. An ocean that melts again).

For years we've been like that, "on the roads" together. Ever since the first conversation (long before meeting Alain) between two café tables across from the Beaux-Arts, an excited exchange of words that lasted until morning, on the changing stage set of the Paris streets, and a June sunrise that paled in his student room. And ever since (more than twenty years), always that same burst of joy, the strong awakening, the architectural insights, the inspiration.

Always only loyalty of a journey, in a disconnected sequence (more lasting than all) of furtive meetings, between other relationships. Beyond my marriage to Alain, beyond his marriage with Charlotte, the birth of Bridget, and, later, his return to an empty house, from one of his trips for our association, when Charlotte left him for the microbiologist from Ghent, taking Bridget with her, and how devoted he still is to his daughter. The unchanging smell of Gauloises from his jackets. And the "very Jewish" intensity of that Flemish man. Inexhaustibly loyal to the struggle for righteous architecture, through the establishment of the association, the projects, editing the journal, organizing conferences, symposia. Only his long, delicate face grew sharp when it grew lined. The clock dial etched around his eyes surveys me in a pensive close-up when we meet again. Following his finger as he drags on his cigarette, redrawing the line of my cheek.

The sound of glass clinking. Brief glimmers in the gloom of the bar.

The movements of the Italian bartender. Next to him, an assistant with a heavy accent arranges the glasses. Russian or Yugoslavian. A smell of lemon dilates the nostrils.

At breakfast the newspaper between me and Alain. Scanning the headlines. "In a speech to the nation, President George Bush announced that the American people must prepare for the possibility of bloodshed in the Persian Gulf. 'The Iraqi aggression is a political test of how the world will be run after the Cold War . . . As long as sanctions don't change Saddam Hussein's position, and the withdrawal of Iraqi forces from Kuwait, the United States has other means. Saddam Hussein must fall.' "

Alain turns the paper to him, stares at me, "Have to take Saddam Hussein seriously," he reads ironically. " 'Dear brothers, now it is your turn to save humanity from the corrupt forces of evil that exploit us, and are led by the United States. That is the Holy Jihad, the just war against wickedness, as written in the Holy Koran.' Got to take him seriously. The Americans don't read the map, nor do the intellectuals in Europe." Ever since he returned he hasn't stopped proving to me, siphoning into political analysis all our inability to hold on to one another.

Alain stands up, pale. "The destruction of the State of Israel will be the first stage . . ." he mutters, leaving the paper on the table, and leaves. And yet, at night, our bodies continue their own conversation. In the stung silence the passion burns, growing darker as the coming of Sayyid and the troupe approaches.

On the way here, on the block between Seventh and Eighth avenues, a group of young men handcuffed, pushed to the fences, their arms raised.

Policemen rummaging in their trousers. Poking them with black rubber truncheons.

Extracting the drugs, the white crystals of despair, the serpent's seed spreading in a glowing dust on the mob.

The fire on the freeway. Rising above the black gold refineries. An eternal fire, day and night, digesting oil that slowly thickens, drop by drop. Flowing into pipes of seed, into sweat flowing from the handcuffed arms, raised on Forty-second Street, along the white erection (fifty storys) of the merciless Grace Building.

Treasures of the globe and its spices crushed in shaded olive oil press, in the world's libraries of passion. Taken to the fire in steel canals and merchant ships. From Dubai, Kuwait, and the cliffs of Hadhramaut.

Fire that burns the few dreams we dragged here in the bundles of those descendants from Canaan: a little wheat, a sack of barley, fodder for a donkey, and our children in camp with us.

An isolated eternal fire above the scaffolding at the gates of hell: ready-made objects held for a moment in the burning lens.

A fire in the skies of the refinery. Writing over and over the big erasure. The crushing of words and names once uttered in silence, in far-away rooms.

On the sofa opposite is a couple. They look Jewish. Middle-aged. From Queens or Brooklyn. (Maybe that's just my obsession.) Resting in the air-conditioning. Stretching out their legs.

"Did you call?"

"Yes, yes. I called. I told him about the medical exam."

"You did?"

"Yes."

"So rest now. Rest a little."

Dressed in ironed clothes, old ones. On the carpet at the woman's feet, a crushed purse and a plastic shopping bag.

Meeting with Claude. Betrayal of betrayal. Of Alain with Sayyid, of both of them with Claude. Though in fact, if there is betrayal here, it's only of you, Father. Forever, with everybody. Or maybe fidelity to your sperm, an eternal flame destroying me. Now, as tanks in Eastern European squares crush monuments to Lenin. When once again history erases the "millions of dead slaughtered wholesale who have trampled a path in the void," in the words of Osip Mandelstam. Yes, I have nights of poetry séances, Father. Mandelstam, Blok, Tsvetayeva, early Shlonsky. "Your" voices. Torn poetry of the individual, amid the emotion of the masses. Broad, wounded voices, writing the secret scroll of the century. The desperate love that burns them, and me within them. Reading Tsvetayeva last night, like "an animal that someone has stabbed in the gut."

At three-thirty I finally go down to the reception clerk.

"Campens, room 215."

The clerk looks at me out of the corner of his eye, turns his back to me, his hair sticky with gel, grunts into the house phone, "Mr. Campens, you have a visitor."

Continuing to write at the end of the elevator lobby, with the notebook leaning on the wall.

Claude appears in the open doors. His face slides over the face of the elevator boy. Profile on profile for a moment (like a detail from Fra Angelico).

Approaches in a summer jacket and denim tie. I see him see me, measuring in writing his steps, and his smile lighting up for me.

■ ■ ■ ■

[Port Authority. I missed the seven o'clock bus.]

I ran all the way to Forty-second Street, past the sex shops, past the drug dealers on the corner of Eighth Avenue and the parking lots, past the homeless gathering around the walls of Port Authority, and nevertheless I was late.

I stop at a snack bar on the second floor. Behind the control room with its rows of monitors. (The only place where it's not so dangerous to wait.) Clutching the bag with all the material Claude gave me, and the souvenirs I bought for the boys: "I'll bring you something before bedtime." For David a pocketknife with a fur-covered case, and for Jonathan a pencil with a rabbit-shaped eraser.

From the other side of the glass wall, a trio of heavyset guards. Riding on the cheeks of their buttocks, the weapons. A baton, a gun, an iron rod, chains. Rising and falling as they walk.

The guards go off amid the cardboard surfaces of the homeless lying at the door of the candy shop, the newspaper stands, the shoemaker.

I collect the crumbs of the bran muffin. Calmed down from the running. Articulating, for you, the moments with Claude in the room above Broadway. Dropping the ash of the Gauloise into a paper cone, leaning his long body on the pillows, and I'm between the sheets, lecturing freely, until he pulls me to him by my neck, "You're so beautiful when you're excited, Lana."

"Let me talk," I get away with a laugh.

"All right, but a little slower, don't forget that it's all being recorded."

"Where were we?"

"At Tsuriel's decision to go back and build in Israel, and Jerusalem at that, after her declarations over the years that she'd never go back." He rests the microphone on his knee.

"Maybe we should forget this confession . . ."

"Look, Lana, I came to New York especially to finish the interview with Tsuriel for the catalogue. I tried to see you in Paris, before you left with Alain and the boys for New Jersey, but aside from dragging me to the theater for five hours, you were too busy applying to the UNESCO competition, and when you went to Denmark, you couldn't find a few hours to stop in Brussels because you still had to work in Amsterdam on the performance with Sayyid Ashabi . . ."

"Okay, okay . . ." I pull up the sheet, and the static of the tape recorder blends with the hum of the air conditioner and the hushed whisper below of Broadway. "So where do we start?"

"Start with your choice to get involved again in a national vision, now of all times, with the fall of the Berlin Wall, the unification of Europe, 'the end of history.' What impels you to seek particularistic, Jewish architecture? Why suddenly turn to a structure like 'Hut,' the Sukkah, or the concept of 'Sabbatical' as an architectural inspiration?"

"Fine." I sit up straight between the sheets, my breasts hanging heavy in the pale light from the window, and speech finally flows like milk. "In fact it all started four years ago with the project of the yeshiva in Strasbourg. I agreed to work on a religious project when I learned that more than fifty percent of the yeshiva students were refugees from the Soviet Union. I decided I couldn't discriminate against refugees just because they're Jews who insist on studying Torah. Refugees are refugees are refugees . . .

"And then I had to start finding out what a 'yeshiva' really was—it means 'sitting,' you know?—thinking about the paradox of Jews who sit down to study in the middle of wandering, on way stations. In Pompaditha, in Provence, in Fez, in Lublin. And also to start finding out what it is to 'study

Torah,' or, in fact, 'to be a Jew.' For the first time, 'I opened a book,' I mean a Jewish book, Mishnah, Talmud, Shulkhan Arukh . . . You must understand, Claude, we grew up cut off. With contempt for those 'Diaspora' 'religious' texts. How can I explain it to you . . . that was part of the auto-da-fé that took place in the Land of Israel. Zionism lopped off every other identity. Arabic, Diaspora, Jewish." The room smelled of air-conditioning and cigarette smoke. The façades of the buildings across Broadway filled the wide window. Claude, leaning along the bed, an afternoon light making his skin even whiter, his thin fingers stroking the curve of his lips in concentration, and the cigarette dangling from them.

"And there of all places, in my hours of strenuous reading in the Jewish libraries in Paris, without any background of how to approach all the talmudic filaments of legal discussions, judgments, that ancient language, there of all places, and from the architectural point of view, I found a stunning model of thought about building, and completely different notions of place, of dwelling. So different from the Western notions of beauty we had learned. Close to what we had always looked for, Claude, an architecture of nomads, guided not by the holiness in beauty or force, but the holiness in the kernel of life, the most intimate movements of human existence . . ." Lecturing to Claude's tense look, with all the sentimentality, all the Russian pathos you bequeathed me.

"Wait a minute, not the whole Torah all at once. Just one example. Don't forget, you're dealing here with a completely ignorant goy . . ."

"All right, all right. Here, I made you a copy of the handouts for the seminar at Cooper Union, with quotations from the sources." I jump out of bed, pull out the papers, and continue with the explanation, wrapped only in the smoke of the Gauloises, waving sketches and hands, as if the room above Broadway were a lecture platform of a revolutionary forum. "Look at the talmudic discussion of Sabbatical Year or the laws of Sukkah. Here you can find the most radical definition of the relationship between nation and land—an unnatural relationship!" I came back to bed, continuing the concentrated lesson in Judaism. "There's a precise formulation here of my old uneasiness with the Zionist story, with all the love of the Land steeped in paganism or

German Romanticism. Here's a definition of place with no possibility of owning it. As it says in the wonderful chapter of Leviticus, 'for the land is mine.' Mine—God's—not man's. The land doesn't belong to anybody! It was given as a promise to the nation that came to it from far away, and the promise is 'on condition.' It will be kept only if the nation is at an ethical level that will justify it. Otherwise the nation will be sent into exile. And how do you stay conscious of that condition? By the laws of the Sabbatical Year! Every seven years, in the year of Sabbatical, the fences around the property have to be destroyed, everybody has to be given food from its produce . . . the poor, the neighbor, the foreigner, even the beasts of the land . . . to let go of ownership . . . I found an amazing explanation of that in the Talmud: that seventy years of exile in Babylon were the punishment for seventy years of Sabbatical the nation had not observed since it entered the Land of Israel! Impossible to be in the Land without letting go of it, without opening your hand." I reached out my hand in that movement of opening the fingers, of letting go of the hand, a gesture I had recently become used to doing while sketching. Claude grabbed my hand and hovered his lips over it.

"That's only on condition, Claude, remember . . ."

"I've already let go."

We laughed.

"And think of letting go of money! What a revolution is that notion, especially today in the global village, with the triumph of capitalism! And as for the female aspect . . ." I reached around Claude, took a cigarette from the pack on the other side of the bed, lit it from the match he held for me while running his other hand all along my back, as if reexamining the topographical data.

"Think about a place that can't be owned! Especially the Land of Israel, Jerusalem, the place everybody wants to conquer, to own! Jerusalem, the longed-for city, the woman, the place of yearning . . . to let go of her . . ."

Unloading everything echoing in my head, my body, ever since our last conversation, Father, in the hospital room in Haifa. "And so, when the call came from UNESCO for a 'Peace Monument' in Jerusalem, with all the condescension, the kitsch, and the Western lip service to 'peace in Jerusalem,' I decided I had to submit something. Working from the start on an idea of an 'anti-monument'—'a Hut, a Sukkah.' A rickety place, not monumental, and not to be watched from outside, but sit in it, live in it. Trying to develop in today's terms the notion of Sabbatical, of letting go. The rest you know already, preparing the site with the Settlement of Huts that will constantly be rebuilt by those who live in them, and with the structures of Mount Sabbatical, the kitchen, the library, and the seminar rooms shaped as spaces in between temporary and permanent, with awning roofs open to the sky. And the site itself, on the edge of the desert, with an eternal flow of water. And that, too, between us, influenced by the custom of pouring water on the holiday of Sukkoth, and the libation. And we've already talked about the feminine terminology of the temporary, open planning."

The trio of guards passes the cafeteria, two black, one Hispanic.

Rows of monitors in the control room of the station.

A capering frame of figments of reality. The silhouette of the controller's back bisects it:

Frame of a monitor with the Hudson News stand.

Ticket offices of Suburban Transit.

Screens above the escalator.

A hall with the statue by George Segal, The Commuters. *(Remnant of a time when you could pass through the station with no fear.)*

Long corridor, a girl's back swallowed up beyond the numbers of the platforms.

At some point, in the heart of the full silence, in the rustle of the city and the air conditioner, I added in a whisper, "It's also my way of being close to my father . . . In fact, this project is dedicated to him. He's with me all the time I plan . . . I think about him, about his dream. How he left behind everything to ascend to the Land of Israel. Try to understand what it is to come out of books, longings for a place you mention three times a day in prayers, a place in awareness, and suddenly to be there for real. In the Mediterranean light, in the strong smells of the landscape. The intoxication, the exaltation of the mission to liberate a nation, mixed with embracing the natives, and in the echoes of colonialism, but above all—the vision of conquering the wilderness, building, paving, planting forests." I was already talking in your terms, Father, "and also simply the faith that it's possible to rest at long last, 'to return home.' That the Jews can stop being the victim. Thinking about the faith that was in my father, a secular faith but a faith nonetheless. In him, in my aunt, Rachel, in that generation. Dreaming in spite of everything . . . sometimes all of us seem to be lost characters in a Chekhov play. Me, too, and Alain, and Sayyid. All of us crushed under the steamroller of history, Claude."

And without looking at him, feeling Claude's close look, and some inundating calm, as in the transparent hours at your bed.

"I tried to explain to Sayyid that it's not us or you. It's beyond ownership, robbery, argument about who was here first, who expelled whom," the words kept pouring out. "If there's any meaning at all to the return of the Jews to their land—that aberration in history—it's to make a new revolution in the concept of nationalism, reformulate the connection between nation and land, give up the passion to conquer, to own . . . In this land, there was always somebody. Always coming from beyond the river, beyond the sea, and wandering back to exile. Nation after nation. Maybe that's what the Jews wanted to expose. The place you let go of. A place of dream, of utopia, a place with another dimension, like a Hut. You know, Sukkoth, the Feast of Tabernacles, is the most universal holiday. On that holiday, at the end of days, all seventy nations of the world will sit in a Hut of the skin of Leviathan."

"Amazing image."

"My Iranian student at Cooper Union built his whole model from this inspiration, and from the description in the Book of Zechariah, of the Mount of Olives, where, on that messianic Feast of Tabernacles, that Festival of Huts will burst open, and ancient water will flow through it to the east. It's a revolution of world order . . . I tried to explain that to Sayyid."

Claude removed from my fingers the cigarette that had turned into a stick of ashes.

"How are things with him?" he murmured.

"I'm getting lost. Completely."

"Don't believe you. You just added another one to your 'mille e tre,'" and he hums Leporello's aria from *Don Giovanni.*

"No . . . This time I'm completely lost." I pulled the sheet up. "This stirs something in me beyond Sayyid . . . Something I didn't know that . . ." I fell silent in his loyal embrace, and the rasp of the tape recorder filled the silence.

"And how are things with you, Claude? How's Bridget?"

"Sixteen and a half years old now. Since May I haven't seen her, even though she was in Brussels. Rebellion. Things aren't great between her and Charlotte, and Bridget takes her frustration out on me. If I were her, I'd be mad at her mother and the microbiologist, but now she's taking revenge on me and my ideals. You know, I've taken her to demonstrations ever since she was born. Believe in early exposure. But apparently all the house slippers with the embroidered reindeer in the snow and the Japanese albums and the rolls with raisins I'd run across town to buy her don't satisfy her anymore." Claude exhaled a path of smoke that twined before my eyes, my head resting on his arm. "She's so beautiful, Lana, short like her mother, and fair. With a snub nose and a face that's looking for trouble. I only hope that girl takes care of herself."

Later we got up, collected the clothes from the floor. Claude took out of the suitcase all the material he had brought for me, "recent publicity about Tadashi Kawamata, from the *Documenta,* number 8. The projects in Grenoble: the squatters' apartment and the destroyed church. Look how close that is to your thinking about the Hut." He pulled out the pamphlets, the catalogues, explaining excitedly, "He wraps abandoned structures, slated for destruction, and in temporary materials of rapid construction: boards, scaffolding. I got him to agree to give a lecture at the conference in New York. He'll try to get to Jerusalem, too, if the situation doesn't get too complicated . . ." The inexhaustible Claude.

And standing now, as I smoothed his shirt, he asked, "How was it at the end with your father? You didn't want to talk about that when I came to Paris."

"I was with him for two weeks. Ella would drop in for a few hours from the kibbutz, but most of the time I was alone with him. He was lucid until the last minute. Just imagine, I talked with him about the project. Even in the hospital. He had a special intensity. Some radiance. When I'd come into the room, he'd feel immediately that I was at the door and would turn his head to me with his white curls, with the smile in the blue look, beaming like a spotlight . . ."

Claude took some little bottles of gin and tonic out of the small refrigerator. Poured, stirred for a long time before he gave it to me. "I remember my visit to him in Haifa, in '73," he said. "It was the Yom Kippur War, but I was cut off. In the Franciscan monastery on the Mount of Beatitudes, I learned the fascistic design of the church, the sweetness of the terraces, the palms, the olive trees in the Italian style, and all the time I felt you in that light, in the warmth of the autumn, in something timeless of 'Canaan.' One afternoon I went to Haifa, especially to visit your parents. Your mother didn't feel well and stayed in bed. I sat with your father on the little balcony facing the bay, above the whole sea of green treetops of the Carmel. He insisted on serving us both tea, went back and forth by himself."

"How well I know that . . ."

"And then he asked me anxiously what I thought. How was the Galilee, how was the Kinneret, how was the Jezreel Valley. He asks about every place in a personal way, waiting tensely for my responses. And I sat enchanted only by the landscape of his face. What a face he had."

"Yes . . ."

"When I said that the landscape of the suburbs on the way here wasn't especially beautiful, he responded eagerly, 'Yes, Ilana is also angry about the housing projects. You know, that was her thesis at the Technion. Housing refugees and the uprooted. And she was very critical, and rightly so. But those were years of mass immigration for a young, impoverished state. We had to build fast, and of course we made mistakes . . . Now Ilana is building for the uprooted, the homeless. That's important.' He looked at me, I remember the look, you could see from it how much he loved you. Only at the end of the visit did he tell me about David. Asked me to tell you . . ."

I turned to the window. Claude hugged my back, even when I talked to him without turning around, afraid I'd start crying.

"The two weeks with him . . . at the end . . . that was a gift. You know, in the hospital, he almost couldn't talk because he was so weak, and yet the nurses, the staff, were drawn to him like moths. They sought something from him. Once, maybe two days before he died, he held my hand like this, between his hands, and with an enormous effort he told the nurse taking care of him: 'This is my daughter' . . ." The façades of Broadway were erased. I went on talking with an effort. "In the end, he simply laid his head on the pillow, with that internal serenity, and fell asleep. I was alone with him. I held his hand. On Friday afternoon . . . yeah, well . . ." I break off. Button up the jacket, hoist the bags on my shoulder.

"Take care of yourself," Claude adjusted my collar anxiously. "Don't take on all the jobs, leave a little bit for the actors of al-Kuds and their director."

"You take care of yourself, too." I wrapped myself in him.

"Hey! I almost forgot!" he ran and took the box out of the suitcase. "This is for your boys. Belgian chocolate!"

"They'll gorge themselves on it tonight. I promised to get back before they went to sleep. I've got to leave you."

"That's all right, I've got three hours until the flight. I'll start transcribing the material from the tape, and tonight there's a game—the Chicago Cubs versus the Yankees," he winked, pointing at the television. "I'll catch the beginning, without having to get up at five in the morning!"

Seven twenty-five. The trio of guards approaches. I'll stick close to them on the way to the platform.

■ ■ ■ ■

[On the bus. Back from Manhattan.]

Tomorrow Sayyid and the troupe arrive. The ridiculous pounding of the heart every time the phone rings. The wild knocking afterward. Unable to put an end to the childish comedy.

The trembling window slicing the sunset, bisecting the lanes of lights capering below.

Beyond the West Side Highway the run-down pier gleams for a moment.

Graffiti with names of the dead. The last meeting place before the river of those with AIDS.

And the bus is already sliding into the tunnel, bearing the end of the day to the river bottom. Swallowed up in the Hudson depths of Hades—river of hell, river of oblivion lapping the shores of Manhattan.

Alain is in Washington. Last night, the phone call from him. The embarrassment in the conversation.

"The boys are sleeping."

"Good."

"And how are things with you?"

"Everything's fine . . ."

I no longer try to hide the agitation from Graciella. She surrounds me with her soft dancing steps. And the boys lift their worried faces to me. Jonathan stands in his crib, rocks it toward me with all his might. Even after the story, and after your songs, that have turned into a tradition, their tension doesn't fade.

[Kennedy Boulevard. Weehawken, Hoboken.]

The lighted profile of the city on the other side.

Evening marshes. Expanses of water burning in the sunset.

And again, parking lots all the way to the horizon. Junkyards. Wallowing car skeletons.

Freight cars, glowing sides of trucks. The evening plops down with heavy udders, drenched in merchandise. And you ride next to me to the roads of night.

[Exit 14A, Jersey City, Bayonne.]

The bus cuts through the shadows of trees piercing the sky of the road, the burst of signposts, billboards flickering in the remains of the day. A snake of brake lights twists its ember tail.

[Exit 13A, Newark Airport, Port Elizabeth.]

For a moment the runways and the spotlights are spread out. A rush of lights like a giant fair spreading fireworks to the end of the dark.

[Exit 13, Elizabeth, Goethels Bridge.]

From the torn clouds on the horizon rises the shadow of your back, Father. Gigantic. Bent a little in the highway skies, above the mass of treetops. Withdrawing from the moving road, with the shaking of a distant embrace.

[Exit 12, Carteret, Rahway.]

The planes, lowering toward Newark Airport, slicing the electric wires, the bridges. Rowing in silence toward dark stubble fields. As if accepting. In resignation to the night that will cover everything with its damp hand.

And in recent days listening over and over to the end of *Don Giovanni.* The attempt "to make him repent." Pentiti! "Repent!" The Commendatore calling, the father returning from Hell as a marble statue. And the hypnotic bass voices growing louder. Don Giovanni's proud refusal, remaining a heretic, free of faith, until his death, "No! Sì. No! Sì. No! No! Yes. No! Yes. Noooooo! . . ."

[Exit 10, Edison.]

The bus slips into the dark. Returns the passengers to kitchen lights in suburban houses, to lattices of light and shade cast on the dark of fields, to lighted windows of a local synagogue.

The edges of night's blanket still rolled up there, at the end of the horizon. Gaping in a last glow.

I go on talking with you, Father, the patriarch. You cross beyond time, beyond the highways, the airports. Passing and entering. Again and again. Abraham, Moses, or Joshua. You pass over to me the Promise. Beyond the borders of death.

[On the bus. Traffic jam coming out of Port Authority.]

Holding to your notebook of snapshots. Writing under the tiny sheaf of the overhead light. The rumble of the bus (still) waiting in the traffic jam, mixing Western metaphysics and Mediterranean pain in me, and all the time Don Giovanni's ironic basso, Chi a uṇa sola è fedele, verso l'altro è crudele. "Who is loyal to one, is cruel to all the rest . . ."

Sitting in the dark auditorium with "the enemy," rehearsing *The Clown.* Flashes of images. The giant masks, the violent pantomime.

And then, in the red light cutting the stage, Iman keening in her white garb. Somnambulant spinning above the straw dolls laid down, covered with sheets. Her voice choking in throaty shouts, swallowed in the incense carried by the masks in the depths. Her body falls under the whip of the red light, risen in cruciform arms lifted by the procession intoning Gregorian chant. Then whirling dervishes fill the stage. And from the amplifiers rises the chant of the muezzin, echoed by the crowd in squares packed with people: "Allahu akhbar, Allahu akhbar . . ."

Sitting there in the dark, gripped by shame and fear. Dizziness of the other, dark side of the dream, the suffering, and the hatred. And Sayyid's breath on my arm, the director commenting in the dark. My thigh leaning on his spread leg, stroking it with my foot. Coming, biting my lips hard, in the dark of the auditorium.

Leaving at the end of the rehearsal, not waiting for Sayyid, as we had agreed. Yet when he strokes my hand in parting, with a movement that betrays the familiarity of touch, I can feel the looks of the actors and actresses at my back start the memory of the shouts of rioting in downtown Haifa, back in the fifties, as we came home from the youth movement. The shouts rising at twilight from the buildings, in the wake of the girl running between the alleys, wild, her clothes undone, "Whore of Arabs! Whore of Arabs! . . ." And then, more than an hour later, Sayyid shows up in the coffeehouse. "Don't worry, it'll be all right, Lana," even now avoiding talk about our plan for the performance in Jerusalem. Shutting my mouth with his lips all the way in the cab.

The bus stuck over the glowing canyon of Ninth Avenue.

A moon cut out in tree branches. Shadows whipping like bats. Pentiti! No! Sì. No!

The bass rumble of the motor.

Sayyid locks the door in the hotel room. The accidental space suddenly includes the imported story. In the bathroom the water gushes in the old sink with an enamel spout turgid as a urinal. The towel is hard, overstarched. The wallpaper is turning yellow. The night-light illuminates Sayyid's face inflamed in the glow of the cigarette. The tears that covered his eyes when he bent over. Averts his head, says slowly, "Whenever I'm with you, I'm afraid, Lana, maybe the next time you won't be there . . . That happened to me only once, with Mirabel . . ." Don't know if he's telling the truth, or whispering to inflame.

And the shutter open to the night. Strikes in the wind the honking of traffic, the fire engines galloping in lower Manhattan. And echoes of his words at the conference at Columbia, an elegant flow in a lecture on the birth of the Palestinian theater. Shaping the national identity of a people. The oppression that created it. The occupation, the refugee camps, Zionist racism, and the new hope with the Intifada's children of the stones. Ignites the audience with the story of the Palestinian Calvary.

And the knowledge that something definite is written in the bodies' lines on the white bed. Beyond belonging to a tribe, a story, a family. His hands lift my groin, gather from it a molten liquid that doesn't stop burning. Entwined and dropping. And again the shudder sweeps away the ends of my limbs, runs over my skin. A thin tiger, circumcised, fills the mouth, the bowels, bites deeper and deeper. And the terror that somebody will open the door, and the sheaf of light will expose the yellowing carpet and us on the bed (I haven't known such fear for so long). And the silence at the distance gaping between us again. Despite his arm, laid heavily on my waist. I bury my head in the hollow of his shoulder. And the lines of Tsvetayeva, "And now I know, where love holds power, death approaches soon, like a gardener." I whisper them silently to you, Father, with the saltiness of Sayyid's sweat on my dry lips.

In the distance segments of light of the Manhattan towers. Chains of lights on cruise ships, along the piers.

Pentiti! No! Sì. No!

■ ■ ■ ■

[On the way back. The last bus.]

The trips back and forth. In a nonstop ten-day whirlwind. And only the whispering to you, Father, sustains me on days torn between the boys and Graciella, and Alain, who came back this morning, and the voices from the stage.

Two other passengers besides me and the driver. The light above the seat shakes in the galloping steel box.

The night of the premiere. Despite the postponement. After the last-minute cancellation of the Public Theater, and the effort to move to the Victory, a derelict theater on Forty-second Street. The storm in the media lasts a week. Attacks on "squelching," on "the need to respect freedom of expression, especially with the spread of the American mobilization in the Arabian Desert."

The auditorium is packed. The mixture of languages of the audience. The excited faces. The actors in the dressing rooms, when I sneak in to wish Sayyid success. Pushing to reach him, among all the other guests. Returning to my seat in the dark. Exposed to the text whispered in the earphones in a simultaneous translation, without the Arabic barrier anymore. Trying to convince myself there's no need to be afraid, those are the same words we said years ago in the radical cell in Paris. But anxiety grows from the first scenes. Iman as a little girl on the stage. Rummaging around in a box, finding a tied bundle and in it the colored glass beads of a curtain. Enchanted, she passes them through her fingers, and runs to show her mother what she found. Farida, playing the mother, grabs the beads from her hands and yells: "Ha, my childhood! Ha, my youth!" In the dim lights, the stage is covered with flecks of color capering over the lamenting body. "The bead curtain that hung in the door of the house in Ramle. The light would pass through the lemon tree in the yard and then be broken by the glass beads, creating an enchanted cave. All my dreams I dreamed there." Her voice flows to the spellbound audience. "When my parents and brothers would go out, I, a girl whose breasts had just started to sprout, would wrap myself in the points of light and dance. I would live it all. All the places, all the loves, all the dreams burgeoning like colored points of light . . ." Farida's dancing stops all at once. Her body is caught in a sheaf of white light. Terrified, she and Iman bundle up things and join the convoy of refugees making its way as a silhouette at the back of the stage, turning dark. Stooped bodies with bundles march to the growing sound of Ibrahim's drumming, as he sits surrounded by a battery of instruments. The shudders, a whispering commotion slowly approaching, with the rhythm flowing from his leaping back, his eyes shut, his shoulders, his fingers strumming, his feet tapping. The ringing of clusters of bells, a soft hand, hard on the skin of the tambourines, the yell that breaks out of his upside-down blind face, slices the stage and the auditorium holding its breath.

And maybe even then, in the hewn silence, in the dark, your voice already echoed, Father. Or something else, approaching still faceless in a searing wave of longing, and receding. And then a yellow light rises on a broken wall, skeletons of cars, tatters of clothes drying on a line in a refugee camp. Ali steals up to the barbed wire at the front of the stage, tells the audience: "My grandfather used to take me to the edge of the camp, hold me with his work-hardened hand, and say: 'Ya, my son, ya, my son.'" He starts as a child, turns into a bony old man. "You see them, ya, my son, their soldiers. They stole everything from us and closed us in a coop, like chickens. My life was broken on one day, like a straw. Ya, my son. There's no limit to the disaster, to our Nakkbah. Everything they stole from us. Groves, almond trees, olives. And we're here like garbage. And instead of our villages—their houses, ya, my son. In Giudida, Mror, Mozza, Tsubah, Harat, Deir Ayub, Saris, Bayt Surikh, Bayt Mahsir . . ." "'Grandfather, grandfather,' I'd say to him, 'I'll avenge your pain, the Nakkbah. I'll be strong as a stone, a child of stones!' That's what I told him. At first, with my friends, we'd let the air out of the cars of the Jewish contractors who'd come to the fence to collect construction workers. Palestinian slaves who go out with heads bowed, with shame, to work for the Jew. My father, too, with ten children, my brothers and sisters, goes to work for the Jew every morning, devoured by shame, not lifting his eyes to me. And my mother, her eyes a knife, looking from the door as he went to build houses for the Jew on the land of her father. In Mror, Mozza, Deir Ayub, Bayt Surikh, Bayt Mahsir . . ."

By then you were standing, leaning your raised knee on the skeleton of an armored car, in the khaki shorts and knee socks of a Haganah member, the secret army formed under the British Mandate to protect the Jewish community in Palestine, taken out especially for my youth-movement field trip you volunteered to accompany: "How many times did we try to break through the siege to bring provisions to Jerusalem. The villages here were especially hostile, held by the brigades of the Jordanian Legion, and incited by the Mufti of Jerusalem. Deir Ayub, Bab-el-Wa'ad, Bayt Surikh, Bayt Mahsir . . ." Standing in your prime, in the shade of the eucalyptus trees, and the palms beyond the prickly pear bushes. A lover I smuggled, dwarfing the clumsy advances of the members of the group, in those five days in a tarpaulin-covered truck of kids, over the dense, dark, and human pulp of sweat and effort and shrill singing, in the smell of farts of canned beans and meat, and the rusty taste of tepid water in canteens, and now and then a sheaf of light with a dazzling strip of landscape darting into the dark. And the bitter offense of solitude in the heart of being together, singing around the bonfire, with yearnings that weren't ours either, but only leftovers from the War of Independence:

Here I am a wayfarer standing at the stone
A black paved road, rocks and ridges
Evening slowly falls, sea wind blows
First starlight beyond Bayt Mahsir

Bab-el-Wa'ad
Forever remember our names.

"Those silent mountains, between Beit Horin and Modi'in, are witnesses to the history of an ancient people," you wave your notebook emphatically, rapt in walking in your Land of Israel. And I, sucking into me your excitement, at the sound of Ibrahim's bewitched drumming, borne on your solemn voice, passing between the Jebusites and Abraham, and Joshua and the Kings of Judah, and the Philistines, and the peoples of the sea, soldiers of Sennacherib, the exiles of Babylon, leading the Maccabees over the mountains, moving the Roman legions. Like a magician, you bring Rabbi Yohanan ben Zakkai and his students from the horizon who make their way from besieged Jerusalem to Yavneh, and opposite Jesus wanders to Emmaus, and Byzantium, and the great Muslim conquest, and the armies of Gottfried of Bayonne, and Salah-a-Din, who expels the Crusaders, until the Turks come, and the English . . . Covering the voices bursting from the stage, as if I were once again listening to you in the heat of the roasted dust, "Here, near the road to Jerusalem, the fighters of the wandering unit gave their lives in the riots of 1929, and the members of the Haganah in the riots of 1936, and the HarEl Brigade in the War of Independence . . ." Your voice flooding me is blended with the Arabic and the English in the earphones, the words buried inside me for years, beneath our bitter quarrels, and my abandonment of the country, and my activities in the leftist cells, "having 'no choice,' the Yishuv, the Jews of Palestine, stood against seven Arab states, the few against the many. Until the gates of the Land of Israel were burst open to take in tens of thousands of illegal immigrants, the survivors, the masses returning to the land of their fathers with a prayer for Zion and Jerusalem on their lips . . ."

"Bayt Jamal, Garbit, Mahsia, Bab-el-Wa'ad, Marj-el-Zarur, Bayt Mahsir . . ." I moved in my seat, at the intensified drumming. Ali, supple as a cat, now scales the iron pole, and a single spotlight follows him. From the top of the stage, above the silhouette of the refugee camp, he says, "I taught my friends how to build the barrier at the entrance to the camp, how to collect stones, when to throw. We here know every stone, every hill. I'm the child of stones for the shame of my grandfather, for the shame-reddened eyes of my mother . . ." Continues above the abyss, to the sound of the audience sighing, sitting erect. And you, lighted for a moment in the flicker of the cigarette on your white curls, look at me intently, when a giant doll descends from the top of the stage, and red flashlights erupt from the holes of its horrible mask. Two actors grab Ali, put a bag over his head, beat him, until bars of shadow descend, and Ali's bound body is dragged behind the sign coming down in English and Arabic: "Al-Anzar Detention Camp." The women return to the stage, gather at the entrance to the camp, wave signs: "Freedom for the Heroes!" To the sound of Ibrahim's intensified, electrified drumming, until the flutterings of the chained body grow weak, and Ali's bound body is dropped like a sack. Wailing bursts from the throats of the women, amplified around the auditorium. Silhouettes of the lamenting women grow bigger, darken the stage, to the sound of applause. And then the final scene. A white light rises on a row of straw dolls covered with a sheet at the back of the stage. Iman wanders around alone in a big white dress, a long whirling. At the top of the stage, Ali in an enormous white cloak, hovers, angelic, and with chains of stones on his body. A chorus of women led by Farida bursts into the concluding song: "Ya, shahid! Shahid! Child of stones explodes like a stone . . . Holy warrior for the liberation of al-Kuds and Harm-a-Sharif of Jerusalem and the Temple Mount . . . Holy warrior for the liberation of Palestine . . ." All of Ibrahim's drums shake and the loudspeakers amplify the voices of the mob in the squares: "Allahu akhbar . . ."

You stood at my side as the audience rose to its feet in a standing ovation. Clung to me even backstage. The laughter, in Arabic mixed with English. The celebration of brotherhood, the smoke of alcohol. Or maybe that was Aunt Rachel, with the cigarette in the corner of her mouth and her hand stuck in the pocket of her khaki pants, erect next to me on the path climbing to the cemetery. Maybe because of her I decided that tonight I would finally dare tell Sayyid about David. And he, in the white silk scarf, surrounded by flashbulbs, slipping out after the cocktail party, with the excuse of an interview with a reporter from the arts section of tomorrow's paper. They scatter with last hugs on the Broadway sidewalk. Sayyid leaves me with polite kisses on both cheeks, and tosses as a bait to me: "So? Tomorrow you'll come after the rehearsal to the Quick Bar, across from the Victory. Update the troupe on the performance . . ." He goes off between Farida and the theater critic in a bright silk dress. And when I turned my head one last time, I saw his scarf flickering at the corner.

The bus leaves the freeway.
Black trees at the sides of the exit.

■ ■ ■ ■

The Transportation Center. The bus to Manhattan leaves in ten minutes.
A family, with two black boys and one fair girl.

"This! This! This!" the black little boy bangs on the chewing-gum machine. "This!" he tries to attract the parents' attention.

The fair little girl pulls up her short dress, exposes her belly and panties and pulls the dress down. Exposes and pulls down. "Fuckit! Fuckit! Fuckit," she repeats stubbornly.

Yesterday when I got back at one in the morning, Alain was still working. He said only that Graciella had left a note in the kitchen. "Ilana hello. Jonathan's nose is running. I set up the humidifier in the boys' room. David wants you to give him a kiss, even if he's sleeping." I made myself a drink, went to the boys' room, and in bed I still listened to the first act of *Don Giovanni* until Alain came in. He undressed in silence, and Mozart's notes were bound up in wordless lovemaking.

At breakfast, Jonathan complained of a sore throat. I made an appointment with the doctor and asked Graciella to take David, too, since he inevitably always catches it soon after, apologizing for not being able to come with them, as I'll be in the city this morning. When the boys left with Graciella, Alain asked casually, "So you're going today, too?" trying to maintain a façade of indifference.

"I've got a meeting with the members of the troupe. I'm supposed to show them the plans for the site," I said without looking up, and I went to the study to pack the material. A moment later I heard Alain's steps in the corridor. I went on packing. He stood in the door of my study. I put the papers in my handbag, hoping that this time, too, with his fanatical formality, he'd stick to our "agreement." That he wouldn't stop me by force. And I was terrified that I really didn't know Alain, didn't know how he'd react when he felt his back was to the wall.

"You're sure you have to go to this meeting now?" he took a step toward me.

I raised my eyes to him, froze at seeing him all white.

"Yes, Alain," I muttered, pretending I was continuing to pack, but I was really only moving the papers from side to side with shaking hands.

Alain was silent. Something seemed to be taking place in him. And when

I stole another look, his long body lost the rigidity that had contorted it until a moment ago.

He brushed aside the hair that had fallen, and whispered, "What's the point in all your monuments, Lana? There's no solution to this mess!"

Only then did I start sweating. I knew the danger had passed, and I listened from the distance to Alain's bundles of words, almost absentmindedly as I prepared to leave.

"Understand, Lana, this isn't a territorial conflict, this is a struggle for existence, you or them! The Muslim world won't accept you there! Where were they, your Palestinians, a hundred and fifty years ago? They're also a creation of Zionism. Another one of the 'twin brothers' the Jews are experts at creating, and that afterward rise up to kill them . . . Ishmael, Esau, the Christians, and now the Palestinians. They're now the victim . . . And everything Israel does to defend itself is immediately defined as 'state terror,' with all the slogans of your beautiful leftists who blame themselves, with some suicidal instinct . . ."

I went into the bathroom to put on makeup and Alain plodded in behind me, continuing helplessly with his speech, in some desperate attempt to convince me. "And what will happen when two hundred million Muslims wipe out Israel? . . . You think the Christian world will rise up and save you? The European Enlightenment? It's only a hypocrisy of the G-Seven. They make a 'coalition' with states ruled by murderers, and still preach morality . . . Yes, fifty years ago it was convenient for the world to silence its conscience for a moment and recognize the State of Israel, but that's over, Lana, over a long time ago . . ."

I didn't dare raise my eyes to Alain's furious face reflected in the mirror, and only my heart pounding, dropping the lipstick from my fingers, knowing something was irreparably breaking at that moment between me and Alain.

". . . Anti-Semitism is only waiting to raise its head, to hate the Jews in all variations. 'Christ-killers,' 'well-poisoners,' 'child-murderers who bake their matzos with the blood of Christian children,' 'capitalists,' 'Communists,' 'cosmopolitans,' 'American agents,' 'colonialists,' the whole list . . ." I go drink a glass of water in the kitchen, knowing I would miss the bus I'd planned to take, and Alain still follows me. "It will all end in the destruction of Israel.

And even then nobody will lift a finger. They'll only mumble a few hypocritical words and shut up. Like then . . ."

I put the heavy bag on my shoulder with the sketches of the site and material for the performance. And only then did I turn my head to him. He stood with his hair dropping on his forehead, his pale face seemed to lengthen even more. For a moment, my eyes held his flooded blue eyes. Something still kept me, waiting until his lips moved. "Lana . . . ," he whispered, "only now did they 'find' in the police archive of Paris the 'Jewish file' with all the Jewish names . . ." His cheeks fell. "There are detailed lists there . . . All the stolen property . . . transferred to the state, to the municipality of Paris, after 'its owners didn't return' . . . a detailed file, lying for fifty-five years in the offices of the French police . . . And my colleagues in Switzerland got awful information about the secret Jewish bank accounts . . . Understand, all of them profited from the annihilation of the Jews, Lana . . ."

He stood in the door of the garage, watching me put the bags in the car and start the motor. I still see his thin figure before the automatic door came down like a guillotine. And all the way to the bus station I pressed the accelerator, stony.

Another five minutes until the bus leaves. The line of people waiting outside.

And on the way to the station, I hit the corpse of a crushed squirrel. Saw at the last moment the splendid tail in the autumn leaves. And then my tires sucked in the dead body.

■ ■ ■ ■

The lobby of the Algonquin. Waiting for Sayyid.

After the meeting with the troupe.

Velvet easy chairs in old-fashioned splendor. Elderly waiters in wine-colored jackets. Like refugees from another time.

The second vodka. The tension slowly fades.

I came late to the Quick Bar opposite the Victory on Forty-second Street, hesitantly pass inside out of the shrill light. Discover them in the inside room, around a circle of tables. Sayyid stands up as I come in, "Welcome, Ilana."

"Ahalan, Ilana, Marhaba," Anton also gets up, the set designer, the only one Sayyid introduced to me in Jerusalem, at the set design workshop of al-Kuds. "What's up?" he holds out his hand warmly, remains standing until Sayyid brings another chair.

Iman turns her childishly round chin to me, looks at me through her mane of curls, with the same excited look she had on stage.

"What's new?" She addresses me with her thick accent, suddenly in Hebrew, tearing up the safe areas of English escape between me and Sayyid.

Ibrahim was folded on his chair on the other side of the table, his soft body didn't betray the electricity flowing in it during the long hours of drumming. Farida was next to him. The mature actress of the troupe, and one of the five or six characters she inhabited in the play was especially etched in me: a monstrous caricature of a settler woman in a tight headscarf and fingers twisting with hatred. She looked at me from her Byzantine profile, emphasized by her straight black hair. And I didn't dare look straight at Ali, despite his warm smile for me. Unable to erase the sight of him hanging at the top of the stage.

Farida examined me from under her long eyelashes throughout the greetings. And then, turning her profile quickly, she continued the discussion that had been broken off when I came in. The words "Public Theater" and "Palestinian" were conspicuous in her argument in Arabic. Sayyid's response was interrupted by the comments of Ibrahim and Ali. Anton intervened, explaining slowly, accompanying his words with rounded movements. Explaining, apparently, the changes of the set in moving from one stage to another. Maybe ten minutes went by, Ibrahim took out a pack of cigarettes and offered them around the table, to me, too. "So what did you think of the play?" he asked in English to acknowledge my presence.

"Very impressive . . . The acting's terrific, so is the direction, and the music . . . And now that I understood the whole text with the translation . . ."

I sought words, or maybe I struggled with the ones stuck to my lips. "I was shocked . . ." My words sounded forced.

"So what's new with your plan?" Anton came to my rescue. His bald head added light to his round face.

I smiled gratefully, took a few sketches out of the case, spread them on top of the glasses and half-full plates, bent over the map and pointed to the site, constantly aware of my outsiderness, the way I stammer the names of the Arab villages around the peak.

". . . As an architect, I only suggested a place for you. Of letting go, of sitting in a Hut. A place that really isn't a place . . . like the name of God in Hebrew, Ha-Makom, He who is a place Who doesn't have a place in the world . . ." The words died on my lips. "I'm trying here a possibility of not-holding . . . a land or a woman who doesn't belong to anybody . . . the ability to let go, an open hand," I hold out my hand to the members of the troupe through the gloom of the Quick Bar, through the cigarette smoke.

"The purpose of the project is to connect the term 'Sabbatical' with Jerusalem, of all places, the heart of the conflict! Facing all the 'consecrated stone fortresses': the first Temple, the second, the churches, the mosques, facing them, to put up a Hut, a temporary structure . . ." I tried to joke, but the tension didn't relent.

> Yes, the words I had pondered so much dropped heavily. I blushed. Clearly I hadn't explained things properly, only the political echo was shrieked immediately, shrill, rising.

". . . The idea of the organizers, and what we tried to sketch with Sayyid Ashabi and Anton, is a framework," I tried again. "Open to all the stories, all the memories . . . in your improvisations for the performance you'll build the Huts with your own stories. You'll shape a possibility of a utopian place. A place of an open hand . . ." Embarrassed at repeating that same movement. I pull in my hand. Finish in a rush, "Everything will be defined during work, that's the idea . . . I'll go to Jerusalem in December. I can help you with the rehearsals . . ."

Sayyid quickly summed up. "Yes, you'll have to return, Ilana. To explain more details of the plan." He switches to Arabic. Explains something in a noncommittal tone, with the words "Hut" and "Sukkah." Apparently presenting to the troupe for the first time what I was sure had been in rehearsal for a long time.

The actors' faces were opaque in the gloom of the bar. Anton tried to say something, but Farida cut him off. Ali also joined. Sayyid raised his hands, broke off the discussion, turned to me with a forced smile, and the white scarf around his neck emphasized the distance between the worldly playboy and the members of the troupe who have borne the daily burden in Jerusalem ever since the beginning of the Intifada, using their theater for mass gatherings, organizing youth groups in East Jerusalem, the radio station. While he flirts with the changing fashions of Europe, changes character with the virtuosity of El-Hakait, as he changed the repertoire of Gilgamesh for the festival in Carthage and then changed again the staging of the play to suit the fringe audience in Amsterdam.

"I'm sorry," I said with an effort, "but I have to get back to New Jersey now, to my family." Farida tossed back her dark hair as the sound of the words swelled between my lips.

I got up. You could feel the relief when I gathered up the papers. Iman waved to me, and so did Ali and Ibrahim, with a courtesy mixed with slight mockery. Anton approached and shook my hand, trying to cover the failure.

"I'm very glad about the cooperation," I added for some reason.

Sayyid kissed me goodbye on both cheeks and said aloud, "Bye, Ilana, thanks for coming," pretending we really were parting now. I turned to leave, and took with me Farida's smirk in the line of lipstick cutting her bold profile.

> Walking out in the prevailing silence, blinded with offense, with jealousy. Feeling the blush spreading to the roots of my hair. Knowing I'm sharing Sayyid's bed with Farida. That we lick his skin on the same sheets. Knowing also that my wounded passion for Sayyid is inflamed at the thought of the other lovers.

Going out to the sidewalk on Forty-second Street, passing from the light to the shadowy lobby of the Algonquin. Waiting impatiently for Sayyid to pass the aging doorman in uniform, bend over me, pick up the glass of vodka with a broad laugh. "I'm dying of thirst," he'll whisper as he leads me outside, stops a cab, and as we glide down Fifth Avenue, his hand is deep inside me through the traffic signals and the traffic jams, as he expertly leads my hand in his pants, darts quickly, still has time to groan with a roar into my tongue, take away my dripping hand while quickly buttoning up before the Sikh driver in the white tarboosh turns his head and winks at us.

The waiter in the old wine-colored uniform comes and goes. A tray of glasses and lemon slices on his big hand.

■ ■ ■ ■

[Between two and three.]

At Jonathan's bed. The house is asleep. Jonathan is also asleep at last. He calmed down only after two. Feverish.

Writing in the children's notebook I found among David's writing materials. (A bittersweet smell of first grade wafts from the pages.)

When I came home, Graciella was sitting with Jonathan, who was writhing with pain in her arms. She replaced Alain, who dropped into bed. For some reason, the antibiotics hadn't yet kicked in. I took Jonathan from Graciella, sending her to bed, too, carrying him in my arms, a bundle of softness and breath.

"Mama, Mama, where *were* you?" clutching my thumb with his damp hand, sliding it back and forth over his face.

I rocked Jonathan until he calmed down. Looking down on the breathing cheeks. A warm mass of sticky sweaty curls, wrapped up in my body full of city smells, taste of Sayyid in my mouth. Cigarette smoke in my hair.

And then, in the quiet that finally prevailed in the dark of the children's room, suddenly bliss. Cut off from everything. Just for the life embracing me. A choking wave of joy. As in pregnancy, when I was suddenly choked on the idea of "the human being" growing inside me.

I brought the CD Walkman. In the earphones the opening of *Don Giovanni.* The tiny light from the Walkman reddens the stars of the children's room. Jonathan's shut eyelids, his flushed face.

And today, in the lull at last with Sayyid between the sheets, the window open to lower Manhattan. Notes of *Don Giovanni* swirling in me. The recent days, until our running to the hotel elevator. Fleeing from the reporter of *Études Palestiniennes,* who has been waiting for an interview with the director of the play. Choking with laughter. Not mentioning my ridiculous efforts to engage the members of the troupe, despite the situation of Desert Shield . . . Laughing again, as when we first met, joking that it would be preferable to wake up and discover that the other wasn't there, that the land was simply empty . . . And when Sayyid teased me, "Now we're the real Jews," we laughed when I came back with, "That much jealousy?"

Close to you, Father. As at the end of nights packed with cigarette smoke of the revolutionary cell in Paris, when I'd suddenly feel so "Jewish" in the Arab-Western Internationale. And the cry of Donna Anna at the fleeing lover, hurrying to get away from the father's body—Padre amato! Io manco . . . Io moro . . ."

And maybe Don Giovanni is also a Jew—after all, Tirso de Molina wrote *Don Juan* in 1630, at the time of a great auto-da-fé in the Plaza Real. Dozens were burned at the stake, and dozens more were burned in effigy, after slipping out of the cellars of the Inquisition. An inspiring spectacle opposite balconies with an excited mob . . .

Maybe Don Juan was one of the conversos, Father. Rabbi Johanan. Escaping from the Inquisition, from the arms of one woman to another. A mystic openly rejecting the story of the Virgin Birth. Spreads among the women of Europe the law of Eros of the living god, renewing the world every day always with his couplings.

Maybe Don Giovanni is the student of Rabbi Akiba, of all those burned at the stake of love. Sings from the fire: And thou shalt love the Lord thy God with all thy heart, Viva la libertà!

David sleeps spread-eagled. Jonathan still seeks rest, with his three pacifiers. One in his mouth and two clutched in his hands.

And after all, maybe we, too, Father, are a belated reincarnation of Don Juan. Wandering with our dreams, burning with longing. Merchants loaded with bundles, haberdashery, fabrics, books, pottery. Bearing the Eros of our stormy tribe. Seized by ecstasy, fermenting dough. Like those beautiful boys who put the sun to shame with their beauty exiled by Nebuchadnezzar, bound in leg irons, "and the Chaldean women saw them and dripped with lust. They told their husbands and their husbands told the king; the king ordered them killed. And still they dripped with lust. The king ordered that their bodies be crushed."

Like Donna Anna, who sacrifices her father to her passion. And the sarcasm in the hasty dialogue next to the father's body, between Leporello and his master—

"Who died, you or the old man?"

"What a question, idiot! The old man."

"Bravo! Two birds with one stone. Seducing the daughter and murdering the father."

After four. Can't get myself into the bedroom filled with Alain's breathing.

From the window of the children's room a strip of road and a lone streetlamp between the lawns.

From the distance, the roar of the interstate. Dew on the plastic chairs in the backyard, on the boys' bikes.

The dawn turns gray in the suburb.

(And in a few hours, back to New York. Final meeting with Sayyid. Before they leave to perform in Minneapolis.)

■ ■ ■ ■

I waited for Sayyid's call after the press conference, so I could leave. Only by chance did I turn on the television.

On CNN, breaking news from Jerusalem.

Riots on the Temple Mount.

"In the middle of Sukkoth holiday prayers, rocks were hurled down from the mosques at worshippers at the Western Wall."

Over and over on the screen a hail of stones pours down onto the crowd at the Western Wall. Women are running in big dresses, suits, covering their heads. Men wrapped in prayer shawls rush from the Wall.

And then smoke rises from the mosques. And shots. Only afterward a few photos of the panicky crowd. A lot of white. Robes. Dust. Smoke of automatic weapon fire.

"Police and Israeli military forces attack the Temple Mount . . ."

By the end of the report, seventeen killed.

Just want to cry. With my head buried in Sayyid's chest.

(And suddenly Mother's image. Her hair pulled into a bun on the back of her neck in the old-fashioned style of a pioneer woman. Her case crammed with fabric for the home economics teachers she supervises. A tiny woman, coming and going gently. A look shrouded in amazement. "The knowledge about her family changed her. She had a breakdown, Ilanka, and the miscarriage in '44, before you were born." You turn me from childhood on into an ally. You're worrying about Mother, did she forget to take her tranquilizer, did she put down the embroidery, and gaze into space?)

■ ■ ■ ■

[In the car. Parking lot of the Transportation Center.]

Coming back from Manhattan. Haven't yet started the car. Sitting in the closed box, on the hot seat.

In the body, the bus is still rolling. The hasty goodbye. The stiffness persisting throughout the meeting. In what is said, and what isn't said. And my weeping in the taxi back to Port Authority. Uncontrollable.

Hot smell of upholstery and metal. The car stood all afternoon.

(Apparently I dozed off, gave in to exhaustion.)

Suddenly softness and quiet. As in hours in the box of the parked or moving car, when Sayyid came to Paris. Dusty windows dotted with drops of light and rain. And the hand passing, like a throbbing, through the hair. A momentary niche, like a hut. Like the lulling dreams, night after night again. Kindling bold visions we'll never experience.

At the end of the asphalt a field of chrysanthemums. Yellow in the fresh gleam of autumn.

Sediment of anxiety. All that happened today. Here and there, in Jerusalem. The nightmare lashing. In waves. And how will I go back home now, Father? To the solace of blood relations, family? To sketches of the site, to the model I'm working on? And all is torn . . .

[In the study. With all the material for the lecture.]
Sketches on the drafting table, the sofa, the floor.

The boys help me, excited to build the model of the Hill of Evil Counsel that I've renamed Mount Sabbatical. A key with the names of the places seen from all around. The sources of water, the aqueduct, the waterfalls. The changing flora on either side of the watershed—olive and pomegranate trees on the east, the vines on the west. The path between the Settlement of Huts and Mount Sabbatical.

David runs to the yard to gather twigs from the trees covered with gold autumn leaves. Planes them, files them, ties them in soft strings, watches me build my first twelve Huts that will be presented with the students' Huts. His tongue thrust out in concentration, Jonathan pastes the little cardboard pieces of the rocks, follows David's progress with cheers. And Graciella fills the house with the bossa nova that once again pours carelessly from her room to this childhood space she and the boys have wrapped me in ever since Alain went to Berlin and Dresden. He won't be back until early December, a week before we go back to Paris.

Sayyid called last night. From O'Hare. The phone rang in the kitchen. Graciella gave me the receiver.

"Ahalan, Lana."

"Sayyid? . . . What's new? How were the performances?"

"Fine," he laughed. "It was terrific . . ."

And after a short silence, he said, "I'm calling to say goodbye, Lana, before I take off for Amsterdam . . ."

"What? You're not stopping in New York?" I burst out like a little girl, and I see Graciella glance at me, then leave the kitchen.

"No, I've got to take a direct flight back . . . You understand . . ." Again his forced laugh.

"So what about the conference? We're supposed to present the plan for the performance together."

"You'll do all right by yourself, you're a big girl . . ."

"And the intro we haven't yet made? . . ." trying to disguise the tremor.

"Just wing it for the time being, Lana. Talk about what we already decided, okay?"

And then, at my silence, he added, "I'll call, don't worry . . ." He laughs and immediately lowers his voice half an octave, "Lana . . . come on, let me feel you once more before the trip . . . ya, Lana . . ."

And despite the pounding of blood that turns the kitchen dark before my eyes, my body responds like a wind-up doll.

". . . Let me feel you, inside—more, yes, yes . . . come, Lana . . ." He grabs my silence, the quickened breathing. "Like that, yes . . . come, come, you're great . . . come . . ."

And suddenly as if something lopped him off, he hurried to finish, "Bye, now," and hung up.

I let the dial tone explode in the receiver before passing out.

And I didn't tell him about the fax from UNESCO that came to the office in Paris. With reference to the postponement of the ceremony, "for the time being until the situation is clarified." And the phone calls with Colette and Fernand, with Jorgenson. "We must consider the danger to the guests, Madame Tsuriel."

A quarter of a million American soldiers entrenched in Saudi Arabia.

On CNN, the apocalyptic musical clip at the beginning of "Desert Shield" news.

Bush declares, with uplifted face: "We are dealing with Hitler revisited. Totalitarianism and brutality that is naked and unprecedented in modern time . . ."

My preparations for the lecture, completely cut off from reality, Father, as in our conversation, started the moment I arrived from the airport. I put down the suitcase, follow you into the kitchen. Immediately surrounded by your joy, forgetting for a moment that I came because of Ella's alarm, that the doctors had lost hope.

"So, let's drink a gleizele tea?" the smile floods your wrinkled face.

"Only on condition that I make it," I dash to put on the eternal kettle, before you start the long operation of getting up from the chair where you just dropped.

"Good," you smiled in surrender, wrapping me in a fresh, blissful look.

"Father . . ." I put the two clinking cups on the table, placed the sugar and the spoon next to you. "Father . . ."

"Yes," you raised your penetrating blue eyes to me, sensing immediately that I had something important to say.

"I won an international competition . . . for a monument in Jerusalem."

"Interesting! Very interesting," you leaned forward, with a jolt that had nothing to do with the effort of bringing the cup with a stiff hand up to your mouth from the body dropped onto the kitchen chair.

"It's a peace monument."

"Peace . . ." Now you were absorbed in my words.

"I brought the plans to show you."

"Excellent, I want to see everything!"

"But maybe tomorrow . . ." I returned to reality. "Rest now. Tomorrow we'll look at everything," I helped him get up from the chair, to find his balance, and then to advance slowly, leaning one hand on the table and the other on me.

"'Give a hand,' eh, Father?"

You smiled, muttering one of your old Zionist tunes between one choking cough and another.

And only to cover up the panic at the sight of your weakness, I hold on to you quickly from behind, "'Give, give, give, give, give a hand, shut your eyes, dance the hora, and we shall now forget it all . . .'"

"Well, what a hora dance," you commented ironically, dragging another step. "'You've got a pain, trample it with your feet again . . .'"

And when we paused between the bathroom door and the corridor, you raised your finger with a puckish smile, still singing, "'Ah, ah, all of us will go mad. We'll live, we'll see wonders and miracles . . .'"

For two days you held on. We pretended that the routine continued between Gabi, the student who comes to wash you and run errands, and Rebecca, "the strong hand," you call her jokingly, quoting Maimonides, for her devoted kneading of your body in physiotherapy exercises, and who kisses you goodbye on your forehead crowned with white curls.

On Tuesday, early in the morning, you had trouble breathing and said only: "I'm weak," before the attack of choking started. And after that, the phone calls, the ambulance, and the panicky hospitalization, and Ella came up from the south, running to take care of all the forms, so much like Mother. And the waiting between the screens, in the turmoil of the emergency room. All the time I held on to the blueness you opened now and then, sitting on the bench next to your gurney. You slowly raised your finger, and only after a while did I understand that you were pointing to the window, to the view of the sea and the Carmel in the distance. "Yes . . ." I confirmed, stroking your hand, the skin hard, smooth, evoking a soft smile on your sunken cheeks. Until you were finally moved to the iron bed with the miserable nightstand and the bedpan.

And yet, next morning, your head leaning on the pillows crowned by the silvery curls like a halo, you whispered through the pallor, "Tell me again about your plan, Ilanka . . ."

All around, the hospitalized men in the room were groaning, the nurses passed by on the other side of the screen. Nothing there reminiscent of an architecture seminar, and yet I was concerned only with focusing my discourse when I started, "The term 'monument' means a 'reminding structure,' a 'structure of memory.' Hence the question, how to remember . . ." You hung on my words. "My plan is not a 'monumental' monument that rules over the landscape and to which tourists are brought in buses, have their picture taken, and go on . . . My site is based on the Sukka, the hut, a completely different kind of 'monument,' the kind you don't look at, but one you build and live in, as a special way of remembering . . . And, moreover, it is a temporary structure. Think what a statement there is here about memory, which is built and destroyed, that has to be rebuilt every year . . ."

"Nice, nice, Ilanka, there's depth to that," you said with an effort.

"The plan is for a 'Settlement of Huts,' and individuals or groups will come to it. They'll build their Huts, and they'll live in them for seven days. People can come from all over the world, without visas, without a police check, it will be an open area. For seven days they'll live like that, in the heart of Jerusalem. They'll leave their normal lives to study, discuss, think, remember. And also to eat and drink, pray or sing, love . . . and to live by the sun, in that enclave of memory, in the midst of Jerusalem . . ."

You raised your eyebrows to me.

"It's a little like your pioneer camp in the Jezreel Valley, in the twenties, eh?" I said.

You confirmed that with a smile that flooded me, knowing that nobody would ever listen to me as you did. And so I continued even when the nurses came, changed the intravenous and turned you over. I clung to the capering of your look, assuming the disputatious tone of the yeshiva: "Well, and the teachings of the Talmud, that's something! A Hut with four walls, fine, but also with three it's possible, in fact even two and a half are enough with openings in completely imaginary walls, a whole mind structure . . ."

We laughed. That is, I laughed, and a flicker trembled on your face. And then you said, chuckling to yourself, "They say . . ." And immediately the coughing cut you off. Struggling with its waves, you went on with lips almost shut. "They say that in a certain city in the fall, during Sukkoth, the inhabitants called the mayor and complained: 'The Jews are violating the law . . .'"

"What?" I bent over.

"Violating the law . . . the city laws," you managed to say before the next wave of coughing. " 'They've enlarged their houses, added some structures in the yard without permission!' " You sneak in an amused look, in the pause before the punch line. "The mayor called in the head of the Jewish community, 'What's this?' he shouted, and you kept up your imitation of the mayor. 'There are laws against unapproved building! I'm informing you that I've issued an order for immediate destruction!' " " 'Honorable Mayor,' " you changed to the voice of the rabbi, in a hoarse phlegmy whisper. " 'You're absolutely right, and I promise to tend to the matter personally! In seven days there won't be a trace of anything the Jews built in their yards. Everything will be taken down! I give my word . . .' " You choked, the cough immediately covering the laugh.

"Great, that's great, Father . . ."

You beamed, raising your eyes to me.

"I promise you I'll add that joke to the project. Great . . ."

You shut your eyes, accepting the compliment shyly, sinking into rest after the enormous effort. And the nurses come in again to take care of you. You're their favorite patient.

The next day, I came back to replace Ella who spent the night in the easy chair next to you. You dozed off and a team of doctors and nurses hovered around you in white coats. I sat in the corridor, among the other people waiting. They didn't let me in until the afternoon. The blue stream of your look greeted me, welcoming without moving your head. And then, as if we were still sitting together in the apartment, you pointed with your eyes to the nightstand with the box of candy Ella had brought, along with the drawing Netta and Nimrod had made for you, encouraging me with your eyes to have some. Three days before you passed away. Only after I filled my mouth with chocolate, to your satisfaction, did you concentrate, try to tell me something.

That day you almost couldn't make a sound. You tried again. With a supreme effort, "I thought about your plan . . . Huts . . . in Jerusalem . . ." I read your lips, "in Jerusalem . . ."

"Yes," I quickly picked up the thread of our conversation, as if we still had time to unravel the whole issue. "Yes, in Jerusalem, of all places . . . And think about the site, the Hill of Evil Counsel. The view from the south . . ." I saw how you passed in your mind's eye the slant of the light on the slopes, the villages, and I said aloud what was going through you, "The view from the Governor's Palace of the Old City, the Valley of Hinnom, the Mount of Olives . . ." You nodded, your face as white as the sheet with the hospital stamp, holding on to the thread of our thought as the thread of life. "Yes, and there of all places, a Hut! And that's the connection with the Sabbatical year. To remind that to live in this Land you've got to know how to let go. A dimension not yet realized in the return to Zion, in Zionism, in the whole renewal of the connection between the people and the Land. And to remind that in Jerusalem of all places . . ." I was afraid I had exaggerated, had offended what was precious to you, but your clear look rose to me, intense, attempting to get to the bottom of my mind, or to the secret chambers of my heart, demanding I go on. "I saw in the sources, Father, the universal dimension of the holiday of Sukkot. Throughout the reading of the Torah and the Prophets during the holiday, from Ezekiel, Zechariah, Ecclesiastes, with images of the End of Days, of seventy nations ascending to the Temple Mount, and when the Mount of Olives will open with living waters flowing out of Jerusalem . . ."

I went on only out of great anxiety, checking whether your heavy breathing didn't require you immediately to have the oxygen mask. "A temporary, rickety Hut of David, which is all a letting-go, a Sabbatical . . ." I hold out my hands in a gesture of opening a fist, spreading my fingers to you.

Silence prevailed between the cloth screens. You gathered up all your strength and through your heavy breathing, I managed to decipher, "You need love, Ilanka . . . love. Love . . . only what you love . . . can you let go . . . love of Jews . . . of Zion . . . of Jerusalem . . ."

Your head dropped onto the pillow. And your hand also let go to the side of the bed. I gathered it up in my hands, stroking the twisted palm, that for months had cleared the rocks of the Jezreel Valley, that plowed, that hoed, that held the pen for so many years. Until the room grew dark. And the nurse, one of those who was fond of you, took the thermometer out of your armpit, wrote down the result, checked the intravenous, and whispered, "He's sleeping quietly."

Yesterday, in Jerusalem, at seven-thirty in the morning, an Arab murdered a nursery worker in cold blood, a girl, and a member of the civilian guard who rushed for help. He got off the bus on Bethlehem Road and started shooting at everybody passing by.

The model presents Jerusalem in miniature. I promised the boys that today we'd paint the water passages in the site blue.

■ ■ ■ ■

An hour ago, the fax came from Erella Hernik, from the Jerusalem office.

"Ilana, I found you an apartment. Two rooms and a kitchen. On Hebron Road, near the site. 'Typical housing-project apartment,' as you insisted, suitable for your research . . . The furnishing is all right, functional (you'll have to add a crib for Jonathan). But do understand that everything here is topsy-turvy. A feeling of the eve of war. It will take time for life to get back to normal. Al-Kuds didn't get in touch with us since they returned from America. Maybe you've heard something? I spoke with the principal of David's neighborhood school. And by sheer luck, in your building, there's a woman who runs a day-care center in her home. I visited her. She's really impressive, and you won't believe, she speaks French, that's so good for Jonathan. She's from Morocco. She's agreed to take him, you only need to confirm . . ."

"Ilana, I found you an apartment . . ." I read the fax over and over. "Two rooms," that is, a bedroom and some space they call a living room, probably a vestibule and living-dining area. "Functional furnishings," surely a living room sofa bed, with old upholstery . . . Erella with her wonderful practicality, friends for twenty years, back at the Technion.

The moment the fax came, I called Sayyid, in Amsterdam. I left a message on the answering machine. (The third one already. Ever since he left America, he's never called. This time I added that there was urgent news . . .)

I haven't yet told Alain. Before he left for Dresden and Berlin, he walked around withdrawn, entrenched in his preparations, packing papers. Almost hypnotized we watched our life together running aground, listing to the side, and the darting waves were already knee-high.

The last conversation was a few days before he left. He comes into my study, talks fast, "Lana, I wanted to tell you something." And I was scared, stiffened in my chair. "I'm thinking about a long trip. To the Soviet Union. Special permission has come to examine the KGB archives in Moscow and Kiev. For me and another investigator from Yad Vashem. Just imagine, all the material between '39 and '46 . . ." He brushes aside the hair that dropped over his eyes, his restraint doesn't disguise his excitement. "Ever since September, trains full of documents have been arriving in Moscow from East Germany. And in Latvia, the offices of the KGB have been packed up after the declaration of independence in August. Everything is in boxes there. Files of whole towns. From orders to names of those shot in mass graves. And in the Ukraine—the material on the extermination machine, on the Ukrainian army . . . This is our last chance to open at least part of that material, Lana! The last chance to stop the race to rewrite history. And there are enough people involved who don't want to be exposed, who would prefer to destroy all the testimony as fast as possible. Shlafman, of Yad Vashem, will bring a photocopy machine, and IBM equipment. That's what they asked for so far in exchange. They don't have a copy machine, just imagine . . . Who would believe that the collapse would be so fast."

I calculated that it would be exactly when we'd be in Jerusalem. And who knew what would be by then between me and Alain, so exposed now, despite everything he was trying to hide in tweed and pipe smoke all these years.

"Where's Czernowitz now? Still in Romania?" I asked.

"No, it's part of the Ukraine."

"Far from Kiev?"

"Not really."

He averted his face. As if for the first time, I saw his thin, delicate profile. And after a moment, I asked softly:

"Will you go there?"

"I don't know . . ." He raised his eyes, and immediately lowered them. Standing with his shoulders hunched like a helpless little boy. And then, as if what surfaced was swept away again in a black wave, he shook himself and said in a different voice: "I'll come back to help close up everything here, and when we get to Paris, I'll have to leave for Moscow at once. I'll stay there until March. You'll be with the boys in Paris then, right?" he concluded tensely.

I swallowed, and then, very quietly, I said: "We're going to Jerusalem, did you forget?"

"What? You didn't cancel the plan?"

"No, Alain. I didn't cancel it," I gripped the drawing pencil.

"You've gone completely mad, Lana. This time you've simply lost your mind," he came to me.

"I've got obligations there, the project . . ."

"I can't stay with the boys in Paris! Can't postpone the trip to Moscow and Kiev. I've got to go! Got to! Wait until the craziness in the Middle East is over, go afterward, in April, May!"

"Alain, don't try to extort promises from me because of your plans. I'm going to Jerusalem, with the boys, as planned! We'll have an apartment, Erella is looking for something, we'll get along . . ."

"I won't let you take the children into a war—you hear? I won't let you do that!" He stood in front of me, pale, drops of sweat covering his face.

"That's my plan, Alain, and it has nothing to do either with archives or with wars."

"I don't understand you!"

"We've never tried to pretend we understand!"

"You're not going!"—"Yes I am . . ." We shouted helplessly at one another.

"We're going as planned on the twentieth of December. Besides, we won't be there by ourselves, you know . . ."

He went out. I turned to the sketches, pretending I was continuing to work. Until he left we didn't talk. Even the end between us could only be spoken in the language of roads.

But in fact the only phone call I'd really want to make now is to you. I'd tell you about the apartment, and I'd immediately be flooded with your torrential joy, "Ilanka! You're coming with the boys! That's good, that's good, Ilanka . . ." I'd try to say that it was only for a short time, that it wasn't what you think. But in fact waiting for the sparks of your enthusiasm, for your solemn pronouncement of a short selection of biblical quotes, "when the Lord turned again the captivity of Zion, we were like them that dream. Then was our mouth filled with laughter and our tongue with singing . . ." Waiting for the adrenaline of returning home (or maybe the adrenaline of danger. We're addicted to it, Father).

■ ■ ■ ■

[After the conference. On the bus from Manhattan.]

Expanses of dark. Plains sown with streetlamps on the dark riverbanks of the turnpike.

Claude rides to Port Authority with me, carrying the bag with the sketches behind me, taking care of everything, as always. "Have a good trip, Lana," he hugs me on the platform. "This one and all the other trips in store for you . . ." The dispatcher, a stocky black man, crossing the platform, hints with a smile that the bus is about to leave. Claude hands the bag up to me, waves with a concentrated smile. "Take care of yourself, eh?"

I stand on the stage before a rapt audience. Presenting the model, the sketches. Turning the lecture into a stand-up routine, entertaining this audience of architects. "Why according to the Talmud must the Hut have a minimum of three walls? By what special architectonic rule?" I thrust the question into the space. "Just because the word 'Hut,' 'Sukkah,' is mentioned three times in the Torah . . ." And then the craziest talmudic examples. The Hut on the back of a camel, on the deck of a ship. The tiny Hut where most of the person is pressed, and the table remains outside. But what really amazed the audience was the lack of any ideal model. Only minimal instructions for building, and endless possibilities, some demonstrated by the students in a terrific exhibit of models. I also told your joke right at the beginning, setting the light tone, the anarchy of the Hut, the Sabbatical Year. Now that the project is postponed, I don't play by the rules. Only by a utopian audacity, to set up some poles of Huts on top of a mountain in Jerusalem, and to leave all those who want to own the city with their tongues hanging out: the leaders of the Greek Orthodox Church, representatives of the Vatican, members of the Greater Israel movement, imams of the Islamic WAKF, building contractors who expect to get rich from the real estate haggling, IDF Border Patrol, UN observers, young members of Fatah, or Hamas activists . . .

And then (swallowing long whole days of waiting for his phone call), I read the poem Sayyid was supposed to have read with me in Arabic and in English translation, before we presented together the binational performance plan, the poem by Abd al-Rahman, the last emir of the Umayyad dynasty who fled to Cordoba in the eighth century, where he set up a kingdom of nomads, Berbers, Jews, Andalusians, and Slavs who were brought as mercenaries. He built the Alhambra, and from his castle in al-Rusafa, he longed for his palm tree in Damascus, on the other side of the Mediterranean. The poem led me to conclude with the Mediterranean basin's special legacy of wandering, and to the ability to give up, to reconcile with the other, which may yet one day ripen in the area, especially in Jerusalem, the disputed city. Object of desire of God, prophets, believers . . . Jerusalem the woman. Loyal, unfaithful, saint and whore, the city of God's lust, the city that maddens all those who yearn to own her, to demand an exclusive claim to her.

"She who belongs to nobody, nobody owns her. She isn't possessed by any tribe. Wide open, abandoned. With long female delight pouring, given her by all who suck the abundant milk from her breasts, crowd into her lap. Find rest in her, as in the shade of a Hut, a Sukkah open to the sky, the stars, the sun . . ." I concluded dramatically, just like you in those speeches at the Labor Council, and, like you, also moved to tears by so much pathos.

The warm response of colleagues from Munich, Tokyo, Milan. The students who stood in line to ask questions, to look at the model up close, to invite me to their studios. And the gathering of the cohort of lovers, who came like a group of veteran guardian angels to my Sukkah. Richard, who came especially from Texas; Henri, whom I hadn't seen since Marseille and "the Trinity"; Ronny Schechter, who came from Milwaukee, from the office he had opened there, with his wife and three children, "Far enough from our cursed place that left me with shrapnel in my thigh, four centimeters short of my prick," and yet teasing me as if he had never left. "What happened to you, Lana, did you repent and return to religion? You do beautiful projects, so why do you need all this drivel from the Mishnah and the Talmud, and who knows where, from Rashi? . . ."

We leave together for the dinner Claude gave at the Yemenite restaurant on Second Avenue. The laughter, the wine, the common jargon, the comparison between the Earth Project and the Spiral Jetty of Robert Smithson and the last projects of Danziger.

"Amazing resemblance," Claude got excited. "Especially with Smithson's great article about Central Park."

"Right, but," me, swept up in the pleasure of arguing, "Smithson chooses places in New Jersey that are non-sites, just a heap of industrial waste, and Danziger is drawn to places steeped in ideology . . . the Pioneers' quarry of Nesher on Mount Carmel, the national plantings on hill 833 in the Golan in memory of the fallen soldiers of the elite squads . . ."

"You're right," Ronny began. And Henri cut in immediately: "Danziger died in an auto accident, no?"

"Yes, on the road to Jerusalem, in the summer of '77," replied Ronny, who had been his most devoted student at the Technion.

The next sentence we recited together: "And Smithson was crushed in the light plane, taking photos of Amarillo Ramp, in '74. Unbelievable . . ."

We stood up, buttoned our coats. Henri said goodbye with an affection that hadn't dulled over the years. "Be careful, Lana. We don't want to lose you now with some anti-monument . . ."

"Take care of yourself in Jerusalem," Richard slid his soft face over mine.

"Nothing will squash your passion for building?" Ronny hugged me to his bosom as we went out into the cold.

"No, don't worry," I declared, surrounded by my guardian angels. "For me it'll have to be something serious—with guns and knives and explosives . . ." We laughed, and the camaraderie covered me like gold, all the way to the station in the cab with Claude. And the escalator, the already empty platform, and Claude's lips, saying through the window of the bus that jolted off, "Kisses to the boys . . ."

Nodding as the bus pulls away from the platform. Seeing Claude hunching over to light a cigarette.

Snapshots before leaving.

Alain returned a week ago. Went immediately to Washington, to finish up. When he comes back, we'll start packing up and moving east. We'll be together in Paris for five days, and then he'll fly to Moscow. A week later, the boys and I go to Jerusalem.

Only travel trajectories are explicit. The rest, one-syllable sentences.

Yesterday, at last, Sayyid's voice burst out of the static on the line. He called his answering machine in Amsterdam and heard the messages I had left. Returning the call. Doesn't say from where.

"So what's new, Lana? . . ."

"I told you in a message . . . I'll have an apartment in Jerusalem . . ." Lucky Alain's not home, I thought, at least I'm spared that.

"So you'll be in Jerusalem all the same, with all the mess?" I hear his forced laughter.

"Yes."

"But everything was postponed, no?"

"We can still go on working . . ."

"I don't know yet if I'll be able to come."

"But aren't Kayyina and the children in Jerusalem?"

"The Israelis will give them gas masks, right?" he laughs. "We're really worried about Kayyina's cousin. Last week he was shot by your soldiers. Took four hours for the ambulance to come. Your army didn't let them through. He almost died from loss of blood."

And then he changed the tone. "Why should you come? There won't be any rehearsals."

I was silent. Understanding that the real reason he called was to try to keep me away from the al-Kuds troupe.

"Now of all times, you've got to sit in a Hut . . . that's our protest, isn't it, Sayyid?" I said at last.

And meanwhile, the snapshots of another story on the screen.

Accompanied by action film music.

Four hundred thousand American soldiers celebrate Thanksgiving in the Arabian Desert with President George Bush.

The UN sets January 15 as the deadline for Saddam Hussein to withdraw from Kuwait, before the U.S. and Allied forces attack. In response, Hussein declares he's ready for war.

Yassir Arafat foresees that war in the Gulf will bring down many Arab governments, exact a high cost in human life, and bring economic disaster by damaging the centers of oil. "Victory in this war will turn to ashes in the mouths of the victors."

A new pact for Europe is signed in Paris.

Food shortages cause despair in Moscow.

Mr. Adams, owner of a building-supply shop in Illinois, says: "I'm certainly in favor of our fight. But I'd like to know what we're fighting for."

The homeless celebrated Thanksgiving with a turkey and pumpkin pie under the bridge of the West Side Highway among heaps of garbage.

And I entrench myself in my travel plan, with the stubbornness I inherited from you.

■ ■ ■ ■

[On the Suburban Transit bus.]
The trip to the city, the last time.

End of autumn. The trees on the side of the turnpike are almost bare.
Deep shivers of cold.

Granite cliffs on the side of the road. Exposing for a moment the rock foundation.

And again with you, in the bus taking me to the big city. Without Alain. Without Sayyid, apparently. The jolting of the bus is so clear, unambivalent. Like passion, blood suddenly throbbing in the heart of the turnpike. Faceless, no ethics. Loathsome, marvelous. And the flooding, lighted silence, in the hideaway of our conversation.

The bus turns to the tunnel facing the towers of Manhattan.
Descends to the vaults of the gates rising at the entrance. Giant iron priests greet with spotlights the might of traffic.

As if we, too, Father, could give ourselves up to the rustle of traffic. The mechanized libido of empires. The powerful seed overflowing through the ovaries of commercial fertility. Possessing, knock after knock, the gates of the city wallowing in the fog, with an open crotch. Babylon, Nineveh, the great city.

> Come hither: I will shew unto thee the judgment of the great whore that sitteth upon many waters. With whom the kings of the earth have committed fornication and the inhabitants of the earth have been made drunk with the wine of her fornication.

So he carried me away in the spirit into the wilderness: and I saw a woman sit upon a scarlet-colored beast, full of names of blasphemy. And I saw the woman drunk with the blood of many saints. And upon her forehead was a name written, mystery, Babylon the great, the mother of harlots and abominations of the earth.

And when I saw her I wondered with great admiration.

And the angel said unto me, Wherefore didst thou marvel? I will tell thee the mystery of the woman.

And he saith unto me, The waters which thou sawest, where the whore sitteth, are peoples and multitudes, and nations, and tongues. And the woman which thou sawest is that great city, which reigneth over the kings of the earth.

For all nations have drunk of the wine of the wrath of her fornication, and the kings of the earth have committed fornication with her, and the merchants of the earth are waxed rich through the abundance of her delicacies.

The words from the Apocalypse of Saint John echo beyond curse or blessing, outside history, when the price of oil soars to forty dollars a barrel, and in the desert, troops are gathering to defend the flow of black liquid to the womb of Madame Commerce.

Lincoln Tunnel.

The line of vehicles advances in the dark. Moves as one block.
The red of the brake lights bleeds on the tile walls.
Manhattan. Cheap apartments near the river. Run-down.
The bus gasps in the lane ascending to the station.

■ ■ ■ ■

[On the subway platform. Almost empty station.]

The ticket counter. Behind the glass window the cashier's head. Below, on a plastic case, a black woman. Holds out a paper cup to collect the change.

Frozen throughout the purchase. When it's over, she rattles the cup. When the passenger goes off, the rattle ebbs until the next sally of the arm and the paper cup.

An ageless black man with wispy hair down on all fours under the steel posts of the entrance. Hits the container of tokens. Collects what escapes. Bangs on one iron pole after another, jerking his body as in a Saint Vitus' dance. Banging diligently. As if hoeing with a small peg an underground plot of land in subway hell.

Three workers earn their bread in the burrow of the station. The cashier, the gleaner, and the hoer. The rhythmic flow of coins. Rattle of the striking metal. The metallic ring of Manhattan.

■ ■ ■ ■

[On the bus back.]

After hours with the students among the drafting tables. Giving final comments on their work, taking their sketches of the Huts for the planned cooperative activity between Israeli and Palestinian students. Leaving shrouded in the nectar of Eros of teaching. The fertile liquid of thought.

The turnpike in the rain. Drops run obliquely on the window, against the direction of the trip. Whitish, turgid swellings.

A truck in the next lane covers Manhattan. Its waving black tarpaulin crops the dank sky.

Spot of an orange streetlight penetrates the gray.

Airplanes in misty spotlights advance slowly.

Wet white body of a plane wallows like a fish in an airport puddle.

Beating windshield wipers. Screens of downpour are pushed aside and poured.

White behinds of two trucks come together and split apart in the lanes in front of us. Leafing pages like steel sheets the approaching end of a book.

■ ■ ■ ■

[In the airport cafeteria. Our hand luggage around me.]

Alain and the boys went to buy notebooks and crayons in the newspaper and stationery store.

Frying smells. Garbage bags hurtling. The squeaking cart pushed by a big-bottomed cleaning woman.

Two flight officers in suits with gold stripes. A worker in overalls cleans the glass wall. The negative of the rag and the spray can is hanging over the brightness. On the runway, steel dragons move slowly.

Overheated. From the television in the waiting room, the announcer rattles: "James Baker . . . Edward Shevardnadze . . . Tariq Aziz . . . Iraqi atrocities in Kuwait . . . troops . . ."

The last days in the panic of packing. Disengaging our possessions from the rented house with Alain. Muttering something into the phone when friends ask if it won't be dangerous, "especially for the boys." Saying I've got to go, it's fixed. Parting from Graciella. The notes of the bossa nova going away with her on the bus.

It's winter now, Father. And there, in the East, the blood's still thick, as on the day Abel was slaughtered by Cain's knife.

There the hatred is still fresh. As between the son of the serving maid, the eldest, and the son of the lady, the chosen. The wound is still bleeding there, with a clenched, bayoneted fist.

There, in the place of the nativity, the star of annunciation doesn't sparkle, and no lord of the eternal kingdom is born. Only crucified blood melts in the mouth of the singers of hymns.

There, in the fields of the Fertile Crescent, crops of blood are harvested and sheaves of black gold are crushed in the lust for power.

There the planes, the launchers are gathered. A metal phallus, hardened in silicone and plague viruses, stands erect every evening on the screens of desire.

In another minute, Jonathan and David will run to me, waving what they bought. And Alain.

Temporary pictures burst from the movement that split open. A street corner in Paris. A slanting, wintry tree. A newspaper stand. The pine tops on Mount Carmel. And the whirlpool that will still sweep us along until, at last, dawn light rises on a pure mountain morning in Jerusalem.

P a r i s

[Café on place du Châtelet.]

The flood of cars circles the square. Flicker of the fountain.

The bare trees fade in the shimmer of streetlamps and the crowd in the early evening.

First moment since landing in Paris that I can talk to you, Father. For days now I've left the boys with Catherine, moving to the office for a few hours, and going through the streets the rest of the time, trying to extricate some personal, fragile moves, from the tangle of the story on the news. From America to Paris it only changed its tone, from an action film to sophisticated moralizing rhetoric. The brand names in the ads are different, too, but the sticky seduction of marketing war and products remains the same. And the photos of the leftist demonstrations in Germany and the Netherlands against the Gulf offensive provide the righteous relief of the performance.

Alain left five days after we landed on a dreary Paris winter morning. The suitcases stood in the entrance as we put the boys to bed at the end of an American night and went into the kitchen. We turned on the radio to the voice of George Bush: "There's a time for talk and a time for war. The time for war has come!"

"Bush has started quoting Ecclesiastes," I still tried to joke. "There's no limit to their kitsch when they have to manipulate public opinion."

Alain looked at me sharply and went out. And ever since then, until he left for Moscow, he buried himself among the files, the names, the dates, the lists. Patiently weaving the web he tightened around the past.

Two days ago he left, leaving behind in the house a bitterness of tobacco and a frightened residue of his toilet articles in the bathroom, his jackets in our closet.

I go through the streets of Paris and Alain's voice pursues me, "What are you talking about, the unification of Europe, Lana? Abolition of nationality? A new epoch? . . ." He twists his lips. "They're all just busy protecting what they plundered, and the rest they bury under slogans of a new future . . . The celebrations of Hitler's birthday in Alexanderplatz weren't enough for you? Or the skinheads' attacks on the Gypsies, or the Turkish workers? Or the desecration of the tombstones in the Jewish cemeteries—the classic beginning of pogroms? . . . You'll still see waves of chauvinism flooding here, a new outbreak of the disease dormant in Europe, deep in the moss, hidden in archives, how it will infect the world again." He looks straight at me under his hair dropped aside that lengthens the shadows of fatigue under his eyes. "That's what we've got to fight now, against whoever sets Saddam Hussein in motion, and not waste time in the Middle East on unrealistic dreams of peace . . ."

On the night he went, we made love again. After a long time. As if we were taking leave together from ancient places. Alain's face above me in the dark. Wet with his tears, with my tears. And the tongues, flooded with salt, wailing of mourning and pleasure. In the morning, when he took the bag and the suitcase out to the elevator, I decided to go with him to the taxi. And even then, dragging the load through the marble entrance, at the flash of the river beyond the dark of the construction sites, all the time until the driver slammed the door and left, the words couldn't stitch together what had been torn apart. I stood wrapped in the big coat over a dressing gown, seeing Alain turning his head a last time in the window, moving away. Or that's how it seemed to me, at least, before my look was flooded again.

Before I could wipe my tears, David and Jonathan jumped on me at the apartment door.

"We saw Papa's cab from the balcony."

"I didn't know you were up already."

"We wanted to tell Papa goodbye. We wanted to see him again," David scolded me, and Jonathan buried his head in my coat, seeking the warmth of my body through the layers of cold fabric.

And in the evening, when I returned to the apartment with a heavy heart, the boys greeted me, along with Catherine, the loyal babysitter, who took two weeks off to be with them. Both of them dressed up as Indians, completely painted, attacking me with battle shrieks. And Catherine beaming behind them, with the transparent silken skin of her flushed cheeks, her blooming beauty, *une jeune fille en fleur* of the Atlantic Coast.

I was abashed, trying to smile. David leads me to the tent they built of sheets. Covers me with a shower of paper feathers. Jonathan lies down on the rug, exhausted with laughter. And I'm already laughing, yielding to the plethora of softness that sweeps us all away.

> I am already secretly looking forward to that, Father. To being with them in Jerusalem. Just them and me, in a closeness we hadn't known for a long time.

The waiter's voice. Clinking of cups and saucers. A jet of beer from the brass tap.
On the floor, around the table, cigarette butts.
Three men at the bar. Talking, gesturing.

Wandering around the streets of Alain's Paris, hidden Paris. The Paris of concierges turning over lists of tenants to the police, of plundered cabinets, of looted collections of pictures, of "the Jewish card file." The Paris of shuttered doors, of a nose twisted at the pungent smell of foreigners, "they" who will always run around with tails and with hooves on their hind legs. Poisoning the air, the wells. Swarming like rats caught in the sewers of Les Halles. (Terrified again on the other side of the rue de Rivoli, on my way here, at the shop of traps on the corner of the rue des Lavandières and Saint-Opportune. "Le Renard Blanc A. Oroz, established in 1872." Strings of rats hanging in the display window. Held in traps, dried, some with broken tails. And above each one a handwritten sign, indicating the year in which they were caught in Les Halles: 1925, 1927 . . .)

And in the afternoon, in the bus stuck in a traffic jam at place de la Concorde, Paris appeared to me through the dripping dreariness and the roar of traffic. There, in the shadow of the gigantic statues of the women wallowing with plaits undone, breasts bared, I saw the Paris that will always be there. The aging Madame who also caught me with her charms.

Paris, lying on marble sofas and brocade upholstery, exposing the marble of her body in indolent indulgence. Moving an aged, powdered hand over her perfumed flesh.

Today I saw Paris surrounded by waiters in black suits, modestly introducing her clients into the small room. And escorting them out a little while later into the back alley, where they quickly button up, wipe a handkerchief over their hot neck, far from the eyes of the next customer.

Today, through the bus window, I saw Paris spread out, bare-breasted, between place de la Concorde and place Vendôme. Paris, where the Germans enjoyed themselves throughout the war. Refusing to obey orders, not blowing her up as they retreated. After all, you don't mar the white flesh of a beloved courtesan, gleaming like gold coins untarnished forever, unmarked by any groping hands.

Today she was lying spread-eagled. The altar of her marble curves offering up a mist to a cold, wet day, and flowing under her bridges, the Seine.

Wandering for hours. Going through the stage set of the city where I chose to live, that never lost its theatrical halo for me. The touch of beauty of the squares, the parks. A rustling labyrinth of life, with a wealth of strata of construction I know inside out from years of study at the Beaux-Arts. Clinging to the window of the bus, the façades, the gray scales of the river, the naked trees along the quays. The barges, the lights of display windows lit at four in the afternoon. Fireflies glowing brightly in the cold. And the abrupt haste increasing then. Fur and mohair wrappings on the women's profiles, men's wool coats, children in tailored hats with rushing legs, scattering into the evening, toward the white aprons of the seafood vendors standing in the doorways of restaurants, among the streetlamps going off to the depths of Haussmann's boulevards.

Passing through the streets, as if searching for the residue of immigration beneath the mandarin comfort of my life today. What was stamped in the exposed, terrified fabric of my first months in Paris, after I burned my bridges with the Land of Israel and left the Technion. A maid's room on the eighth floor above the rue de Rivoli, and a "Turkish" toilet shared with the tenants of the attic rooms. My effort to kneel over it without wetting my panties stretched across my crotch. And the little garret room that closed on me like a straitjacket. With the echo of the deaf old lady's radio on the other side of the partition. "Raskolnikov's old lady," as I called her, following with bursts of sadism the gray braid wound like a mouse tail on her neck, when she bent over to scour the crappy shared toilet with a straw broom. And then fleeing from the little room and pounding down the stairs, going out under the hostile look of the concierge, passing by the trap shop with the rats, and calming down only on the bridge, on the way to the Beaux-Arts. Drowning there for a moment, in the grayish flash of the water mirror, the longing for the blue expanse opening in Haifa Bay. Swearing to devote my life to the struggle for justice, to building for the wretched of the earth, to the struggle against the lies of the old language that betrayed.

Going through the streets of Paris for hours, Father, a city where you never set foot, and yet in its streets I locate pockets of your presence, of Mother and you: the Bank Leumi branch on the boulevard des Italiens, where you'd send me the small sums from your savings account that you changed into francs as a "student allowance," standing behind me despite the pain of my leaving. And on the other side of place de l'Opéra, Galeries Lafayette, where I'd buy you gifts for my "homecoming" vacation. And around the corner, the El Al offices, where I rushed in panic last year when Ella called me to come. And also the waves of pain at the end of last winter, when I returned after the seven-day mourning period, walking for whole days in the streets pursued by guilt, as if a building I put up collapsed on its residents. And the heart pounding, spinning, the butcher shops, the antiques shops, the illuminated glass cages of the cafés, the telephone booths I sneaked into to call Sayyid, looking around to make sure nobody saw me, still trying to spare Alain the knowledge of what happened in Jerusalem.

And then, a few days before the trip to America, a phone call from Uncle Yehiel. And the sight of the dark river from the windows of the apartment when he told me, in a heavy voice, of Aunt Rachel's death. "Suddenly. In her sleep. In her room on the kibbutz." He asked Ella for my phone number to tell me himself. "Now that Aaron isn't here anymore . . ." As I face the lamps of the barges slowly crossing the necklaces of light of the bridges, knowing I'd have to go back to Israel for the anniversary of your death. (And only afterward thinking about how long to stay, about renting an apartment.)

Finish the cup of coffee. I'll go down to the Métro now, to the bitter air of the burrows, to the hurling of the packed trains at rush hour. And in the exit, the small station. A grocery store of an immigrant family open till midnight. A bakery where I'll stop to buy a baguette for dinner. And the dark excavations along the riverbank, in the shade of the bridge.

Even the construction sites are familiar. Already turned into a source of solace, Father.

■ ■ ■ ■

[In the office.]

At the table, the runway for so many dreams of construction.

The intimacy of work habits with Colette and Fernand. Maybe my most precious station of all.

Stealing a few days of concentration, not answering the piles of mail—proposals for bids, invitations for lectures, seminars, interviews.

Colette at the computer. Translating to three dimensions her plan for the "Green House," a day-care and rehabilitation center for critically impaired children. A form of a friendly, organic milieu. "Vegetal structure," with branches of wings, roots of stairs, garden corners between the wings. And the flora covers the façade like a wild, living part of the construction. Her intense face is bent over the diagrams, now and then she pushes aside strands of her hair that come undone. Fernand takes care of the urgent calls to our international association from transit camps in Germany, Denmark, and Holland. Waves of immigrants, refugees. He sits at the wide window, and his rust-colored sweater shimmers in the winter sun that reddens the office.

A few days of work with them, between the jolt of parting from Alain and the trip to Jerusalem. They wrap me in friendship from the moment I arrive. Bending over the model, admiring the tiny Huts I built with the boys, bursting into laughter at my stories of interrupting shouts from the audience at the lecture at Cooper Union, considering my latest ideas.

"I want the site to bring the desert to Jerusalem, to recall the border of dryness crossing it," I said. "I worked here on the presence of water, or more precisely, on the presence of the messianic yearning for water in a city on the edge of the desert. The apocalyptic water that bursts out of the Bible prophecies."

"Yes, your idea of reviving the ancient aqueduct crossing the site," Colette went on.

"Exactly. Here, right here"—I pointed to the trajectory. "I'm in touch with the archaeological crew. I'll let you know about their new discoveries from Jerusalem. Yes, the tension between the memory and impermanence already exists, too," I went on, thinking aloud. "But I haven't yet finished articulating the implementations. For example, the temporary form in compositions of the Huts and of the structures of Mount Sabbatical—using special kinds of connection, supporting poles, registers . . . And I still have to emphasize the presence of anarchic, underground humor in that anti-monument . . ."

"How did they respond at Cooper Union to the 'unnatural building'?" asked Fernand.

"I only had time to touch on it quickly. To say that the temporary notion here comes to undermine the direct connection between man and nature. For example, in the talmudic instructions that the materials of the Hut will not be natural, but a human construction: "even its covering cannot be the natural shade of a tree but branches cut off and then laid on its roof." I also managed to talk about the profound humanity of the Sukkah in the Talmud . . . Yes, I'm sinking more and more into those ancient texts. Coming to the Bible, the Mishnah, the Talmud, as if they were concrete poetry, which also formulates questions of architecture within a system of gestures, relations, behavior." I savored our rare space of conversation.

Fernand listened intently as soon as I started quoting. I remembered that even before my trip to America, he had declared his intention to go to a Jewish bookstore to find a French translation of the texts I mentioned. And from his shy smile, I understood that he had already done that.

"For example," I went on, "how in the middle of the most detailed discussion in the Talmud of the Hut's dimensions, just when it seems that the whole issue of the tangle of foliage is to symbolize the Clouds of Glory, the divinity—there of all places the rabbis saw a need to emphasize the absolute separation between heaven and earth, between God and man, in order to preserve the freedom of man. The total opposite of the Greek-Christian yearning to build a bridge between heaven and earth . . . my 'quarrel' with Heidegger . . ." I moved my hand between the drafting tables and the rolls of paper, and if I had had a beard, at that stage of the sermon, I probably would have stroked it.

"Yes . . ." murmured Fernand.

"It's precisely in the traditional explanations that I find the boldest sayings about the relationship between a nation and a place. Rashi, for example, envisions that the legitimacy of Israel will be undermined as it settles in a place already settled from the first by others, who will claim against them, 'You are robbers.' Because the promise of the Land of Israel isn't natural, it's only settling on condition."

It's not clear when I started feeling how much my solemn tone, the excited gestures, were like yours, when you'd get swept away in a flamboyant Zionist vision or when you'd translate something from Yiddish for me.

"You understand the radicalism? The People get the Land to let go of it, get a place that will never really belong to them. You get an estate and every seven years you have to remove the fences around it, so that anybody who wants to can come in and eat from its fruit. That's the freedom in the ability to give up, despite the fear of 'what shall we eat the seventh year?' . . ."

The light in the office began to grow dim. The short winter day withdrew from the windows. Colette played with a pencil.

And maybe it was only because of the intense unbroken silence that I added: "I see that with the boys now. How I'm slowly learning to keep my distance, not to hold on to them, to let go of the umbilical cord between us, despite the fear. To send them gently, with faith, to their freedom . . . especially now that I'm alone with them . . ." Moving my eyes from Colette to Fernand, and back to Colette. Their eyes hung on me, waiting attentively, even when I shrugged and added, "I feel quite alone with those thoughts. Far from the ideologies of the right, far from my friends on the left, far from the dream of the Zionist founders, like my father, and also far from Sayyid's dream of independence, which doesn't even begin to deal with the multilayered uniqueness of the Land of Israel, and remains in the original definition of ownership, tsumud, a jihad liberating the Muslim holy lands . . ."

By the end of the afternoon, when we went back to the drafting tables, sitting in cones of lamplight, Colette addressed me as if casually: "Lana."

"Yes?"

"You know, you really can postpone your trip to Jerusalem until the situation is clarified."

Fernand nodded from his table. They had surely agreed on those words beforehand. "The UNESCO decision delays the preparations, including the cornerstone-laying. You know, Jorgenson canceled his trip in January, and the UN is evacuating all nonessential personnel from its bases in the region."

"Yes, Lana, maybe you shouldn't take on too much risk, especially with the boys . . ." Fernand's soft voice crossed the office. Among the photos on his drafting table was the picture of the boys in the Luxembourg Gardens. One-year-old Jonathan with full cheeks, sitting erect in the stroller and looking at David pushing a sailboat with a stick, leaning into the central fountain pool. The picture that stood on your desk, in Haifa. Only after the seven-day mourning period did I remove it and put it in the bag. The only photo of the boys I've carried ever since.

"It's not too late to cancel," Colette repeated almost in a whisper.

I stroked the sketch of the Hut's rope hinges and said into the space between the drafting tables, rolls of plans, and photos of projects we carried out together in all those years of friendship: "It's hard to explain . . . I need that trip now. Before the year of mourning for my father ends . . . I've got to be there. Something's wrong inside me . . . Maybe I can call that the need to enter the Hut myself, or to let go . . . I've got to renew some connection. Maybe so I can let go . . . And maybe it's all the same thing." I raised my eyes to them. "And that Saddam Hussein decided to invade Kuwait just now doesn't really have anything to do with my trip."

Fernand looked at Colette, and she said in her deep, musical voice: "Lana, the rental in Jerusalem is part of the business expenses of the project. You can decide after a week or ten days that you're coming back. And besides, the insurance premium is based on an emergency rate. And that allows a sudden cancellation and a refund. So feel completely free."

"Thanks, thanks for the thought." I changed some connections of the ropes in a corner of one of the Huts.

Silence prevailed, and the scratching of drawing pencils on paper. Fernand made another phone call, Colette came back from the kitchenette with a glass of water.

"What's happening with the al-Kuds troupe?" she asked furtively. "Have you heard from them since they returned from America?"

"No, not really. Everything's stopped . . ." I answered with an effort. "I think they were relieved by the postponement. There was tension there around the binational event . . . I'll see in Jerusalem if something can be done."

"What about Sayyid Ashabi?" she continued.

"Haven't heard from him either." I stifled the pain, the disappointment.

I delayed a little more. Continuing to sort out what I'd take with me. And then came the phone call from Claude, from Brussels, with another breeze of friendship and concern, and the laugh that still succeeded in sneaking in when he declared, "That's it, in the classical style of the Middle East, you've decided to finish under the ruins of some Iraqi Scud." And yet, after the laughter, he also asked, how are "my guys," and it was clear that if I had dropped a hint, he would have come from Brussels immediately.

On leaving, as on every evening, Colette got excited, as if I were already going away.

"Really, don't make a thing of it," I hugged her. "A little fireworks of a war will make the 'trip to the East' sexier. And if you feel like some colonial Orientalism à la Chateaubriand or Flaubert, you can stay with us, and drop in on Jericho for a cup of coffee in the shade of the palm trees and bougainvillea in the middle of January. Think about it seriously, it's only four and a half hours by plane."

Fernand goes down with me. Helps me drag the material I packed to the cab. Stays on the sidewalk, waving, and his rust wooliness fades in the halo of the streetlamps, between the façades of the ancient street.

■ ■ ■ ■

[Cheap Indian restaurant. Behind the Gare du Nord.]

Remnants of the meal on the table. Clementine rinds. Lentil dough. Curry. Scarlet, amber, glowing spices. Pungent smells from the kitchen.

On the way, shops with silk fabrics in dusty windows, fruit and vegetable shops, Indian groceries. Immigrant quarter.

Yesterday, when I came back from the office, along with the rest of the mail, the concierge gave me the letter from Sayyid. A crumpled envelope. I thrust it in my coat pocket, withdrew to the elevator. Entering, I evaded Catherine and the boys, closed myself in the bedroom, and there I tore open the envelope.

One page, no postmark, a French stamp. And Sayyid's deep whisper:

Lana,

Hope things are going okay. I won't be able to get to Paris. Leave the plans for me at the offices of the Alliance France-Palestine (63 rue Paradis, second floor, third door on the right). I'll try to go on with the work until the next time we meet (who knows when or where . . .)

Ciao,

Sayyid

> I reread, and in my ears Sayyid's laughter on the phone in the last conversation from America, evasive when I asked him if he'd be in Jerusalem in January—"If the Israeli cops at Lod let me in . . ." And since then the long ring at my repeated attempts to call the studio in Amsterdam. Addicted to the barren dialing even after the operator at Gilgamesh said he hadn't called to get his messages for two weeks.

And since yesterday, again the volcano, no point denying, "until the next time we meet . . ." Standing half the morning at the photocopy machine with the drafts of the project, bursting out laughing at every comment of Colette or Fernand, chatting with Claude on the phone, infecting them with my excitement. Adding a brief note to the file of the plans, "I'm traveling on Monday with the boys." And the address of the apartment on Hebron Road, with the phone number. Feeling the blood rush to my face when I write the numbers.

The secretary of the France-Palestine Alliance, a well-groomed woman with tight hair and a sculpted face, took the file from me.

"Thank you, Madame," she said drily. As if she were expecting me.

Clearly, that polite remark was all I was going to get. Yet I couldn't resist: "Might you have some message for me?" I blushed down to my neck.

"No, madame."

"Fine, then . . ."

"Au revoir, madame," and then her smiling mask went on.

I turned to leave. From the depths of the corridor Alonzo burst out at me. Thin, silvery hair, ironic ever since our first encounters at the conferences of architecture students more than twenty years ago.

"Look who's here!" he called in artificial surprise.

"Alonzo . . . You work here? . . ."

"Somebody has to take care of building Hebron and Gaza . . ."

I was silent, feeling the secretary's eyes on my back.

"So? You're happy? There'll be an attack on Saddam Hussein, eh? And I just now planned a vacation in Basra, with a few friends who are doing scientific development there," he hissed with the same mockery. Never did he forgive me for being Israeli, returned glowing from his trips to the Fatah training camps in Lebanon, from the military stroking he gets there for his ego.

I turned again to leave.

"Tell me, Lana, what's with you and Sayyid Ashabi?" he blocked my way.

"Something political, cultural . . . and personal."

"Keep your hands off him. You'll end up softening him."

"Meanwhile, I'm hardening him," I replied provocatively at the flicker of blue in his steel-gray eyes. "Don't worry," I added, "it's a joint project with the al-Kuds troupe, sponsored by UNESCO, and the Dag Hammarskjöld Fund. A monument to peace in Jerusalem."

"There's no limit to Zionist hypocrisy. You're geniuses in always turning the story to your side—and calling that 'a joint project for peace' to boot . . ."

"Okay, Alonzo, I've got to run."

"Why are the Jews always in a hurry?" he muttered as he bent down to slide his cheek against mine, and the door slamming echoed behind me all the way down the steps. On the sidewalk of the rue Paradis, a memory from last year, on my return from Israel, washed over me. The celebration at the release of Nelson Mandela, which turned into a conference of veteran activists of revolutionary cells, where I last saw Alonzo. Colleagues who came from Eastern Europe for the first time, drunk on their new access to the West. Spending hours in cafés in Montparnasse, Saint-Germain. Members of the dissident architects' group from Prague, Solidarity activists from Poland, loyalists from Hungary. Claude also came from Brussels, passing out leaflets to the participants on transit camps for refugees from the Eastern bloc, on our association's emergency committee plans for building and reconstruction. In a few sentences I told him about Sayyid, the meeting in Jerusalem, the plan for the performance. The rest he certainly understood from my tone of voice. And Peter Brook's production of *The Mahabharata,* with an invitation Sayyid arranged for me. "Say that the ticket's in the name of Ashabi, of the Gilgamesh troupe," he told me over the phone, and while my knees were still shaking, he added, "I'm dying to hear what you think of the show, Lana . . . No, don't call . . . tell me by mouth, mouth to mouth, yes . . ." I heard his laugh. "I'll get there the day after tomorrow, by car . . ."

Sitting for the long hours of the play on sack seats of the Théâtre Bouffes du Nord. Facing the cascade of colors, the torches, the costumes sparkling in a crimson flash. Flooded with the sounds of bells, conches, cymbals, stringed instruments. The actors dancing across the stage, bursts of wheels of fire, bold battle scenes with drawn bows, fluttering lances. And lines of heroic poetry recited in solemn French, to the flushed faces of the Parisian audience.

And the wall of distance that didn't melt around me throughout the play. As if the audience, the actors, the emotions that stirred the audience, that whole bold wave of hope that greeted me when I returned from Israel to a new Europe didn't belong to us, Father, to the story left unraveled behind me, when the plane cut off from the shores of Israel. Wandering around Paris like a sleepwalker, continuing to search for you. Jonathan has changed so much, is already starting to talk. And David's face has grown long. And all the "drawings of Grandpa" he made since I left. In some of them you're lying in bed, and I'm looking out the window. And in others, after Alain told them you died, only I, or you, on a blue or brown background. Wandering around the streets like the blindfolded Gandhari, looking blind at the death of her sons, the death of her nephews at the bloodshed. And the words of the beautiful Lebanese actress rip me: "The land is burning as in the End of Days."

Only the next day, in the hours with Sayyid in the car, in our silent driving, was I close to you again, Father. Sayyid picked me up at the office, for an aimless drive. Going through Paris between rain and sun in drops on the windshield. And the windows covered, inside, with the mist of breath, and Sayyid's warm hand under all the layers, with the pace of the bodies quenching the thirst ever since we had parted in Jerusalem. The hair is bound, squashed to the upholstery of the seat. Dozing in the wool coat. And the naked poplars on the quay of cement and plaster warehouses, at the entrance to the ferry port.

"Yes, Gandhari . . ." Sayyid's eyes stare into the distance, and my fingers are bound and unbound in his curls. "Until the last minute, the role was kept for Mirabel. A personal invitation from Peter Brook . . . Even for Peter she didn't return, didn't break her vow of withdrawal . . . it's been eight years now since I've seen her. And I can't get her out of my body. Once, in Tunis, I saw her in the distance, crossing the street. I couldn't budge. Couldn't even yell. You understand? I was sick for a week. Sick. Maybe that's why I agreed to work at the headquarters. To be with her in that city. To see her in the distance. Sick with her . . . I never loved as in those days and nights of the shelling of Beirut, in the summer of '82. Every centimeter of her skin I licked. From the tips of her toes to her hair. Licking so slowly. Like the body of a goddess. Learning from it everything I'll ever know about a woman's body. Feeling it even now, Lana . . . And then, I returned to al-Kuds, to Jerusalem. To keep my parent's promise to Kayyina's parents. And to work with the troupe. We decided after the fall of headquarters in Beirut, that that was the time to move the struggle back home. When I returned to Beirut, I found the apartment empty. No trace of Mirabel. Only a page with two lines: 'There's no compromise in struggle, and no compromise in love.' Since then she left the stage. Went underground. Only does secret activities . . ." And when he bit my lips, he whispered: "She'd spit in my face if she knew how I am with you, Lana . . ." Lifts my body in his arms, turns me over him, with a rustle of breathing that filled the silence again. And the roar of the distant traffic bursts against the windows of the parked car. And your voice, Father.

Yes, your voice once again poured then, in tatters. Flooding the shaking of the sweat-soaked body. The melted voice Sayyid plucked from my lips.

The heart is hungry, the heart's insane,
The heart will shout and cheer with pain,
Hallelujah, hallelujah, on and on,
Torn are we, worn are we . . .

Leaving the offices of the France-Palestine Alliance, instead of going down to the Métro, I cut away from the cascade of light on the main streets, turning north, to the dark among the immigrants' shops. Just to be with you again before I go back home. Men congregate, their hands in their pockets, their faces impassive. And the restaurant where I stopped to eat. Four tables. Paper tablecloths. The pungent taste that permeates.

A black couple stop at the window. They peep into the restaurant together. Two masks of amazement with raised eyebrows. In nylon coats zipped up to the neck and wool caps.

At the end of the dark street, the bridge hanging above the railroad tracks. Open to the cold, the smoke, and the mist of streetlamps going off along the tracks.

■ ■ ■ ■

[At the open suitcases, escaping to our conversation.]

A monotonous rustle drains from the city to the glass walls, to the quiet in Alain's study, the long corridor.

The suitcases with our unraveled insides. Rag dolls, panties, picture books, cotton shirts, airplanes, Jonathan's collection of crushed pacifiers I asked Catherine to pack in advance. And in a second pile, the tight jeans I bought in the last sortie to Manhattan, the red wool scarf, the rolls of sketches, the books. Cultures of life to survive in Jerusalem. In the first trip without a phone call to you as soon as we land, and your voice lit up at the other end of the line, like your big wave and smile, darting from the mass of people waiting at the airport.

The trip east. To "the mother of all wars," Father. Trying to silence the worry about the boys. David sorts out what he'll take. Excited at the idea that he's going "where the planes are." Winging his collection of planes into the suitcase, "I'm killing him! I'm killing him!" And Jonathan toddles behind him with outstretched arms—"illin im, illin im."

Until a little while ago I was waiting for a phone call. Not knowing from which one of them. For a call from Alain, from Moscow, or maybe for still another call from Sayyid. After midnight I stopped waiting. Sinking into the silence surrounding the apartment, me, the boys, and fragments of the conversation with you, coming close and swallowed up again in the night leading to the trip.

A gray cover hovers over the towers of the neighborhood, the winding river. The lights open to the horizon, to the pale pulp of the suburbs. To Montmorency and the fields seen from the orphanage directed by Madame Heller until her death, two years ago.

And the thought that tomorrow evening we'll be in Jerusalem. In the rented apartment.

The imagination refuses to shift itself there, to be cut off from the space here that still holds our lives.

I stayed in the children's room for a long time. Bending over their beds. Jonathan's beautiful face in the crib. The high line of the eyebrows, the wonder, so innocent it makes you shout. And David, wrapped up over his head. His long legs always finding a way to burst out of the blanket. What's in store for them in the coming weeks there? (The only moment I admit the absolute madness of the trip, now.)

And suddenly a childish joy at the trip. Out of the blue. Despite the danger. As at the start of pregnancy, the start of a new love. Maybe like the impulse that made you leave everything and go to Palestine.

And the blue sky that will spread tomorrow instead of the dreary gray of Paris.

Three o'clock. The bags are zipped. Standing at the door. With a pile of backpacks.

I finished the last of the chocolate in the refrigerator.

The hushed swarming outside. The apartment seemed to sail off already, in a countdown, until six-fifteen. When Catherine will come help me dress the boys and we'll leave for the airport.

Jerusalem

[On the plane toward Jerusalem.]

Masses of clouds over Europe. An opaque woolly covering.

David at the window. Putting together the puzzle he got from the stewardess. A thin profile on the glowing background. His resemblance to Alain. In the tremor of his lips, the straight line of his eyebrows.

(He's careful lately. Not to talk about Papa. Or about what's in store for us in Jerusalem. Packs the fleet of airplanes, the Lego boxes. Slowly absorbing, with his pensive look. Bursting into rollicking laughter only with Catherine. And last night, on the table in the children's room, I found his notebook with basic Hebrew exercises. And I who was afraid to mention the school in Jerusalem.)

Jonathan sleeping on the seat between us. Finally. His cheeks flushed. Wrapped in the airplane blanket. Sucking movements pace his breathing, the tremor of his big eyelids, covered with sweat. Waves of dream go over them and his high eyebrows.

The space around us, between two rows of seats. Empty plastic cups. The boys' shoes between coloring books, the bags on the floor. And the CD Walkman with Don Giovanni, *still flooding with the shadow of Europe's lust.*

Smell of wool steeped in cigarette smoke. Wrapping me like your jacket.

The boys sit straight up in their seats for landing. Jonathan strokes my trouser leg with one hand, and with the other, he holds on to Lolo the rabbit. Finally calm. The strong sucking apparently eased the pressure in his ears.

(When he woke up, he wanted to "show the plane to Lolo." Toddles between the seats with his legs spread. And the French stewardess is taken with his charm and follows in his wake.)

A kind of seriousness descends on the passengers. A tense silence. Disturbed only by the racket of buckling and fastening. David hugs his backpack. Concentrated.

The shoreline. Beyond the heads of the boys clinging to the window.

A distant strip of foam in the wintry pallor.

And the heart pounding. All at once. Over the citrus groves and the plowed furrows quickly coming close.

"Well, what's there to fear here, Ilanka? . . ." you hum amused.

"Torn are we, worn are we,
In honor of the holiday adorned
Patches on patches
Hallelujah on and on
And the heart is hungry, the heart's insane
The heart will shout and cheer with pain . . ."

The boys at the baggage claim. They left me to watch the cart and ran ahead. Drunk with some unraveled relief that fills the arrivals hall.

David zigzags in and out among those waiting around the baggage carousel, still for now. Jonathan runs after him with outstretched arms.

I lean the notebook on the cart and the hand luggage. Go on reporting to you, against all logic. Apparently this way avoiding bursting out with the brace of songs of the first settlers, "Here in our fathers' delightsome land, we shall do all that we have planned . . ."

First images here. The slumping posture of the passengers. Their sharp turn of the head. Overly made-up women. Some passengers pushing their carts. Fighting with those who got a place next to the baggage carousel. A few hesitant, restrained tourists, in fine clothes. And billboards, in Hebrew.

Suddenly the look is drawn there, to the distant corner of the hall. I didn't discover them immediately, Father. As if they were wiped out under the racket. The new immigrants from the Soviet Union . . .

Sitting in families. Coats zipped up. Women, men, thin-necked children. Old people in berets. Surrounded by heaps of suitcases. Weary faces, tense with worry. Like passengers whose train is stuck in the middle of the track somewhere between Ukraine, Moscow, Israel, Brighton Beach, São Paulo. Waiting resiliently. Anyway, there's nothing to do until things are cleared up.

I'm drawn to them. With the embarrassing sense of immediate closeness. Something in the gestures, the Russian sound. And maybe only a delusion because you're not here. A mirage in the insane staging of history.

The baggage belt moves. A rolling heap comes around. A sudden push. Voices rising all at once.

David and Jonathan squeeze in front of the carts. Bend down to identify our bags. Shout something to me.

I open the notebook again. While walking. Use Jonathan's backpack, puffed up with games and toys, to write on, to share the sight with you. Hear you whisper, "New immigrants from Ethiopia . . ." And already, like you, moved to tears, and expressions like "thy children shall come again to their own border" and "ingathering of the exiles" fill my head.

Jonathan was the first one to see them and tugged on my coat. They pass in a procession. In families. Long figures, in white cloaks with gold hems waving.

Walking with faces raised. Men, women. Airy groups of children. As if the wind of the plains puffs up their holiday dress.

And again the intoxicating joy. As if all the passengers pushing carts are pilgrims hastening on the road to Jerusalem, to some international mass meeting, on Mount Sabbatical, being built on a hilltop in Jerusalem. Outside time, far from war, on a day that is all Sabbath . . .

David jostles my elbow. We're already causing a traffic jam. And Jonathan whines, "Coke!"

■ ■ ■ ■

[The apartment on Hebron Road.]

Late. The boys are in their room. Sleeping.

Through the window night comes in. Noise of roads behind the ridge, of distances in the dark.

And all the time expecting the tread of your steps in the corridor, your voice calling "Ilanka?" when I turn my head.

Yaron Matus comes to the airport. His height makes him stand out from the mass of people waiting. "Hey, Lana! Hey, boys!" And despite the broad grin, the taps on our shoulders, the hugs, his face is stiff as he navigates the loaded cart between the cars. And then, all at once, the winter light of the Sharon Valley, the oleander bushes, shadows of eucalyptus, the hibiscus at the entrance to the parking lot. And the curves of the road going up to Jerusalem, familiar as the folds of the body. The fields of Beit Shemen, the sunset-covered hills, the yellowing treetops, graying quickly at Sha'ar Hagai, at the entrance to the Judean Mountains.

When we climbed the road at the war monument, Yaron said, "Danziger."

"Yes," I echoed, in a regular rite, apparently, silently or aloud, of all of us students from the same class at the Technion. "Yes, Danziger . . ."

It was David who asked from the dark of the backseat, "Do you build Huts, too?"

And Yaron, who until then had spoken to them only in the plural, "boys," glanced at him in the mirror. "Yes. I help your mommy."

I thanked him silently for not mentioning the postponing of the project, so as not to get dragged into talking about the war.

"Me, too," announced David. "I help Mommy too!"

By the time we entered Jerusalem, it was night. Erella was waiting in the apartment, ran to bring snacks for the boys, took off their coats. Yaron finished bringing up the endless pieces of luggage, then said he had to run. I followed him out to the stairs to thank him. When I hugged him, he put his arms around me for a long minute. I should have understood, but the neglected staircase of the housing project distracted me, and I pulled away quickly.

Erella went with me into the little living room with the sofa bed, the boys' room, the kitchen. Making the beds, putting away a few pots and plates.

"Erella, you're awesome," I clutched her arm.

Only then did she stop. "I'm glad it's all right," and a tired childish smile flooded her face where the traces of beauty could still be seen.

"I didn't know until the last minute if you'd come, so I prepared at least the minimum." And she smiled again like a successful little girl, reminding me of Mother's endless cares, and tears rose in my eyes, with that sentimentality I had inherited from you. And then we all crowded around the kitchen table for dinner. With the small "Israeli" cucumbers, and all the lumps of cottage cheese that Jonathan gathered up from the corner of the plate, and the yogurt with jam that Erella pulled out of the old refrigerator. "And now something hot to drink. I brought an electric kettle, let's see if it works right. There's tea and coffee, and cocoa for the boys!"

The domestic racket nearly covered the knock at the door. Erella blurted out something and ran to open it: "Mrs. Ben-Harush. Allegra. The neighbor from the ground floor, who takes care of children. She's got a day-care center in her home," she announced solemnly at the woman who filled the doorway like a regal statue, with her thick eyebrows and straight nose, handing me a cake pan covered with a cloth napkin.

"This is for welcome, cake!" She warms me with her smile.

"You really didn't have to." I was immediately captivated.

"Au plaisir, Madame."

Immediately addressing the boys, with throaty French and a musical flicker of Hebrew:

"Vous venez jouer chez moi? D'accord? Come play in my house, there's lots of games."

"We've got games, too," declared David.

"Wanna see?" Jonathan already grabbed her dress.

"Of course I want to see! Faites voir, chéris."

The two of them ran to the bundles. Jonathan pulled out Lolo, put him in Allegra's arms.

And she, like a magician who already sprinkled dust on the hypnotized audience before continuing the performance, addressed me practically.

"The little one's in my day-care center. That's good. There are good children, and the yard is nice, you'll see. And if you're not at home, I can pick up the big one from school. He can eat lunch at my house. I've got a son, a year older. Il s'appelle Yossi. They'll be friends. Don't worry. Vous pouvez compter sur moi. I've been taking care of children for many years now."

The boys didn't let her leave before they arranged a toy show for her, and David told her in quick French about Indian costumes and planes.

> And at the door, as she softly shook my hand, you also stood with me, smiling at her with that family spirit in which you'd connect with people who won your heart, in the street, in the line at the post office. You come home and reconstruct the conversation, if not really in Yiddish, at least with the connecting sentences, "zogt mir . . . zog ikh . . . he says to me . . . and then I say to him . . ."

"So see you tomorrow, Allegra." I imitated your tone of voice.

"Yes, Ilana." She came down hard on the *n* in my name.

> You also remained when Erella gave me a long hug and left, and afterward, too, when I went into the bathroom with the boys, and when I turned out the light in their room, and together we looked at the spots of light coming in through the shutters, wandering over the ceiling of the room. Then, too, you gathered up with me the slivers of the moment in a transparent net.

I bent down to kiss David, inhaling his soft smell.

"Mommy, tomorrow after school, I want to go back home, not to Allegra."

"Of course, David. Don't worry. Anyway, tomorrow you can stay home. You don't have to start school."

"That's all right, Mommy, I'll go tomorrow," he said and clenched his jaw.

"I saw that you were going over the alphabet . . ."

"Yes . . ." he whispered, and turned his head.

And something filled the apartment with a rustle. Maybe Jonathan who fell asleep breathing heavily, strips of light fluttering over his face. Maybe your voice saying softly, "Ilanka." Maybe the smell of Sayyid on the narrow mattress when we let go of one another like two lobes of fruit that burst.

The phone call from Yaron came as I was leaving the children's room, still dazzled by the light in the living room. The pulse throbbing in my temples, even when I understood that it wasn't Sayyid, silenced Yaron's panting voice, "So, what, you want me to come, Lana?"

"What?"

"I thought of dropping in on you a little. What do you say?" he chuckled.

Only then did I get it. "Drop it, Yaron . . ."

"What do you mean?"

"Drop it now."

The effort of recent days hit me all at once.

"Come on."

"Enough, really. We'll have enough joint projects . . ." I tried reluctantly to appease him.

Sitting at last in the night space of the apartment in the housing project. First look around.

The old furniture. The peeling plaster near the ceiling.

And in the bathroom drawer, the hairpins of former tenants.

(And all day long, I haven't heard any news.)

The distant rustle of the city. And the soft tread of your steps, Father.

■ ■ ■ ■

Almost midnight. I dialed Sayyid's apartment. I couldn't help it.

The body completely awake. Bursting with excitement. And writing to you. Choking.

I would go out for a walk. But I can't leave the boys alone. The apartment is like a cage. Not even a balcony. The sliding window in the living room only opens halfway. Brings in a pure, crisp cold.

I introduced myself with a fake name, as a television producer from Paris. Only then, in panic, did I quickly apologize for calling so late, for disturbing.

A woman's deep voice, not young (Kayyina's mother?), "Moment. Moment."

And the silence full of rustles coming and going. Finally, a woman's hushed voice, in a British tone.

"No. He hasn't come back. Sorry. No, he didn't say when. You want to leave a message for Sayyid?"

Did she suspect. And the pronunciation of the name "Sayyid," with a soft glottal. And the jealousy. The jealousy.

And in fact, from the moment I attached the number of the apartment in Jerusalem to the plans, I went to meet Sayyid, already calculating the hours until he'd call, would come. Spreading the map of lust with our holy places: the traffic signal on Hebron Road, where we burned in the car, leg against leg. The driveway to the Scottish Hospice, where he rolled the syllables of my name, "Lannna . . ." when I barely made it to the gate with melted legs.

And the suitcase of material I brought, in spite of everything, to the Israeli-Palestinian seminar for the architecture students of Bezalel and Birzeit.

Starry night. In the distance, the octopus of lights of Gilo. The schematic urban planning exposed at night.

Behind the mountain, the road to Bethlehem is swallowed up.

A tremor of cars slices now and then.

The breathing of the boys from the open door.

And your voice humming, "The heart is hungry, the heart's insane . . ."

■ ■ ■ ■

[Dawn. The red bursts into the room, floods the sheets.]

Sunrise burns on the faces of the housing projects, sidewalks of Hebron Road, the road climbing south.

To wake up in the light I saw for months in my mind's eye while planning the Hill of Evil Counsel. In every one of the stages. Starting with the sketches and ending by illuminating the model. The light etching the slope to the desert, the library, emphasizing the materiality of the Huts, the wood, the cloth, the straw mats, the flicker of water.

A stormy sleep on disheveled sheets.

(Till late at night I struggled with the mechanism of the sofa bed.)

In a dream, a white cliff, amazingly beautiful, drawn out of a greenish turquoise lake, maybe the Dead Sea. Behind it a rise, with a few cypresses darkening in the distance. And there, beyond the bend, Sayyid and I among the flower beds, going into a meeting with Jurgenson. Whiskey at a window overlooking Bethlehem, and the two of us present the plan for the performance. Still only the "architect" and the "director," starring in a European show in the Levant. He still hadn't touched me. But with a flicker of his eyes, he licks the words from my lip, rolls them on his tongue, changes their color, puffs them out in multicolored rings around the table and the glasses.

Jurgenson gets up to leave, shakes hands with a toothy grin. And right after he goes, the two of us walk together, among the flower beds; in the pungent smell of earth, he rubs a handful in front of my face.

"You see that earth?" He walks close to me, winding around me like a sheet and the clods crumble between his fingers, scatter over the whiteness. "The earth is mother and wife. With us, the wife doesn't have many husbands. One husband with many wives—that's possible . . ." He bursts out laughing. "But a wife of everyone, that you let go of, 'sabbatical,' 'shmutah' . . ." Only dust remains on his hand. "Here's the new song of the al-Kuds troupe." He chants in his throat, and after a few words in Arabic, he switches to an improvised translation:

Oh, earth, earth of Palestine, the Franks lay with you,
And Saladin freed you by slaugher.
Oh, holy earth, the Franks lay with you,
Your honor we shall restore with our blood, the mother, wife, and lover,
Oh earth, earth of Palestine—

The laugh hurls his body wound around me, moves my body stuck to him. And everything's spinning. The flower beds, the cypresses, the fences of the camp, the guard tower with the Israeli soldiers. Everything slides down the slope, into the deep abyss. To the erect cliff, flowing with salt. Laps with its warmth the sparkling rocks, the shoulders, the silken neck. Licks the smooth skin. Bites part after part, hair, sweat. Down to the deep layers of the mountain. To the gushing, in the smell of thorns and dust. Steaming mist. Sweetness winding up in the smoke curling from a forgotten cigarette. Veiling the look. And already the shadow of your voice envelops the rolled body: "Read you, Ilanka?" you say slowly, "The story you love best?" Leafing through the shroud of parchments around me, slowly uncovering my ear and whispering:

"I woke up with the first lines of light of a new morning, Ilanka . . ." The rush of words gushes from the shadow bending over, inflaming the tunnels of the ear: ". . . we were ready, Ilanka. We lined up in twos, twos and threes, on our shoulder a hoe or a pickax . . . we rise to conquer a new point! We headed to the wilderness. To the uninhabited land . . ." You go on lulling me softly, and from the thread of saliva sparkling in the dark between your lips pop up riders, loaded carts, shouts of "Dio"! Men in Russian shirts, girls in flowing dresses, popping up and marching among the rocks in the morning mist. Into the valley. Marching on soft, warm ground, and their voices echo in the distance. "We rise and sing, we rise, sing and rise."

You bend over, move your lips, strum words I never even imagined were buried in me: ". . . we marched and we sang, Ilanka, the sun rises, everything shines . . . I swallow the landscape in deep breaths, want to blend into it . . . in the distance flickers a hill, shouts of 'Here, here it is, this is the place' . . ." You chuckle, your voice moves me but I can't budge, rolled in white, while the marchers climb up, paving a new narrow path in the black earth. "Who knows when the foot of a Hebrew person trod here last? . . ." you whisper, as the first marchers reach the hilltop, and the clatter of hoes is heard, the banging of pickaxes. "First contact with the earth, Ilanka . . ." The pale light, when in dream or in the hallucination of waking, your warm breath smoothes like silk, in growing, reddening rustle. ". . . And they stood-shoulder to shoulder and spread out their arms. The fatigue vanished, the feet pounded, the faces lit up . . . And the circle kept growing: "God will build the Galilee, God will build Jezreel, the regiment will build the Galilee, the regiment will build Jezreel . . ." A flame fused of words flows on the skin, on the sheet blazing in the campfire, and the dancing silhouettes are darkening around it. "Night fell," your voice grew distant. "The Arab villages are already sunk in sleep . . . And maybe they peep at the hill, don't understand what dead of night, who wakes that hill from its long slumber? . . ."

Only a red hovering on the white with the hazy voice, retreated from the body lying on the sheets, spread for a moment on the peaks, from one side of Jerusalem to the other, in a trembling of rising light.

I stood for a long time at the window.

On the mountaintop the Mar Elias Monastery. Overlooking from the line of the watershed, south to Bethlehem, north to Jerusalem. All glowing in the direct light of sunrise.

■ ■ ■ ■

[Seven o'clock news. The announcer's polished voice.]

"Violent clashes between demonstrators and security forces erupted yesterday in the eastern neighborhoods of Jerusalem. In a march in the village of Silwan, stones and Molotov cocktails were thrown at members of the Border Patrol. A response of tear gas and rubber bullets inflamed the riots. The disturbances were quashed only late at night."

"Following the murder in Jaffa last weekend, an expulsion order was issued against four leaders of Hamas in Gaza. More than seven hundred activists of the organization were arrested."

"Baghdad rejects the offer of the American president to hold joint discussions. In an announcement received yesterday, Iraq declares that she will go to war."

"The number of immigrants from the Soviet Union now stands at twenty thousand a month. Our correspondents report long lines at the aliyah offices in Moscow and Tashkent."

The light now washes the sparkling buildings of Gilo, behind the industrial district of Talpiot. The cranes. Construction scaffolds. And in the middle, near the solitary grove, the houses of Beit Tsafafa.

The light shimmers now, two kilometers from here, on the cars rising early from East Talpiot, Arab-a-Sohra, Tsur Bahar, the UN camp, crossing the peak of the Hill of Evil Counsel. Their radios open to the

seven o'clock news. Announcers' voices, in various languages, Arabic, Hebrew, the foreign stations in the UN cars, slicing the site of Mount Sabbatical—the dream that still connected us, Father, before your hand was cut off from mine.

Through the slit of the door rises the boys' sweet breathing. They haven't yet left the land of dreams.

I'll go wake them now. For their first morning here.

■ ■ ■ ■

[Eleven a.m. On the bench facing the grocery store. In the neighborhood shopping center.]

In the plastic bags cornflakes, yogurt, bread, oranges, and a few vegetables.

A square patio between the buildings. Arid. From the park planned here, probably, all that's left is a pine with a twisted trunk, casting a spot of shade, and a few dusty bushes. In the sharp, splashing light.

Without the boys, for the first time after two whole days in a row. David insisted on going to school this morning. All the way he clutched my hand. We walked across the schoolyard together. The shrieks, the children running. The busy principal, the secretary filling out forms. And then the bell. Teachers rushing out of the teachers' lounge. Hand in hand, we look for classroom A4. We stand in the doorway, David at my side. The teacher, Hadassah, smiles at us vaguely, the children raise their heads. David's hand drops. The teacher addresses the class in a thick voice: "Say hello to David. He's a new boy who is joining us."

I saw him sit down in the second row, next to a curly-haired boy. He put the blue-and-green backpack on the table, and then the door shut. I stood in the empty corridor. The roar of voices swelled behind the classroom doors. On the walls, colorful cutouts of jars, dreidels, Hanukkah lamps. Pictures of a Makhzor in black and white. Signs on Bristol scrolls: "Honor thy Father and Mother," "Jerusalem of Gold."

> And a twinge of guilt all the time for deserting David like that. Dragging him into our complicated story, Father.

I returned to Allegra, to be with Jonathan, as I promised. At the traffic light on Hebron Road, I was suddenly terrified that Jonathan had been sitting in a corner crying all the time, that he fell off the teeter-totter. I almost started running in the sun beating down even though it was late December, arrived panting at the door on the ground floor, ringing the "Ben-Harush" doorbell.

Allegra quickly returned to the five children sitting with her around the mosaic table in the backyard, under the awning of vine and lemon tree tendrils. Drinking juice and eating cookies. Jonathan, too. His fair curls standing out. Rapt in gnawing. Sees me come out to the yard behind Allegra and doesn't budge. For a moment, I drank my fill of his beauty from a distance, until he got up and ran to me, hugging my legs hard. And the softness washes over my limbs. Even when he breaks off and returns to his place on the bench, immediately absorbed in chewing another biscuit. As if he knows that that's what he has to sink into now.

I sat down far away, in the shade of the lemon tree. Jonathan smiled at me hesitantly, and the hair dropping on my face hid the tears of my answering smile. I stayed there even when the children ran to play in this hidden paradise in the back of the housing project, with chickens running around the coop, and flower beds and the vine. Jonathan took over the carousel for himself, alone, his curls sparkling in the quick spinning. Abandoned to the pleasure. Leaning his head on the pole of the carousel with a drunken smile, even when I called goodbye to him.

"Venez voir," Allegra accompanied me from the yard to the kitchen. "I'm making courgettes farcies for lunch, venez, venez." She lifted the cover off the pot of meat and vegetables. A jet of steam shot over the windowpane, on the starched curtain, on the tears that once again fogged my eyes at the woman who was only a few years older than me, who had already adopted me and the boys. Le petit est très gentil, Ilana. The little one's very nice."

"When he rests he needs three pacifiers . . ."

"I remember . . . here they are, ready!" She pointed at the heavy cabinet covered with a lace cloth. "Don't worry, everything will be fine."

Eleven-fifteen. In three-quarters of an hour, I'll go get David from school.

The morning drags on, despite the strong light. Over even before it started. Pours through unknown passages, Father. And the alienation is even more oppressive because of the closeness.

On the bench on the other side, next to the post office, a man sat down. In coat and hat. Leaning on a cane. Sunk in sun.

A woman comes out of Ben-Shoshan's grocery store with full bags. In a flowered dress. Now a young man comes out. Maybe a student. With a light step. He has a bag, too. The woman is swallowed up on the right in a narrow passage between the housing projects. The young man crosses the square in a baggy black T-shirt. A few boarded-up display windows. Maybe workshops. Shops for housewares and hardware.

The older man still leans on his cane, gazes into the distance.

And suddenly the words of Robert Frank about his New York photos from the summer of '58. I hung them over the drafting table when I started working on the site: "The Bus carries me thru the City, I look out the window, I look at the people on the street, the Sun and the Traffic Lights. It has to do with desperation and endurance—I have always felt about living in New York. Compassion and probably some understanding for New York's Concrete and its people, walking . . . waiting . . . standing . . . holding hands . . ."

Like the people walking here and in another place. The man across from me, who sat down to rest, some jumble of languages humming under the warming hat on his bald head? Hebrew? Romanian? Turkish? Maybe Yiddish? And the woman with the bags, going off on the bare path, maybe also going down to the port in Saloniki, or to the square in Marrakesh? And I, in the first moment of silence, at the end of the whole journey that led here.

Ben-Shoshan came out of the grocery store, dragging a carton inside, "Some sun, eh?"

"Right . . ." And his smile completely reconciles me with the short morning, the neglect in the square.

■ ■ ■ ■

[Café Cobalt. On the fourth floor of the industrial building where the office is.]

Downstairs, workshops and stores. A mattress shop. A carpenter shop. A housewares shop. A dance studio on the second floor. A creative center for autistic children on the third. The architects' offices on the fifth. And a bakery for pitas and borekas—the boys assault the hot plastic bag with its pastries—behind the building.

From the porch, theater students in masks enter the café (an enclave of Jews and Arabs). Noise of building stage sets rises from the workshop.

Late December. The glowing light drips day after day. Warm, especially in the winter clothes, worn stubbornly according to the name of the season. Drought. And, despite my guilt feelings, I bless the blue every morning.

After a week here. In the office of Yaron and Erella, I already have a desk. Yaron is working on the model of the technological greenhouses: "The future in our harsh area is in economic profit. Pragmatics and economics, that's the name of the game, Lana!" he admonishes me. Erella won the competition of the National Park Authority. She brings to "Mount Sabbatical" her precious knowledge of the local landscape and flora. Eran, her older son, was drafted into the army four months ago. And ever since, she's become more fragile. The tablet of despair of his basic training hangs over her desk. "Lucky your sons are still small," she drops her eyes and changes the subject.

Gil, Yaron's apprentice from the new department at the Bezalel art institute, works next to me. He immediately got hooked by the project. Starts planning his own variation of the twelve huts. Questions me about the Huts of the Cooper Union students. Urges me, despite the situation, to set up if not a regular seminar between Bezalel and Birzeit, at least meetings with a small group of Israeli and Palestinian students and artists. "Screw it, Lana. Meanwhile we'll, like, work on parts of the plan, as like personal projects." I put him in touch with Anton of al-Kuds. They agreed on a tour of the site, and afterward a working meeting in the office. Yesterday, when we were working together, Yaron passed by, and looked at us for a moment. Gil didn't notice, went on explaining the strips of shade of the thicket. "Well, well!" Yaron blurted out. "Look at the excitement here . . ." I cut through in a loud voice that Yaron would hear, "Gil, let's check how that's integrated with the performance of the cornerstone-laying staged by Sayyid Ashabi . . . Here, right next to the first Hut you planned, the actors will lead the audience . . . in a combination of texts and song . . ."

Yesterday, another polite, evasive fax from the Dag Hammarskjöld Fund. "International ceremonies cannot be held in the coming weeks. But, of course, nothing fundamental has changed . . ." And from the office in Paris—faxes every other day. Always with some amusing detail, some soft word. Now that I've gone, in spite of everything, at least I should laugh. I tell them to postpone all invitations for the time being. "For how long?" "For the duration . . ."

And last night, the phone call from Claude, from Brussels. After asking how the boys and I were, he tried to distract me (or himself) from what's about to happen here. Tells in his quick speech about our architects' association organizing an activity in Angola. "With the end of the Cold War, there's hope for a ceasefire in the civil war there. They're planning to restore villages, bridges that were blown up, and there's a plan for a hospital in the suburbs of Luanda . . . Now that the Russians have lost power, we've got to act fast, Lana. The West extracts oil there up to its neck . . . Yes, some of your plan for a global Sabbatical wouldn't hurt for the oil wells and the diamond mines of Africa. In general, the time has come for the world to completely turn the laws of Sabbatical into the basis of economics . . ."

Claude's excited voice, and the smell of Gauloises that filled my ears as if they were nostrils.

After a week here, Ben-Shoshan, from the grocery store, greets me like an old customer. And the boys are relaxing their hold on me. Already swallowed up in their own reality. David goes to school with Danny and Ido, the sons of the Levi family on the second floor. Yesterday, he told me excitedly how Guy, the boy who sits next to him, showed him a nest of ants in the playground behind the school, at recess. "Big, black ants, came and went into a hole in the ground." In the afternoon, he plays soccer with Yossi, Allegra's son, who takes a bus home from his religious school. David returns home with a dry branch of squill, or of sticky elecampane he picked in the lot behind our building. Jonathan, curlier than ever, drags everywhere "Bobo," the dusty stick he found in a nearby construction site. Totters ahead of me on the steps to Allegra's day care. Stands on both plump legs on one step, sends out one foot and then another, and stands on two feet on the next step. At Allegra's, he's followed everywhere by Hila, the little girl with thin features and gigantic brown eyes. "Jonathan! Jonathan!" she runs after him as soon as he comes in. And this morning, after he and Hila went off, Allegra laughed and told how Jonathan led the children yesterday in a game of hide-and-seek with the chickens.

Waves of joy that sweep me and the boys away, Father. Bursts of sudden laughter of all three, for no reason. See you smiling, like me, at the sight of their movements that become more angular, and at the sound of their Hebrew permeated by French as they hunch over the gigantic puzzle together.

And in the afternoon, the shouts of the children rise among the housing projects, "Mama! Maaaamaaa!" reminding me of childhood in Haifa, the chorus of women's voices from the windows and tiny balconies, "Yossi . . . Baruch . . ." pouring into the twilight.

The phone call from Alain came yesterday when I was out. I returned to the office in the afternoon and Lilach and Smadi, Allegra's grown daughters, babysat the boys. When I came in, David said, "We talked with Papa."

"Where did he call from?"

"There."

"Where there?"

"I don't know."

"What did he say?"

"He asked how we are."

"Yes?"

"That's all."

A thick wave hurled me. A mixture of relief that I avoided his rage, perhaps shouts, and of unexpected tenderness for Alain in his solitary journey in the depths of the archives of the collapsing superpower, seeking another strip of paper, another name in the lists of the dead.

And Sayyid's long silence. I plow through the newspapers. Follow the news of the headquarters in Tunis, Arafat's militant trips, the definite support of the Palestinian street for Saddam Hussein: trying thus to extract information about what's happening with him. And every single evening, the body renews its expectations.

■ ■ ■ ■

[Alone in the car. Hill of Evil Counsel.]

Parking near the UN camp at the Governor's Palace, outside the fence around the grove, near the remains of the Shepherd's Inn, the café that was burned down a year ago, in the Intifada.

Every single morning on the way to the office, I turn east, to the site, with the secondhand Fiat I bought in the car lot in Talpiot. "Now you've come here? Everybody's going and selling. And you're buying . . ." The lot owner didn't calm down, a virile man with a broad body tilting to the side.

Driving to the site. Stopping each time at another point of the three hundred sixty degrees of the open site. Give myself to the deceptive, bitchy beauty open to the gleaming ridges around the Old City. And in between the turrets, domes, roofs rising inside the walls. And the descending slopes of dry streams; the Valley of Hinnom, the Kidron, the Shiloah.

> At my feet, the steep slope is etched by the river Etsel. A grade of more than sixty yards. Here I planned the library and the seminar rooms of Mount Sabbatical. Overlooking Mount Moriah: a direct view of the Foundation Stone, but with the distance necessary for thinking of Sabbatical, of aiming at, with no holding.

I move the car another hundred meters to the east and the landscape changes completely. Like a new deck of cards in the hand of a seer.

North, the last houses of Silwan, Ras el Amud, Abu Dis. And from there, to the east, the yellow ridge slipping in the slices of the mountain descending to the desert. Cones of hills rise from the floor of the valley, revealed only from here, once behind the flank of the mountain. Yellow-pink hills, surrounded by terraces, and at the top—like pillars of a pistil or a circumcised penis—the turrets of mosques.

The desert is open to the horizon. The Syrian-African rift draws it all the way up to the abyss of the Dead Sea. And behind it hangs the transparent ridge of the mountains of Moab.

Start the motor again. The next point.

I take you with me, Father. Or maybe it's you who are taking me on an ancient route you've drawn . . .

The observation post at the end of Meir Nackar Street.

The slope opens to the south, to the cut ridge of Herodion, crowned with Herod's Palace.

According to the plan, that will be one of the ridges around the demarcated area, where a beacon will be lit on the first of every month, on nights the moon is born—the circle of time and water surrounding the mountain, granting Jerusalem an awareness of the cycle of the year.

What an intoxication at slowly opening, while driving, the folded infinity of the place here, confronting dream with reality.

The stone buildings of the Jewish neighborhood of East Talpiot. Broad sidewalks on Avshalom Habib Street. The young trees haven't yet shed their leaves, in the belated winter.

Under the wall of the observation post, the road to Jabl Mukabar.

A grocery shop. Minibuses of transport companies. A boy runs out from one of the alleys. Goes around the grocery store. Is swallowed up between the houses. Domes of mosques in grayish blue. A steep road down the slope.

This is the place that, for all the months of planning, was for me the multinational urban texture surrounding Mount Sabbatical. What was supposed to become the community of local support for the residents of the Settlement of Huts. The Jewish and Arab groceries that would supply food. The electrical and water connections. The paths going around the site, alongside the neighborhoods, connecting them with gardens, in the shade of groves and water fountains. And the community projects that would run together between the international groups that would live in the Huts and study on Mount Sabbatical and the inhabitants around the mountain on the other. A first pilot group for the "establishment of a life of Sabbatical" . . .

And yesterday, there were "disturbances of the peace" here. Stones were thrown from Jabl Mukabar toward the buildings of East Talpiot. The windows of an apartment and a car were shattered. The car's driver, a pregnant woman in her fifth month, was interviewed from her hospital bed on the evening news.

I continue the conversation with you, as if everything (like the deceptive presence of your absence) were conducted here by different laws of time. The news about Operation Desert Storm also comes through a thick glass. Yes, there's news about the American ultimatum for Iraqi troops to leave Kuwait by January 15, about immunizing the Marines against biological weapons, even the estimates that the fighting is liable to reach here. But as if they're made-up horror stories, nothing to do with reality. Because of the tone? The formulations? Maybe the instructions from on high to spread fog, lull the population with cynical descriptions of hoarding food, buying plastic sheets, like news about an ants' nest in the grip of terror, somewhere, far away from here.

Only the daily news about the violence between Jews and Arabs has any reality. It continues to set the pace of the story here.

Two days before we came there was a triple murder in an aluminum factory in Jaffa. The two murderers were members of Hamas, from Gaza. One of them worked in the factory. When the secretary, Iris Asraf, arrived, they followed her in and stabbed her all over her body. A cutter who came to work was stabbed to death. Joshua Hakmaz, a worker from a nearby upholstery shop, who came when he heard shouts, was also stabbed brutally, and collapsed in a puddle of blood.

And the rest of the list since we came. In the Gaza Strip, five killed and two hundred fifty wounded. Soldiers in Rafiah opened fire on young men painting slogans, killed two of them, and in riots that continued for hours afterward two more were shot and killed. A woman died in uncertain circumstances. Two Israeli soldiers were slightly wounded.

This morning, Yaron went to the Arab villages around Jerusalem with members of Amnesty International. They'll pass through Isawiyya, Silwan, Bayt Jallah, and here, too, among the residents of Arab-a-Sohra, Jabl Mukabar, and Tsur Bakhar; they'll collect evidence about plots of land that were sold, and on which Jewish neighborhoods were built. They're checking the bills of sale. Interviewing the landowners, who now regret the deal and are getting threats from Fatah headquarters in exile. A year ago I would surely have gone out with them. Yaron raised an eyebrow when I declined.

"What's going on with you, Lana? I don't understand you anymore."

"Beyond pragmatism and economics, I'm trying to influence another layer of time and place here. To build a texture, in other words, Yaron . . ."

"What do you mean?"

"How to explain it to you? . . ."

"Maybe it's your love affair with the director from the Old City?" His breath comes close to me. "If there's equality—then put out for me, too, not just him . . ."

"Can I still talk with you beyond vulgarity?" I insisted, out of loyalty to something old between Yaron and me. "Can you still imagine a revolution in thought, a radical change of every notion of ownership of place? Of saying, for example, this place belongs and doesn't belong to me, and of just living that way? . . ."

"I don't understand you, Lana. I tell you to come on the standard tour of the refugee camps, to see reality, to report. After all, there's no need to explain to you . . ."

"That's exactly what I'm trying to tell you, if you'd only listen for once," I went on, perhaps to be close for a moment to the terms of the project that was disappearing. "I'm at a stage of one step beyond the symmetry of hatred, of mutual victimhood, or of guilt feelings . . . I'm at a stage of opening a new reality, with dimensions of letting go of the hold on this bloodsoaked place. I want to show that the place par excellence of envy ownership can exist beyond the hold of human beings—as the Bible says, 'then shall the land keep Sabbath . . .'"

"You'll turn into a fanatic right-winger with all your Jewish junk," Yaron protested.

"You're so stuck in definitions of left and right. It's much easier to communicate with Sayyid Ashabi than with you . . ." I lied.

"Okay, okay," he cut me off. "Drop it."

Returns to me sarcastically my own expression on the phone the first night, turns his broad back.

And meanwhile, here, in the site of Mount Sabbatical, there isn't even a sign about the plan. Nothing disturbs the wilderness of thorns and rocks of the peak, nothing augurs the crowd of pilgrims on the holiday tumult this city longs for so much . . .

(And yet, here of all places, alone, in the dryness between the rocks, in the late morning, the dream is dizzying, Father.)

And once again, I'm choked by the joy of belonging to this place. That "atavistic" feeling I've tried to deny all the years. For how to deny what this place does to me. Now, for the first time without an excuse of visiting Mother or you. The body is charged all the time, and the heart suddenly rises, as at a meeting. Never have I denied the beginning of love.

The noise of a motor rises from Arab-a-Sohra. Fear immediately grips.

(I can't ignore the fear either, Father. The living border, always gaping, of fear, here.)

I went on driving south. The broad circle around Mount Sabbatical. Arab villages. The armored cars passed me. The land of the Intifada. The land of quarrel, hatred.

I park on the side of the road.

A flock of starlings bursts out of the stubble. Circles.

A deep shadow of a vineyard in the strong sun.

Olive trees dot the pink slope, and a shepherd tramps behind the herd to the distance of the yellow valley.

A man in a leather jacket bends over a faucet to drink. Raises his mustached face to me. Watches the Fiat, parked here in the middle of the morning.

At the top of the slope, at the curve turning to the mosque, a woman walks uphill in a long dress and a red kerchief.

And in the village I drove through, the walls are covered with graffiti, in English. Jews go home! Fuck the Jews! (And on Hebron Road, on the pedestrian bridge across from our housing project, the graffiti is: Death to the Arabs.)

I park at the bus stop at the foot of Herodion.

Two Arab children next to a mule loaded with bags. Sitting in the shade of the bus stop. One of them is lacing his canvas shoes.

Flies buzzing. The children spur on the mule, which refuses to budge. Lift their eyes to me. A little older than David and Jonathan. Their eyes go beyond, don't turn the Fiat into a target for stones.

News on the car radio.

"A terrorist was killed when she tried to set off a pipe bomb in the Jewish market of Mahane Yehudah.

"Serious turmoil in the villages of Jilasun, Dahisha. A child was killed. In Jerusalem, fifteen vehicles were set on fire in recent days.

"In the territories, people say: 'We'll fight along with Saddam against the Zionist enemy.'"

Last look south, from the hill above Bethlehem near Mar Elias Monastery.

On a family outing in '67, when we stopped here, in the Arabic neighborhoods, on our way to Herodion, you stood still, with manuscripts that would later turn into the "Places and Sources" pamphlets, and explained loftily: "Look at this landscape. The same flat roof where a goat fell down or a jar—it's right out of the Talmud tractate Nezikim. And here, here is the courtyard and the cistern, and the fruit trees, all of them together as in the Talmud tractate Baba Qamma."

Leaning our tablet on the steering wheel. Continuing our conversation, Father.

Soon I'll cross the watershed. The sight of Jerusalem will suddenly burst forth there.

■ ■ ■ ■

I returned from Haifa only now. The boys are still at Allegra's. I arranged for them to stay with her in the afternoon.

Sitting by myself for a moment. To calm down. Before I go down and take them.

Afterward I'll call Ella. I'll tell her I was there. That the apartment is all right. Her practical, protective voice. Like Mother passing silently by the door to your study, seeing you reading to me, and going on, without disturbing us.

Three hours of driving each way. With traffic jams in the middle of the country. And then the Zikhron Yaakov junction. The valley open from the cliff of the Carmel, the palms, the strip of sea behind Atlit. Areas of childhood. Now also areas of death. Mother and you are in the cemetery at the foot of the mountain, behind the old road. And driving up the Carmel. The display window with the bride and groom dolls, flickers from between the thickets of pine. And the slope of our winding street, with the shade of thick trees. Walking from the car with the steps from back then. Careful not to step on the grass that always grew in front of number seven, in the crack between the paving blocks. The stairs of the entry. The staircase. Your mailbox full of junk mail. Heart beating when I stick the key in the lock. Ten months after. And the gloom, until I bang the shutters open.

(My need to repeat all my activities to you now in the empty space of the apartment.)

In the kitchen, the faucet is leaking. Got to take care of it with Ella. (Thanking her silently for her willingness to postpone the dismantling for a year. To wait until I come back. And also for cleaning devotedly. The glasses and the plates are arranged in the kitchen cabinets. Even your kettle is standing on the stove.)

I didn't go into the bedroom. Afraid to tear the veil. And in the bathroom, between the spots on the mirror, my tense face flickered, instead of your bent face, covered with foam. "Papa's wearing a mask!" I used to beg you to let me dip the brush in the cup of foam, to put a white ball on your nose. And in the end, your effort to stretch your neck to the mirror with the shaver I bought in Paris. Leaning on the sink, moving the wheels over the sagging skin. And then opening the medicine chest with the round wooden handle, the color of antique ivory. My recoil today at holding out my hand, finding the box of Nivea cream in the cabinet and your bottle of cologne.

In the door of the study, the smell burst out like a live body. Steeped in tobacco and old age, wool, paper. Jackets were still hanging in the closet, and on the left, above the shelf of shirts and underwear, all your writings. Some in office files, paper envelopes, and some in colorful plastic bags. I took out one of the personal notebooks at random. Pages written in your dense, round handwriting. Words spin before my eyes. Throughout the week of mourning I didn't go to the closet. I was afraid to find your notes, and I was even more afraid of not finding them. Everything that was your world in the last years. Maybe, at the last minute, you decided to get rid of everything, to leave no traces . . . Postponing the verdict. And all those months, I only envisioned, on the roads of New Jersey, I only imagined you taking the notebook out of the yellow shopping bag, looking at me hesitantly, "Well, Ilanka, read a little?"

Leafing through writings from the sixties in the notebook. When the members of the party thwarted your candidacy for secretary of the labor council. Your decisive reaction. You preferred to resign publicly, despite their pleas. And the new secretary is now serving instead of you, and yesterday's supporters turn their back. The eyes read furtively. Pages in a slow, emphatic handwriting. I read in panic, "Today I find myself in a hopeless situation. At the end of a long way, with many torments, many upheavals. Deserted by companions, colleagues in the party, leaders I looked up to. Woe is me that I came to this, woe is me that my eyes see and are not extinguished. In the morning thou shalt say, Would God that it were even! And at even thou shalt say, Would God it were morning. And I fill my mouth with water and am silent. I keep silent about what floods the heart. Betrayal of colleagues. Betrayal of an ideal. Because of envy and lust for power, and despondency of pettiness. I won't reproach and I won't smear. In the name of the greatness of our task. Oh that my restraint will silence the spirits and help calm the branch and the movement."

And then the page dripping pain. A few words, next to the date and the title: "Today I concluded my public function. A great deal of insult I have known . . ." And the long quote from the tractate Baba Mitzea about the insult of Rabbi Eliezer, and his prayer of despair which brought the death of Raban Gamliel. Your voice spreads in the room full of the smell of old clothes. Shouting alone, to yourself.

Reading with an effort. As if uncovering your nakedness. How you aged then, all at once. Chest covered with white hair, bent over the sunken belly, over your bruised might. Closing yourself up for days in the apartment. You and Mother existing on a modest retirement pension (only because of comrade Givoni's intervention), and on Mother's salary as a supervisor of vocational education in the northern district. She traveling hours in buses between village schools in the western Galilee and the towns around Haifa to prepare the annual exhibitions, to supervise personally the student works that were selected, the quality of the embroidery, authenticating the colors, the kinds of cloth, checking whether they didn't need another colored background of jute for the stained-glass windows. Always with her swollen black briefcase. In any case, you lived modestly, "unpretentiously," as you put it, in an apartment that always looked like a room in a kibbutz. Making do with the beauty of a pebble, a thorn Mother dried in the closed balcony, or one of her "Bedouin style" embroideries.

And I avoided seeing what was happening to you then. Steeped in studies at the Technion, in radical leftist activities before the Six Day War against the military regime of the Arabic population, the expropriation of Arab land, demonstrations. Giving myself like a queen bee to lovers rustling around me in parallel, subsequent, crisscross encounters. Creating honey, hoarding, sharing. Applying first of all myself, the "matriarchal profusion" I articulated then. Seeing you retreating. Maybe feeling something. But in my youthful egoism I didn't stay around to understand what was really happening with Mother and you. Closing my eyes. Turning you, then of all times, in the depths of your weakness, into my source of attacks about Zionist mistakes and failures in mass settlement, the transit camps, the housing projects. Cutting you with "facts" that prove better than you what really was. And then getting up and going to Paris, leaving this corrupt place, without asking myself what would become of the two of you. I find today in your closet a file of drafts of your weekly letters to me in Paris (the letters that wandered with me in a shoe box from one student room to another, from Alain's scholar's apartment to the back of the closet in the apartment on the Seine). It didn't occur to me that you prepared each of your weekly letters like that. With two or three drafts. Holding on to the story of my leaving Israel, reformulating for me betrayal as loyalty. "I read carefully the plans for workers' housing you sent us, Ilanka. I was deeply impressed. How important is your struggle against the humiliation of the immigrants, their alienating isolation, their transformation into the slaves of the new age. I'm proud to discover how much you continue the same tradition of the patriarchs . . ." I read, and blood pounds in my temples.

And even when I came to visit from the Beaux-Arts after '67, with some uneasiness "to understand what I had left behind," I wasn't interested in what was storming in you. I avoided your explanations about the Allon Plan for partial withdrawal—that you supported it along with a minority in the party, loving the places and giving them up. I dismissed all your talk as total nonsense. Also stayed remote during the "family tour" you organized in Uncle Yehiel's pickup, with the "women" pressed in the back, Mother, Aunt Rachel, and me in my Parisian suit that got covered with dust more and more during that long day.

We traveled according to your map of yearnings to the ancient Hebrew landscapes. Bethel, Levona, Hebron, Herodion, Rachel's Tomb, the fields of Bethlehem. Your elbow leaning on the window, your white hair in the wind. Looking intently. Harvested fields, Arab women bent over in the stubble, soft slopes of mountain roads. All dizzy, you enter the gates of Jerusalem, go deep into the alleys of the souk, greet the vendors like a son returning home, blind to the suspicion, the hostility, or the violence inherent in our tour there. You still believe in the possibility of brotherhood among the inhabitants of the Land, in one bustling shared texture of life, one vitality. And then you touched the stones of the Western Wall. In the distance, I see you slowly approach, stand, your head bent a little, in enormous excitement. And that very night, I went to Eilat, to settlements of flower children from all over the world, who filled the hills around the bay, the beaches of Sinai, Nueba. Sinking there, at the bonfires, in the smell of hashish and the sound of guitars, our skin drenched with sun and delight, diving into the great orgy of hope, youth, blue flicker, colorful corals.

And maybe the weeks of that summer, in excited tours with members of Compass, the anti-Zionist organization, with Palestinian colleagues, in refugee camps around Jericho, around Gaza, in the shadow of battles, victory, humiliation, shame of the defeated and disgrace of the victors, coming out of the battles with booty and inevitable dishonor—maybe the weeks of that summer really were a dizzying moment of bursting borders, of mutual revelation, still charmed, in the place flooded by rivers of Eros. The Eros of the victors, the Eros of the vanquished. Butterflies of dream in colorful clothing. Devoted to this forbidden love between victors and vanquished on magic beaches, in wadis. Sunk in a holiday that washed over the summer, that we will pay for, one slash after another. In my dreams, in Sayyid's dreams, devoured by nostalgia under the ideologies. And the voices of Simon and Garfunkel, Joan Baez, Pete Seeger, Bob Dylan, *the answer is blowin' in the wind.*

The material for the pamphlets "Places and Sources" was separate, in brown cardboard office files. Sources from the Bible, the Mishnah, Aggada, and Midrash, copied into notebooks. And stenciled pamphlets for field trips of the Haifa labor council, filed according to the parts of the Land of Israel. And the opening words on the first page (apparently written near the time of the crisis in the labor council): "My only refuge in these days of personal distress is reading our sources, our ancient sayings. First and last. And I am especially satisfied when I read sensible things about our Land and its heritage."

Then I went down to ask Kleiner in the grocery for a cardboard box for everything I'll take (for the time being leaving part of the material in the closet, postponing the rest of the classifying until the next trip). Only at the corner of the street did I "remember" that the grocery had been closed for years, replaced by a small supermarket. An energetic young man greeted me at the check-out and sent me to the storeroom. And there, of all places, facing the storeroom worker, a Russian immigrant in an old jacket, I got stuck. No, he doesn't speak Hebrew. And he doesn't have a box, no box! His eyes dart at me, as if the KGB supervisors had come for an inspection. And only after persisting in monosyllables accompanied by gestures, did he agree to give me one of the most damaged boxes, piled up in a corner. And yet, the tingly, bittersweet smell of "products" in the storeroom was like Kleiner's old grocery. And when I bought the newspaper from the smiling young man, I missed you standing next to me and declaring: "Newspaper shmewspaper, Ilanka! You know the Ukrainian joke about what a newspaper's for? For wrapping herring. And if you don't even have herring, then from a newspaper and a little tobacco, you can always roll yourself some paperossa."

On the way back, the bride and groom dolls stood out in the display window. And suddenly the strip of sea. And the emptiness that grew while driving south. And the evening that descended all at once, on the ascent to Jerusalem.

In the city it was already night. The gasping buses and the trucks on Hebron Road. Always at that hour, traffic increases in both lanes. And all the time, my growing worry about David and Jonathan.

■ ■ ■ ■

Late at night. At the open window. After two glasses of vodka.

Addressing you as a witness, a judge.

I sat next to the boys even after they fell asleep. Then the phone rang. At first, I thought only of you. And then Sayyid's voice burst out, "Lana . . ."

"Sayyid? . . ."

"Ahalan . . ."

I didn't dare ask him how he was.

"Did you get the material? . . ." I went on breathlessly.

"Yes, they sent it to me . . . It looks excellent."

A silence fell. "Have you gone on . . . working?" I asked.

"A little hard now, you know."

"What will happen to the performance?" I whispered finally.

"If I may remind the famous architect, the performance is now a war, not a monument to peace . . . but . . ." His voice slid, immediately wrought havoc in my guts. "You've already gotten under my skin . . . Lana . . . like a dog, I search for your smell . . ."

"With your lovers in Tunis? Baghdad." I tried to save some self-control.

"Yes, even with them . . ."

And once again silence prevailed.

"And what's going on with you?" he asked.

I was silent. Hearing only the pulse beating in my temples. What shall I tell him, that today I was in the apartment in Haifa? That I took your writings?

"Have you got somebody?" he cut in, tense.

"In fact, I do, Sayyid. Somebody from the past. We're back together. I've got his smell on my whole body now."

"I'm from your future, not the past. Remember that."

I wanted to say, "There is no future without a past," or to ask, "Why did you call?" But sadness paralyzed me.

"You think you'll come?" I asked.

"Yes, maybe at the end . . . Wait for me there."

"We'll see . . ."

And until the end of the conversation, there was only heavy breathing, shaking the night that separated us.

And when I picked up the boys from Allegra, Jonathan clung to me, as if confirming over and over that I had indeed returned. At supper, he freaked out, pushed away the plate and the table, and didn't calm down until I sat "alone with Jonathan." Body clinging to body. Letting him rock us from side to side.

"I was in Haifa today," I said to the boys when they were in bed.

"Yes, Allegra told us," said David.

"I went to bring some of Grandpa's things."

"Did you?"

"Yes."

"Great."

And after a silence, he said, "Sing to us now, Mommy. Sing, Mommy, sing."

And for the first time since we came, I sang to them, sitting in the dark room, with flashes of light running from the window to the ceiling: "Fields in the Jezreel Valley welcomed me this morning . . ." "Blue is the sea, comely is Jerusalem . . ." "Nevertheless and in spite of all, the Land of Israel . . ."

David held my hand all the time, until he fell asleep. Jonathan sucked and breathed deep, rubbing the other pacifier on his nose, not moving his wide-open eyes covered with a thin scrim of sleep, until the gigantic, transparent lids dropped.

■ ■ ■ ■

[Three in the morning.]

I woke with a start from Sayyid's arms. And then, in the moment before waking, from the dark of the corridor, the boys burst through the door. Jonathan, with a frozen look, leaning on Bobo the stick, his curls dusty, as if he came from far away. David's hand on Jonathan's shoulder. Wearing only pants, the ribs protruding on his exposed torso. Only then did I see that David's eyes were covered with a white film and were staring at us blindly. Was he going blind? And Jonathan, leaning on the stick, maybe his eyes were also turning turbid? I quickly pulled the sheet up to cover our naked bodies, trying to hold out my arms to the boys. But the weight of Sayyid's hand dropped on my waist, pinned me to the mattress. Trying to shriek, I woke up.

Four. I opened the window.

The singing of the muezzin cuts the night. I hadn't imagined how strong it was.

Dragging to bed the yellow plastic bag from the cardboard box of your writings. Wrapping myself again in the blanket. Leafing close to the body.

A bag with your photos from the meetings of the labor council. Of the commissions. Members around tables covered with green cloths. You're delivering a speech. Holding a bundle of papers in front of you. Photos with Ben-Gurion. With Eshkol. A speech of Golda Meir.

And then, in an old envelope from the Health Plan, family photos. Separating them from the album, according to some plan you apparently didn't have time to carry out.

Photos of David. The two of them. An old photo of David riding on Ruhamka. Curly-haired, in the white, embroidered rubashka. And next to him, on the saddle, Uncle Yehiel, a two-year-old baby. And then a photo from '71, maybe '72, of David the officer in uniform. Smiling. And in that same envelope a small notebook with your stormy notes. From '74. After the war. I opened and closed it immediately in panic.

Suddenly drowned in what was silenced, what I tried from the first to excavate from Sayyid's body. The last, secret meeting, when I came to David in the summer of '73. When I came especially from the middle of the Marseille project. On a short international phone call, we made arrangements. With no need to explain. The meeting of the leftist architect and the commander stationed at an outpost on the Suez Canal. What both of us needed. What isn't known to anybody in the family to this day. I disguised the meeting in a visit to you. That summer you went to a rest home in Kibbutz Ma'ale Ha-Hamisha on the mountain near Jerusalem. Mother got treatment, and you'd go into town to the National Library to collect material on Jerusalem and the Valley of Hinnom for your pamphlets. I rented a room (for the first time) in the Scottish Hospice and from there I came to visit you. You quoted to me from the sources you filed in your cardboard case, made me promise to go through the Shiloah Tunnel, "which we didn't manage to do on our joint tour . . ." And thus, in a heavy heat wave, I arrived, covered with dust, at the bottom of the valley, walking in the dark of the tunnel, in the sudden chill of the waters of Gihon in the heart of the hot day, returning soaked to the room facing Mount Zion. And the next morning, a direct flight to the electrifying heat at the airport of Sharm al-Sheikh, and David waits for me with a broad grin. I'm immediately pierced by the daggers of blue penetrating from his sun-darkened face, and the panther sloppiness of this familiar yet unknown man. He drives me in the military jeep across from the hallucinatory blue of the Bay of Eilat. The Blue Hole and the Straits of Tiran, shores of Sharm al-Sheikh. And the blue that finally flowed in hungry acrid salt mixed with saliva and blood and sweat, and dry breezes that console my tears that flowed all the time, "from excitement, it's only from excitement."

And what of that was exposed to the eyes of the MP when we returned, two cousins with faint limbs. "Hey, girlie, you came to visit our post of bones?" He tosses up his hand in a coarse movement he camouflages from the commander behind an eastern wiggle of his ass:

"A bullet from here, a bullet from there,
In the end we're all bones.
And it don't make no difference when the meat rots
Between the bones from here and the bones from there.
The Canal, the Canal—a bullet from here, a bullet from there
The Canal, the Canal—the bones of here and there."

And his coarse voice that was suddenly pulled out at the sound of Claude's words, a few weeks later in Paris. I go over and over in my memory the landing at Sharm al-Sheikh, the ride in the jeep, and that last night, when we didn't touch one another: David takes me from the guest hut and then, for hours, we walk in the starry, desert night. And he talks. Deposits in my ears the words that go on resonating. About something uneasy in him, comes from far away, imprisons him. Doesn't let him give himself. Devote himself. To any one of his girlfriends. He tells how when he gets out of the army in the fall, he'll go to a settlement his friends are establishing on the cliff above the shores of the Dead Sea. "Close to the Essenes." Want to get some distance, learn what's in a grain of sand, in the seed we came from. And maybe to write . . . to wash away all that. He runs his hand over the moonscape of cones of crags rising to the night. And it's that sentence that keeps coming back to me: "To read a lot. Without a framework. To learn what there is in the seed we came from. To wash away all that . . ." And also the envy that sliced me then for what would happen between him and the pages, how raptly he was drawn to them. Also knowing how he would love, when he loved, with that same self-forgetting. As revealed to me then, on the rocky slopes, at the height of his beauty. Looking into the distance and laughing, and the pale night light carving his face.

The voice of the muezzin echoes from another direction. Maybe from Beit Tsafafa.
A breeze of sharp cold strikes the rickety glass pane.
The boys' calm breathing, from the door I opened.

And the yearnings for Sayyid, Father. Or perhaps I seek in him the yearnings for David on that night before the flight to Sinai, in the room in the Scottish Hospice.

■ ■ ■ ■

[Another car ride to the axes around the site.]
Whatever can be snatched in the time that's left. Five days until the end of the ultimatum.

Waiting for the evening news. If nothing comes out of the round of talks in Geneva (sold in advance? staged?) between Tariq Aziz and James Baker, I'll have to give in and go to the station of Reargard Defense, take "defense kits" for the three of us, gas masks, atropine injections . . . buy the absurd list of supplies for the "sealed room." Plastic tape, a battery radio, a flashlight, a plastic bucket with disinfectant powder for a chemical toilet . . .

Sparkle of glass slivers on the slopes of the site. Rustle of thorns in an oppressive summer that goes on without a drop of rain.

The dryness absorbed from childhood. A precise quality of place—smell, light, touch on the skin, that no sketch, no photo, can convey. Only sitting now, in the morning sun, in the dust that fills the nostrils.

And the thrill of planning the flow that will burble again on the back of the mountain, will cover with netting the rustle of the water the twelve lobes of the Settlement of Huts, will pass in paths through the library, fall in cascades from Mount Sabbatical to the new pool I added at the bottom of the Etsel River valley, between the groves—for bathing, games, outdoor meals for the local residents and the residents of the Settlement of Huts. All that I still had time to tell you.

Excitement shook the lines of your face sunk in the hospital pillow, and a soft smile illuminated them when I whispered to you, "Here, Father, this is what you taught me. Everything started when you read me the prophecy of Zechariah . . ." And you nod. "How did that go, exactly?" And over your almost paralyzed lips the verses skimmed: "And it shall be in that day that living waters shall go out from Jerusalem, half of them toward the former sea, and half of them toward the hinder sea . . ." I concluded, and you went on nodding emotionally, "in summer and in winter it shall be," and the two of us recited together, word for word: "And the lord shall be king over all the earth: in that day shall there be one Lord, and his name one." And you add something else that I identified only the second time, "Hezekiah, of course, the inscription of the excavators of the tunnel," and I hear you in my mind's ear, reading the verses when we stood, in the heat of the summer and the chill of the water, at the entrance of the Shiloah Tunnel: "The excavators struck, each to meet the other, pick to pick. And there flowed the waters from their outlet to the pool." Then on that same family tour, when for the first time I also heard you talk about the ancient aqueduct. "An impressive technological achievement of the Second Temple period; an aqueduct carrying the waters along dozens of kilometers from the sources at Mount Hebron all the way to the Temple."

And then the nurse came in, waiting with enormous patience. And the smell of drugs, and the day shrinking in the windows, less than a week before your death.

Yes, Father, I've recently planned another stage. As "Desert Storm" approaches I'm sunk furiously in this plan—the most utopian of the project: building an addition to the ancient aqueduct, which will renew the flow into the walls of Jerusalem, to the holy places. I haven't yet completed the planning, I'm formulating it for the first time, talking with you. I didn't have time to tell you about that vision. Perhaps it came out of our conversation or out of everything that happened in these recent months, Father. A plan for a waterline that will lap the holy places, spray its chill on them, renew the suckling of the holy Mount Moriah from sources in the mountains, surrounding Jerusalem all around . . . This is my interpretation, in feminine architecture, of Sabbatical, letting go of the flow of Deliverance. Not the waters of the Prophets' rage, but an eternal flow, throbbing, from the source of the Gihon from the depth of the tunnel in the bottom of the Foundation Stone—this living womb of Jerusalem.

The first stage will be to excavate a continuation of the Shiloah Tunnel to the depths of the dike Herod built, that dirt platform on which the Second Temple was built, and on its debris the caliphs of Omayyia built the Dome of the Rock. The tunnel will pass near the threshing floor of the altar of Araunah the Jebusite from whom David bought Jerusalem, over the legendary abyss of the Foundation Stone ("A symbolic passage, charged," I see you nodding in wonder). From the bottom of the mountain, a shaft will be hewn and through that, by force of the siphon of interlocking instruments, the water will burst to the height of the springs at their starting point, near Hebron. The pillar of water will dart from the stone fountain in the heart of the vestibule of pillars of the square of the mosque of Harm-a-Sharif, this jewel of architectonic beauty, the most recent layer of holiness. From there, I planned three veins of flowing. One, through the Muslim fountains at the square of Harm-a-Sharif that will gush among the group of worshippers, flow along the eastern wall and the Gate of Mercy, and overlook on its way the Mount of Olives, the ancient cemetery, Gethsemane. A second vein will turn north, through the Mugrabi Gate. On its way it will resupply the cisterns from the Hasmonean period, the two ruined pools between the city walls: the pool of Israel and the pool of Beit Hisda, and will flow along the Stations of the Cross of the Via Dolorosa to a basin that will be built in front of the Church of the Holy Sepulcher. There it will sprinkle the air for the crowds of pilgrims. The third vein will flow in a parapet of water to the west of the square of the mosques, to the Robinson Arch. There it will fall in a thin cascade, "the eternal cascade," whose slivers will dampen the stones of the Western Wall, perfume the dry air, thick with dust, echo the murmur of prayer.

I work from maps dating to the beginning of the British Mandate. The last moment when the partial mapping of the archaeological layers of the Temple Mount was done. I work without checking. Or without any permission, for the time being. Will have to get a long list of agreements: from the Muslim authorities, the Vatican, the Ministry of Religion, the Ministry of Defense, the Antiquities Authority. And the beginning of negotiations of the Dag Hammarskjöld Fund with the representatives of the Greek Patriarchate in Amman, were also broken off completely.

The car turned into a box of hot upholstery and tin. The block was covered with dust.

The dream already streams the chill of water, relieves a little, Father, wards off for a moment the threat closing in.

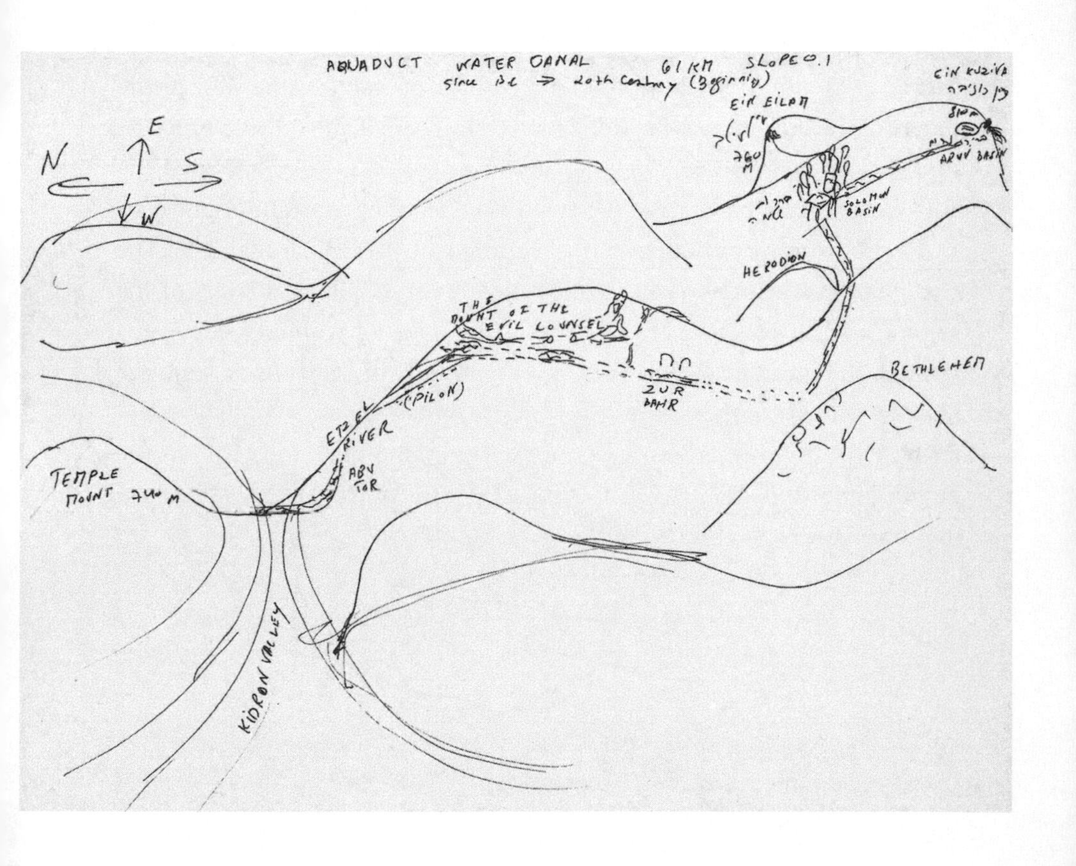

AQUADUCT WATER CANAL 61 KM SLOPE 0.1
since BC → 20th Century (Beginning)
EIN KUZIVA
EIN EILAM
760 M
ARUV BASIN
SOLOMON BASIN
HERODION
N
E
S
W
THE MOUNT OF THE EVIL COUNSEL
ZUR BAHR
BETHLEHEM
(PILON)
ETZEL RIVER
ABU TOR
TEMPLE MOUNT 740 M
KIDRON VALLEY

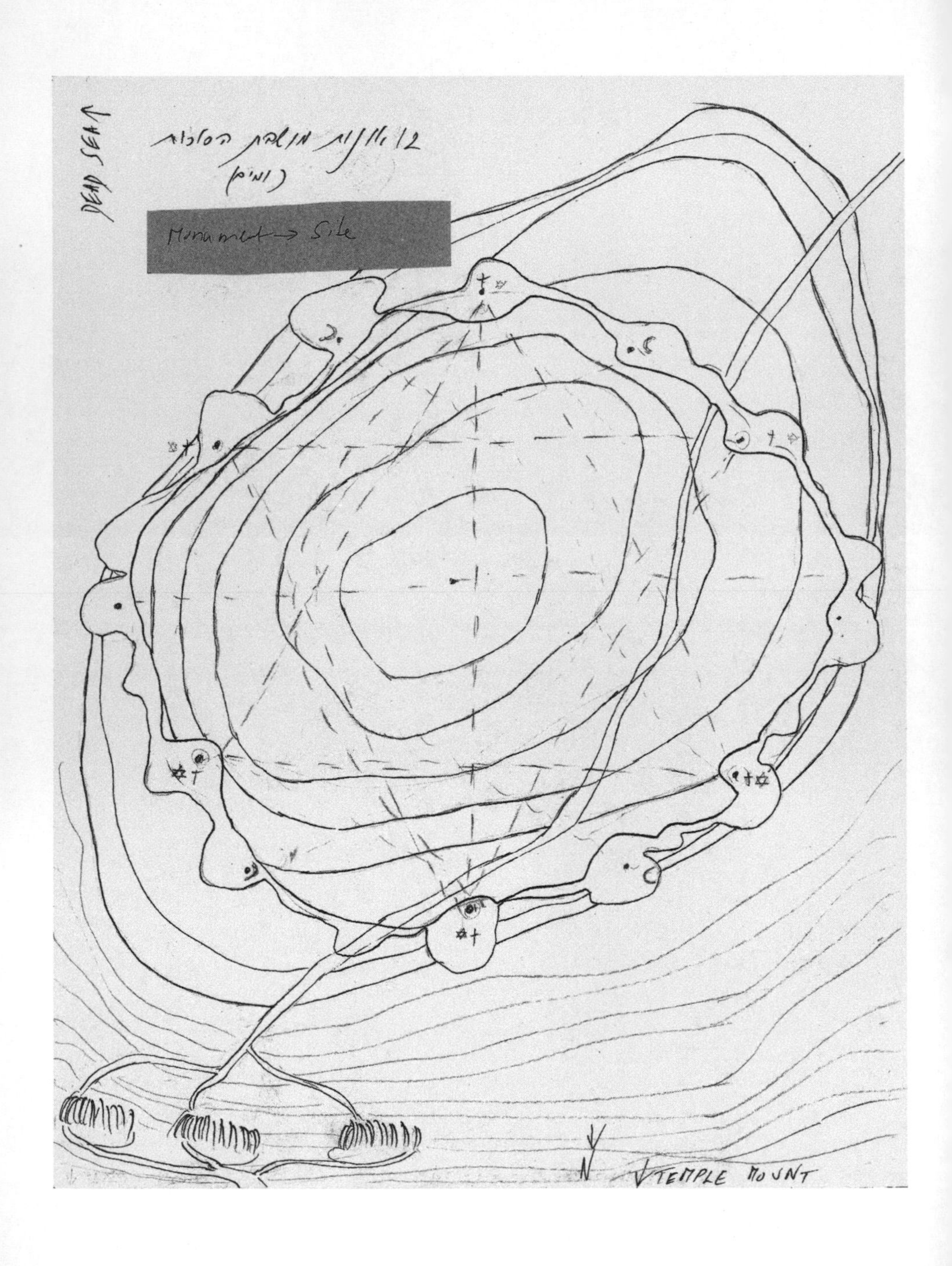
DEAD SEA
Monument → Site
N
TEMPLE MOUNT

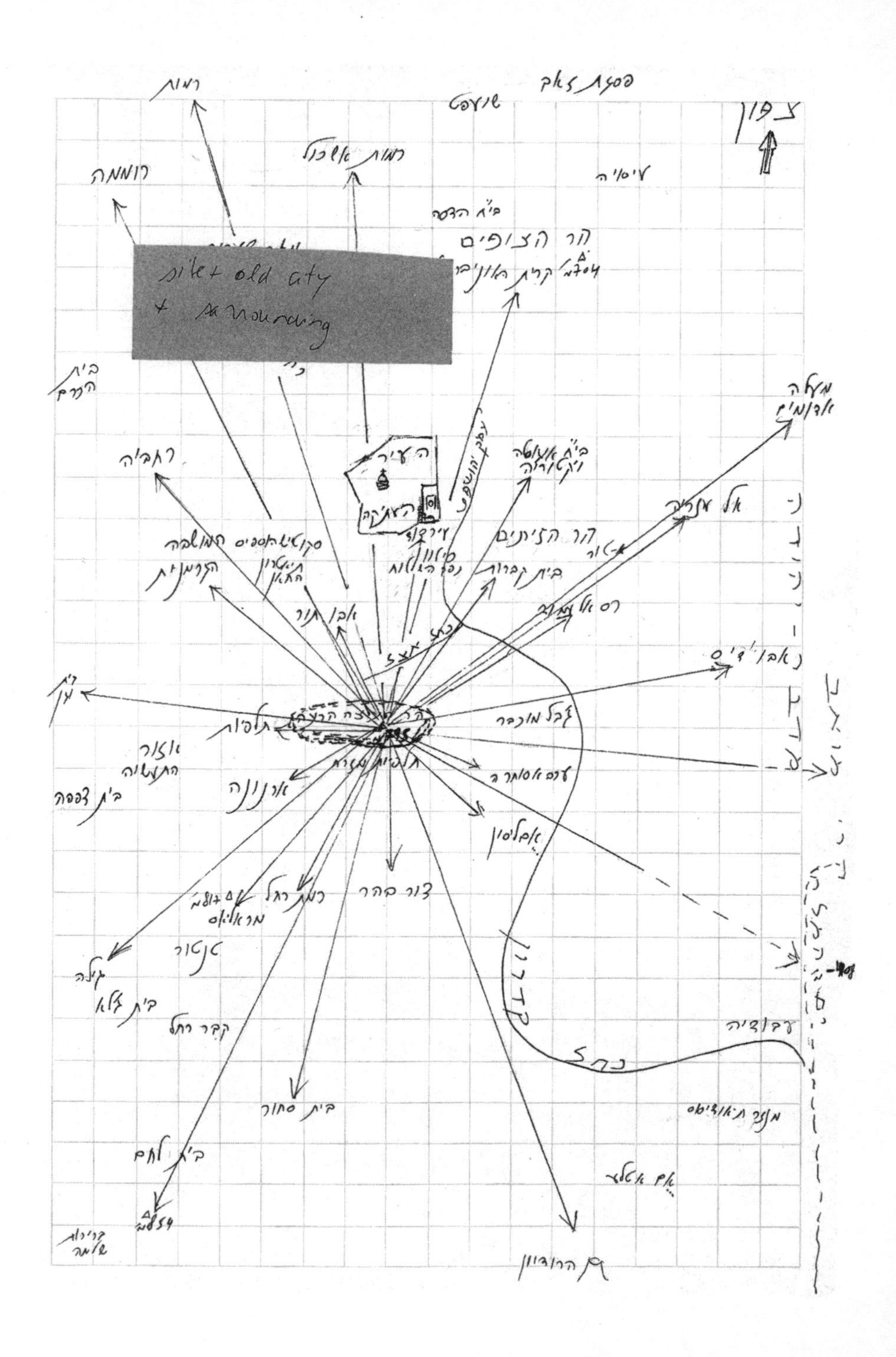

צפון
רמות
רמות אשכול
רוממה
הר הצופים
site + old city
+ mourning
רחביה
העיר העתיקה
הר הזיתים
בית קברות
מעלה אדומים
אל עזריה
אבו דיס
תלפיות
ארנונה
רמת רחל
גילה
בית צפפה
קבר רחל
בית סחור
בית לחם
הרודיון
כביש

North

Mount Olives

Mount Scopus

Hebrew University Tower

French Hill

Ancient Jewish Cemetery

Augusta Victoria Tower

A Tour Tower

Ras-El-Amud

Abu Dis

East
Amman
Moab Mountains
Mount
Nevo
802
Jordan Valley
Jericho
Abu Dis
-400
Dead Sea
East
Slope
793m
796m
WEST

South

Dead Sea

Mount Herodion

Kibontz Ramat Rachel

Bethlehem

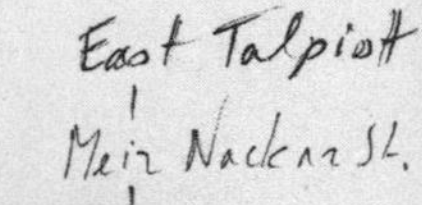

Arab-a-Suhara

The South Slope

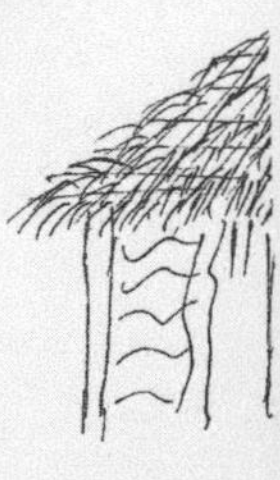

North

Baker's first words on the noon news, "I regret to . . ."

And then I went out immediately to the "Station for Rearguard Defense." Giving in at last.

I didn't believe we'd come to that, Father. To giving in, to being dragged in stages into the war. Writing to pound on your chest with weakening fists. As if you could defend, a dead and buried Commendatore.

Writing to you as in a story by Rebbe Nakhman of Bratslav, that you told me. About the king and his deputy. When it was discovered that anyone who ate the next year's harvest would go mad, they thought about what to do. In the end they decided they would eat the harvest of madness like all the other citizens of the country. But first they would put a sign on their forehead. So that when one of them saw the other, he would remember they were mad.

At Ben-Shoshan's, I bought the afternoon paper, and scanned the printed type where our lives have been shrunk.

The Geneva talks failed—five days are left for peace or war. High alert.

The Iraqi foreign minister: We will definitely attack Israel.

The Geneva talks lasted six hours, but the Iraqis refused to budge: they talked about Palestine, but not about withdrawal from Kuwait.

The U.S.: That's "total rejection." In Washington, preparing for a national emergency and mobilization of "up to a million reservists."

Generals call on Bush to threaten Iraq with nuclear weapons.

Saddam: We'll make them swim in their own blood.

Israeli chief of staff Shomron: We're ready.

Prime Minister Shamir will probably address the nation today on radio and television.

Israeli minister of defense Arens: The citizens of Israel will have to listen to the radio for instructions.

I found the note for the "Distribution of Civilian Defense Supplies" between the pages of the passport, where I had stuck it at the airport. I went to the industrial area, seeking the "Station of Rearguard Defense," behind a commercial building, under an athletic shoe factory, in the cellar. Concrete stairs. And then, suddenly, in the middle of the morning, a crowd of people crushed in forced partnership. Women soldiers in the distribution corners. A fitting room made of military blankets.

In front of me in the line stood three young women in tight clothes. Giggling all the time. Out of dread, apparently. After three minutes I knew they worked together in the motor vehicle bureau and had come down during their lunch break. "I kept telling you to come before," complained one of them. "Don't exaggerate, Lili," answered her friend. But she, too, the laughing one, also lost her gaiety in the pulp of waiting.

Across from the woman soldier stood a Russian family. A middle-aged couple and an elderly man, the grandfather apparently. Erect, in a flannel shirt, neatly tucked in. Completely lost, probably immigrated to Israel a few days before. Lingering a long time across from the woman soldier, with a short gray-haired woman who volunteered to translate the military bursts into Russian falsetto. Meanwhile an argument arose. The grandfather insisted on something, the couple disagreed with him. The old-timer's patient smile didn't help, either. The old man stood tense at the contents of the kit presented to him. The injections, the mask with the black straw for drinking, the rubber straps. He inhaled and stood at attention across from the woman soldier.

"Ikh bin in krieg geveyn. In Stalingrad!" He tapped his stretched chest. "Farshtayst? Farshtayst?" he declared his experience in World War II to encourage the woman soldier, and turning to the rest of the waiting line as well. "Ikh bin in krieg geveyn! In krieg!" But the couple already grabbed his elbows and this time one round of translation was enough, until they finally paraded to the exit, hoisting the cardboard boxes.

Now the three young women, giggling in embarrassment, approached the pile of steel and black rubber skulls, and the woman soldier who recited indifferently, "Release the clasps of the straps and put the mask up to your face with both hands . . ." Finally the soldier turned to me, turning my old ID from side to side.

"You're with two children? Sons? Where is the husband? Not in Israel?" And then she added, "Why are you all coming only at the last minute?" pouring all their tension on me.

On the way out, I passed by a few of your old-timers, standing with civilian obedience, and in their eyes that tense, pensive look. It had been a long time since I had seen so many of them all together.

> Suddenly they make me remember the black-out siren in the Sinai Campaign in '56, when you served in the Civilian Defense, in your khaki shorts from the Haganah, the pre-State defense force, which you insisted on wearing again. And how you returned home in a blend of shame and joking and told that at your age all you could do was shout: "You there, on the third floor, put out the light!"

On the way home I bought the pitas the boys love, and I stopped in a housewares shop. Sitting behind the counter, the exhausted shopkeeper pointed to what remained of the piles of supplies. I left with plastic sheets, duct tape, a pink bucket . . .

There was almost no merchandise left at Ben-Shoshan's, either. "Tomorrow yogurt in glass jars will come. I'll put some aside for you, don't worry, Ilana."

"But the boys love chocolate pudding and that's in plastic cups . . ."

"What can I do? This time they drove us nuts. Only glass resists chemical weapons."

And on television, photos from Baghdad. Mobs fill the streets, the market alleys. Also supplied with the same colored plastic buckets, pitas, loaves of bread, rice, oil. And night falls fast. There as here. In the same strip of land. The sunset that starts there, in the east, and spreads up to here to the sky opening above the industrial area.

Our defense masks, David's and mine, and Jonathan's "Defense Device for Children (DDC)" I pushed under the sofa in the living room. The warm pitas in their plastic bags spread their strong smell, mixed with the thickness of fear. Here, as there. And Jonathan passes through with his Bobo stick, aims it at the pictures on the screen. "I'll shoot 'em."

> That's what the struggle was about all the months, Father. Try and defend ourselves with a dream of temporary Huts, Sabbatical. As if even in Mesopotamia, in the Shiraz Valley, in the shadow of the towering madness, the fist could be softened . . .

■ ■ ■ ■

[Morning. The boys have already gone.]

Last night, David insisted on watching the news with me (my pathetic attempt so far not to expose them). He sat tense, shouting encouragement at the warplanes swooping from the destroyers. "Galaxy! F-16! B-52! Tornado!"

"How do you know all the names?"

"All the boys in the class know them. But I'm the best."

Clasps his bony knees, waiting for the planes to come back after the photos of Bush and Yeltsin, and the lines for plastic sheets and masks.

Jonathan also joins in. " 'Cause Bobo's already sleeping and Jonathan's not tired." He clings to me, covers my eyes with his plump hands. "Mama, not levision. Mama, Jonathan."

"You're right," I hugged him, letting him "rock" our clinging bodies, as he loves.

Afterward, drinking in the noises of the boys getting ready for bed, filling the apartment with the pleasure of routine. David growls at Jonathan not to step on his planes, and Jonathan puffs out his lips at him, runs to get to the bathroom first. Climbs to the sink on the plastic stool, holds the glass with one hand, and with the other clutches the brush. Only then does he remember that he has to turn on the faucet. Puts down the glass, turns it on, picks up the glass . . . And David, impatient, from behind, pinches him. Jonathan yells, as usual: "Hey! Stop! Mama, tell him!" Doesn't hurry. Until he finally, slowly, turns from the sink, buries his face in a towel with an embroidered rabbit, and his pajama top is now soaking wet. From a distance, I enjoy this texture of life, the real battlefield, the one they don't report on the news.

"What's there in Grandpa's things?" David stops at the cardboard box.

"Notebooks. Grandpa's writings," embarrassed that I haven't yet found time to take care of them.

"About what?"

"About Israel. About himself."

"Maybe you'll read us what Grandpa wrote." He lifts his eyes to me and picks up something.

"It'll take me time to find Grandpa's notebooks . . ." I tried to evade him, not remembering what exactly I had finally taken out of the cabinet in Haifa and what I had left.

But David didn't relent. "So now you'll read," he sat up in bed when I came in. "We're ready." And Jonathan, with the three pacifiers, looks at me from behind the wooden bars of the crib.

"I won't find it now . . ."

"But you promised!"

"I can tell . . ."

"Fine, tell."

I sat down on David's bed, like you when you'd make up one of those stories about me, "Ilanka and Brownie the Dog" or "Ilanka and the Robbers."

"Grandpa used to tell me about how he was a little boy . . . back in another country, in the Ukraine. He lived in a small town with his father and mother, grandmother and grandfather, and his big sister, Aunt Rachel. The grandfather and grandmother lived on the ground floor of the house. He loved to go to them, to eat the plum jam his grandmother made, and to sit next to his grandfather, who would open the Torah with Rashi, and study with him. They would read together, letter by letter and word by word. Grandpa Aaron knew the alphabet already, from the age of three, he went to kheyder every morning. His grandmother would put a hot cup of tea in front of his grandfather, and so the commentary of Rashi tasted like hot tea and jam. Grandpa's town was on a hill with a river flowing at the bottom. A big road, the highway, went through it. Small wooden houses stood on both sides of the road, ditches were dug along it and over them were bridges to the doorways of the houses. After the rain, a lot of water flowed in the ditches, and flooded below, to the river. When Grandpa was a boy, your age, he didn't know where the road led. The grown-ups said it went far far away, from Warsaw to Moscow! . . ."

"Moscow?" David interrupted. "On the phone Papa said he was in Moscow."

"Yes. That's in Russia. Today they call that the Soviet Union."

"Is Papa with Grandpa?" Jonathan's voice suddenly burst out.

David giggled. "Grandpa's dead!"

"Notso."

"Is so, he's dead!"

"Notso, notso . . ." Jonathan insisted, sucking excitedly on the pacifier.

"Yes, Jonathan, Grandpa passed away," I said.

His face twisted. "Want Grandpa, want Grandpa, want Grandpa . . ."

"Well, Mama, go on already," demanded David. And Jonathan sucked down his tears in the pacifier.

"Grandpa would tell," your voice continued gushing from my lips, "how the whole town sparkled when the rain stopped, when it cleared up and the sun came out, warming, drying. He and the other children would run around in the ditches between one bridge and another, rummage and find all kinds of coins. Most of them copper, but sometimes they found a real silver coin! They would also collect rusty nails, buttons, everything the rain swept up and brought . . ."

"Want Grandpa's nails," Jonathan started again. "And buttons."

"Yes, yes . . ." David was swept up after him.

"Grandpa's nails, Grandpa's nails," Jonathan pestered, ready to go on like that for a long time.

I was amazed that I hadn't taken anything from the apartment for the boys. Not the green stone from the ancient copper quarry in Timna lying dust-covered in the library in front of the volumes of *The Book of the Haganah*. Or the pin you got at the convention of veterans of the Labor Brigade. Or your watch, with the reddish leather band in the drawer of the table, next to the old pens, and the tobacco box you filled with paper clips.

"Next time I'll bring you something of Grandpa's from Haifa. And now to sleep." I got up to turn out the light.

Jonathan's voice burst out of the rhythmic sucking: "It's good that Grandpa."

Something in his determination stopped me. "What's good, Jonathan?"

"That Grandpa died."

"Why, Jonathan?"

"What don't you understand?" David burst out. "Because of the war."

"But . . . there won't be a war."

"You're just lying!" shouted David. "Everybody says there'll be a war. Even teacher Hadassah, and Allegra, and all the children in the class. And on television, too!"

"On television they haven't yet confirmed it."

He looked at me in the dark and was silent. And only when I was tucking him in did he say, "I miss Grandpa."

"Right, it's very sad that he's not with us . . . But he'd be happy that you're in Jerusalem," I whispered as I bent down to kiss him.

"I said that on the phone to Papa."

"What did you say to Papa?"

"That we came here to be with Grandpa."

I turned my face and inadvertently the words went on flooding from me in the dark between the beds, continuing to tell. "Ever since he was little, Grandpa dreamed of coming to the Land of Israel. His grandfather, too, who was a Hasid with a long white beard, also dreamed of coming to Jerusalem. Every Sabbath afternoon the Hasids in the town would hold a Sabbath meal. They'd sit around a table and sing sad songs of longing for Jerusalem. Grandpa would go with his grandfather, sit next to him, surrounded by Hasids. At the end of the meal, before they'd sing 'When the Lord turned again the captivity of Zion, we were like them that dream,' the Hasids would hide the big knife to cut the challahs under the tablecloth so they wouldn't stab themselves out of grief that the Temple was still destroyed."

Only the breathing of Jonathan's pacifiers was heard, and the echo of my voice between the beds. "Father and Aunt Rachel came to the Land of Israel. But the rest of the family didn't . . ." And I stopped. Not to bring down all of Jewish history on them all at once.

> Morning. Your presence, Father. Sitting here, inhaling the "half-cigarette," which you put out a moment before in the eternal struggle to stop smoking. The cloud of smoke covering you for a moment. You sink into silence, humming. Spread the newspaper, close to your eyeglasses and the thorough reading. Quoting to me in a loud voice, as if only you read that news, as if only from your mouth did it get the full historical majesty, framing for me snapshots of news items from the paper:
>
>> Shevardnadze's resignation intensified the political thicket in the Soviet Union. Chaos is expected. Fear of Gorbachev's fate. Airbus for a mass exodus of immigrants to Israel.
>>
>> Evidence of a rising wave of anti-Semitism in the Soviet Union. "Anti-Semites cut me with a knife in five places in my body. Then they fled," said D., a new immigrant, aged sixteen, who came to Israel yesterday.

> A new peak. Five thousand immigrants from the Soviet Union landed at Ben-Gurion Airport over the weekend. In the reception hall, orange slices were distributed along with biscuits and small sandwiches.
>
> The rate of immigration increased. One hundred seventy immigrants arrive every hour. The 200,000th immigrant arrived on Monday. There are preparations for 400,000 in the coming months.

And you probably wouldn't have read aloud the next news item: crowding at the airport. Foreigners and many Israelis gathering at the offices of travel agencies hoping to find a seat at the last minute on a plane out of Israel. People prefer to sleep at the airport so they can get on a plane before the ultimatum, in another three days.

In the staircase, voices in Russian. New immigrants. Three generations squeezed into an apartment on the third floor. They came a few days after we did. They go to ulpan every morning.

Once again, the staircase sinks into silence.

■ ■ ■ ■

Late at night. I finished sealing the living room.

The screech of the tape pulled from the roll, the sticking. It was especially hard to do the crumbling wooden sash of the sliding window in the living room.

From now on, every attempt to ventilate the room will require ripping up the whole construction, and taping it back up.

As I was working on the sliding window, it took me time to decipher the giant spider whose silhouette fills the whole rectangle of light on the other side of Hebron Road. I watched its monotonous movements and finally recognized a man with a potbelly, legs akimbo and arms spread out to the windowpane. Taping his sliding window, right in my reflection.

What's clear is that, because of the impending war, I get to know my neighbors fast. It feels like some strange military unit taking shape. The first one was Mr. Schleicher, from the third floor. A week ago, he knocked on the door, standing slightly stooped in his ungainly posture.

"Yohanan Schleicher!" he introduced himself, in a German accent.

I had seen him only from a distance, supporting his wife on their slow climb down and up the stairs, apparently taking her for medical treatment. They were careful to whisper on the stairs to keep from disturbing the neighbors.

"Mrs. Greenenberg!" he declared. "I apologize for the disturbance, but I must protest . . . ," he began in a severe voice. "Now that everybody's apartment is the front, and establishing means of communication is vital . . ." and he concluded solemnly: "And damage to others' property, Mrs. Greenenberg, is irresponsible!" He stares at me from under his eyebrows poking up from his head like antennae.

It took me some time to understand that the boys had hit the Schleichers' antenna cord and their television screen was covered with snow. The boys closed themselves in their room, afraid to come out until he left. They explained to me afterward that they decided to train for the war with the water pistol. David cut out a cardboard circle and drew increasingly smaller circles on it. Unfortunately, he decided to fasten the target with a clothespin precisely to the Schleichers' antenna cord dangling along the side of the building.

For the next half hour, I went with Mr. Schleicher to reinforce the connections of the antenna and to hang it again, with his box of fine tools and my basic engineering, from the compulsory course at the Technion.

This afternoon, another knock on the door, and with the same bow: "Mrs. Greenenberg, perhaps I can help seal a room in your apartment, according to the instructions?"

I soothed him with the information that I had just brought home everything I needed, "according to the instructions," and when the boys went to bed I would use all my proven engineering skills to carry out the sealing.

"Hah, that's excellent, Mrs. Greenenberg," he retreated, relieved. "Perfectly fine! Perhaps I can bring tools . . ."

"There's really no need."

"Hah, good, perfect," and still he lingered, concentrating, before he declared: "Mrs. Greenenberg! The young gentleman can come up to us. We can play chess."

"I love chess!" David burst out of his room, addressing Mr. Schleicher directly. Their relations had apparently improved since the incident of the antenna. "Papa says I play good."

"Whenever the young gentleman would like!" A mischievous caper cut through Mr. Schleicher's gray eyes, and once again he bowed officially.

Across from us is the Lerner family. An elderly Romanian couple. He limps, scares the boys with the beat of his cane on the stairs, and she has soft, submissive eyes. They've got a seventeen-year-old daughter, Aviva, a mentally retarded dark-haired beauty. She hangs around all day, heavily made-up, peeping furtively from the crack in the door with a seductive look. When she sees me, she declares: "Hello!" Until Mrs. Lerner pulls her back with an apologetic smile. (Will have to tell them not to hesitate to ring if necessary.)

On the second floor is an empty apartment. Three American students left before we came, in the middle of the semester. They're still paying rent. "They'll come back when it's all over," said Allegra. "Before there was a weaver, Amalia, living there. She left a year ago." And across from them, the Levy family—Isaac, a policeman in the northern precinct of Jerusalem, and Sima, a hairdresser, with short blond hair and a tiny well-built body in a tight shirt. Danny and Ido, their sons, go to school with David in the morning. And in Ben-Shoshan's grocery shop now, Sima asks me how David and Jonathan are. "How are they fitting in with us here?" And she immediately answers her own question: "Looks good, no?" She's also concerned about Avi, the delivery boy from the grocery, and wants to know if he's gone back to school: "What do you mean you're not in school? What will you do without a profession? I know your parents want you to go to school, and we here in the neighborhood will pester you, too, pester you to death." She leaves him with his eyes gaping at the blonde going off.

And on the third floor, across from the Schleicher family, are the new neighbors, the immigrants from Russia, the Solomonayvitch family. Old parents, a middle-aged couple, and a daughter with a husband, Draganyetzki, I think.

They always go out in a group. The older ones dressed properly. The women in wool coats, wide-heeled shoes, heavy makeup, the father and grandfather in hats. Only the young couple wear jeans. They go to Hebrew lessons at ten to eight, return at one. Fill the stairs with Russian. In the afternoon, they do errands, gripping notes in their hand.

A week ago, all three generations were standing outside the building: even though they had started a vigorous procession, they suddenly stopped and started a discussion. I happened to see the scene from the window, but I heard details from Allegra, who had gone up to them with a cake the first night, and the next day took them to Ben-Shoshan, "who already gave them on credit, and made deliveries to them, the Russians." And when they stood in the entrance, Allegra went to them, and they immediately surrounded her. Mrs. Solomonayvitch took off her father's hat, pointed at his ear and said: "Viktor, ay. Ir?" "Ear," Allegra helped her. "Doctor," explained Mrs. Solomonayvitch, and Allegra replied with the same noun-language: "Clinic!" "Clinic, clinic!" They all nodded energetically, recognizing the word. Allegra went with them to the edge of the yard, pointed right, "Public Clinic!" And then left, beyond the housing projects, "National Clinic!" "National!" they confirmed with sudden expertise. "Wait a minute." Allegra went in and came out again in a coat, vanishing with the whole Solomonayvitch family at the corner.

A few moments ago Claude called. He calls almost every night, and always the expectation that it's Sayyid, and then "Hello, Lana," in Claude's voice. Tonight I admitted both the joy and the disappointment, "Because you thought your director took time during intermission between the acts to call you . . ." Claude understood immediately, and we laughed. We simply laughed together a moment. As if quietly inhaling the bitterness of a Gauloise.

"I'm coming back from a demonstration. Seventy thousand. 'No Blood for Oil.' Everybody was there. The members in Berlin and Paris also demonstrated. There hasn't been anything like it in Europe since the early eighties. The left is heard again . . ."

"I wish," I went on joking. "But wait until Alain exposes how those demonstrations were also financed with money from selling weapons to Iraq . . . You know, Claude," I went on after a silence, "I feel that we, here, have already gone through a different reality, far from Europe. There are neighbors here, adults, children. All of them closed up with tape and plastic, counting the days." And I immediately found myself telling Claude about Allegra, Mr. Schleicher, carried away with descriptions of the Solomonayvitch family, even talking about the concern for Lerner.

"Good, at least you're surrounded . . . do you want me to get on a plane and come?"

"Thanks, Claude. Take care of Brussels for the time being. I think each of us will live his own story in the near future. But telephone calls are gladly accepted, and especially a fresh stock of jokes. You hear?"

"Yes, Commander. And kisses to the guys. First thing in the morning, don't forget."

Late. On the window the flash of the tape neatly frames squares of night.

Vodka from the freezer calms the body. And the snapshots to you, Father. Without thinking. To hold on to strips of reality with you, with loosening fingertips.

■ ■ ■ ■

[Morning.]

Even though I made an appointment with Gil, I didn't go to the office. Stealing finally, from a countdown, a few hours with you, with the file of sources you collected for your Jerusalem pamphlets. Going out with you to corners of the city, accompanied by your excitement and the quotations you collected from the Bible, the Aggada, the poetic liturgy, listing all the names of the city, Zion, the Holy City, Joy of the Earth, the City of the Great King, and the materials you collected about Jerusalem in Christianity and Islam. Quotations from holy books, journals of travels to the Orient and Jerusalem, copies of engravings, old photos . . .

And for a few moments it seems to me that you're the only one who would understand, without questions, what I'm doing here now.

And last night, two phone calls. From Yaron in uniform and Alain in Moscow. Their residue this morning.

"Hey, Lana."

"Yaron?"

"Calling from a phone booth across from the city commander's. Going to reserve duty. The whole brigade. It's serious now, eh? . . ."

He blew a blast of laughter in the receiver.

I was silent.

"So, don't you have anything to say to a soldier going off to battle, some good word, eh?"

"May it go peacefully . . ."

"No, not like that," another burst of hoarse laughter.

"Really, Yaron . . ."

"Let me put on an act, Lana. This is all so ridiculous anyway. 'National glue,' you could puke. With orders to hoist flags, as if anybody cared about that rag. And for now, they're not distributing gas masks to the Palestinians, not even in annexed Jerusalem. Like they're air, Lana. You hear? What happened this morning? You didn't come to the office. I thought I'd see you again before I leave."

"I stayed home to work. I went over my father's legacy." I tried to change the tone.

"Right, Aaron Tsuriel. I remember him from the Technion. He died last year, didn't he?"

"Yes . . ." and I didn't mention that only a week later, Yaron had hit on me, pleading, and ever since then I haven't been able to get over the disgust when he approached me.

"Yes, he died almost a year ago."

"In fact, you're a little bit like him, with all your monuments on Sabbatical. Another beautifying metamorphosis of Zionism," he shook with coarse laughter. "Watch out, it's all stories. There weren't even any swamps. The historians have already proved that. They didn't drain anything, just manufactured a little mud to feed generations on myth. The hell with it all . . ." His voice dropped. "All the years wasted on wars because of that shitty story. All the friends who crapped out next to you. Fuck it all. I want a little peace in life, a Volvo and an apartment . . . you hear?"

"Yes, Yaron. I always hear. Anything else?"

"Last request. A tiny one, Lana."

"Well?"

"Devote five minutes a day to thinking of me. That's not much. You can even masturbate then. Why not? Make it more fun . . ."

He catches the laugh that blurts out of me.

"You're fabulous, Lana sweetie. I always said I could laugh with you."

As soon as I hung up, the phone rang again. It's Sayyid, the thought sliced through me.

"Hello, hello . . ."

I whispered with an excitement that apparently evoked hesitation, or perhaps parallel excitement, in Alain's distant voice.

"Lana . . ."

"Alain?"

"Yes . . ."

Silence.

"How are you? And the boys?"

"Fine..."

And he exploded immediately: "You've got to bring them back from there!"

"From there? What is it, now you also boycott the leprous place? You've given up on the place here?"

"Don't talk to me like that!"

His voice cracked.

"What do you understand at all..." I shouted, choked. "You never believed in the possibility of peace, of agreement. And here that will happen someday. My father built in his way, and I build in mine, with huts in the heart of the war. Just to believe, Alain. Understand that. Without that belief I can't live... That's my life, and that's also what I want to pass on to the boys!" I was swept up into defending something very broken in Alain, or in me, or in you, Father.

"Don't talk to me like that, Lana," Alain's voice beat in the distance. "You and your spoiled left, the childish, blind left, that collaborates with the worst of the enemies, supports the claims of the worst murderers. And now, with all your sentimental claims, you dare expose the boys to danger. If you want to commit suicide—go ahead, but give me back the boys. You hear?"

"Shut up, Alain, shut up," I trembled. "You never could really be with me... to help... to participate... not even to dream together... never..." and I slammed down the phone, horribly tired.

■ ■ ■ ■

[January 15. Six in the morning. Writing in the kitchen.]

Returning from Tel Aviv. Blocks of mountains slide out of the night. The dawn turning pale at the entrance to Jerusalem. Deserted streets. Last wave at Gil, Shirley, and Assaf in the alley in Nahlaot.

Yesterday, in the office, Gil mentioned the "end-of-the-world party" at a club in a Tel Aviv suburb, starting at midnight and lasting until the morning of

January 15. The velvety flicker between his eyelashes kindled some wild impulse in me to cut the impotence in the final hours, with the broadcast, all afternoon, from the mass prayer at the Western Wall, "a shout to the Creator of the World for the danger of war and the stopping of rain."

Gil's precise fingers at work. Executing in recent days his own twelve Huts he planned for the site. Reading whatever he finds about the workers' neighborhoods, the Marseille project, the Yeshiva project. "I'm doing research on you, Lana . . ." he says with a shy smile. And last week, he organized the first seminar, "Before they take me to reserve duty, too," he laughed, bringing in Shirley and Assaf, his classmates at Bezalel. And Anton came with Nabil, from the architecture department of Birzeit University.

And suddenly the office turned into a classroom, with two connected drafting tables, and plates of dried figs and dates, among maps of the site and the sketches. With comments on my presentation of the project. With exchanges in Hebrew and Arabic. Nabil was especially interested in the presence of thatch and water in the library. Assaf promised to get in touch with his friends, who returned from India and lived in a small village in the Galilee: "When the mess is over, they can be a first group of settlers in the Huts on the site." In the discussion Gil started, possible echoes of Sabbatical in Islam, and in Christianity. Anton and Nabil hesitate to reply, promise to do some initial research by the next meeting. A fragile promise, like our meeting. We interrupt the discussion at four. Nabil's pass expires at dark, and before then he has to get through the police barrier.

"I'm dying to go to that party," Gil laughs, lowers his eyelashes.

"I'll contribute the services of the old Fiat," I offer half-jokingly. "On condition that you take me, the driver, along."

And so, we left, after eleven at night. Leaving the sleeping boys with Smadi, Allegra's pretty daughter, who appeared with her hair pulled back tight. Melting my anxiety with her melodious accented speech, like the best student in the class.

And then, the smack of smoke and noise on entering the club in Tel Aviv. The bony jaws of grown-up children, shaking in a metallic beat. Soldier boys with steely arms intent on dancing. Heads thrown back, in the sweaty flash of spotlights, waving their arms, stamping. And the body does violent things to them in the dark, rips with the whips of rhythm, with the spasms of the head, the belly, the legs. The teenage girls made up like divas, femmes fatales of a leather-and-steel youth. Throbbing in anticipation of quick sex in the bathroom, in a car at dawn in the industrial area. They will take off their makeup on the stairs before they go back to their little-girl rooms, with foam rubber sofas and schoolbooks. And the song bursts out from the crowd,

End of the world party end end end
Give more gas, boy, end end
Gas rocket full of gas, end
Straight line to hell, end end end

And on the stage, in thundering smoke, members of the band in leather pants and bare chests. Banging the battery of instruments, puffing up the big animal sprawling at night over the suburbs of the city.

End of the world party end end end
We've been in the last war
And we'll be in the next war
Peace here is only a short breath
Pass the joint, dummy, and together we'll get high
Check the gas, check the gas,
Check the record, check the gas
We'll be in the next war, too,
I I I I I hate hate hate hate you

Round and round goes the wind in the same rhythm, over and over. A snake's head stands erect, spits fire, in the shadow of death that walks in the Tel Aviv suburbs. Tossing the rest of the beer in the empty plastic glasses, the cigarette butts, because there's only one step between here and there. End of the world end end end. Hit and punch. Whip and cleanse. Night of the end of the ultimatum of the war of Gog and Magog, on the altars of Babylon the great whore, in the depths of dawn of the Arabian Desert.

Round and round goes the wind and in its spin the wind returns in slivers of verses from Ecclesiastes I collected every morning for the project from the Torah reading of the holiday of Sukkoth. Goes to the south and spins to the north, round and round goes the wind, and on its rotation the wind returns. End of the world end end end. As on Hoshana Raba, when stones of fire and tears flooded the square of the Western Wall and the square of the mosques, bursting from the spring of hatred in the abyss of the Temple Mount.

End of the world end end end end.

Gil's face emerges from the crowd. I look at him from the side, in a halo of smoke and spotlights. Finish the vodka at the bar, careful to hide from him what I'm going through. Seeing him moving alone to the beat, his arms waving in denim overalls and an undershirt, baring a damp armpit, muscles washed with flashing. Dancing with his head thrown back, and a necklace of sweat pearls sparkling on his open lip, along his eyebrows, hanging on his heavy lashes, in the curls stuck to his neck. Gulping the beat with eyes shut, like Jesus in Caravaggio's painting.

And then the total night driving back, in the moonless dark of the first of the month, after the eternal light of the spotlights on the turnpike.

[January 15. Seven in the morning.]

The boys in their beds. Their heads on the pillows floating on the milk of sunrise flooding the room.

The body agitated with alcohol. The muscles crushed with dancing.

Maybe I'll go to sleep for a while.

[January 16.]

Beyond the ultimatum.

Late at night. Traffic on Hebron Road has stopped. A strange quiet.

The boys are finally asleep. All day long they clung to me. The school shut down this morning. I took David to the office, and Jonathan also insisted on coming. The first time he refused to go down to Allegra, holding on to my trousers all the time. Only in the office did he calm down. Toddled after Erella. Cheering her up just as much as she took care of him. David helps Gil build the model. Pastes toothpicks, tiny strips of cloth with his patient precision.

On the one o'clock news, in the office, they announce the murder of Abu Ayyad in Tunis. Murdered along with his bodyguard. Apparently by members of the PLO, at Arafat's orders. (As far as intelligence sources can be relied on.)

And all at once, panic for Sayyid. The shadow of Abu Ayyad that shrouded our encounter from the beginning. The similarity between them, a generation apart. That same personal charm, eloquence, the natural touch with the media. And the aura of Abu Ayyad ever since Eric Rouleau's book of conversations with him, *Without a Homeland.* The trail of romanticism of the wandering hero, one of the founding trio of the PLO, architect of the murder of the Israeli athletes in Munich. And the tape sent to the leftists in Israel, kindling in the members the dream of brotherhood—real or calculated. And hours of arguing about him in Paris. Maybe the beginning of my distance from the organization, which led me in a roundabout way to the project of the yeshiva in Strasbourg, and from there to Jerusalem.

At one-twenty, I broke down, knowing how close Sayyid was to Abu Ayyad, worrying about which side of the barricades he was on now. So, instead of lunch in the popular restaurant in the industrial area, as I had promised, I went home with the boys to wait for his call. Waiting all afternoon. He had certainly called before we came back, I explained his silence. There's no answering machine. He couldn't leave a message. Torn between worry and anger.

As the hours passed, the expectation faded, I receded. As if reality here were cut off from the mooring, and was already sailing to an unknown place.

At supper, I decided to confront the swelling threat of battle with your humor. I made the boys a performance of "planes taking off." I leaned back, puffing out my cheeks, waving my arms to the sides with sounds of rumbling planes taking off from "the runway" on my stomach. David immediately joined in, also darting airplanes from his belly, and Jonathan, choking with laughter, cheers us on, "More! More!" The flight exercises dissolved the thought of Sayyid, and we even managed to finish supper without the usual fight: David didn't explode, and Jonathan didn't run away from the table.

Claude phoned at the end of supper. Chatted with the boys first, and then, when they went to the bathroom, he asked tensely how things were, and continued with uncharacteristic worry, "Who would have believed that, after all that, war would burst out tonight! Today, in the 1990s! With blood and bombs, and that the West would be involved!"

"Yes." I nodded wearily, feeling how Claude was also left behind on the shore we were already cut off from. "I played a game of 'air force' with the boys," I said.

"What?"

I gave up on the explanation. And even Claude's friendly whisper was only static on the line, without any delusion of closeness between Brussels and the apartment with the sealed room in the housing project on Hebron Road.

[Eleven-twenty.]

> The unbearable style of CNN. "Desert Storm": a commercial entertainment, down to the last detail. Hasty photos from Israel. And the reports from Baghdad continue a few minutes. I turned off the TV when they got to interviews with scared people in shopping centers in the U.S. Filling carts with duct tape, masks against chemical warfare, cartons of canned goods, and American flags and war souvenirs. I could no longer bear the getting high on "war games."

A grainy night, chilly, around the housing projects swept into the war, exposed to the missiles rising in the east. From the Arab villages, around the Hill of Evil Counsel, waves of hatred rising. Rustling around the small apartment in the building on the road. Rachel's weeping rising from behind the ridge, beyond Mar Elias Monastery. Or perhaps filtering from your writings, Father.

> I know it's impossible to dream, even not of the Sabbatical or the Huts, without risking your life, exposed to danger, in the transparent hut of plastic and duct tape.
>
> (Talking with you relieves a little.)

At midnight, the Israeli army spokesman announced that it was necessary "to prepare equipment for a real alarm."

I find myself in the silence of the living room, acting like a robot. Taking the cardboard boxes out from under the sofa. Pulling out the masks. (David's hood has an extra blue rubber gullet.) Tearing open the packing case of the big DDC, and setting up a transparent plastic bunker in the living room with breathing holes, straight from the trenches of World War I, or from the civil defense shelters of the Cold War. I also prepared the wet rag next to the door, and the pink plastic bucket with disinfectant for a sanitary toilet (for some reason the pink bucket is the most terrifying thing in all the hollow quiet now).

Ella called. Our relationship doesn't justify a call after midnight, but both of us clung to that brief conversation, understanding, perhaps for the first time, that now, even though we're almost a generation apart in age, we're two orphaned sisters.

The ticking of time. The announcer continues guiding the public from the screen. That recurring cycle of slides with details of "means of defense," and instructions "in case of a real alarm." "If you get caught in a bombing, lie down on the floor. If possible, go under a table or a bed . . ."

I've now finished the phone conversation with Uncle Yehiel. Ella encouraged me to get in touch, despite the hour, she said he and his wife sounded terrified. "He's not young anymore. Even though for us, he'll always be 'Aunt Rachel's son.' " We laughed together.

His voice brightened when he heard my voice: "Nice of you to call, Ilanka!" . . . "No, we're not sleeping." And then, in a thick, measured pronunciation, he tells me that he sealed the whole house. "Yes, not just one room, the whole house," and that they're sitting in defense suits. "What's that?" "It's made of plastic. Plastic pants and jacket that you put on. Yes. They said this is safer. No, not only in the street, also in the house." I didn't argue. Not even with the declaration that he relies on our army, and that whoever has to will do his job. I just found myself imitating your style of speech, Father. Trying to restore some formula of family encouragement.

And then, in the middle of the conversation with Uncle Yehiel, a moment of panic—how are you getting along? Did you seal a room? A black, blinding flicker. How come nobody's with you now? That you haven't called yet? And the effort to calm down, for the sake of reason.

Twelve-forty. More defense instructions. Like the last bells before the play starts. After the Hebrew version, the instructions in English, Arabic, Russian, Swahili.

One-forty. On the transparent screen. Aerial photo of Baghdad. The voice of the CNN reporter: "The skies of Baghdad are full of strips of shooting."

Slide of a river winding through Baghdad. Pictures from Washington. Press conference with a White House spokesman. Reporter in a close-up. Figures in suits. "I've got an announcement for you from the president: The liberation of Kuwait began in cooperation with Coalition forces! Desert Storm has begun!"

(Writing to you to keep from yelling at the unreal nightmare, like an entertainment program on television.)

Slide of an empty street. Voice in the background. "From north of our hotel there are explosions. The sky is illuminated. We heard a whoosh that filled the sky. It's really exciting. Looks like a Fourth of July celebration at the Washington Monument."

Three in the morning. The announcer from Atlanta or Baghdad or God knows where announces that SCUDs are falling in Saudi Arabia. Pictures of Marines running, wearing gas masks.

Outside, it started raining. At last. Striking the windowpane beyond the plastic sheet and the strips of tape. Flooding the street. A fresh smell that stays outside the walls of the "sealed room."

■ ■ ■ ■

Four in the morning. After the all-clear.

Until a moment ago, the television flickered. Now the screen is dark. For the first time since the sirens wailed and tore the night.

The boys are in bed now. In the living room Jonathan's gaping plastic kennel. Filled with a heap of sheets and stuffed animals and a bottle with some leftover water and a wet diaper. And in my bed, crushed sheets where David was curled up, clinging to me.

The day passed sluggishly, the boys spent long hours at Allegra's, and then came up with Danny and Ido, the Levy boys, to watch television. The office was also closed. But nothing happened yet. Not even when I put the boys to bed and went to sleep myself. When the alarm went off I was sleeping. An unfamiliar creature darted from the bed, acting mechanically. I ran to the boys' room, plucked David out of the blankets, shrieked at him, "Hold on tight to me." Turned with him to Jonathan's bed and lifted him out with the blanket. David collapses onto me in his sleep. Maybe five seconds now, maybe ten. It takes a SCUD thirty-five seconds to get here from Iraq. Muscles tensed with fear. "Hold on tight to me, David," I plead. We dragged all the way down the corridor to the living room. In my arms, Jonathan wakes up. Turns over in the mass of the blanket, almost drops. Twenty seconds now, maybe twenty-five. Maximum fifteen seconds left. Or ten. Pushing Jonathan's slumbering body into the plastic cage. Cramming the blanket in after him. Immediately terrified that he'll be too hot, that he doesn't have enough air with all the quilts inside. Eight more seconds. Maybe seven. The muscles tremble. David curls up on the bed. His eyes gaping at me. He sits petrified despite all the practice drills they did in school, his whole body trembling. I take hold of his face, transparent with fear, try over and over to press it into the iron and glass stocks. And only his eyes follow me behind the mist-covered glass, with the smell of rubber, and acid. My fingers stumble, tightening the straps of the gas mask. Get entangled in my hair pushed onto the face. Don't forget the valve. And the valve. Got to open the filter. Don't forget the filter. Not to choke. To seal the door. The clear tape. A wet rag to close off the threshold. Three more seconds, maybe two. Can't count anymore. Two more seconds. One more, maybe. The muscles explode. The creature with the iron beak threads an arm into the plastic sleeve on the side of the DDC. Puts it on Jonathan's leg. David's hand is sweaty. One more second. A half-second. Until the end. Not to breathe. With paralyzed muscles. The heart stops beating. Only a still mass with a breathing beak. Until the end. The last moment. An iron rat raises a blue look to me through a steamy and choking mask. A body being wiped out behind the plastic wall, already blurred. The last moment. Together.

And heartbeats that burst only now. After twenty-four, twenty-six, thirty seconds beyond the limit.

Sometime, in this age of iron creatures, defense instructions in several languages came on the screen. Wiped out in a wave of sweat that burst from all pores. And only the ringing of silence from the dark street. Yes, here it's absolutely still. It's not here. It fell, but not here. Not here. The screen of my sweat wipes out Jonathan's curly head, laid like a rare flower in the plastic greenhouse. David crawls into my lap. His iron skull is stuck in my thighs. Only then do I notice how much he's trembling. I hug the skinny limbs, see through the steamy glass the tears running down his face, blended with streams of sweat. Maybe a half-hour later comes the announcement that a SCUD missile fell on Israel. In District A or B, I didn't catch that. Only that it's not here. A chemical missile? I didn't catch that. Only that nothing exploded here. Not in our street, nowhere around here. Here it's quiet, for the time being. No gas. David's body relaxes. He falls asleep, folded inside me. Jonathan didn't respond to the soft tapping of the plastic sleeve on his back. Lay with his eyes wide open. Not sucking.

The announcement of the lull came an hour later. I released the sleeping David from the straps of the gas hood. He goes on sleeping, landing on my shoulder, even when I pick him up, put his soft body in bed, and tuck him in. As if an envelope of down and cotton will carry to him my endless love and compassion, and my shame and guilt. I return to Jonathan in the kennel. Silent. Eyes expressionless. Even when I drag him out by his legs. Only when I wrap him in my arms does he finally bleat softly. Rock him, so close. To make up to him for something irretrievable that happened. Sit for a long time at the boys' beds in the dark room. Finally I cover up, in my bed, over my head. Trying to warm the petrified body.

The second alarm was at three-thirty. The creature once again bursts like a machine. With Jonathan, and David collapsed on me. This time Jonathan crawled on all fours to the DDC. Submissively, "like a trained animal." He lies down with an emptied body. Doesn't look at the stuffed animals I spread out for him. Looks with those frozen, expressionless eyes. David weeps silently. He can't put on the gas mask hood. Fights me and tries to help at the same time. Jonathan also starts fighting with the hut. Tears the plastic doors. I fight with his unraveling fingers through the plastic sleeve, roaring vague syllables at him.

After I put the boys back in bed, the call came from Alain. From Vinitsa. He couldn't get a line. On the Russian media they announced that SCUDs fell on Tel Aviv. "Tel Aviv?" "Yes, that's what they said," his voice faded. Exhausted, I said that the boys were sleeping and I was going to sleep now, too.

I curled up in the place molded by David's body in the bedclothes. Pulling the blanket to me. Taking your notebook with me, Father. Another snapshot in the story of our rifts.

On the screen the photos of shooting continue. Crosshairs homed in on a black spot, stopped, and then the crumbs covered with smoke.

Another series of slides with the same defense instructions. I turned the volume off. Only the announcer's moving lips. Update for the journalists in Washington. People running. No, not here. In Saudi Arabia. Crosshairs homing in. Black crumbs.

■ ■ ■ ■

Morning. Next day. (During the alarm I thought tomorrow morning would never come.)

At home. Instructions to the population to remain indoors.

The boys are glued to the television. They slept late. Got up wrinkled, as if they hadn't slept at all. Wandering in pajamas to the unventilated living room. Gazing at the children's programs, at the announcers' artificial giggles.

I called Erella. She sounds as if she's in a pit. Guy, her husband, went on reserve duty yesterday, and all night long she's been on the phone with his elderly parents in Givatayim, just outside Tel Aviv. "I worked on them for an hour," she relates in an exhausted voice. "Finally they agreed to come. They announced a lull until two. So I'll go to Givatayim and we'll come right back."

Nissim, Allegra's husband, was the first one to knock on our door. I opened the door in a robe and nightgown.

"How did things go with you, Mrs. Ilana?"

"Fine. And you?"

"Thank God."

He holds out a bag. "Sesame rolls, for the boys. Ben-Shoshan just got a delivery . . . Yes, on the way back from the synagogue. War or no war, you've got to pray. At first we didn't have ten men for a minyan to pray. We waited half an hour. Finally, thank God, they came . . . No, no, no need to thank me." He's in a hurry. "If we don't help each other here in the building, what will become of us?" He is about to leave for city hall. There, in the main comptroller's office, they work during emergencies. And then he concluded: "Allegra also sent me to invite madame and the boys to the Sabbath meal."

Afterward, Moshiko, Allegra's older son, came up here to ask the boys if they want to come down to them. But they preferred to stay in pajamas in front of the television. Got to see what's happening with the Lerner family.

■ ■ ■ ■

Two. I returned from the grocery. Like landing from another world.

On the way I dropped in on Allegra. The living room is full of piled up mattresses, and the door to the garden is sealed.

"Yes, you're with us for dinner. Vous venez! No argument! You won't stay alone for the Sabbath eve, with all this mess of the plastic and the crazy wet rag on the floor," she burst out in her broad, sweeping laugh. "Yes, come with the masks and Jonathan's plastic box, what can we do! That salaud Saddam Hussein isn't going to ruin our Sabbath."

I gave in. "Fine, so what should I bring?"

"Nothing. I've got everything."

"In that case, we can't come . . ." I shift to threats.

"Good, chérie, if they still have any, buy challahs. Bring five. Yes. Here, thank God, they eat. Smadi! Go up and stay with the boys, Ilana's going to the grocery."

Despite the cloudy day, the light was dazzling. Hebron Road turned into a vacant lot, and in the neighborhood gazing shadows wander around, wrapped up in army tunics, house slippers, sweat suits. One night is enough to turn the residents of the neighborhood into wretched refugees, as if the essence of Jewish life were refined in them.

At the entrance to Ben-Shoshan's grocery, a long line twined all the way to the bench, paralleled by a line to Marciano's newspaper kiosk. Only after a few minutes in line did I realize the strange total silence of the two lines. An obedient, scary silence. Warming the fallen faces in the winter sun. Thawing out a little. Not exchanging impressions of everybody's dread of the sealed rooms.

In the second line, next to me, stood a young man in unlaced sneakers and John Lennon glasses. He had already shopped at Ben-Shoshan's, and was waiting with a case full of cans and six-packs of cola. Only after I myself emerged from my fuzziness did I realize that the young man had been holding more than twenty kilos in his hand for ten minutes.

"Why don't you put it down."

"Eh?" he looked at me in amazement.

"Why don't you put the case down on the ground?"

"What?"

"It must be awfully heavy."

"Oh, it's all right." He swayed, went on clasping the case with the cans and the cola, with a smile that stretched, then died out.

At Ben-Shoshan's, nothing was left. I went on to the only supermarket in the neighborhood. All the aisles there were blocked with customers, and there weren't any carts, either. People swept everything off whatever shelf they happened to come on. Laundry detergent, instant soup. Candles. Lentils. Even insecticide, as if they now had to prepare for a chemical attack against Saddam Hussein. The challahs had sold out long ago. Only crumbs were left in the bread cases. Fortunately, in the supermarket bakery, they had prepared braided dough to bake at home. I got four. I didn't have the heart to take any more among all the outstretched hands. In the checkout line, the nervousness increased. One-ten. Less than an hour before the end of the lull. Three hours before the Sabbath begins.

At home, it didn't help that I had opened the kitchen window. The compressed air from the night still stood in the living room, glued to the glassy eyes of the boys, covered with crumbs of the snacks they had been munching all morning in front of the television.

Out of habit, I leafed through the weekend paper. Spots of print dissolve before the eyes.

Headline all across the front page: "Eight Iraqi Missiles Fall on Israel." Photos of destruction, houses with walls missing, furniture hanging over the abyss. Two Emergency Equipment men next to parts of an Iraqi missile. Crushed cars.

"Four citizens died from heart attacks. The Magen David Adom evacuated hundreds of terrified people last night." "Ambulances with increased forces were sent to help evacuate the wounded and the injured." "Twelve patients injected themselves with atropine in panic."

Reading bent over, glued to the precise descriptions, full of the exultation of dread. And an Italian journalist's report: "I arrived a week ago, and I feel that things change here from one hour to the next. I file reports, and don't know what I'll be writing from one moment to the next. Hysteria is disguised here as rationality."

Returning from the grocery, I meet Mr. Schleicher on the stairs. Without his eternal jacket. Wearing only a pullover. Trudging heavily.

"How are you, Mr. Schleicher?"

He stands still, gripping the banister. "Fine." And for the first time you can't see his youth in the Bar Kokhba sports league in Berlin.

"And how is Mrs. Schleicher?" I asked warily so as not to intrude into the private realm.

He lifted his eyes to me. Serious, penetrating, gray eyes.

"Not simple."

"Yes," I echoed, finding myself again listening attentively to what was kept silent, as in our last conversations, Father.

"Gerda's not in perfect health, and . . ."

"Yes?"

"She's got fears. You know, during the war she was in Europe . . . in the camps . . ." His fingers moved on the paint spots of the iron banister. "It was hard for her to put on the gas mask. She was terrified." And then he straightened up. "It's a good thing I'm a volunteer nurse at Magen David, able to give the necessary treatment."

"Yes . . ."

"Got to be strong, Mrs. Greenenberg, that's our job!" he concluded with an exclamation, looking me straight in the face with his gray eyes. "And the chess player is still invited. Now that he's on vacation from school," he called from the top of the stairs.

Soon it's Sabbath.

■ ■ ■ ■

The neighborhood on the Sabbath.

From the window, I see Nissim with Eitan and Yossi and Moshiko, walking to the synagogue, holding the velvet bag of the tallith in one hand, and all of them hold cardboard boxes with gas masks in the other.

Yitzhak Levy, from the first floor, runs after them. Buttoning his jacket, straightening the kippah he put on his head. Every Sabbath he goes to the Betar soccer game. Today he's changed his routine.

Last night, a wartime Sabbath meal took place, with a large group, as at a Passover seder. At the head of the table was Nissim—"Nichem" to the family—with his three sons, and across, close to the kitchen, Smadi and Lilach next to Allegra. And the guests: the boys and me, and the three generations of the Solomonayvitch family. "This is their first time at a Sabbath meal," Allegra whispered to me. "I went up to them this morning and I saw immediately that something had to be done." They shake hands officially and present the box of candy they probably ran around during the whole lull to find. They sit down at the table. Viktor and Lusia, the aged parents, Masha and her husband, Yeffim, who assumed the main burden of the conversation, and the granddaughter, Natalia, with her engineer husband, Boris, who came to Jerusalem to try his luck in a computer company.

At the entrance, the cardboard boxes of gas masks were piled up. Yeffim pointed to the pile and laughed: "In USSR, at door, shoes. Here, at door, Protivo gas, gas mask . . ." He persists in telling a joke in a blend of Russian and Yiddish and a few words of Hebrew he learned at the ulpan.

We put the open DDC next to the sofa, where it takes up the rest of the space. Jonathan hangs on to Allegra all the way to the kitchen, brings the warm challahs, stands next to Nissim like a member of the family during the trilling of the blessing over the wine, goes from Lilach's lap to Smadi's and back, plays tag with Eitan, the child of Allegra's old age, and David also is slowly drawn out of the slumber that has clung to him since last night. The first siren was in the middle of the fish. We all ran together to the cardboard boxes. Yeffim insisted on helping Allegra stick tape around the door, put a wet rag on the threshold. On the rug, next to Jonathan in the DDC, Smadi and Lilach stretched out in long Sabbath skirts and masks. All the rest returned to the table, sitting around, silently, with the iron and rubber beaks. Generations of Solomonayvitches, erect as at a parade, Masha's broad fingers moving the slices of challah on the tablecloth. David held my hand all the time, sweating, especially ashamed in front of Yossi, his football companion in the neighborhood. Because of the Sabbath, we were spared the flickering of the television, only the radio was on in the kitchen, finally announcing the all-clear. Nissim gave the signal to put the masks back in the cardboard boxes. We return to the table, to the abandoned Moroccan fish with the bitter red sauce.

Yeffim's booming voice cut the embarrassed silence: "In USSR, I work SCUD," he began ceremoniously. "Work, how you say? Make, made . . ." He consulted with Boris and Natalia a moment. "Make! I make SCUD, Iraq. Now I new immigrant, Izray! I SCUD on head!" He demonstrated with a theatrical gesture. "Now on my head—my SCUD!" And he switched to a flood of Russian that wrested laughter from the group in the middle of the table. Until Allegra and the girls cleared the fish plates and served the rice and meat. When the next siren came, half an hour later, there was a general shout of disappointment. And once again, like a trained unit, we ran to the cardboard boxes, the rag, and back to the table to the meal of rats. Eitan had to go to the toilet and started crying. The rats hummed together to keep him from being ashamed, so he would do it in a bowl. He stands in a corner with Allegra, nobody looks.

The end of the meal dragged on heavily despite the Sabbath songs Nissim trilled with his three sons. David didn't understand what a false alarm was. Refused to eat. Fell asleep on the sofa. Jonathan sat on Nissim's lap, gazing at his fist beating time. The Solomonayvitch family didn't make any more attempts at conversation. Exhaustion is obvious even on the faces of Lilach and Smadi. We leave with the Solomonayvitch family. They help me drag Jonathan's DDC, pacifiers, and cardboard boxes with the masks upstairs. David's walking in his sleep, swaying and collapsing on me and on the banister.

Seven in the morning. Suddenly winter weather.

The site is also flooded now with the morning light. And the residents of Arab-a-Sohra, of Jabal Mukhbar are airing out from the night and the alarms. And once again your voice returns to me. For the first time since everything turned upside down two days ago. Shrouded in cigarette smoke: Sabbath mornings you'd smoke with special intensity. The weekly news show on the radio in the kitchen, and you bending over lists of "Places and Sources." Setting off for other strata of time.

A group of people coming home from synagogue. Surrounded by children in white shirts. With cardboard boxes of masks. And yet, the Sabbath light gives a little relief.

■ ■ ■ ■

Morning. The boys are at Allegra's. Last night was another hard night.

From the moment he got up, Jonathan has clung to my leg, "like a koala." He shrieks when David gets close. "Jonathan has stomach ache. Here," he drops his pajama bottoms, insists that I look at his navel, just so I don't answer David.

"I can't find my sneakers! Last night I put them next to the bed. I'm sure. I'm sure!" David kicks furiously. Finally he finds them under the sink in the bathroom.

There was general relief when Smadi came up and said the boys were invited. David ran and packed up all his Legos, puzzles, and workbooks.

"You don't need so many things, David."

"I do, I do," he clasps everything.

Jonathan imitated him, pushing crayons, pencils, pencil sharpener into a bag, pulling Bobo the stick from the bed.

"Go to Allegra, go to Allegra . . ." and he's gone already, strumming the banister with Bobo.

"Jonathan, you're disturbing the neighbors . . ." I run after him with David's defense kit and the folded DDC.

The call from Olaf Jurgenson caught me as I came out of the shower, taking advantage of the boys' absence to condition my hair, which I shampooed for the first time since Wednesday night. Fortunately, accustomed to the sealed room, I had dragged the phone to the bathroom door with me, to the end of the cord.

He called from Sweden. To apologize. His flight to Israel was canceled. "And it's very hard to find other flights, Madame Tsuriel, you know."

"There's no need for you to come now. After all, everything is on hold for the time being . . ." I found myself calming him, and the wet towel I wrapped myself in didn't protect me from the chill filtering from the ramshackle window.

"How long will you stay in Jerusalem, Madame Tsuriel?" And the distant rustle of a wood-paneled northern morning, well-heated, echoed from the hesitation of the diplomatic voice into the freezing cold.

"As planned . . ." I muttered.

". . . I'll get in touch again . . . if that doesn't disturb . . . to encourage . . ."

"Of course, Mr. Jurgenson . . ."

Afterward, Erella called. Says that in Givatayim, in Guy's parents' neighborhood, nobody was left. Those who didn't fly abroad went down to Eilat. I dragged to the kitchen some plans from the office, along with Gil's material. On Sunday, on his way to reserve duty, he'd passed by to drop off his sketches of the site. Just then I was in the grocery. David gave me the material, with the note: "Hi, Lana. Hope to get a good grade. Bye, Gil." I spread the sheets on the small table, trying to concentrate, but worry scratched my forehead like steel wool.

And then the phone again. I was glad for the call, especially when Colette's and Fernand's voices burst out.

"How are you all, Ilana?"

"I'm with the children . . ." I started, and didn't know how to go on. "They went down to Jonathan's kindergarten teacher . . ." And there was a silence. As if all the questions had already been asked. And that silence of the three of us was enough for something of the warmth of the office in Paris to filter through.

"I sleep with the radio on," said Colette. "The Jewish station broadcasts from Israel all the time. At the first alarm I tried to call. The international line was busy. All the time."

"Me, too," echoed Fernand.

"Yes, yes," I wasn't really listening, just enjoying the nearby voices.

"Olaf Jurgenson asked for your home number."

"He just called."

"It's very embarrassing for him."

"Yes. He apologized."

And once again, silence prevailed. I started doodling a lattice of ink on the paper in front of me.

"We checked," Colette said hesitantly, "but for now there are no seats on planes out of Israel. Though with Jurgenson's intervention, it's possible to get a seat with the diplomatic cover . . ."

I went on doodling, back and forth.

"Did you think about that?"

"What?"

"Ilana," Fernand continued, always willing to deal with difficulties, "we're trying to get you and the boys seats on a flight."

"No need. Thanks. When school starts again, David will go back to school."

"When will school start again?"

"They haven't announced yet."

The sheet was black with hatch marks.

"And how are you . . ." I know that Colette didn't finish because of emotion.

"Not easy . . ." I whispered. Then the set sequence of farewell sentences, spoken slowly, emphatically.

And the conversation last night with Alain, after the second alarm, after the boys had gone back to bed, maybe at three. He called from Kiev. Not clear whether from the hotel or some office. Immediately aggressive, in a tense voice.

"Ilana, you've got to send the boys back to Paris."

"What do you care about the boys?" I exploded. "What hypocrisy . . . you're a coward, a coward . . ."

And his terrifying silence, with the heavy breathing into the receiver.

"You know, the boys almost don't mention you," I went on in fear. "Fortunately they're in bed now. I won't tell them you called. That will simply upset them. Even so, it's hard for them . . ." My shouts cut through the apartment. "Jonathan wept constantly after he talked with you the last time. I couldn't calm him down . . ." I choked.

"Well, then, goodbye . . ." I muttered, without waiting for an answer.

From the window, a pure light between the clouds. Striping the industrial area.

On the Hill of Evil Counsel certainly a clear view of the mountains of Moab, within reach. And beyond them, only crossing the desert, missile-launching pads gleam. Casting their shadow here.

Time is completely unraveled. With no recess of privacy. Heaps of words in newspapers, on television. The whole present is sucked into a rough heaviness.

Expecting now the voices of the boys as they climb the stairs. Laughing with Smadi, who will help them drag upstairs the games and the DDC.

■ ■ ■ ■

[After two in the morning.]

On television, pictures are still running on CNN. Account of the fall of a SCUD in the Tel Aviv area. The reporter, with makeup: "An Iraqi SCUD hit a residential area." Photos of police cars, people running, the destroyed front of a building. And back to the reporter in the studio in Atlanta.

The newspaper is crumpled from so much leafing. "The money markets asserted: The U.S. has already won. The price of oil has dropped more than ten dollars in one day."

"Iraq set fire to the oil wells in Kuwait." (Photo of thick smoke to the horizon.)

"Hundreds of children appeal to the open line of the Ministry of Education. Many of them aren't absorbing the information conveyed by the media and express great fear. Some of the questions and appeals yesterday also concerned the fate of pets."

I turned down the volume. The singers on the screen. Shaking their heads and rolling their eyes with frozen smiles.

[After three.]

I can't fall asleep. I returned to the blanket with a glass of vodka. At long last quiet. Half an hour after the boys fell asleep, there was another alarm, and everything all over again.

Sitting with the notebook of snapshots in bed, still warm from David's body. I can't do it anymore. Disgust wafts from the exhausted body. A woman with two children who were raped once again—tonight, too. And tomorrow we'll be raped, too, and the day after. I and Jonathan and David, and the neighbors from the housing project on Hebron Road, and those huddled in rooms in Baghdad. All of us will be raped with the monstrous arms of the mother of all wars.

Writing to you to say that the abominable seed has penetrated the blood, spread in the tissues, sprouted a perverse embryo of horrors that will change shapes and forms. Writing to tell the defeat. How everything I planned all the years in "Lodgings of Life" around the bed, how everything is befouled, Father.

(Will it be possible ever to wipe out what happened? To dream of a Hut, of Sabbatical?)

Gathering the exhausted limbs and holding on to the memory of your attention to tell how, while running with the boys, I was surrounded by the breathing of mothers. Running around me in drooping nightgowns, with sticky hair, clasping their children to their bodies. Running outside of time. Running in the only time that exists, the time of the child crying in their bosom.

And the impotent wrath at the ancient, incurable disease that again infects the men excited by battle cries and waving phallic weapons, by ejaculating shots from rifle barrels, cannons, the devastating erection of missiles and soaring of planes into the night.

And the smell of the scared victim's fear only inflames the mad disease.

And the fathers, too exhausted to go out with the battalions, turn their aged bodies' shame into shouting matches, incitements inflame hatred with their tongues, fuel it with that oil pressed from the ancient olive grove. They stand at the side of the path going down from the village, and, plowed with wrinkles, they follow the marchers raising dust on the roads.

(And you, were you innocent of this curse?)

And the women? Let's not pretend, Father. How they distill the poison of revenge from fear, mad with groans of pain and dread. They make the men, the sons, swear, send them to die for the mother, the wife, the soil. And when they return, the women will wait at the side of the road, drugged with pain, and on their lips songs of battle and heroism. Covering the shame, the guilt.

Will I have a chance to tell that to Sayyid? To tell him about David and Jonathan clinging to me? About the nausea, the fear? To ask him what happened to Kayyina and the children—did he ever ask himself, beyond the slogans?

And how I was silent in the dark hall at the murderous shouts of hatred of the play *The Clown*. Understanding, liberal . . . How I didn't dare talk there of Huts, Sabbatical . . . I didn't dare, Father.

(And maybe that's why we found ourselves clasping body to body? Hallucinating that one day we'd weep together for our story of shared blood?)

The sweet smell in the boys' room.

Sitting there in the dark, on the edge of David's bed.

To calm down.

And once again the night vapors in the studio over Prinzengracht, leafing slowly through Rembrandt's etchings. Close to you, and to the death that is still so fresh. The thought then of Sarah. After three years of her rising milk. Sarah roaming around, weaning. Empty, and the pain cutting her nipples. And then she sees Ishmael, leaning, swarthy, curly-haired, looking at the people celebrating, and laughs. So immediately a wave of dread for the future that rips Isaac from her breast, brandishing him like a slaughtering knife. And her harsh expulsion of the mother and her son. Then, in Amsterdam, I also understood, for the first time, why the story of Hagar is read at Rosh Hashanah, along with the story of Hannah. She who knew not to hold on to her son, "because he lent him to me." Lets him go with the weaning, returning him to the one who lent him to her.

■ ■ ■ ■

[Home at last.]

The boys are waiting for supper. I make the spaghetti Bolognese they love so much. They're playing together. One of the few moments when David lets Jonathan touch his planes.

(I leave the cooking a moment to talk with you.)

After two nights without alarms, I decided I could take the boys out a little today. For a week now they've been dragged out of their beds to a morning spread between our apartment and Allegra's. Even the rain that finally came didn't change the weather in that sealed space. This morning David said with a look of amazement that he had had a dream about an airplane that was burned in the sky: "Blue and green fire came out of it." "That's a sun jumping," called Jonathan. "You dummy, it's fire," David attacked him, kicking him. Jonathan burst into tears and took a long time to calm down. And yet it seemed that life had somehow returned to some routine. Hours of the day with activities, and a quarter of an hour before sunset the streets empty out.

When we went down to Allegra, she declared: "Come on, Ilana, we're going out!" and immediately melts the siege with her deep voice. "We've opened the door to the garden." Adding, with full authority, a military interpretation: "During the day, they don't dare put their heads out, the Americans see every movement. At night, better not to know . . . may it only pass quietly, with the help of God."

I found myself nodding a kind of "amen," turning immediately to the boys: "Let's go out! We'll go buy something special for supper, and a surprise for everybody!"

"Awesome!"

The two of them bounded out, getting to the car long before I drag myself to it, with David's and my kits and Jonathan's folded DDC, which I put between them on the backseat. Getting out into the air after a week was dizzying. Smells of winter, of fresh sprouting grass. Trucks on Hebron Road belching soot, in a joyous weekday bustle. And the almond trees scattered among the heap of buildings in the industrial area were covered with a transparent blossoming.

We stopped first at the sporting goods shop, and I smiled to myself because I had first found it when I went to the Rearguard Defense Station in the cellar of the same building.

"Mommy! You're buying me new sneakers?" David was choked with gratitude.

"No," I preserved formality. "Not sneakers, soccer shoes. I think you'll be needing them in the near future."

For a moment he was upset by my tone, but because of our exposure to Schleicher's dry humor, the smile quickly returned to his face.

"And for Jonathan, all-purpose ones."

"All-purpose, all-purpose, all-purpose," Jonathan got himself out of the straps of the child seat, leaping into the shop with Bobo the stick.

We were the only customers in the shop. The clerk trudged slowly amid the towers of shoe boxes, shuffling back and forth, as if he hadn't yet come out of his sealed room. He even wrote out our bill half asleep. The heap was increased with sweat suits, a yellow one for David, and a blue one for Jonathan, and some extra-thick cotton socks. We were about to leave when Jonathan had to pee. Not until I came back with him from the employees' toilet, in the depths of the stockroom, did David mention that he had to go, too.

"Why didn't you think of it before?" I couldn't help scolding him, knowing that by the time the clerk accompanied David to the bathroom and back Jonathan would get restless, and if he didn't actually untie all the laces in the shoes on the display table he'd at least mix up their order. And, anyway, it was getting late.

I waited helplessly at the counter. Jonathan was content to run among the rows of shelves. On the counter where I was leaning was an evening paper.

And even before I understood what had caught my eye, my heartbeats had darkened the headline all across the front page: "Saddam Has Arsenal of Bacteriological Weapons of Mass Destruction." The details of the diseases and the names of the viruses were already covered by darkness.

Through my dizziness, I saw David and the clerk. I gripped the counter to keep from stumbling. Back in New Jersey, I had read articles on biological weapons, and although I'd absorbed little in the way of details back then, I'd understood enough to now register this thought: We're defenseless against a biological shelling. The gas masks wouldn't help at all. And in fact, how can you defend against plague viruses that would fill the street, the roofs, the trees, the puddles, that would condense and fall like rain for weeks after? And I just recited to myself that the boys mustn't see me like this, that I mustn't infect them with my terror.

I held Jonathan's hand, and this time the very sight of the Rearguard Defense Station deepened my nausea. It was almost three. I decided to return home immediately, I tightened Jonathan's child seatbelt with trembling fingers, and he suddenly announced:

"Want pita, pita, Mama!" And he clapped his hands.

"And salads from Rahmo for supper!" added David in the same exalted mood.

I hadn't yet said a word. I moved stonily. I knew that if I tried to answer I'd immediately start weeping uncontrollably.

The sun slanted between the buildings. Around the industrial structures the air smelled of wet earth, pure cold. The boys were drunk with joy. Jonathan hit the stones with Bobo and sang; David ran ahead with outstretched arms, hurrying down the path around the building, then returned, slicing the air with whistles of flight. The bakery was empty, too. At the borekas counter stood the vendor, a yeshiva student in a white shirt and wavy ritual fringes, deep in thought, a serving spoon hanging from his thin hand, his long-lashed eyes gazing straight ahead. I paid quickly, dragging Jonathan, who was holding the warm pitas.

"Now we go home. No salads. Everything's closed. Come, come quickly."

The low sun struck the bare concrete walls, the signs, the trash on the climbing path, with a swath of red. Clearly we had lingered beyond the allowed limit. In Iraq it was already after sundown. No reason the Iraqis wouldn't decide to shell immediately tonight. All means of defense, David's and my masks, and Jonathan's DDC, were still in the car, a twenty-minute climb on the asphalt path with Jonathan's slow toddling. We, a mother and two small children, would make a perfect exposed target.

"Jonathan," I pleaded, grabbing David, too, laboring up the path with the two of them. One of three possibilities. Either the explosion would bury us immediately under the rubble. Or it would fall a few streets away and take twenty, twenty-five seconds for the fungus of poisons to darken the graying red. Or third, the explosion would include viruses, and because of the especially clear air, in ten seconds they would penetrate the mucous membranes, the lungs of the boys, who were still breathing innocently, would quickly be carried into the blood vessels, would spread to the brain cells. And then the contortions. The saliva. The melting bones, the hair falling out—first the eyelashes and eyebrows, and then from the head—immediately or in a year, or five, when the disease explodes. I tug at their hands, my body turning to stone. Almost pick up the meandering Jonathan, who continues tapping the path with Bobo, reciting some nursery rhyme, as if he understood something that only made him linger deliberately, out of fear, made him heavier. "Jonathan . . ."

"I got a stone in my shoe," David insists all of a sudden.

"Come on, we'll fix it in the car!" I shriek, pulling him.

"Hey!" he yells in panic, his voice choked with tears.

"Come on. Now!"

Pushing the boys to the car. Rattling past the housewares shop where I bought the pink bucket. And again it looks like a bazaar in Baghdad, in a whirl of keening voices in Rayyida's slow dance, or maybe a Yiddish song I once heard.

We were the only car on Hebron Road, in either direction. I sped all the way. At the building I almost hit a gas tank. I ran to the entrance with the boys, in a race to get there first. And only on the stairs did I let my legs start shaking.

The fear, Father. What we thought we could leave behind, there, with the Jews abandoned to the rioting mob, setting fire to the straw roofs of the huts, slitting the quilts, stabbing the white bodies with pitchforks. The fear they dragged behind them, as the rat drags bread crumbs from house to house, from city to city.

We thought we could bury the fear, or the hate. We believed that "Here in our fathers' delightsome land, we shall do all that we have planned."

Writing to you in the kitchen. Cooking smells. Cutting the onion slowly. The dash of spices, the lumps of meat in the thick steaming sauce.

And the relief in our defense Hut. Life rustling. As in the Mishnah Sukkah's definition of what constitutes life, of the commandment to stay, to live in the Hut, to live, seven days: food, sleep, and study. "The rabbis taught: All the seven days one must use the booth as one's regular domicile. How so? If he has fine utensils, he shall place them in the Sukkah; if he has fine bedding, he should transfer it to the Sukkah; and he should eat, and drink, and walk only in the Sukkah."

Late. The boys are already asleep, after a real celebration meal. I opened a bottle of wine, was delighted with Jonathan, who wiped the sauce from his plate, and even the frying pan, with a pita, his cheeks covered with red spots of warmth and tomatoes.

Your voice lulls me back to sleep. I'll try to fall asleep now. To seek in dreams the smell of the cypress and eucalyptus branches from the thatch of the Hut you built in our yard, and I'm helping you, as you used to help your own grandfather "to bring thatch." And how proud we were when the neighbor children would come see the decorations I made, the lamp you hung (threading an electrical cord back to the house, the entire length of the building), to light the perfumed space.

■ ■ ■ ■

Echoes on the stairs. The Lerner family's door closes and opens. Mr. Lerner went to the hospital last night. The ambulance siren woke us half an hour after the second alarm. Yohanan Schleicher, the nurse in the building, went to the emergency room with him. This morning, at seven, he knocked on the door to report that Mr. Lerner had been transferred to the cardiac ward.

"It was a heart attack. The last days have been especially hard on people with health problems," he summarized, standing erect, before he gave in to my plea that he needed to rest, too.

Work in the office has resumed for a few hours a day. Yaron and Gil are still on reserve duty, but Erella comes. The battles continue beyond the time declared. The Patriot missiles, greeted with cheers, turn out to be like a flaccid erection. Off the mark, or if they do chance to hit, only adding their slivers to the blast of the explosion. Peter Arnett reports from heavily attacked Tel Aviv: "I can only say that a SCUD fell in a residential area. People say, 'I was never so scared,' 'What we saw here was hell.' " And in the newspaper, psychologists explain that fear is a kind of emotional infection. Convoys are leaving Tel Aviv. People are packing up, cramming into cars and leaving. Whole families. "There's nothing to be ashamed of, we're leaving because it's dangerous to be here." Others return to Tel Aviv to work, and leave before dark in long traffic jams.

Two other families have crowded in with the Levys after the second SCUD attack. Levy's elderly parents from Ramat Gan, and her sister and family from Or Yehuda, both near Tel Aviv. In the morning, generations emerge from there, join the neighborhood people sitting on the benches around the shopping center. Or they go downtown with the other refugees from the coastal plain, who wander the street mall with their defense kits. A soccer team organized in the building. David and Allegra's sons, Moshiko, Yossi, and Eitan, and Danny and Ido and their cousins, who brought a different rhythm to the game. Especially Reuben, tall with a trace of a mustache, who thunders commands to the little ones. Every afternoon, they go to the shopping center, drop their defense kits in a heap, sometimes go off to the abandoned neighborhood playground. They come back dripping, their sweaters tied around their waists. And David, flushed, in the sweat suit and new shoes, dribbles the ball with his fingertip, with a dexterity he acquired in the backyard in New Jersey. At three the space begins to close. And at four the streets are empty.

A week ago, I tried to persuade Allegra to let me raise her monthly fees now that David goes down to her house, too.

"Stop it!" she scolded me.

"But it's more work, and you've also got expenses. Food and . . ."

"What are you talking about?" she was truly offended. "What is this? Aren't we at war? And anyway, he's a wonderful boy, il m'aide beaucoup avec les petits, he's my main assistant."

Nissim works half a day at city hall, after early-morning prayers. And Eitan runs among the rooms with the fringes of his short prayer shawl waving, begging David to coach him in soccer, watch him kick.

Yesterday, after their chess game, Mr. Schleicher brought David home. The two of them stood in the door. Mr. Schleicher, tall, his nose thrusting, a bit stooped, and David all absorbed in the doormat. After an update on Mr. Lerner (yes, he admitted when I pressed him, it was he who took him for check-ups), he began: "Mrs. Greenenberg!" (He still refuses to call me Ilana.) "Mrs. Greenenberg, we've got a proposition!" And he winked at David, who was absorbed in his shoes striking the mat. "We've got a fellow here, how shall I say, who's definitely not a fool, and who isn't going to school as long as the guy with the mustache from Iraq plays with bombs, eh?"

If he only could, David would have sunk into the mat.

"And we've got a neighbor here with a little education in the humanities, classics, and sciences, and master of several European languages, although he must admit that his French has a Berlin accent," he opened his gray eyes wide to me under the antennae of his eyebrows. "The two of them, the young fellow and the neighbor from the third floor, get along pretty well together. That's how it seems to us, no?"

David nodded, apparently according to agreement, allowing Mr. Schleicher to straighten up for the conclusion.

"And so, they've got a proposition! To establish a home school. They propose a little arithmetic, geography, English conversation—to maintain the level, which is definitely satisfactory, of the young man—and work on the basic reader. And to expand the Hebrew vocabulary—reading some of the favorite books of the neighbor's son, and the grandson also enjoys them when he comes to visit: *Hurray, We've Got a Flag!* and *The Balloon Seller of the Zoo.*"

Mr. Schleicher tapped David on the shoulder, clicked his heels, a throwback to his prewar German education, and announced, "So tomorrow, the young man is invited. First lessons, and then a game of chess." And at the landing, he added in a scolding tone, "And the young master is requested to try not always to win, the neighbor is beginning to develop an inferiority complex."

Only then did a smile spread over David's face. He entered the house, confused, but also clearly proud. That same enjoyment at the end of a thought process that makes Alain run his hand through his hair. The unconscious movement that had attracted me in our very first conversation, when he approached me after the lecture in Munich.

And at night, during the alarm, when he clung to me, sweating under the mask, I whispered to David, "Congratulations. Looks like you're the chess champion of the building."

■ ■ ■ ■

With the mask on my face. They haven't yet announced the all-clear. Stink of rubber and sweat.

Five minutes after the alarm, the skies of a city burst on the screen illuminated by an explosion. Buildings destroyed. An excited reporter. Police cars. Ambulance. Two young men carrying a stretcher. Running up to the camera. The first crosses the screen with a grimacing face, apparently shouting something. And immediately the reckoning, though here it's quiet. And a wave of sweat that burst out. With relief.

And then the screen was filled with a woman on a stretcher. Lying in an open, bloodstained bathrobe. Thick, wounded legs, approaching the camera.

At the top of the screen, the electronic crawl, moving from left to right, above the crushed legs: "Immediate response of the New York stock market to the fall of the SCUD missile on Israel. The following are up-to-the-minute quotes . . ." And beneath them, the open bathrobe continues passing by, with rolls of blood-stained flesh, a head lolling on the stretcher, gray hair.

The young men lift up the stretcher. The woman and her legs are pushed into the ambulance. The numbers are still drifting across the screen.

Who knows the price on the stock market of the legs of a woman, who was sitting with a gas mask on, when the wall of her home collapsed on her, mutilating her legs, her stomach? What is the price of her blood in a crushed bathrobe and disheveled hair, with stock market rates crawling across her head?

And at the same time, I (why lie?) breathe a sigh of relief that we are spared, once again, the three of us. That the fate passed over us, that it caught somebody else. I run my fingers over David's damp hair, move Jonathan's blanket with the plastic sleeve as he lies in the DDC.

And then the disgust, a caustic, undermining internal knowledge that there is no empathy. Only a bestial rejection of anything that might connect the woman with the wounded legs with David and Jonathan. The pity is only pretend, self-pity, another facet of relief, of the selfishness of the survivor. Nothing distinguishes me from the hypocrisy of viewers in Atlanta or Paris. Except the blood of the woman from Ramat Gan is translated into figures on some exchange, and the proximity of danger raises the price of the blood in my account.

The Israeli army spokesman. At last. A censored version. "A SCUD missile fell in the middle of Israel in an inhabited area. The all-clear has not yet been received. Inhabitants throughout the country are to remain in the sealed room."

David falls asleep with the mask.

I gently put his head on the pillow, straighten his cramped legs. Jonathan lies without moving. Sucking. His heavy breathing isn't heard through the sides of the DDC. The flicker of the screen capers over his face, flushed like the face of an angel.

■ ■ ■ ■

[Maybe there won't be an alarm tonight.]

When I returned home from the office today, it was quiet. I was sure the boys were at Allegra's, or that David was at the playground. But the television was on, and the box with David's hood was on the sofa. And then I saw him in the door to his room, looking at me. "Mother," he said quietly, "I prepared." And something in the way he was standing worried me.

"What did you prepare?"

"It's in my room."

"What is it, David?"

"Come see."

A bit of light burst between the slats of the shutter. At first I couldn't make out anything. Only when my eyes grew accustomed to the dark did I see a red strip drawn on the floor. And then two more curled strips, leading from Jonathan's bed under David's bed. A big sheet of drawing paper with lines and squares covered the bed. And under Jonathan's bed, lined up, with noses bursting forth, were all the planes.

"Here, it's ready."

I leaned on the wall, not yet understanding.

"Out there, behind the window, they're going to attack. But here, on the runway, hiding in the dark under the bed, the whole army is waiting to destroy them. The F-15 Eagle shoots from a distance of eighty miles. AWAC 5000 destroys radar, spots missiles from a distance of one hundred sixty-seven miles. B-52s bomb from long range, carrying two thousand bombs. An Apache helicopter . . ." He picked up each one of the planes, leading it in a wide circle, and putting it back gently in its place in line.

". . . And here, that's the Patriot battery," he pointed to a Lego structure between the beds. "Look, there's a SCUD advancing, advancing, advancing . . ." He moved his arm from the window to the sheet of drawing paper on the bed. "And it's immediately in the crosshairs, like that. And here it blows up! And furthermore," he added with a thin smile, "I prepared escape routes. Come, look." He pulls me with his thin hand. "Here, here's where we get out, and go fast beyond the range of the SCUD." He dropped to the floor, continuing along the red lines. "Here, the chemical mushroom catches us, and here, this is the biological cloud. But we manage to escape and get into the caves." He pointed to the line that disappeared under his bed. "Everything's ready there, here, I drew blankets, and a flashlight. I saw that in the valley, near the Arab village, there are holes in the ground. That's caves, Mommy! You can see them behind the playground! We'll hide there. That's the safest. Not like here. I heard them say on television that the sealed room and the masks we got don't really help. But in the caves it's safe."

Jonathan has been slipping out of my hold, Father (holding on a few days to those words inside me, and only now, because of talking with you, do I dare say them). He annexed Allegra's apartment. Stays there until five or six. Refuses to return home. Only after I go down once or twice does he get up reluctantly and clamber up the stairs after me with Bobo. At home he's silent, appears silently, observes me from under that cascade of fair curls. And at the alarms, he sucks from the plastic hut the flicker of the screen, and his eyeballs are drowned in pallor. Jonathan is a stranger, transparent, suspicious. As if a wall had come down between me and him.

Yesterday, in the room, before going to sleep, he sat and drew with his tongue poking out. I bent over him and saw the sheet covered with a giant sun, with stick figures; above the stomach a round face with curls, and in it—tiny stick figures and hooks for hair.

"What's that, Jonathan?"

"That's you, Mommy?"

"And who's inside."

"Jonathan, David, and that's Allegra."

"And this?"

"Daddy. Telephone."
"And why are they all inside?"
"All in Mommy. That's in Mommy."

New programs on CNN look like repeats. Over and over photos of the cormorants trying to take off, stretching their necks, toddling to their death with wings stuck. Turned into a symbol of this war. The rest of the images remain on the screen only a minute. Photos of a shelter shelled in Baghdad. Mutilated bodies. Women wringing their hands and screaming.

And in the newspaper a photo of a couple and a little girl who won the "contest for the nicest sealed room." And the caption: "The Lippes family came from Moscow two months ago. They integrated nicely, despite the war." Sitting close together on the sofa. Each one of them holding a gas mask on his lap. At the front of the photo, on a low table, a box of cans, a transistor, a thermos. On the sofa, between the father's spread legs, a piece of carpet with a pattern. The only detail that softens the photo.

After three weeks in the sealed room, the weakness mounts up, Father. Some change in the body, the movements, the gaze. I lean over the sink to wash my face in the morning. In the pungent taste of the local toothpaste.

Before, when I trudged back to the table, holding a cup of coffee, I was thinking:

"Just like you."

You're sitting with me here, drawing on the "half-cigarette," long exhale, lips thrust out, the cloud of smoke covering you a moment. And then raising your warm look.

"So, we'll drink a gleizele tea, Ilanka?"

You're getting up and trudging to the kitchen. To the long operation of boiling water in the kettle, steeping the tea in the pot of aromatic black leaves, pouring. One glass for you, another glass for me, despite my protests that I don't really want to drink a glass of tea now.

■ ■ ■ ■

[After three.]
Over Gilo a flattened half-moon hovers. Soon it will sink.

Tonight Jonathan refused to go into the DDC. Like an echo of my refusal to get up for the alarm. Ignoring the siren, deciding out of exhaustion not to drag the boys this time. Calming myself with the thought that Jerusalem won't be shelled. And then David, who woke up, was sure something had happened to me. He burst through the door, yelling, "Mommy! There's a siren!" He ran back to Jonathan. "Get up! Get up!" Hurtling him with shrieks.

Jonathan burst into tears. And when I ran after David, and picked Jonathan up out of bed, he clung to me hard and refused to crawl into the DDC. I left him next to me in bed. Wrapping him in a hug and a blanket. But David yelled through the mask, "Go into the DDC. Go into the DDC." Hitting Jonathan's and my hugging body. "It's all right, David . . ." I roared at him, mask to mask, until he weakened, he, too, clinging to me, his shoulders shaking.

We stayed like that, the three of us hugging, even after the all-clear. And then the call from Alain. A slow, reserved voice. I gave the phone to David, who started saying something about airplanes. But after a few words, he muttered "goodbye" and let go of the receiver with a humiliated look. Jonathan squabbled a few vague syllables. Not clear to me whether out of weariness or on purpose. Holding the receiver far away, hiding from Alain, wanting to offend him, in his own way.

"How are all of you, Lana?" Alain addressed me in a forced voice.

"And you?" I maintained my distance. It took me time to recover from the jolt of the last conversation, and this time I tried to be more careful.

"Fine, thanks," he answered.

"And the work?" I garnered all my forces to add.

"There's a lot of material." And then he went on, almost in a whisper, for fear of the censor, or out of emotion, talking fast. "We started going over the

KGB archive, material sent from the Red Army archives." He stopped again, and, foreign to Alain's usual eloquence, the silence seemed to go on forever. "... Even children's journals. In Yiddish. From a camp near Vinitsa ... They were encouraged by a young teacher, who also added a preface. She writes that that's how they kept up activity. At night before they cleared them out, they buried everything under the floor of the hut ... I and my colleague from Yad Vashem are the first Jews to open this material. At any rate, the first non-Soviet Jews ..."

I was silent. Knowing that was Alain's way to share what we were going through, silently thanking him for not exploding. And yet I couldn't, in reply, describe the boys nestling in my lap.

"Everything's quiet here now," I only said.

"So take care, and goodbye," he immediately retreated to the tame tone. As if he had said more than he had intended.

"Goodbye, Alain."

We sat hugged around the dead receiver for a moment. Jonathan was the first to leave us, going back to bed alone. And then I walked David back, holding his hand. Covering them up, stroking their heads, and singing. Yes, tonight I sang. At two or three in the morning. "At Kinneret, on the sands, there a splendid palace stands, there a garden grows so sweet, there each tree is tall and neat. Who lives there? Just a lad ... And there he learns his Torah, too, from the Prophet Elijah." Caressing Jonathan's hand, the crescents of his tiny fingernails, and singing.

This morning, I decided to continue going over your writings (in another week it's the anniversary of your death, and the need to talk with you doesn't subside). Opening notebooks, stenciled pamphlets. Leafing through. Words dart to the eyes. From the 1960s, 1970s. Can't really read.

Taking out of the bundle of writings the notebook you'd sit and read to me from. On the first page, the opening words are emotional: "For a long time, perhaps too long, an internal impulse has existed in me to put things in writing. To open my heart. This need frequently appears in me. I don't mean experiences concerning my present life. In these pages, I will write down events from my childhood in the small town, and from the fifty years of my life and work in Israel. Those chapters in a long route with one common denominator. Love of Israel, yearnings for Israel and building Israel. In all of us, old hands and young, both wittingly and subconsciously, there exists a profound and lofty sense, the great privilege we have earned: the establishment of a homeland for the Hebrew people."

And among your writings, also a thin notebook (apparently an uncopied draft). On the title page: "To the memory of my parents, my brother, and my sister, who remained in the town, and were killed in the slaughter of European Jewry." And a comment to yourself, "To continue to ask Ida about her family. Maybe I can bring forward a few lines of their images. Pious Jews with generous qualities, from the little bit she said. Her father a scholar. Her mother taking care of the big family and the needy of the community. Maybe it will make it easy for Ida if I write about them a little."

A half-moon is behind the ridge now, and the other half is tilted on its side, like a ship with an erect stern.

■ ■ ■ ■

[Another morning with your writings.]

Leafing through. Slowly. Letting the voices spread. Spreading out the contents of the box. As if for classifying. But in fact, only to touch, to caress.

Your immigration certificate. From 1921. Signed by the Mandatory authority.

Histadrut workers' association membership booklet, from before the establishment of the State.

[Photo with your official expression.]

Food ration books. From the world war. From the rationing period after the Israeli War of Independence.

And then, drafts of speeches, greetings, official letters, from your time as secretary of the board of the Labor council of Haifa. Four, five drafts that you went over with a fine-tooth comb, back and forth, your formulations of current events, urgent issues, "absorption of the mass immigration," "from the state in the making to sovereignty," "implications of the Sinai Campaign . . ."

Stunned again at the early nude pictures. The splendor of the well-carved, relaxed Michelangelo body, forceful. Lying on your side with sparkling tanned skin, so young, all dreamy. And the photo with a white suit and a cap, the revolutionary dandy, with colonial glory and a bold wink. And a later photo, in khaki, next to a dirt road. (On the Burma Road to Jerusalem under siege in '48? In the northern Negev?)

I go on sorting. Spreading indiscriminately what I took out of the closet in Haifa. Stenciled pamphlets of "Places and Sources," clipped together, with a note in parentheses: "Led by Aaron Tsuriel." The quotations from the "Sources," "brought from home," and your modest notes about the "days of revival: from the days of the first settlers to the battles of the War of Liberation." (And among the notes "not to be published," I also find, to my amazement: "And that problem we haven't yet fathomed, about the sabbatical year and the abandonment of the Land." The surprising, embarrassing similarity between what I've thought for years was the annoyance of the old-timers of the Labor council and my own projects.)

And your preface to the notebook with the story of your arrival in the Land. "Lines devoted to Ella and the grandchildren and to our Ilanka, who, despite the distance that has separated her from us for years, is always in touch with us, with her letters and the letters of mother and me to her." (And your voice rising in me all this year. Impregnates me with your story, our story, without any difference anymore, Father.)

I went to the window. Don't dare open it, tear the strips of tape.

Stick my face to the pane. Clinging to the calming cold.

The sparse traffic shakes the glass. Dark clouds hanging over Gilo, casting a shadow on the industrial area, going south to Mar Elias, Har Homa, Bethlehem—names of the places that were on your lips.

In a notebook with a yellow binding I find your writings from '67. The exaltation in the wake of the redeemed land and meditations on the problem of water, on integration into the area, "now that the Arab states know they won't defeat the Jewish settlement by force of arms." And next to them your excitement about the opening of the gates of Russia, the waves of immigration that come. May they come. Yes, now, in retrospect, I understand how big was the hope that jolted you in those months after the Six Day War. Binding you again—beyond the personal crisis and the mediocrity of the party—to the great story of yearning of the people for the Land, to the prayer of generations that was granted. I read, and the words are covered with a scrim. With no shame, for the legacy of longing, Father.

Among the writings, I also found the pictures I took on that "family tour," in the summer of '67. I gave them to be developed when I came back from Paris in the fall and haven't seen them since then.

A group photo at the top of Tel Herodion, Herod's palace. Mother in a flowered dress and broad-brimmed straw hat, already fragile, Aunt Rachel with her hand in her pants pockets, and Uncle Yehiel stooping a little toward you.

And another picture, so "relevant" now. The little group at the entrance to the Shiloah Tunnel. You're glancing at notes, pointing with your outstretched arm. Mother and Aunt Rachel turn their heads after you to the shadow of the pool, and Uncle Yehiel holds the bottle of Jordanian lemonade he had just bought in the kiosk in Silwan.

Yesterday on the news, Kamel Mustafa, the English literature professor from Birzeit University, was arrested for spying. "He informed the enemy about the location of the fall of the SCUDs, helped with targeting. In his house, a fax machine was found from which the information was sent." We were supposed to go to him with Sayyid, to prepare the list of invitations together. I blush to read in the paper how he was also swept up in the intoxication of the summer of '67, when he came to Jerusalem on vacation from school in London. He volunteers for an international group of dusty young people in the archaeological digs, going with them to the bakery at Nablus Gate for pitas and hard-boiled eggs, for nightly swims in the Dead Sea, falling in love with a professor's daughter, with her thighs in shorts.

Yesterday, when I went to take the boys, Nissim commented, "That's how an intellectual dances on the roofs when a SCUD falls on Jews. How he marches with half a million demonstrators in Rabbat Amman for Saddam Hussein." And how would you put it carefully? "The abyss of the struggle between two peoples, Ilanka. A thin border separates treason, loyalty, and coexistence."

At the site now, instead of a ceremony for laying a cornerstone, abandonment. And Sayyid, who's wandering around somewhere in Tunis or Libya—we're cut off, each one engulfed in his own story.

■ ■ ■ ■

[A hummus restaurant at Jaffa Gate.]

Chill drafts burst in from the glass door. The smell of chickpeas. A cool oilcloth on the table. And a glass of Turkish coffee. The cloudy sky floods the wall of David's Tower, the stone façades in the square of the gate, with gray.

On Saturday afternoon, the ultimatum of the land attack will run out. Estimates of forty-five thousand dead in battle. Meanwhile the massive air raid on Baghdad. Three hundred sorties at night. The thirty-second SCUD fell on Israel. In Kuwait, the Iraqis are systematically burning the oil wells.

Morning with Anton and his assistant, Samir, in the workshop of al-Kuds. A work meeting on the maquette, the accessories, the costumes. Whatever can be advanced in the meantime. Meeting them at New Gate, they take me to the theater in a clear, thin rain. The ridges in the distance: Mount Scopus, the Augusta Victoria Tower, the Hebrew University, the ancient pines on the illuminated horizon. Each walking with the cardboard box of the protective mask on his shoulder, like the backpacks of food toted by kindergarten children. We walk in the zone of hallucination between SCUD attacks, deep in the threat of the Intifada—in a kind of truce between strata of fear. On Suleiman the Magnificent Street shop signs in Arabic, English. Anton tells about his father's wood-carving shop on the Via Dolorosa. "Everything's from him, all my work," a smile lights up his round face.

And the entrance to the theater. A year later. Anton's workspace, with all the tools neatly arranged, wood shavings on the floor.

"There's no heating in the auditorium, either," Anton rubs his hands.

"So we'll keep our coats on," I declared optimistically, tying my scarf, and adding gloves as well.

"Everything has stopped since the mess has started. The audience doesn't come. From Ramallah and around there because of the curfew, and people in Jerusalem aren't in the mood. We canceled all the performances in February. There's a little work only with our joint production with the Dialogue Theater in Jerusalem. Yesterday I put up a set for them in an auditorium in Kfar Saba. I heard that in Tel Aviv the theater is working. And concerts, too. They stop for the sirens and then they go on. Bravo for them. Really."

"It's good you came, Ilana, terrific!" The smile flashes again on his eyeglasses and in his soft eyes.

"Of course, Anton."

"How's Gil?"

"Fine. He sends regards. He called from reserve duty. I promised to tell him about everything you show."

"Say hello to him."

"Of course," and we laconically sum up that part of the conversation.

We sit around the high worktable. Samir meanwhile aims a spotlight at the model of the hill. The explosion of colors in the straight, geometric blocks of Anton's design. Miniature strips of fabric on the slopes, along the paths. Red, yellow, green, black. Blue veils for the aqueducts, for the wooden bridges.

Samir carefully rests his cigarette on the edge of the table, then drags on it again, his dark cheeks swallowed up in the long sucking that lights a ball of fire in the grooves of his face. He helps Anton spread out the sketches, one picture after another. The entire performance. Reviving all at once the hours of thinking with Sayyid. In Jerusalem, Paris, at his studio in Amsterdam, in the shadow of his library shelves with Sartre, Brecht, Anouilh, Camus, Genet, Pirandello. Planning the ingathering of the audience. The musicians dispersed on the ridge between the lobes of the Settlement of Huts. And the narrator with the musicians leading the audience from station to station. First, Cain and Abel. Composition in simple colors. Yellow for Abel the shepherd and his flocks, green for Cain working the land, whose inheritance encompasses the whole world. Cain darkening with rage at the sight of his property becoming food for Abel's herd. And then the altars, and the waving banners: "And the Lord had respect unto Abel and to his offering; but unto Cain and his offering he had not respect." Writing the banner in Hebrew on a tiny strip of paper that Anton prepared for me, and he pastes it next to the signs in Arabic and English. His careful fingers lift the strip of cloth off the tiny model of the altar, and dangles over it a strip of red cloth for Abel's spilt blood. And then, the expulsion of Cain. Carrying the mark, the curse on him. Wandering. Leading the audience to the second station. And the drumming of Ibrahim from the top of the ridge, when Cain sets up his Hut, the first city. And in the next station, the departure of Abram, Abraham, Ibrahim. "Get thee out of thy country, and from thy kindred and from thy father's house, unto a land that I will shew thee." The writings rolled in banners made in a blend of arabesques and Brecht. The chapters from the Koran on the birth of Ishmael. The chapters from the Bible, which I brought to Sayyid, on the birth of Isaac, on the expulsion of Hagar.

Anton spreads the sketches of the next station on the table. The two of us lean over the picture of the Binding of Isaac. Today for the first time I see the concrete, spatial rendering of the versions of the Bible and the Koran on the Binding of Isaac and the Binding of Ishmael. Our arguments, our shouts, the laughter, and again the conflagrations. Anton's colorful sketches. With abstract lines emphasizing the heart of the drama, around the altar on

Mount Moriah, that altar already stained with the blood of Abel. The moment the knife was raised on it and not lowered to slaughter: the first act of letting go, and it leads the performance to the final scene, in the last lobe. Palm fronds and the sheets of the thicket rise to music, song. A Hut of peace, the Hut of David that falls, the Hut of the skin of Leviathan. It covers the audience following the performers. Ibrahim with the drums in the shadow of the antenna of the UN camp. And Rayyida's dancing at the remnants of the position of the Jordanian Legion. And on the slope of Mount Sabbatical, where the library will go up—the baskets of refreshments. Bread and salt and water. And the conclusion inspired by the joy of Beit Ha-Shoeva.

Anton released the "dam" of the miniature tank, and a drizzle of water went through the aqueduct, in cascades, to the sound of my shouts of admiration. And together we mentioned the beacons to be lit on the surrounding ridges. And the dovecote to be opened from the navel of the slope. Releasing a white gust on the yellow, green, red, black, and the song.

"That's great, Anton," I whispered at the end. "Really, extraordinary. I didn't expect such a shock of beauty . . ."

"Thanks, Ilana."

"It's just too bad my little boys won't see it."

"It was very interesting to work on the project. Too bad it won't come out now." And after a silence with downcast eyes, he added almost in a whisper, "Maybe this performance will be done someday after all . . ." And the light once again capered behind his glasses.

Anton brought coffee in little cups that steamed in the crystalline cold of the workshop, the aroma condensing on our faces.

As we left, we passed by young men sitting in the theater café, buttoned up in army jackets. At the gate, Iman passed by us, amazed to see me in al-Kuds, her lips spread in a chilly greeting.

"How have these days been for you?" I asked Anton when we were in the street.

"Hard," he answered with his eyes down.

"Have you got a family?" I dared address him personally for the first time.

"Yes. Four children."

"Four!"

"We live not far from here. In the Armenian Quarter. I sealed a room in the apartment. My wife's parents and my parents have moved in with us for the time being."

"Yes . . ."

"We didn't get masks until the second week. In the first days, I made cardboard masks for the children so they'd have something to put on during the alarm," once again a smile washed over his face. "You know, it's not sure I'll stay much longer. It's hard for Christians here, and even harder for Armenians. Problems with the Muslims. We may join our family in America."

In the passage near New Gate, before we parted, I said, "The next meeting can wait until Gil comes back. He won't forgive us if we continue without him."

"Yes, of course. We'll wait."

And we didn't mention Sayyid throughout the meeting.

Cold drafts whenever the glass door of the café is opened. Almost no traffic in the square of Jaffa Gate. A few German tourists, exceptional in their foreignness, come in and go out.

Photos of the mosques on the walls. Framed.

(Meanwhile, in the margins of "your notebook," I sketched a few drawings of Huts. Something in my architectonic language has sharpened lately. And new materials. Plastic sheets, cardboard tablets.)

Last look at the pale light striking the hewn stones. Quality of wintry white that will come back to me someday, maybe in another year, one morning, far away. In Paris, perhaps.

■ ■ ■ ■

Evening. I returned from walking Uncle Yehiel to the bus stop. He absolutely refused to let me drive him to the Central Bus Station. "You won't leave the kids alone."

At home, the boys are playing quietly, already in pajamas. The calming influence of his visit.

"I'm coming to be with the young folks." That's what he announced on the phone in his heavy intonation. Rejecting my worry that he'd get tired. "That's something I've got to do, Ilanka, you've got no right to interfere."

He arrives after two, after changing buses four times since morning. The boys cling to him. He taps David on the shoulder, and despite his seventy years he lifts Jonathan into the air. Deposits in the kitchen the fresh-picked oranges he brought from his farm—"for Tu b'Shvat, even if it is a little late. Here. And a jar of olives and some grapefruit wine. Homemade.

"So, does the sealed room hold? There's a little knowledge of architecture here, eh?" he decreed. "We sleep in protective suits. Well. The plastic rustles a little in bed." But when he picked up David's terrified look, he quickly tapped him on the shoulder. "Fine, boys, let's play a game? Who has some math paper for me?"

The three of them bend over the squares of the game of submarines he sketched carefully. David bursts out laughing, a laugh so much like yours. And Uncle Yehiel, with the deliberate movements of a farmer, his square face lights up with laughter, he raises his eyebrows and the lines of his forehead and puts on a look of amazement. Jonathan sits on Uncle Yehiel's lap, sprawls against his broad chest, rubs the sleeve of his checked flannel shirt, and watches the game.

I cling to them, too. Have a hard time again with the riddle whose solution I've kept forgetting since childhood, about the shepherd guarding a ewe, a cabbage, and a wolf, and they have to cross the river in a boat with only two places. Who will he take with him so that none eats the other, not the wolf the ewe, and not the ewe the cabbage? And an early supper before Uncle Yehiel leaves. All of us crowded around the little table in the kitchen, with cut-up vegetables, and cottage cheese on whole-wheat bread. The same smell as when you'd make vegetables and fresh bread for Aunt Rachel's visit. We turned on the radio to hear the news, at Uncle Yehiel's request. Interviews with those whose house was hit by the SCUD and were staying in a hotel, and with a wounded father: "Enough! For three weeks now everything's in a mess. This isn't life. The children are already climbing the walls. They said it would be over in a few days." And details about the plan for the land invasion. The boys grow nervous, as always with the news. David started kicking Jonathan, who pushed his vegetables through the pile of cottage cheese off the plate. Until I simply got up, apologizing, and turned off the radio. As if you could just turn off the story.

And the sweet moments when I served the oranges. Uncle Yehiel teased the boys about whether they knew how to "really peel." "Want to learn?" Before their trusting faces, he shows how to made a perfect mark all around, and then, "you lift the hat," and "open the doors." And the two of them, after him, thrust a finger into the small space in the center of slices: "The finger is the main thing," he lectures very seriously, and Jonathan cheers when his whole little hand is swallowed up in the orange. "And now you open." They spread the slices on the plates in juicy flowers of translucent yellow and juice, flooding the palate with cool, sour juice.

David still insists on showing Uncle Yehiel the fleet of planes of the "members of the coalition." I was afraid he'd go on and demonstrate a Patriot hitting a SCUD, and especially that he'd mention the caves. I knew it would deteriorate into a stubborn inquiry of Jonathan, who was absorbed for the time being in stroking Uncle Yehiel's big hand, kneading his knuckles, clinging to it. I interrupted David's demonstration, saying that Uncle Yehiel was in a hurry, that he had a long trip ahead of him.

"It's no big deal, I arranged for a neighbor to come pick me up from the bus station in Hadera."

At the door, bundled up in a military jacket and a scarf around his neck, Uncle Yehiel tapped the shoulder of each of the boys who stretched up to him. And on the stairs, his painstaking grasp of the banister, with that upright posture, that only became even more erect after David was killed. I watched him descend the stairs with the heaviness of someone who works the land, turning to me with his wondering smile that unravels his face's furrowed landscape.

Waiting at the bus stop on Hebron Road. In the cold, as evening fell. Uncle Yehiel was buttoned up; I had my hands in my pockets. And then, in that same slow voice, he said directly: "Ilanka, I wanted you to know how much I admire that you're building a monument to peace."

"It's not exactly a monument, and for the time being I'm not actually building," I tried to joke. (And did not dare to hug him, to tell him it was great that he came and did not put my head on his tired shoulder and weep.)

"Ilanka, I wanted to tell you something." He was silent a moment, his face raised to the twilight above the industrial area.

My heart started pounding. I was sure he was going to talk about David.

"There are two events from the War of Independence that won't let go of me," he continued, sunk. "One is the Battle of Latrun."

"Yes," I recoiled. These are well known, and it's too bad Uncle Yehiel feels like stirring them up before his long trip. And why doesn't he talk about David?

But he went on in a pained voice, hesitantly. Not to renew, but to say aloud, perhaps to me, perhaps to himself: "Going into a misbegotten battle with the Holocaust survivors. Straight from the ships. Coming from the camps in Cyprus, from the DP camps in Germany. We turned them into soldiers with a little training with brooms led by members of the illegal immigration, Aliyah Bet, in the camps, and sent them to the campaign right from the boats. And then the shit. And they didn't speak a word of Hebrew. To this day, I hear in my head shouts in Romanian, Polish, Yiddish. Shouts of names. Only names. In the dark. I broke down then. But you couldn't talk."

I looked at Uncle Yehiel's withdrawn silhouette, his profile protruding from the scarf and the army jacket, and the time getting late until the bus came. I had left the boys alone in the danger zone that had begun ticking, and hadn't told Allegra. But Uncle Yehiel didn't yet relax.

"And the second thing is Campaign Danny. Expelling the Arabs of Lod and Ramle," he went on.

"Yes," I wanted to apologize and leave. Unable to hear anymore, in the last moments before Uncle Yehiel also left.

He didn't notice and went on thinking aloud. "There was some small clash of forces with a few rioters in the middle of Ramle. That was a pretext, and then the expulsion. Children, old people, pregnant women, we took them out of their houses and put them on trucks. Took them in the dark across the Jordan. Dropped them off there. Thousands. You know. I grew up among Arabs, in the Galilee. I knew that Father's murderers came from one of those villages. And there were years of attacks on the roads, in the fields. But there were also neighborly relations. And respect. Who knows . . ." He raised his face to the full dark now, with the lamps of the industrial area striping the horizon like a desolate fair. "Maybe someday we'll be able to shake hands. With them or their grandchildren. Peace has to be learned very slowly. So it's important, what you're building, Ilanka. A place of learning, of thinking . . ."

And from the frightened silence I recognized the family sign of lopping off the conversation, when David's name is liable to be mentioned. I thought I heard the bus rumbling in the distance.

"You know, I started going over Father's writings," I only said.

"Aaron wrote very well."

"I brought a box full of material from the apartment in Haifa."

"There are letters from Aaron to Mother. For sixty years. Aaron was the family scribe."

He turned to me, his face unraveled in a childish, apologetic smile that swirled all his lines. "I never could write . . ."

"But you've got a collection of stones," I replied. Just to hold on to David for another minute, how I used to come to them on vacation in blue shorts with an elastic waist and an embroidered shirt, and David peeps at me playing with Uncle Yehiel's pile of stones in a corner of the courtyard. "Maybe you'll lend me some for the cornerstone laying ceremony. I'll put them on the central path of the site. Family cornerstones."

He lifts a flattered look at me. "Fine, if you insist."

"Yes, Uncle Yehiel, for me that will mean something."

"All right, Ilanka. It's a deal!"

We laughed as he waved goodbye to me. Uncle Yehiel never was accustomed to hug or kiss. Just another wave, and turns his back. And the choking that floods me when the bus leaves. Seeing him making an effort to grip the pole next to the driver, waiting for the ticket.

■ ■ ■ ■

[Mid-February. Fifth week of the war. Ground attack.]

I peeled an orange from Uncle Yehiel's pile, careful to push my finger in the center to make slices. Bring the plate with the celebration of yellow and juice back to the table.

In the cafés downtown, tables are full of refugees from the coastal plain who migrated to hotels, family, friends. Sitting in the alternating winter sun and chill, with their cardboard boxes of gas masks. Trying to have fun in the time spreading out. It's clear to everybody that Saddam's missiles won't strike here, in Jerusalem. The mosques protect us all from becoming a target.

The Russian immigrants on the sidewalk mall. They emerged when everybody was behind plastic sheets and duct tape. Suddenly they're here, in their strange, proper clothing. The women in wool coats with fake fur collars and wide-heeled shoes, the men in dark suits and hats. Gathering together with straying eyes. An accordion player, bound to his instrument, leaning over to work the bellows. Playing ticking adaptations of Mendelssohn, Chopin. Collecting money. On his worn-out jacket, a Red Army hero's medal. Opposite, an old woman with sparse hair gathered with a hairpin, dancing a stuffed monkey made of nylon fur, tied to a wooden beam. A green monkey, skinny, dancing stiffly to the old woman's chirping voice.

The tension eases. In recent days I've gone out on tours of Jerusalem, to take advantage of the time until we return to Paris, at a date set in advance, "when the Passover vacation begins." Walking in the traces of five notebooks of "Places and Sources" devoted to "periods and neighborhoods in Jerusalem." The stenciled pages are clipped together with descriptions, quotations, rare maps, and photos of etchings you put together, with simple printing, too black.

Yesterday, when I came back from a tour, I saw David playing alone in the distant corner of the playground. Kicking the ball to the wall of the playground and running to catch it with another kick. He didn't feel me watching. All concentrated on the ball ricocheting toward him, harmonizing with his running. His face was flushed, his straight, fair hair falling on his sweaty forehead. I won't call him to come home yet. Let him play some more in the lengthening shadows, climbing with the desert chill.

The ball rose and landed beyond the playground. David carefully lifted a layer of old wire, maybe from the British Mandate. Puts his feet, step by step, between the thorns, the stones. Keeping his balance, he gets to the place where the ball landed. Hugs it in his arms. And for a moment, when he stood up, his long face appeared in its concentrated gravity, and also in the savagery that could burst out any moment in a fragmented, trumpeting laugh.

He came back through the thorns and rubble. As he stooped to get through the wire, the ball fell and rolled off in my direction. Only then, when he turned his face, did he see me standing at the edge of the playground. I pick up the ball, throw it back and he catches it with a thwack, appreciative of my participation, and runs back to the playground.

"Come up in ten minutes," I tell him in a thick voice, and see the two of us enveloped in this moment that belongs here and not here. Like the sight of David and Jonathan kicking, from the window of the house in New Jersey. And how much we've all changed since then.

And with the same terror, also the hand reaching out to our notebook, to the words of another time. And my decision, a few days ago, to continue renting the apartment, to return here every year, as a "pilgrimage." To continue the tours on foot, by car, in the folds of the city, in the formations of the mountain around the site and the Huts changing on it. Knowing that the place was already permeating in me, digging another space in me, Father. Beyond everything I'll ever build here.

Alain returns to Paris in another week. Last night, in a dream, his body came into my body. Even the thought about Alain has changed. As if the body, with its seasonal cycles, is already open. Like another station on the route of our wanderings. Alone. Together.

The return to Paris at a fixed date seems natural now, too. The place can be dropped. To take on the roads a place that has no place in the world. Jerusalem is open like a thicket to the stars, the sky.

■ ■ ■ ■

[The Old City. Jaffa Gate.]

I park near the Kishle, the police station that went from the Turks to the English and from the Jordanians to the Israeli police (a safe place to leave the loyal Fiat, without having to worry that I'll find it burned in a fit of nationalism).

Leaving that tour to the end. Postponing to the last minute entering the heart of the place. Carrying as a compass your pamphlet "Jerusalem, the Old City," with its opening words: "Jerusalem, the city to which all my thoughts are devoted, its history, its beauty. To it I have been drawn ever since I came to the Land. For many years I wanted to make my home there, and could not. For many years it could not be visited. I shall make my pilgrimage through the generations of steps and words."

Casanova Street. A quiet corner. I dare to take out the notebook, stop, write.

The shops of postcards and crosses on the Christians' road are half shuttered. The alleys are almost empty. Across the way a photography shop, behind it a shop of leather goods and embroidery, rugs, leather floor pillows. And at the end, the clear light of Moristan Square. Silence. I play the tourist in Lancôme sunglasses. I need this walk now to cut the fear, the siege, as a way of drawing, in the heart of fear and siege, my plan for the aqueduct that may someday gush here.

My footsteps plod in the alley to the Church of the Holy Sepulcher. Once again I examine the proportions of the plaza, the optimal height for the pool of my planned fountain, the light and shade that will be cast by the rustling water on the paving stones. I move in thought, with your sketches, the alignment of domes, towers, crowded roofs. The roof of the Church of the Holy Sepulcher, above it the roof of the Greek church, above it the roof of the Ethiopian church, above it the bell tower of the Moristan, and even climbing to its top doesn't let go of the stone fist I'm trying to soften by Mount Sabbatical, in the Settlement of Huts.

Esplanade of the Temple Mount. Harm-a-Sharif. I stop in a corner. Collecting for you.

I'm drawn in ever-tightening circles to the heart of the place. The magnet of danger. Madness. Holiness. Can't silence the sense of sneaking into something close and forbidden. And the white, frozen light.

"Temple Mount holy mount," you write. "The esplanade is a splendor of Islamic architecture. It is found today on top of the Mount of Time." Attaching the schematic sketch you did, with cuts of strata: the abyss with the Foundation Stone, the Jebusite threshing floor, the first Temple, the mound and the arches of Herod's Temple, Iola Capitolina, Byzantium, the palaces of the Omayyias around the mosques, the Lord's temple, the Crusader "Templum Domine," and the synagogues in the Jewish Quarter. You stand here surrounded by Labor council tourists. Old-timers in cloth hats. Reading out the descriptions of the building, the lamentations of Destruction.

The paving stones gleam in the winter light. Black spots of cypresses on the white. And the avenues of arches open the gates to heaven.

To the east hangs a grove of pines, facing the Mount of Olives. The light grows hazy there around the trunks, and a path leads to the wall, winds down to the Gate of Mercy blocked by stones.

The morning silence. The slope of the Mount of Olives is seen from here. The flash of tombstones covering it. Gray, sparkling. "More than two thousand years a Jewish burial ground," you write. "Including those who want to bring their body from far away. To spare the torments of the metamorphosis of forgiving, and they are buried opposite the Gate of Mercy."

Some Arab women with children sit in the shade of a tree. Resting for a light meal. A plastic can is passed from hand to hand. A veiled woman raises the scarf a moment, hoists the can, and a transparent jet of water hastens to her full lips. A little boy puts his head in her lap. His fingers snag the fringes of the scarf swaying above him. The weight of the stone in my heels. Near Al Aqsa Mosque, heaps of stones. Dust. They're building or excavating something. (Now? In the middle of the war?) And yet, something is opening there, in this jumble of stones. Some breathing. In the stone surface.

Behind the building, a guard watches. I hadn't noticed him before.

"Go! Go! Not here," he yells angrily at me.

I retreat. How far down does the excavation go?

An unemployed guide clings to me. Amazed to discover a tourist in the heart of the empty place. Trudges a few steps. Finally gives up. Once again alone on the edge of the whiteness, near the shade of the cypresses.

The Western Wall. A collection of illustrations you bring. Sketches of the Temple, dimensions, vessels. And the engravings with Jews huddled in prayer in the alley next to the Western Wall.

I pass by the soldier dozing in the hut, on the dirt path connecting one holiness to another.

Fern and castor oil plant hanging on top, above the few worshippers. Tables with prayer books. Chairs. And the broken arm of Robinson Arch in the rib of the wall. Above the site of the archaeological excavations.

I sit on a low wall to continue the conversation with you. From the Western Wall, isolated voices.

The winter light bends west, sharpens.

Leaning the notebook on the cardboard box of the kit. Holding not holding. Snapshot. For you.

The deceptive closeness of your absence. Reading with bated breath your preparatory outlines for the pamphlet "Gehenom and Moriah in Jerusalem," with the subtitle with the Hasidic and messianic echo, "Descent for the Sake of Ascent." You're drawn down to Tophet, the place where Jerusalem was founded. You try to contrast the Moloch rituals on the blood-soaked slopes of Mount Moriah and the Binding of Isaac at its top. Trying to compose a believing, hesitant interpretation: "It was hard to uproot a primordial faith, steeped in terror and blood. Even from the heart of the Israelite, it was not easy to uproot, even when the Temple was built on its mound above that valley, where animal sacrifice and offerings of oil and flour were exchanged for human victims. Even when the waters of sin or the waters of the libation ceremonies from the Temple flowed to the Valley of Hinnom, when the blood of the sacrificed victims irrigated it, watering the plots of the Levites, even then the altars of Tophet went on smoking with human sacrifice. In the words of Jeremiah: 'For the children of Judah have done evil in my sight, saith the Lord: And they have built the high places of Tophet, which is in the Valley of the Son of Hinnom, to burn their sons and daughters in the fire; which I commanded them not, neither came it into my heart.' The kings themselves sacrificed their sons and daughters on the altars of Baal. Ahaz, Menashe. Only Isaiah broke the altars and scattered their ashes around here, in the Kidron River. Slowly, over hundreds of years, the custom of terror was uprooted from the heart. The lesson of the Binding of Isaac was stamped and learned. And here, the new history began: the shift from belief in gods of rage demanding human sacrifice, to belief in the ethical God. But the place has not yet achieved complete salvation. Ever since then, the slopes of the Valley of Hinnom have known blood and hatred. Crusader battles, Muslim slaughters. And today, too, we're far from peace and brotherhood. May He uproot hatred of man for his fellow man from the world. May He also ease the ancient grievance against the Jewish people and their children. Amen."

The end of the essay, the most personal one you wrote. In heart's blood. Shortly before David was killed. What was supposed to have been the crowning piece of "Places and Sources," your "Repair." And then you hide it all. Without a word. Just add the date on the last page. Without explanation. Just the rip. David's death broke something in you. I felt that when your arguments at the repeated attacks I brought from Paris grew weak. As if, soon after David was killed, we made a pact of silence, our common mourning. And even today, I didn't dare go through Dung Gate, continue on to the Valley of Hinnom, to the tunnel of Shiloah, to the source of the Gihon.

A piercing cold. The diminishing light reddens the stones of the Western Wall, kindles the crests of the cypresses in the square of the mosques dominating it. Here, the shade now laps.

The fingers are freezing. Hard to write, to hold on for you anymore, Father. Only the tops of the cypresses blush in the bluing shell of the evening basin.

To the car parked at Jaffa Gate is a fifteen-minute walk. I won't get to Allegra's before sundown. She'll certainly worry. David is with her or with Mr. Schleicher. (What he'll read in me when he lifts his eyes, questioning.)

[Purim. The war is over.]

The boys went down to Allegra, in their costumes. For the first time without dragging the DDC and the mask. The two of them wanted to dress up as cowboys. In black cardboard hats, studded belts, toy guns. I couldn't convince them to dress up without weapons. In fact, I gave up quickly.

On the news, the army spokesman announced that the "sealed room" could be dismantled. For two hours I sat at the sliding window in the living room and peeled off the ribbons of clear tape, like a monkey picking lice. Two hours of madness. Pulling off strips of tape, one by one. And then when it turned out that the adhesive all remained in an opaque film on the windowpane, I scratched at the glue, millimeter by millimeter, unable to let go. Taking out on the window of the rented apartment all the wrath over the impotence, the pretense of protection I had used to delude the boys. The official declaration of the end of the war. The politicians declare a "happy ending," a crushing, decisive, just victory. And the smoke from the refineries burning in the Gulf, the destroyed cities in Iraq, mushrooms of smoke from the explosion of chemical-weapons dumps, and the responses of the stock markets in New York, Tokyo. Last night, an interview with Bob Simon, the CBS reporter, who was released from Iraqi prison. His face covered with stubble, eyes darting. "The jailer opened his mouth wide at me, spit a gob of spit into my throat and cursed, 'Filthy Jew.'" And this morning, a TV reporter declares joyfully that life has returned to normal, "even here, in Tel Aviv!" Around him, a few children huddled for the camera with lost looks, made-up as clowns in yellow and red satin clothes. And once again the screen is covered with confetti and battalions returning from the Gulf.

I drew mustaches for the boys with eyebrow pencil before they went down to Allegra. There's softness between us now. We don't talk about what was. We talk only about Bobo, who "decided to dress up" with a hat and kerchief, or about David's last victory over Mr. Schleicher. And the words between us, Father.

At some point, I managed to bring out the CD Walkman with *Don Giovanni.* After so long. Pure gold. And the soprano pleading of Donna Elvira, trying to rescue Don Giovanni, to save his soul: "Change your life!" Still believing, even in the middle of the revels and the whips of mockery.

Da Ponte's irony about the passivity of the woman fighting for the man she desires. She only pleads, powerless. And even now, at the end of the war, the silence of the women. Here, in Baghdad. They leave no mark.

I should have contacted Kayyina. Not to look for Sayyid. Just to ask directly how she is and how are the children—beyond conventions. Beyond boundaries. Will I ever dare? Will she dare?

I haven't even seen a photo of her. Just the image of a woman in a long skirt, jacket, and hair gathered above a shaded look.

■ ■ ■ ■

[David is building in his room. He's calm now.]

Last night the announcement on the news of the "reopening of educational institutions with the end of the Gulf War." I didn't react. David raised his eyes and said, "I'm going." We were silent. Even when I prepared his backpack in the morning. Putting the sandwich in the front pocket, packing the cowboy costume in a plastic bag, "in case they decide to have a belated Purim party." We were silent, too, when we left Allegra's, leaving Jonathan there. And as we advanced in the dusty light along the housing projects, I, too, with my hand tight in David's hand, turned into a six-and-a-half-year-old girl on my way to school, and the pit of fear in my belly grew deeper. At the traffic signal where you can already see the building, we knew from the silence that we were late. From the empty yard, we passed to the gloomy corridors with the shouts of children behind closed doors. And in the hall to classroom First Grade 4, we came upon Teacher Hadassah. Hurrying with chest high, her rollbook waving in front of her, she passed by, not recognizing us.

"Hello," I said to her back.

She stopped, and after a moment she blinked, "Oh, David! . . . Come come come. We're starting immediately." And was off, mobilized to present herself to the children, without wasting time on the outsider who came here only for a short time.

We went on a few more steps, and we stopped. David's hand was sweaty. When my eyes met his blue look, I only hoped he didn't feel my own heart pounding.

"David, if you'd rather stay home today, that's all right," I whispered. "I'll call the office and tell them I'm not coming. We'll stay together."

He dropped his eyes, clenched his chin, his blue-and-green backpack trembling with the silent weeping that shook his shoulders.

On the way back, the light rested clear on the street and the trees, and a screen seemed to lift from the cars at the traffic signal. We stopped at Ben-Shoshan's to buy fresh rolls. And as soon as we got home, we sat down in the kitchen to devour them with chocolate spread. Swallowing the sweetness with the last bit of oppression.

Sound of pounding Legos.

In ten days, the Passover break will begin, and we'll pack up and go back to Paris.

■ ■ ■ ■

[Morning. In the apartment.]

I stayed to finish sorting your writings. Before we leave, I'll go back to Haifa to bring what's left there. Using the project, which will certainly start again soon, to justify the whim of keeping the rental apartment in the housing project in Jerusalem. And in fact planning to go on reading your writings when I come back here in late May.

And then, half an hour ago, Alain called from Paris.

The last conversation had been from Moscow. And at the end of it, the traces of his harsh voice, steeped in bitterness, remained in me.

The first moments were covered with alarm. His voice was also different. As if it were washed. He didn't wait for me to reply, and said quickly, ". . . Yesterday the cleaning woman was here. She prepared the boys' room. She straightened up everything . . . No, so far she hasn't come. Ever since I came back, I haven't been able to arrange with her . . . And I also left the mess, as you all left it," and he laughed (the first laugh I heard from Alain since autumn). "I felt all of you in the house like that, with the mess . . ."

"How do you feel . . . after the trip?" I asked at last, in a choked voice, to my complete amazement. The tears were unexpected, too. For so long they hadn't burst out from talking with Alain.

He was silent a moment. The beats of silence in the receiver. And something that was opened, climbing up into the throat. Something that had been buried a long time.

"I don't know. It's complicated."

I waited.

"Difficult material in the archives. Lists of mass graves . . . Takes a lot of strength to cope with that . . ." And then his voice hardened. "And also the name of my parents. And Leah . . ."

"Where?" I whispered.

"In Pichora."

"Did you go there?"

"No. I didn't have the courage, Lana . . ." He ended in his special way of chanting the *l* in my name.

We breathed together. As much as possible on the phone. Admitting our fatigue more than our yearnings.

"I'm expecting the boys on the date we set . . . The plans haven't changed, have they?" he finally said tensely, afraid of my response.

And then, casually, he asked softly,

"You're coming back with them, aren't you?" And all the anxiety and loneliness and bruised softness penetrated Alain's caution.

The trip is less than a week away.

And everything that has changed here, Father. Downtown, the people slowly pass by the display windows that haven't changed for weeks now. They burst out dizzily from months of dread, gazing at products as if they had forgotten the calming lust to buy. I look at them as intimates, those returning from exile in Eilat, from cheap hotel rooms in Europe.

And the texture of life in common in the neighborhood that got us through. The Ben-Harush family's lemon tree loaded with yellow, shading the kids who run around in the yard again. Nissim made it a habit to bring us rolls every single day on his way back from morning prayers, and on the Sabbath he fills the stairwell with the sweet trill of the chants. Mr. Lerner finally came back home, after a complicated catherization. "It was a long stay in the hospital," reported Mr. Schleicher, who himself looks exhausted lately. He runs around buying medicine for Gerda and worrying about his grandson, who's looking for a place to study the hotel business. "He speaks many languages, I worked with him," he explains to me bending over in the door, bringing David home from the daily chess game, which they've kept up even in peacetime. The Levy family returned to the limited group of Danny and Ido, without the support of the elite players of the neighborhood team. And Boris, the son-in-law of the Solomonayvitches, got work at a computer company on Mount Hozvim. He and Natalia started looking for an apartment, and the grandfather repeats proudly to anyone who will listen the sentence he memorized: "Boris work in Izrail: Good!" And once again, when I bring the pile of yogurt cups from the refrigerator to the counter, Ben-Shoshan makes sure I haven't forgotten the chocolate pudding "in a plastic cup!" that the boys love. He says that he was at the funeral of Mrs. Gillis, from the block opposite. "She had a heart attack. In the end. At the thirty-eighth missile, maybe. Rabbi Levy gave the eulogy. Called her the 'victim of the neighborhood.' She used to buy here, back in the time when my father ran the grocery." And with a warm smile he hands me the bill.

The spring light is already here, Father. And the almond blossoms at the foot of the site. The valley lapping the fields of Ramat Rachel between Arab-a-Sohra and Tsur Bahar, all crowned with a gilded white. Like every year, when the Carmel was covered all at once with the sweetness of blossoming, and you would point excitedly, "Look, Ilanka!"

■ ■ ■ ■

[Tantour. Enclave of Protestant culture in the outskirts of Bethlehem. A tourist cafeteria.]

Waiting for the representative of the Dag Hammarskjöld Fund, "To agree on what can be done before you go, Madame Tsuriel," as Jurgenson said on the phone from Sweden. He sends one of those blond good-willed angels fluttering on their missions among the natives.

The place is desolate. The locals still define the Middle East as "dangerous for tourists." Two plump German women run the snack bar and souvenir shop. They stared at me as I paid.

On the way to Tantour, I stopped at the garage in the industrial area to arrange to sell the Fiat. Smell of motor oil, black floors, cars hoisted on lifts. And the workers in blue overalls, Jews, Arabs. Maybe the only binational place that went on functioning throughout the war.

Ibrahim and Bassam approach, shake my hand.

"Hey, Ilana, what's new?"

Avi, the supervisor, waves to me from the distance. "So, how's the car?"

Ibrahim, Erella's faithful mechanic, concludes a brief inspection. "The carburetor needs cleaning, and the brakes need servicing."

"And what about the interior. A little neglected, isn't it?"

"Don't worry about the upholstery, we'll recover seats. There's an excellent upholsterer in Bethlehem, not expensive," Bassam promises.

I leave a set of keys with Ibrahim, arrange to meet at the post office bank to transfer ownership.

At the office, I pack up the worktable. Last look at the flat concrete roofs of the industrial buildings, the workshops, the trucks, and the smells of the pita bakery. Yaron fills the office with his presence. Walks around in a denim shirt open to the third button.

"So, Ilana, until UNESCO and Tunis open the Jerusalem file again, we won't see you?"

Ever since I refused to sleep with him, even when he returned from reserve duty, he hasn't missed a chance to tease me.

"Who knows?" I limit my response, making Erella swear not to tell Yaron that I decided to keep the apartment.

"Come on, look," he taps the sketch spread on his worktable. Straight lines of a long structure. Free drawing, the medium in which Yaron always excelled, and the sensitive line betraying his vulnerability under all the masks. "Look, two projects that just came, all at once. You should hear, you should know what's happening here. I mean, what's *really* happening, not the war games, with all the bullshit about sealed rooms and Patriots and a Greater Israel that's not worth a fuck, while you sit in the valley, a whole squad, and the missiles pass by over our heads . . . Here, look, a commission for a technology campus in Herzliya. On expensive land. Something big, high-tech, computers, the twenty-first century! You should remember, Lana, economic boom is the name of the game!" He goes on pounding on the sketches. "Our integration into the region is only a question of time. In a little while, we'll be getting orders to build shopping malls in Dubai and Kuwait. There'll be a different, new Middle East here . . . and that's the only way to ever make peace here, Lana . . . not with a selection of fundamentalist quotations from holy books, or dreams about Huts and Sabbatical . . ."

And the whole time Yaron is lecturing like that, waving his arms, in the depths of the office, Gil, who returned from reserve duty, goes on sketching. Looking at us, and bending over again. Silently strumming his movements on a different string.

> He's preparing with friends to construct the first twelve Huts at the site on Passover, adding to the project a "pilgrimage" from Sha'ar Hagai to Jerusalem. "Journey of internal meditation, of self-preparation." He raises his long-lashed dreamy look.

Last night, after we worked late, we went out to eat in a pub in the Russian Compound. A space full of cigarette smoke and bare-shouldered young people devouring life with a zeal sharpened by weeks of war.

"So tell a little about yourself."

"There's not much to tell . . ."

"Childhood, father and mother, grandfathers, grandmothers . . ." I listed in the tone of an interview.

Gil's sharp face on the other side of the table. Barely hearing, through the noise and loud music. "Well . . . so, childhood in Dimona. You already know that. Family from Morocco. Meknes and Rabat. All of them in Dimona. Those who got off the trucks at night and in the morning found themselves in the middle of the sand . . . Today we're the old-timers. Father manages a section of the department store, and Mother's a teacher in the district grammar school. She was very beautiful. One of those from the famous song 'Simona of Dimona' . . . Am I boring you?"

"No, no," and I shook my head with a smile Gil picked up.

"Well . . . So let me tell you where architecture really started for me. With my grandmother, Masoudi. At first, when Dimona was only sand and more sand, with lots of despair, she held them all together. That's how my family tells it. My grandfather, who didn't go to work for two years, and all their five children, with my father, the youngest of them all. In Rabat they left a two-story house with servants; and here . . . a desert. It all started because there was no cilantro, there was barely the parsley of the Ashkenazim. And so Grandmother decided to plant cilantro in front of their windows, and from that came the most amazing garden you can imagine. When you come to Housing Project 5, where the road rises to the dune, you see in the distance the purple of my grandmother's passion flowers, covering the whole block . . . When I was a little boy, I'd help her in the garden, pulling up weeds, watering—that was my first experience in landscaping . . ."

We laugh together, gulping the vodka we ordered with the salad. And Gil ducks his head, embarrassed at the candor.

"In high school, in ORT, technical drawing came easy, but I had nothing but contempt for that. I'd go out to the hills all around and draw. Drawing wasn't exactly my parents' dream for me, and it didn't make me any friends, either." He fell silent, seeking words.

"After high school, I had to prove myself, you understand? Three times, I took the exams to raise my army scores. Until they took me into the elite Golani Brigade . . . You really want to hear all this?"

"Yes, Gil, I want to hear everything about you."

He raised a quick look, which he erased with a toss of his head, rocking back in his chair, and then he leaned his face on his hands, examining me with a question, and the quick whisper burst out from under his lowered eyelashes—

"How to explain what happens to you at nineteen, when you come back from a night of duty in Lebanon, encounters with terrorists, and your friend doesn't come back with you? Died in your arms. How to describe the darkness that hangs over you afterward? A choking smell that doesn't leave your breath. All that confusion. Ever since Gabi was killed, yes, his name was Gabi, Gabi Horn . . . I'm not the same person since."

He stares at the glass of vodka clasped in his hands, grips it.

"And then, the Intifada exploded, they took us out of Lebanon and sent us straight to Nablus in the hardest time, at the beginning, with all the surprise, and all the anger of the system caught with its pants down, and the orders to go in with force. You know, the period of Rabin, with 'break their arms and legs,' and all that . . . After three weeks in the Nablus sector, they took my unit down to Gaza. A gift for the end of service, ten months in the Jeballiyya refugee camp."

He clenched his jaw, his eyes fixed on the glass of vodka.

"What haunts me from this is this one thing—a nothing, an incident. Probably not recorded anywhere. Just a day at the entrance to Jeballiyya. The order was to watch for anybody who tried to smuggle weapons. And every morning it was the same thing. Searching all the men who went to work . . . Finally, they arrested somebody. An old guy, maybe fifty. They found a knife on him. A simple kitchen knife. But our commander made a big deal of that. They tied him up, with his hands behind him, put a bag over his head, and interrogated him. He said he had nine children, and that it was just a table knife. He repeated over and over that he had nine children. This old man, and they left him there at the fence, tied up with the sack over his head. In the sun. From six in the morning. At two or three they came back to him. The commander decided to have a little 'fun.' He took a pipe and poked him in the back. 'You've got a rifle in your back,' he told him. 'And you've got two choices. Either confess or we'll kill you on the spot.' And they kicked him so he'd understand. The man simply became hysterical. His whole body started shaking. Crying in Arabic, which nobody understood, and shaking. And the commander wouldn't take the pipe out of his back, and the translator keeps repeating to him, 'Confess or we'll kill you.' In the end, they put him in prison for a month. But I fell apart there. I stood at the fence and vomited up my soul." He averted his face, his head borne on his thin neck, the jaw line moving intensely. "Afterward it just dragged on and on. In the end they lowered my score, and until I was discharged they stuck me in the administrative unit of the brigade. It took me a year of traveling in the East to get away from that . . ."

His eyes held me a moment, then drifted again into the distance. "It was in Nepal that I calmed down. In weeks of silence in a monastery above Katmandu. And then in treks. With a few others. That was where I started drawing again. What had almost completely died inside me . . . I didn't have to hide it anymore. You could just walk in the mountains and be . . . I'd go down to Katmandu only to buy more paper and pencils. And when I came home, without asking anybody I enrolled in the new architecture department. Well, and then, you know . . . school, internship with Yaron Matus. And then you . . . the Huts, Mount Sabbatical, and the war, and all the madness pouring in again . . ."

He goes on rocking, listening to something inside him, until finally he shakes his head, which was caught in the smoke of the spotlights.

"You feel like moving a little? Come on, Lana, come on, let's dance."

"Not now, Gil. It's all right. Go, dance," I whispered. Watching him turn slowly in the denim overalls, his eyes shut, moving in the small group of dancers on the platform of the pub, as if he were still listening to something, and his sharp jaw supporting his spread lips, like a pomegranate blossom.

When he returned, his look had cleared. Smiling slowly, putting his hand on the table, next to mine, which opened to interlace my fingers with his. In a silence that thickened immediately. We got up without a word and left the glass door of the pub ringing as it slammed behind us. Going out into the starry night sky above the Russian church on the way to the car, and the lights going on behind the treetops—from Mea' She'arim, Mount Scopus, the Mount of Olives. And the silence that continued in the car when I didn't start the motor right away. And the sounds of musicians, of Hasids singing in the night in the distance. And the piney smell of Gil's sweat.

"We should get some sleep now, Gil," I whispered at last. "I'll take you home."

I drove dizzily up to the entrance of his alley in Nahlaot. The streetlamp lit the stone ledge, a cat running on top of it.

"You should get some sleep now," I whispered again, as if all the other words were forgotten. And then driving through the empty night streets back to Hebron Road, the echo in my temples. Through the gushing, the trembling. That I'd now have to teach Gil the wisdom of surrender, of letting go. The constant sprouting that changes forms, like the planning of one Hut after another. To reveal to him the secret of this feminine place. And the tremor that went up the line of his cheek under the streetlamp when he turned around and waved goodbye before he was swallowed up by the alley.

In the apartment, Smadi extracted her dozing body from the sofa. Said that only Erella had called. "She said it wasn't urgent, that you'll talk tomorrow in the office. And the boys were awesome!" I looked at her slender body, her straight black hair, as she collected her books and notebooks with a sleepy step, leaving behind a breeze of beauty, and as she disappears in the staircase. And all the time, the murmur of the heart is still, and the distant weeping. Sprouting. As always when love touches me, with the farewell written from the start. The last one, from you, more than a year ago. "Only what you love can you let go of, Ilanka." It's after one in the morning and I'm opening your small notebook. Leafing through the first pages. David's name leaps to the eye immediately. I close it before I find out which David you mean.

Another four days, then back to Paris. The day after tomorrow I'll go to Haifa, for the last time.

The view opens to the east above Herodion, as far as the abyss at the bottom of the desert. In the pale light already a breeze of spring. Heralding the thick smells of sage, of sticky elecampane, and the rustle of thorns when summer assaults.

A blond man in a black suit and carrying a James Bond attaché approaches on the path to the cafeteria. Now each of us will play his part.

■ ■ ■ ■

The phone call from Sayyid. A few minutes ago. (Now, after everything.)

His voice, over street noises, passing cars.

"Lana? . . ."

"Where are you? . . ."

"In Jerusalem . . ." he laughed tensely. "I just got here. I said I was going down to buy cigarettes and I went out to call."

"Sayyid . . ." I uttered wearily. ". . . Sayyid."

"So what's up?" his voice rang.

I was silent.

"Say, when do I see you?"

"We're leaving the day after tomorrow," I whispered.

"Tonight I'm with the family. And I've got things to do in the morning. So . . . tomorrow evening?"

Paralyzed, I agreed on a time and place where I'd come by in the car to pick him up. Silent even when he went on and whispered quickly.

"I'm holding you, all of you, Lana . . . I'm kissing your body for all those months, Lana . . ."

He laughs, drunk, through the hoarseness of the phone line. And the lights interlacing in the window. Points of lights of Beit Tsafafa, a necklace of streetlamps of Gilo along the line of the ridge.

> And the whole time, I calculated the hours until our flight in two days. With packing, going to David's school to say goodbye with him, as I promised, and the children's party for Jonathan at Allegra's on the morning before the flight. Knowing that tomorrow I'd give up the trip to Haifa, the hours I planned to be in your study. And immediately a hot salvo of shame down to the roots of my hair, as if tomorrow evening, I wouldn't meet Sayyid, but you.

And the syllables of farewell in a long breath, like a sob.

"So we'll see each other tomorrow."

"Yes, tomorrow . . ."

Leaning my forehead on the cold windowpane, the receiver still hanging in my hand after the last words. And the busy signal like an all-clear siren, until I hung up the phone. And the silence sawing even after the second vodka. Wandering between the four walls of the small living room, finally taking our notebook out of the handbag. Gazing at its pages open to the night. And again, as from the beginning, the betrayal, and the lack of choice, in the name of some loyalty I'm not sure I succeeded in explaining to you during all the months of conversation on the other side of your death.

The rustle of the cars on Hebron Road.
The boys' breathing. Sleeping on the other side of the corridor.

■ ■ ■ ■

[Once again, open suitcases. How many times this year?]

Jonathan insisted on taking Bobo, which ultimately also turned into a SCUD launcher, with him. "Bobo patwiot boom!"

"I take Bobo, I take Bobo," he burst into tears when I tried to hide the stick, and kept pushing it, with all its dust, between the clothes in the suitcase, whining, "Bobo go too, Bobo go too . . ."

Until I gave in and wrapped the stick in two plastic bags, one on each end, cramming it to the back of the suitcase.

David spent an intense afternoon packing, again and again checking the drawers, the closet, the hiding places of the caves under the bed. It may have taken him an hour to dismantle the Lego airfields, to arrange the parts in boxes. His eyes were wide with tension, he raised his clear look to me, until finally he asked:

"Will Daddy meet us at the airport?"

He didn't wait for an answer, immediately defending himself by searching for his sports shoes and socks, lying prone under the bed and yelling: "I want them to be close to me, the socks, too. Everything should be ready!"

Stuffing his backpack with coloring books, games, and all the candy he had accumulated from gifts, restraining himself until the trip, guarding them jealously from the rummaging of Jonathan's sweet tooth, counting them one by one again, and closing them again in the pockets of the backpack, as if the flight was going to take two weeks and not a few hours.

> And only there, looking at David's immigrant's pack, did I get some distance, smiling to myself at the little wanderer I had raised, Father. A second generation? A third? A tenth?

And then I put the boys to bed for the last time before we fly away from here. I tucked them in, in the room with the flecks of light on the ceiling.

> *Smadi will come up soon. And I'll go out. I told her only that I'd be back late. I'll take our notebook with me.*

■ ■ ■ ■

[Back in the apartment. Smadi has left.]

(The need to report to you.)

The hours with Sayyid. In between. "I can't get back late," one of the first sentences he said. "Slima has a fever, and Kayyina, after all that's happened . . ."

I stopped across from the Khan Theater. Across the street I see Sayyid talking with one of the people from the theater company. Standing in the shade of the lighted mulberry tree of the Turkish inn, which had also turned into a stage set for our drama. He's leaving with a laugh, with taps on the shoulder, and stops in the arch at the entrance. Squinting, not recognizing me at first in the parked car.

I start the motor immediately. Not knowing where we're going. Just shifting gears with a trembling hand, and Sayyid's hand is already on me.

"Got an idea for a place?"

"I hadn't thought."

"Then, come on, let's drive a little . . ."

The hallucinatory driving from one side of Jerusalem to the other. The night before we leave. Outlining a secret map with the turns of the steering wheel, in a last attempt to explain something to Sayyid. Yet what stood between us throughout the drive remained unsaid. Growing. Dissolving only in talking with you, now.

Turning the Fiat onto roads that go deep into the west, in the chill of fields and the rustle of dark in the groves of Ein Karem. Stopping on a dirt path leading down to the valley. And there, stripping in a rush. Back, chest. Armpit panting between the folds of the shirt. Pressed in the small car, and the windows covering with vapor. Headlights of a car approaching on the slope. I start the motor with melted legs, wide open on the accelerator. Driving with clothes unbuttoned through the city spread out to the night, and Sayyid's hand traveling between my thighs. Crossing the broad streets, neighborhoods dimly lighted, since the war, the withdrawn looks we get at traffic signals. Going deep into old alleys, the sounds of Jews in caftans and black hats, unwitting wedding attendants, hastily scattered in the dark. Finally turning onto the road up to the site. Clutching the steering wheel so as not to lose control. The UN camp, the governor's palace, the top of the Hill of Evil Counsel. Plots of dark, lighted windows of the buildings of East Talpiot. Rows of streetlamps in Arab-a-Sohra. The mosque. As if spreading out one after another the dozens of maps, in various scales, that I sketched, with Sayyid's hand strumming the wind in the slopes of dark, the stubble, the thorns, rolling down from their place, the rocky ground on the open slopes, fold after fold.

Only then did I take a road I hadn't dared enter all those weeks. One turn of the steering wheel, then the steep descent to the Valley of Hinnom. Steering the little car between the rocks on the narrow dirt road, down to the bottom of the Kidron River, olive trees, the crevice of the valley that goes down to the spring of Gihon. The tunnel of Shiloah, the pool, the sweet, moldy smell. Pressing the accelerator, my lips clenched, as Sayyid draws with devouring gulps the gushing evoked in me again, outraged. Flowing forth in a thick, deep flow while driving. And then your voice burst in me, singing from a distance, leading the way to what will always remain hidden to Sayyid, the wayfarer who accompanies us, Father. And in the dark, for a moment, the little group was revealed, Aunt Rachel and Mother and Uncle Yehiel, standing around you and listening. And the rumble of the car shattering the silence to the top of the steep road, in a course in which the waters of the aqueduct will stab the heart of the mountain, will stream its pure waters into the maze of the temples, between the alleys. And only my and Sayyid's heavy breathing pours down on the road around the walls. And from the east, the ridge, covered with tombstones, turns white. And there, bowed, your short grandfather, pressed between the mourners of Zion weeping over the destruction of Jerusalem, their voice swallowed behind the churches of Gethsemane, on the road that splits the Jewish cemetery in two, climbing to the turret of the mosque, scaling with the prow of the car the summit of the Mount of Olives.

Navigating on the path to the dark gateway of an ancient grove, and the lights of the city spread in a wall of spires, mosques, church towers, in the gleam of the spotlight on the golden dome. Only then did I turn off the motor again, in the stormy rustle of the wind in the crests of the pines. The seat moved with the rage of limbs, the hasty sucking, a hand clutching the ceiling, a leg between the pedals, subsiding breaths. Silencing in the dark all the places we had been. The stories. The words. The dreams. Your voice going away then, leaving me in Sayyid's arms, in the smell of cigarettes and sweat. But the foreignness didn't dissolve from his sunken cheeks then, either, from his open look, from the bitter, unfamiliar cologne he had slathered on himself. And afterward, the hand rising to turn on the motor, navigating slowly through the dark and the tombstones to the shuttered cafés in the streets of A-Tur, in the extinguished gold shadows of the Russian church, and the throbs of the messiah growing distant.

I drove then on the dark dirt road at the top of the Mount of Olives, facing the desert and the Dead Sea. "Look, Lana, our project is hard for me now." I didn't really hear what Sayyid was saying. "There were always differences of opinion within the troupe. You knew that. And in Tunis, at the headquarters that 'artistic collaboration' was first accepted as a tactic for the Swedish, but now . . ." He spoke as if to a little girl who needs to have things explained to her. "We're working now in the troupe on the right of return. A story about somebody born in a refugee camp in Lebanon, and after he escaped from the massacre of Sabra and Shatila, he infiltrates the Galilee disguised as an Israeli soldier. He gets to what is left of his family's old village. A few prickly pear bushes next to the houses of the Jewish village. And an abandoned, desecrated mosque. The Israeli secret service catches him there. They kill him on the spot, even without arrest . . . What do you think, eh?"

The snarl of the Fiat's motor went across the summit, in the white of the waning moon of late Adar, when I finally spoke. "I did here everything that I was able to do with Anton and Samir," I said to myself more than to Sayyid. "The plans are more or less finished."

I stopped at the corner of Suleiman the Magnificent and Salah-a-Din. And even then the cologne formed a screen of foreignness, like a border clearly marked. Still, setting up another brief meeting for tomorrow, before our flight, if only out of a sense of oppression, of fear of admitting. Sayyid slammed the car door behind him. A single snack bar lined with bottles of Pepsi-Cola was still lighted. He passed by it, didn't turn his face toward my hinted wave. In the mirror I see him straighten his belt as he walks. Going off with his supple, swaying buttocks. And the mirror is already cut off as the traffic signal changes, dashing to the road around the walls.

I'll continue packing now until dawn. Once again I'll fasten in the suitcases everything that was opened here for a few weeks.

■ ■ ■ ■

[Airport. After everything.]

Departure lounge. Sunset floods the planes, the navigation flags, acres of citrus groves in the distance.

After everything. Parting from Allegra, final kisses. She gives the boys party bags of candy, for David the honeyed peanuts he loves, and bubble gum for

Jonathan. "Bon voyage!" she waves to us through the window of Yaron's car. For he did insist on taking us. "Thanks for everything, Yaron," I still manage to say, and he nods with his jaw clenched. The boys are packed between the bags in the back, with Bobo, which Jonathan insisted on taking out of the suitcase at the last minute. He clutches it on the trip, drags it through the airport lounges, between the luggage carts, the bundles, passport control, and the American woman who scolded him when he almost tore her nylon stockings.

The last moments here, Father. This morning, after I took David to say goodbye to his class, we hurried back to Jonathan's "bon voyage party" at Allegra's. He sits beaming with a wreath of greenery and flowers in his curls. And then the phone calls. From Erella, and I convince her that she doesn't have to come to the airport, too; and from Gil telling excitedly about the progress of the plan. "If not at Passover, try to come at Shavuoth. The gang is dying to meet you." Another hasty conversation with Ella, Uncle Yehiel, and his drawled pronunciation, "Ilanka." And Mr. Schleicher, who knocked on the door with two gift-wrapped chocolate bars, "One for the curly-haired little boy, and one for the chess player!" And then I told David I had to go someplace. "I'll watch the suitcases," he declared as I went off. He stayed in front of the TV screen with the children's announcer with the yellow wig and cherry mouth.

I waited for Sayyid in the garden café of the Jerusalem Hotel. The only foreigner among all the Arabs. Businesspeople, two women in white kerchiefs, and waiters, who filled my water glass twice before Sayyid appeared, half an hour late, splendid in the leather jacket and white silk scarf, swaying his loins before my eyes, which didn't move from his eyes.

He had time to smoke five cigarettes. The butts placed in the glass ashtray. We were silent most of the time. Exchanging a few words, lip service to politeness, leaving a black sediment in the coffee cups. And only our knees touching. Sayyid's fingers brought the jet of smoke from his lips close and pushed it away, my fingers rolled the hem of the tablecloth. I etched in my eyes his carved face, the long lines next to his cheeks, the lips clenched around the cigarette. At five to one, twenty minutes late, I almost ran out, knowing we had skipped our parting ceremony, the scheduling: "Where and when will our paths cross again?"

At home, Allegra was sitting with the boys for the last lunch. And my guilt at being late for the meal Mother was now serving, and you also raise your eyes to me in a question, just as David examined me as I went to the bathroom to wash my face. And Sayyid's look, shadowed by fatigue, when we parted.

The bustle in the interim air of the waiting room. And in the windows, the flush of sunset inflames the edges of the clouds.

And I didn't visit your grave on the anniversary of your death, and I didn't go back to the apartment in Haifa. All that was postponed to the last minute, and was finally abandoned.

David returns from his tour. He walks around the hand luggage, the chairs loaded with winter coats. He sees me writing quickly in the little notebook. Perhaps tries to investigate what's going on with me.

Jonathan runs up with Bobo. Amazingly nobody has yet taken the dusty stick away from him. He stops, too, raises his laughing face to me.

I smile at them. "No, they haven't called us yet."

And shame suddenly flooding. Shame, Father. Guilt. As at every parting from you, with the last phone call from the airport. And the meaningless panic at the last minutes in Hebrew, before the plane leaves the shoreline.

The flight to Paris is announced. I'll call the boys.

For a moment, still trying to figure out the melody echoing inside me. Not one of your songs, and not *Don Giovanni.* Maybe another song by Simon and Garfunkel, or maybe the elegiac voice of Leonard Cohen, echoing Yiddish as he strums the beat, "Hallelujah . . ."

Paris

[Morning. In Paris.]

I left the notebook of snapshots next to the bed. The only item I unpacked.

The dark bedroom.

Alain's breathing on the other side of the bed.

And you're in the dream. Standing at the bed in the room overlooking the dark bend in the river. Maybe in Paris, maybe somewhere else, with shadows of strange furniture. I lie without moving. So you won't know I'm awake. And also so that whoever is lying next to me won't notice that you're standing there. And only, in silence, drinking in the sight of you close by, taking the blanket off me, running your eyes over my naked body. And then, carefully, lying down next to me, as in the photo on the rock. Your skin, cold as marble, hovering over my skin. Without movement. Body along body. Enormous excitement. I woke up in the dark of the bedroom in Paris. The curtains are pulled down. Alain's breathing, curled up with his back to me.

Landing yesterday over the darkening river, light of a slow sunset, low, on plains of combed avenues of poplars. Europe. Parading with the boys in the glass corridors, passenger lounges, smells of espresso, the clink of coins, the perfumes. Movement of suitcases on the baggage carousel, the hushed rustle of people waiting. And Alain with the two boys. Bending down to them, surrounded by their jumpy prattle. Thinner than I recalled, in a tweed jacket, a lock of hair dropping on his forehead. Picking up the suitcases, adjusting the backpacks, and pushing the loaded carts, and the boys on either side of him. Only then does he stop, lifts his eyes to me, looks, and pallor draws his sunken cheeks.

"Come on home with the boys now, Lana, you'll see afterward . . ."

"Home . . ." The expression goes on resounding, cut off from all connection, alone, in the second cab loaded with baggage, following the cab with the boys and Alain. "Home . . ." At the structures bursting out of the dark beside the roadway, the overhead bridges, signs for shopping centers, factories, small towns. And on the intercom the voice of the cab dispatcher warns of a traffic jam at the entrance to the Périphérique, "Élysée, Élysée. Trente-six, Clichy, Clichy. Quarante-quatre, République, République . . ." "Home?" The dark street, the marble and glass entrance, the fluffy carpet in the staircase, in the elevator. And the unrecognizably neat apartment. With all the details of life I designed so carefully. The living room with the glass wall to the bend of the Seine and the lights of the distant hills, the boys' rooms, the bathrooms, the kitchen. Only in Alain's study is paper strewn about, the only room he goes into, no doubt sleeps on the sofa there. And in the bathroom, flushing the toilet with a strange, old movement. "Home?" Alain gives the boys hot chocolate with a buttered baguette. And French rings out between them again in the different tones of voice, the twists of the mouth, the gestures. They get into beds in their separate rooms, and Alain and I go tell them goodnight one after the other. Again. Anew.

And the weariness that descended on me at the heap of suitcases. I opened only the one with the boys' pajamas, and the few clothes that poured out I folded and put in the empty closet. And then Alain's hand on my shoulder.

"Come on, Lana. Let's go to sleep now."

At the mirror in the splendid bathroom, through the heaviness and the distance, I surveyed the strange landscape of my face. And then Alain came in.

"Sorry," he withdrew.

"That's all right. I'm done," I said, leaving him the sink.

And in the bedroom, when I took off my clothes, he sat down to undress with his back to me.

"Anything new in the plan of your site?"

"Yes," I answered after a silence. "There are basic developments . . ."

Startled to rediscover how connected Alain is to my dreams of building, he moves me in his own way.

And before turning out the light, I made an effort to indicate the time that gaped.

"Do you have the children's diaries . . . what you told me about? . . ."

"No," he whispered, gazing a moment. "No, that went to Yad Vashem . . . I can ask for a copy . . ." He brushes aside that lock of hair.

And the groping. Like going down old paths. Fringe of hair, interlacing of knee and calf, shoulder, back, turning over clasped beyond the hovering bubble of the flight, a body still hurling, before landing, on the nocturnal slopes on the edge of the desert. The weeds, the chill. And the separation at the end. And smells of wood and wool of the bedroom, the breath, the phlegm. And dull heartbeats, as if something very dim has shifted, filling the dark. And then, all at once, the dive, like a bucket cut off from the mouth of a well, to the depths of sleep. And the dream, and at the end the waves that rose around the bed. Very close to us. Lapping the glass door opening onto the banks of a white cliff. Tongues of water, slivers of dark.

Rustle of the pen in the hushed room. Alain's back to me.

■ ■ ■ ■

[Night. Alone with the boys in the apartment.]

Alain went to Zurich for three days. With American lawyers, to investigate dormant Swiss bank accounts of Holocaust victims.

Meanwhile at home. With the excuse that this is how I'll help the boys find their balance. Waiting for confirmation from Jurgenson on the renewal of the plans in Jerusalem before I talk with Alain.

On the weekend, I went with him and the boys to the Seine. Sitting on a bench, looking at them. The boys running, Alain with his jacket off, waving to say something. And a flow of yellowish light flickering between the buds of foliage, between the bushes dotted with buttons of flowering. The three of them bending down, maybe over some beetle. Alain folded between the poles of David's body and the flecks of light of Jonathan's curls. Looking at them with a weary body, from afar.

I also parted from our snapshots, the umbilical cord of the conversation. I'll let you rest at last on the slope of the Carmel. Under the dust of receding time.

Jostling you for the last time back in my bewildered return. The ears detach slowly from the whistle of a siren. Get used to the Parisian rustle. And yet, the wild heart pounding when an ambulance passes by in the street or a truck backfires. The crack in the diving bell into fear isn't yet mended. The cormorants still toddle in black oil.

And the knowledge, Father, that this time, too, the mother of all wars has won. With all the lies told in her name. The news they converted into "the reality of a live broadcast," though it was nothing but a made-up story. Pictures of death on the floor of the cutting room. "The death was off camera, so it wouldn't sway public opinion." Censored are the sights of destroyed cities, heaps of corpses of Iraqi soldiers. And it's still forbidden to report on the thousands of American soldiers who were wounded by "a not-yet-discernible factor," and flown, hidden from the media, to a base in Europe. And those who come out of the shelters in Iraq bury their dead in the shadow of poison clouds and giant pictures of Saddam Hussein.

The mother of all wars has won again, Father, with cheers and counting the profits from sophisticated instruments of war, that easily hit the "natives." And Bush, his face aglow, said on television last night, that American forces have once again been victorious, that America has proved itself the unequaled military power in the world. Number one, and don't you forget it. Already the cynical abandonment of the rebels in Kurdistan, day after day news of thousands fleeing Iraqi forces, huddling in tent camps in the snow. And evacuees from apartments destroyed by SCUDs have not yet been moved from the cheap hotels. Waves of refugees continue to rise even at the end of our torn century, Father. They join the millions who wandered from one end of it to the other, rotting with a few blankets, wrinkled clothes, pacifiers, dolls.

> And knowing (nauseating, as during the time of the alarms) that if our place, "there," is wiped out from the shelling of a chemical or biological warhead, after a few days of exciting horrific sights on television, everything here will go on as usual, without a break.

Trail of fatigue ever since coming back. Walking around like a raw nerve-ending between the bakery and the grocery, under the bridge of the elevated Métro. Amazed at the "Bonjour, Madame" of the newspaper vendor, or the greengrocer, who added "How are the sweet little boys?"—I hadn't imagined I'd become part of their texture . . .

Hard to concentrate in the office. Sorting the mail that's piled up. Still postponing the projects that have been awaiting my return, the bid for the European Parliament in Strasbourg, the residential quarter in Toulouse, the final plans for the experimental village in Senegal. Yesterday I went with Colette to Créteil. A street gang set fire to garbage bins across from where the "Green House" is about to go up. It took three hours for the fire engines to come. Meanwhile the fire spread to the nearby housing projects. Hundreds lost all their property in minutes. Colette said that the evacuees, most of them African immigrants, stood there all night watching the flames.

I manage to work only on the materials I brought from Jerusalem. To summarize them for the opening lecture at the association convention, which Claude organized in Munich. He wants me to talk about Sabbatical, with all its implications, political and architectural. "This is the moment, Lana . . . Send me copies of the final sketches from Jerusalem . . ." He calls the office every day at three, "The members of the association are confused, don't know what line to take. On the one hand, euphoria at the fall of the Eastern bloc, a new united Europe, America drunk on prosperity. And on the other hand, the ebullience in the Arab world, the battles in Africa, and recently worrisome news from Yugoslavia . . . This is the moment to present your breakthrough, Lana, the plan for a Settlement of Huts and Mount Sabbatical in the eye of the conflict . . . Hey, you can title your lecture 'Architecture in a Sealed Room' . . ." We laughed. He holds me with his anxious joy, his potato accent. The contact with Sayyid had sunk under the skin. Like a distant echo. We haven't talked since I've returned. He hasn't called and I haven't gotten in touch, either. Not with the studio in Amsterdam, not with Gilgamesh, and not, with some bureaucratic excuse, with the offices of the France-Palestine Alliance. Yesterday, I saw in the program that Alonzo will also participate in the association conference in Munich. Wonder if he's in touch with Sayyid, if he'll report to him on my lecture.

And through the shadows of the chestnut trees budding on the boulevards, yearnings for the light that floods the apartment on Hebron Road in the morning. The voices of Allegra, Nissim, Smadi. The children of the day-care center gathering in the garden behind the building. Danny and Ido going to school, bouncing the soccer ball between them. Mr. Lerner not going back to work for now, he has to rest. Mr. Schleicher reporting for voluntary guard duty at the hospital. The three generations of the Solomonayvitch family beginning to scatter. And Gil staying in touch with Anton, reporting on the first pilgrimage.

> The Huts to be erected among the rubble on the ridge. And the voices around the bonfire at night, a moon flooding the folds of the desert with its glow. And strumming the guitar, the oud.

This evening, without Alain, the intimacy between me and the boys was renewed. I was reading them "The Blue Jay," a story they love, when David suddenly cut in, "Mommy, tell the stories about Grandfather," saying aloud just what was going through my head.

"What to tell?"

"Go on from where you stopped."

"What, where?"

"You don't remember? The gutters, near the houses!"

"Oh, right. So Grandpa was a curious child, as you already know," I started. "And when he and Aunt Rachel would walk hand in hand from the house to visit their grandfather and grandmother, it didn't matter how much Aunt Rachel prodded him, he'd stop again and again and pick up everything he saw on the way. Snails, pieces of stone, coins swept by the rain to the gutter beside the highway . . ."

"And nails, and nails!" cried Jonathan.

"Yes, and nails. And Aunt Rachel would pull him, 'Come on, Aharonchik, come on already, Grandfather and Grandmother are waiting for us.' But he said: 'No, look at this thing sparkling there, that must me a real gold coin.' And he was already going down to the gutter. And even if he came back only with a copper coin, or a piece of broken glass that could reflect the sun and shine like drops of gold, he was happy, and thrust everything into his pockets."

David said that a piece of broken glass really does catch the sun, and Jonathan was already pestering that they had to try that. And then I stopped telling. Because there, your face would always cloud over. And after a long silence, you'd add in another voice, "From '39 on, it became harder and harder to get information. A letter took a few months. With all the seals of the censor . . . The last letter came in '41 . . ." And your silence then. Out of a feeling of guilt, that also passed to me. Otherwise, how come it didn't occur to me to send Alain the names of the family, to ask him to try to find them in the archives in the Ukraine?

I'll also let go of your notebook of snapshots now. As if to end a year of saying Kaddish. And bless and praise and glorify and exalt. Rest in your resting place in peace, Father.

I'll keep the sights together with you. May they flood my eyes.

■ ■ ■ ■

[Café. Sitting to calm down.]

I have to resurrect you . . .

I bought a pregnancy exam kit in the pharmacy next door. I did it in the bathroom of the café. I was afraid to return home, to run into Catherine or the boys coming out of the bathroom.

The test was positive.

Positive . . .

I knew from the beginning. Even before my period was late. Allowing myself to be with Sayyid, and with Alain, even though I had stopped taking the pill sometime in the middle of the war.

I'm pregnant, Father . . . there's nobody to laugh with, as you would say. Pregnant. Now . . . you've got a new grandson in my belly. You, a blue-eyed grandfather . . .

(I don't know what I'm writing. The hand moves over the page by itself.)

Ten minutes later. The body heavy in the chair.

Only here and now.

At the next table is a couple. Whispering together.

Heart pounding. And yet, some calm. Confidence.

"And proclaim liberty throughout all the land unto all the inhabitants thereof; and ye shall return every man unto his possession, and ye shall return every man unto his family . . ." The verses of Sabbatical echo in the head . . .

The bitterness of the espresso. Gathered into a sediment of reality.

■ ■ ■ ■

[Roadside restaurant on the exit from Strasbourg.]

After one a.m. Another four hours of driving to Munich. On the way.

A group of truck drivers. Eating sauerkraut. A heavy smell of sausage, pickled cabbage.

Behind the glass wall, the night grows dark.

The compulsion to drive from Paris to Munich, instead of taking the train. I need these hours alone on the road to feel Europe in my body, before the lecture tomorrow evening. I left late, until the last minutes arranging slides, and the final drawings, some of them Gil's. And wrinkles of waves flickered in the sunset. Finally I took whole files of material. I'll finish sorting it in the room Claude reserved for me at the Hotel Palatz, after he made sure it had a big table.

The life twitching inside me, Father. Yesterday an ultrasound. The technician's hand slides the instrument over the layer of cold gel on my belly. On the monitor a millimeter of tissue with a throbbing vein. The life that for the time being I've whispered only to you.

Carrying with me again, for a while, your snapshots.

In Munich, I'll tell Claude, the first one. When he comes, as we agreed, with a breakfast tray, so I can sleep late. He'll pass his hand over my belly, love the fetus in advance, perfume it with smells of Gauloises.

Before the trip, I left a message on the answering machine in Sayyid's studio in Amsterdam. I asked him to get in touch.

And something has changed between me and Alain. Maybe he felt. He carefully suggested, twice, that maybe, nevertheless, I should take the train, "the infamous European means of transportation." He stood in the corridor as I came out of the boys' room, telling them goodnight before I left.

Another three drivers come into the restaurant. Laughing, talking in loud voices.

They pass by, too, with trays loaded with pickled cabbage and sausage.

They bring the expanse of the road in with them.

Slowly, strength returns to me. After hours of driving, and the traffic jams leaving Paris.

It's lucky I remembered at the last minute to take the old CD of Don Giovanni. *Measuring the distance between the cities by the arias.*

While driving, I spread the presentation out in my head. Hoping it won't be "built," either, but will exemplify in its moves a model of temporariness. An open-ended lecture, striking a different chord in each of the listeners. (I can't help giving you a whole lecture while driving. In the end, I'll read the words from your snapshots . . .) I'll start by talking about the holy place that is never whole, incomplete by definition, as Solomon says at the moment of inaugurating the Temple: "behold the heaven and heaven of heavens cannot contain thee; how much less this house that I have builded?" And then I'll mention the other open holy forms: the tabernacle, the Sabbatical, the Sabbath. If I can, I'll linger a moment on the idea of the Sabbath and will emphasize how, even in the formulation of the sanctification of the wine, the blessing is for the ability *not* to complete, to stop in the middle of the task, the freedom to let go: "And God blessed the seventh day, and sanctified it: because *in it he had rested from all his work* which God created and made."

(And maybe I'll dare talk in the name of the fear of the first nights of the war. And in the name of the mothers. Lead the talk to the softness flooding my body. And only Claude, the only one in the hall, will know what place I'm talking from . . .)

And meanwhile, until the genetic test, fantasizing that you're the father of the child. That your seed has impregnated the Hut of my womb . . .

The drivers finish their meal. Get up, move chairs.

Glance at me: sitting alone at a table and writing at such an hour.

After two now. Got to go.

We'll continue our conversation on the road, anyway, Father, galloping in the night through Germany.

And the notes of *Don Giovanni* on the roads. The words of the Commendatore—"Your laugh will turn silent before dawn"—to Don Giovanni, who laughs until the end: "Long live freedom!"

From the distance, beyond the restaurant parking lot, the headlights of the passing cars slice the dark.

Again and again volleys of light approach, magnify the shadows of the bushes, and go off.

■ ■ ■ ■

[I stopped at the rest area at the side of the highway. Exhausted.]

The rain started after the border crossing. A black screen of vapor and water covers the road. Hard to see. The coating of spray off the trucks, blanketing the car for their whole length, gleaming for a long moment, blinding.

I lock the car from inside. It's really irresponsible exposing myself like this, a woman alone.

I seem to have dozed off. Maybe ten minutes. Fatigue won out. And now the softness. Spreading in the body. And I was overcome by a memory of the boys' arms, hugging me before I left. Jonathan clung "hard hard," holding me around the neck, and David whispered something in my ear, choking with laughter, covering me with a warm, sweet breath.

> I dreamed you were standing in an illuminated landscape of brand-new furrows. Wrapped in a prayer shawl. Before sunrise. I run behind you among the clods, see in the distance the pale wind ruffling your white hair. You show me something. Explain, perhaps. But I don't hear. Just a sweet thickness of a layer of seed poured on the tongue, filling the gullet. And the yearnings. A sharp blow.

I munched the chocolate bar I bought in the roadside restaurant. I already fastened the seatbelt, to start driving into the rain, which will go on all the way to Munich, it seems. And, again, taking the snapshots, only to tell you the joy now. For our whispering, Father. For all that is promised, spread out.

A flooding, gushing joy.

The body speaks in its own language. So soft.

I'll take our whispering with me on the road.

A p p e n d i x

Drawings and Maps
of the Site
of Mount Sabbatical and
the Settlement of Huts
on the Hill of Evil
Counsel, Jerusalem

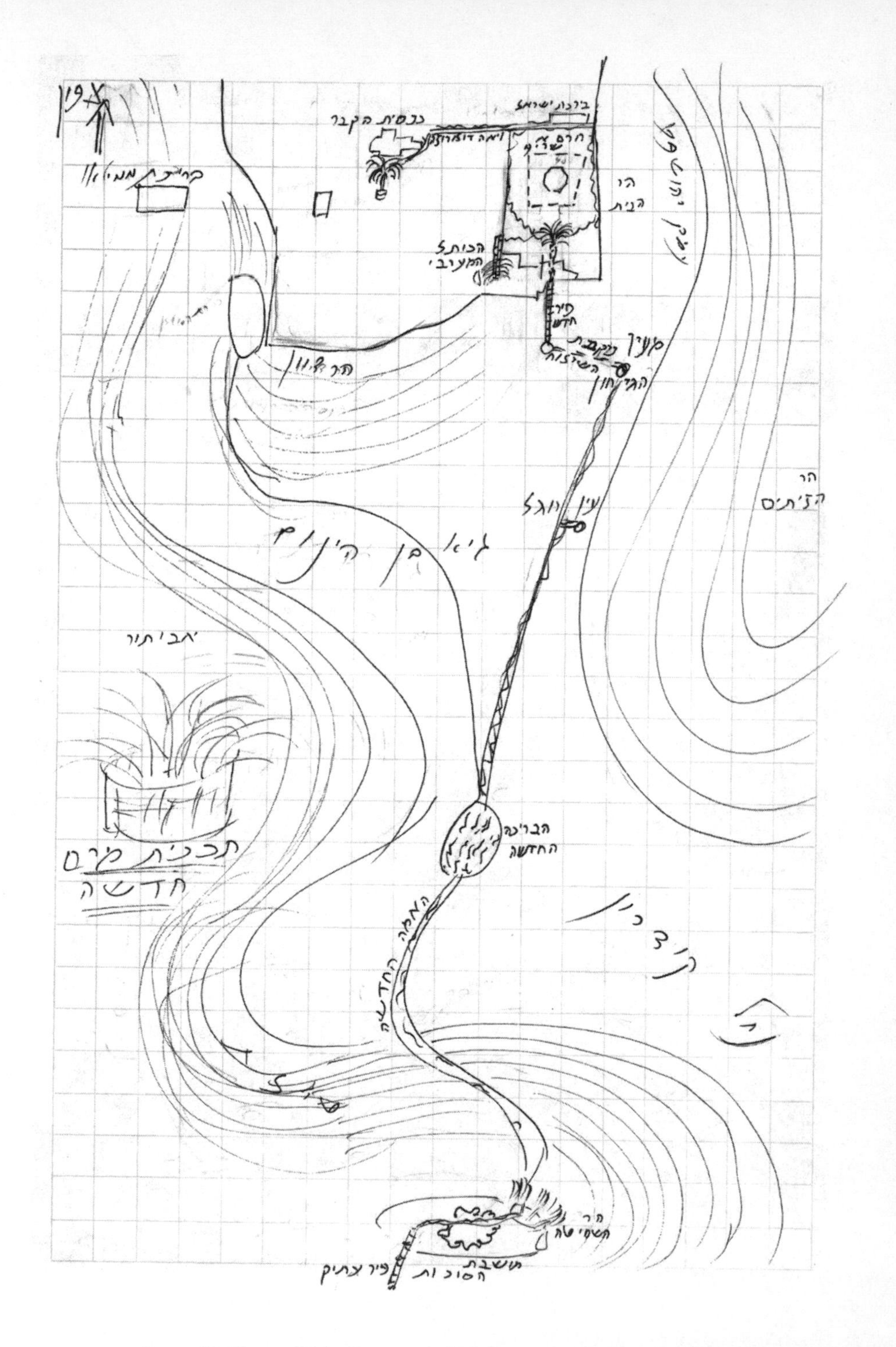

Site, Valley, Old City, and water, with fountains at Haram a-Sharif, Western Wall, and Saint Sepulcher

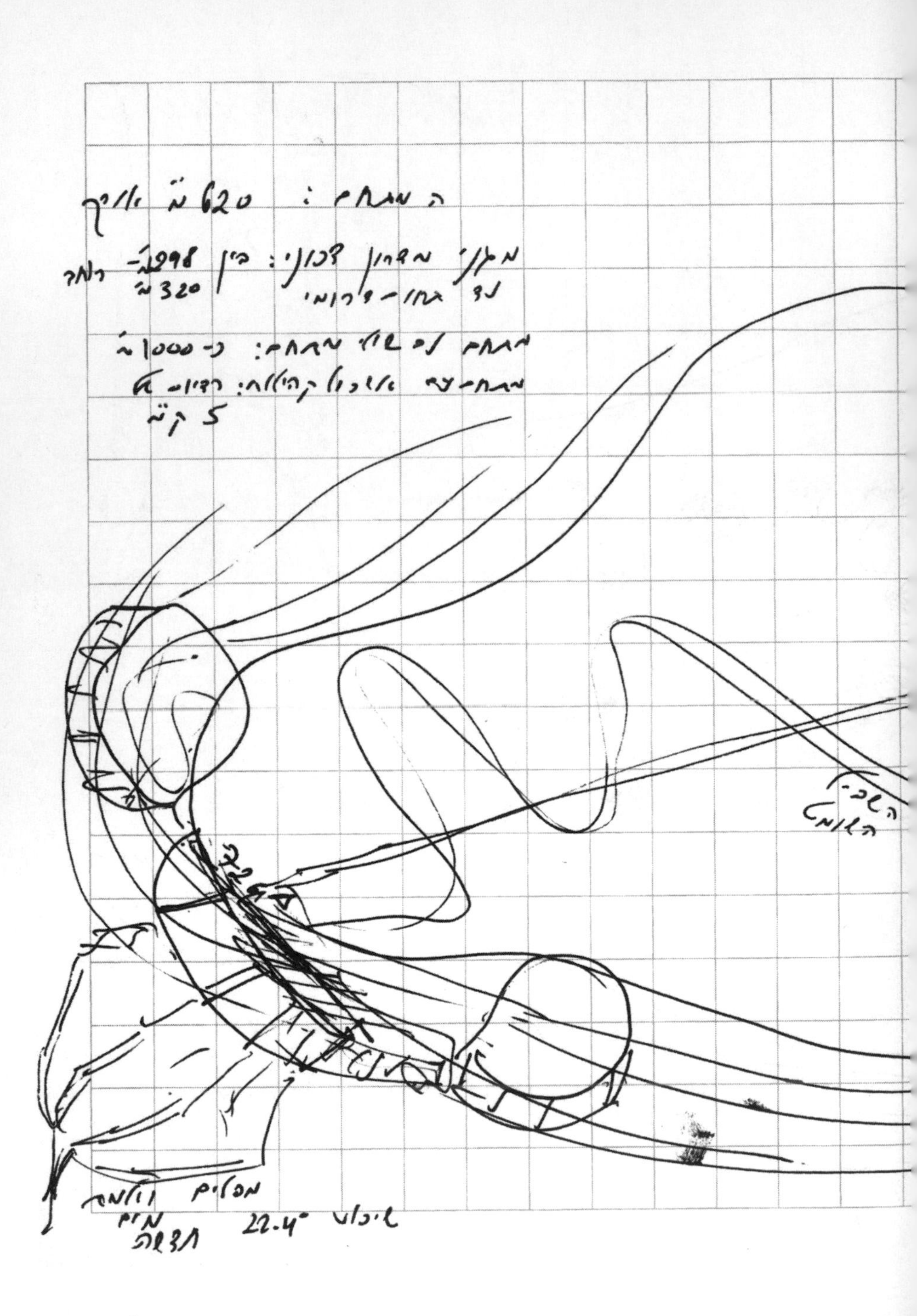

Site and water

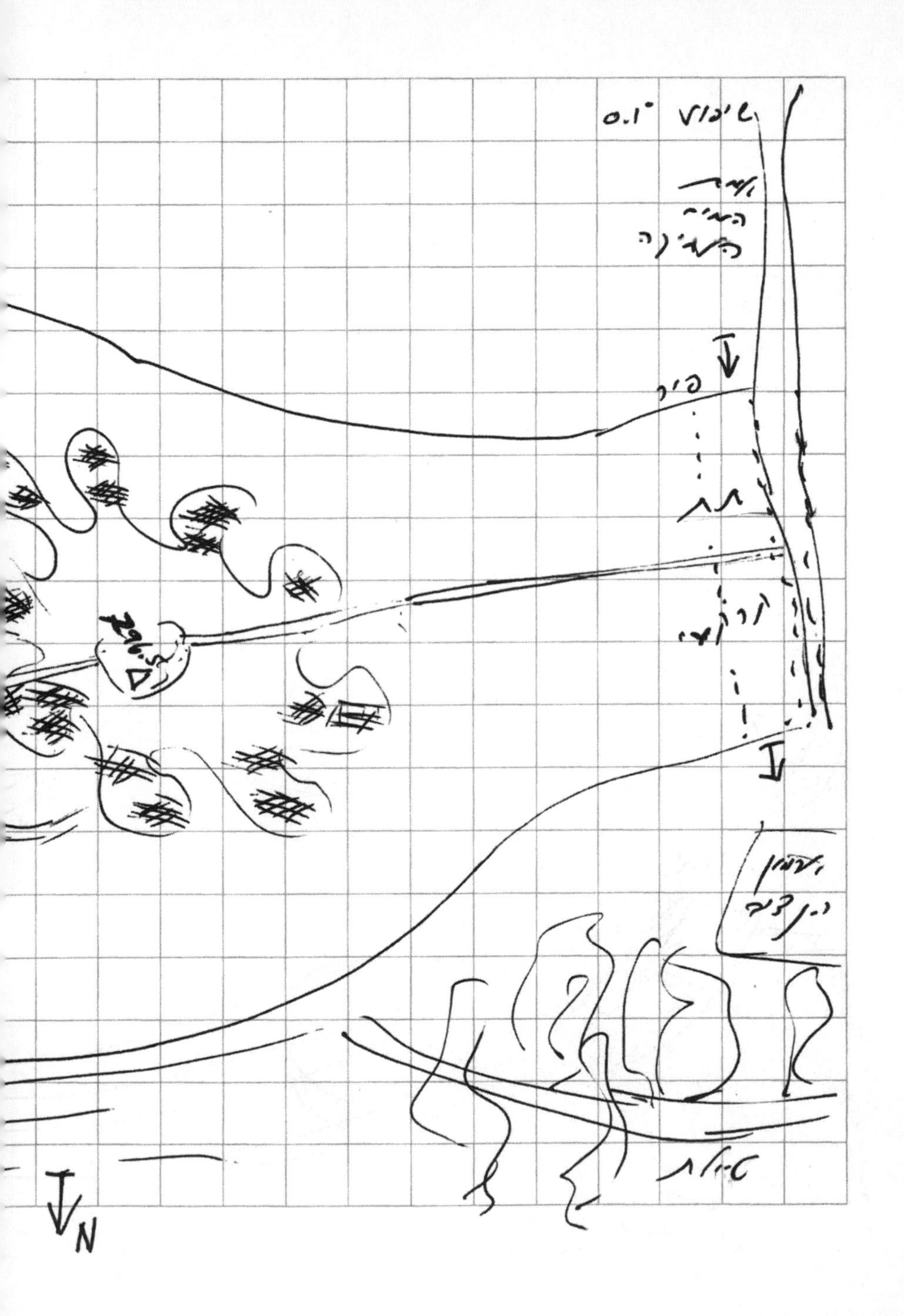
N

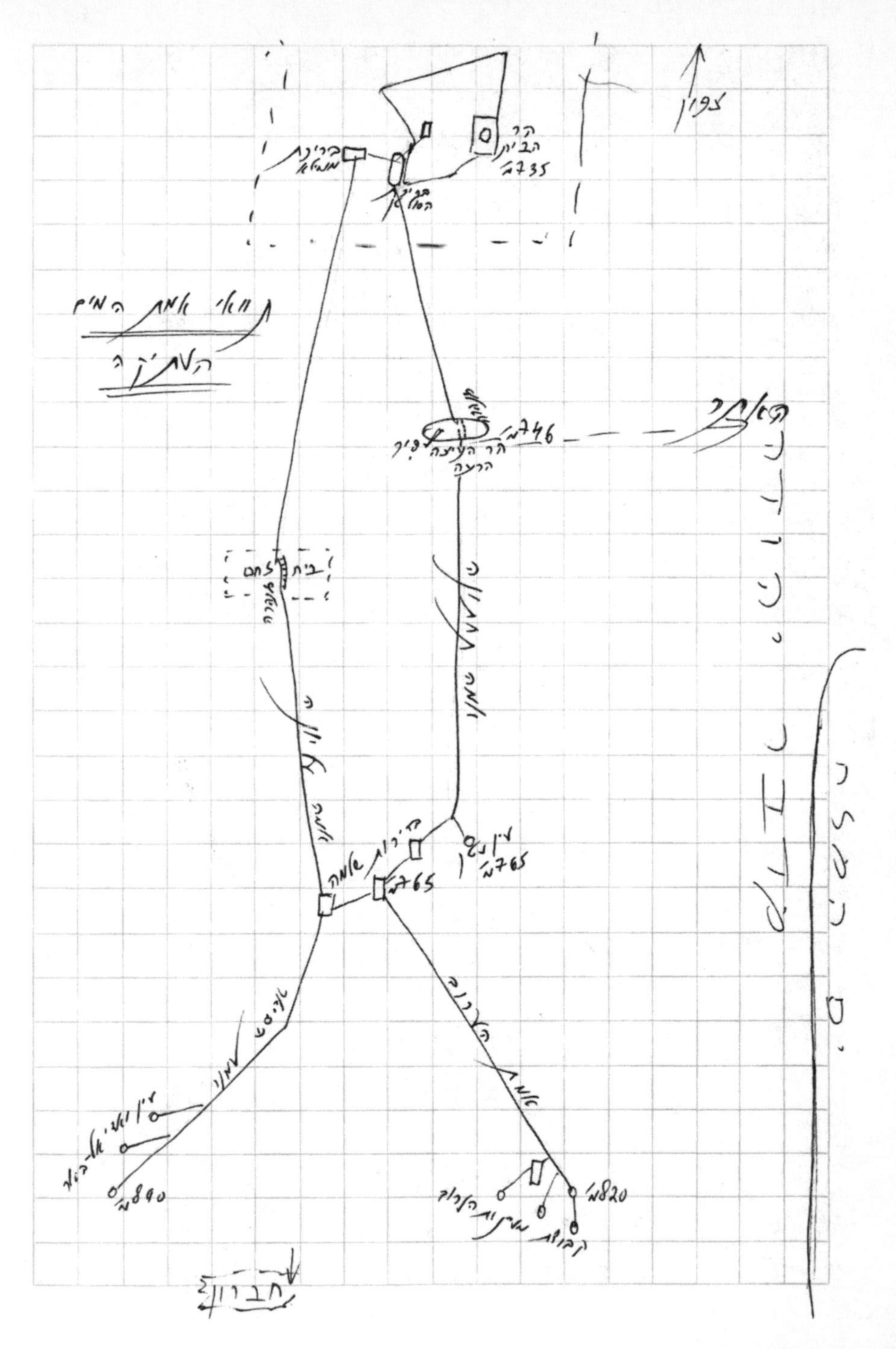

Ancient aqueduct from Hebron, via Bethlehem, to Temple Mount

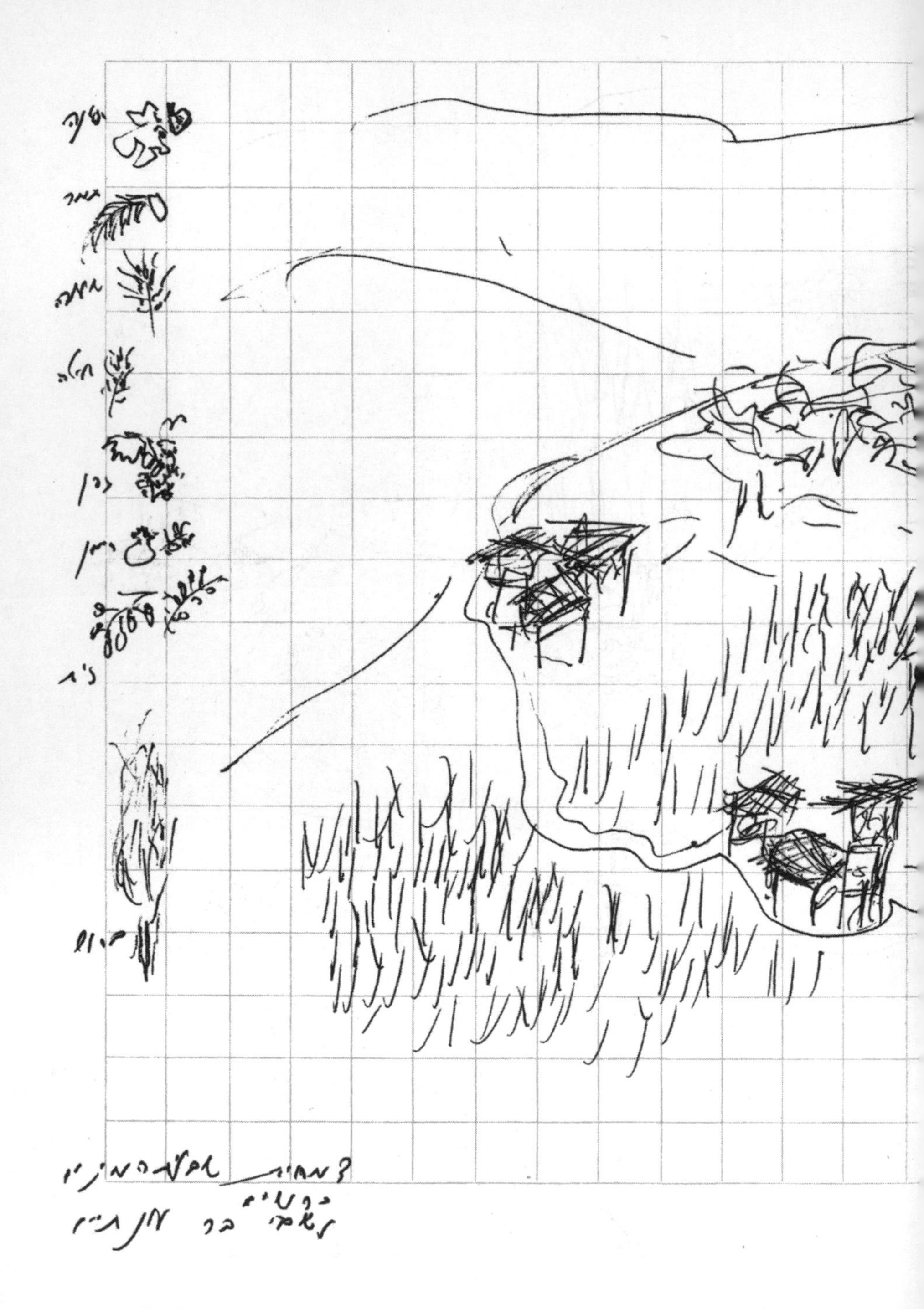

Site and plants

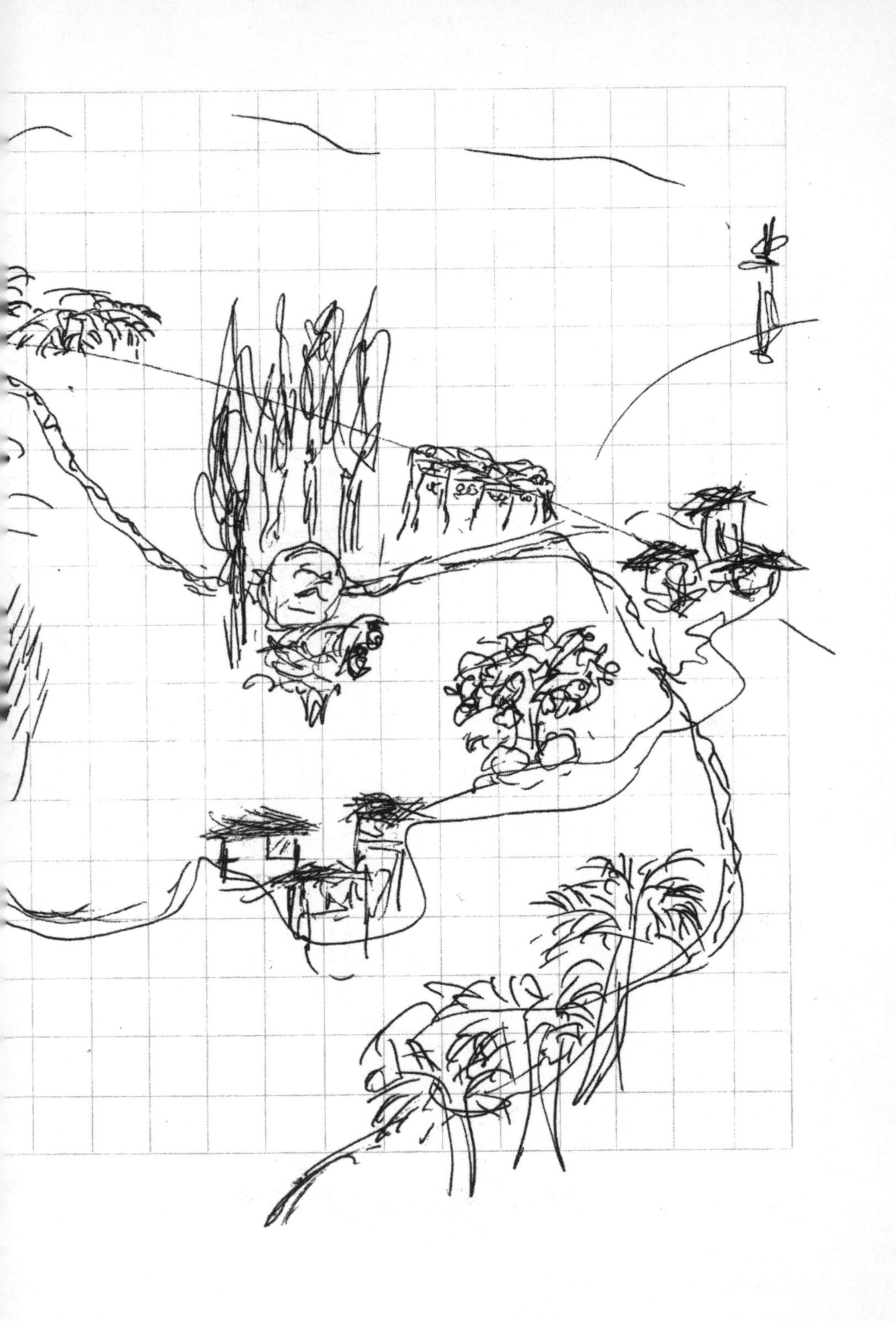

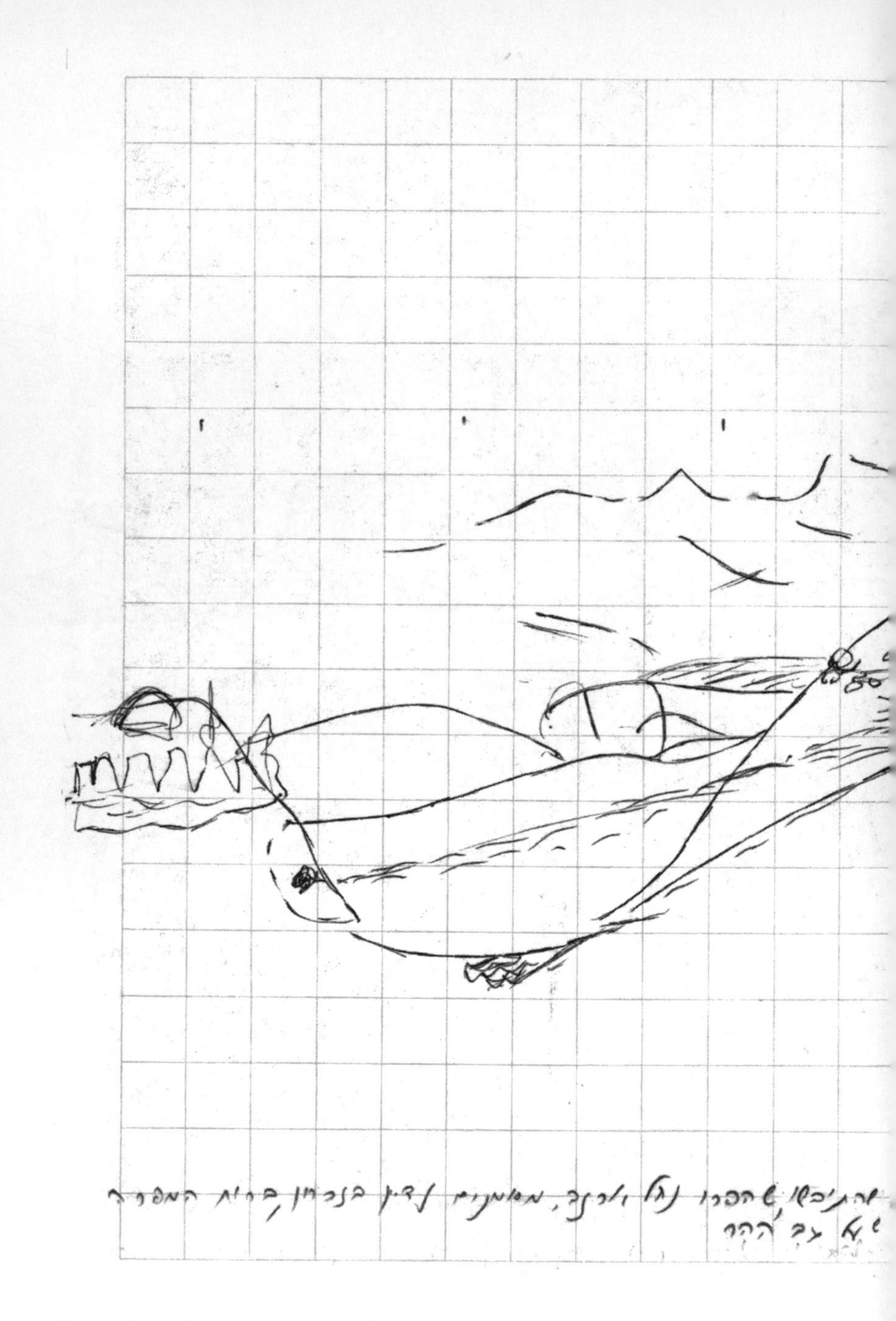

Site, Temple Mount, Moab Mountains

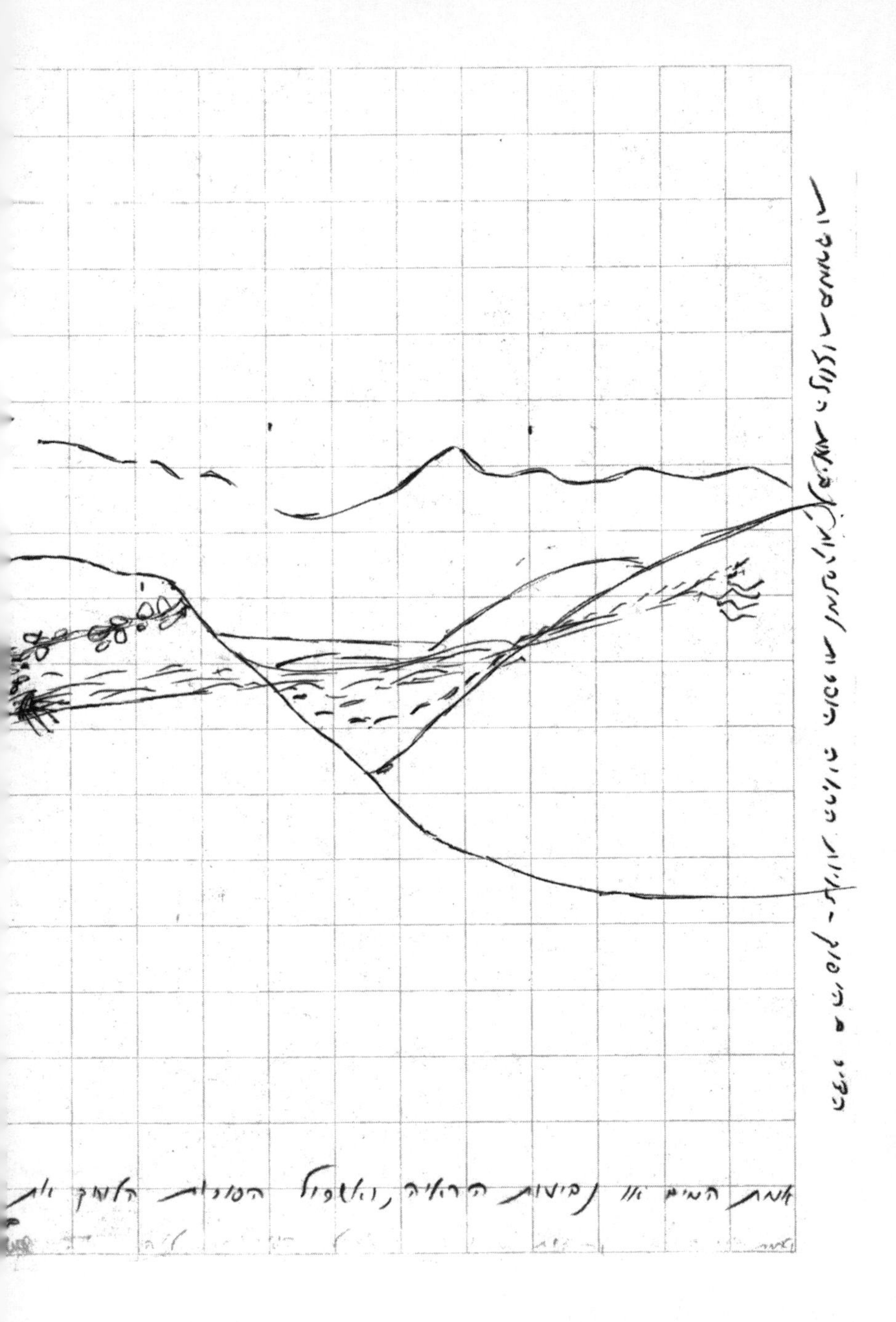

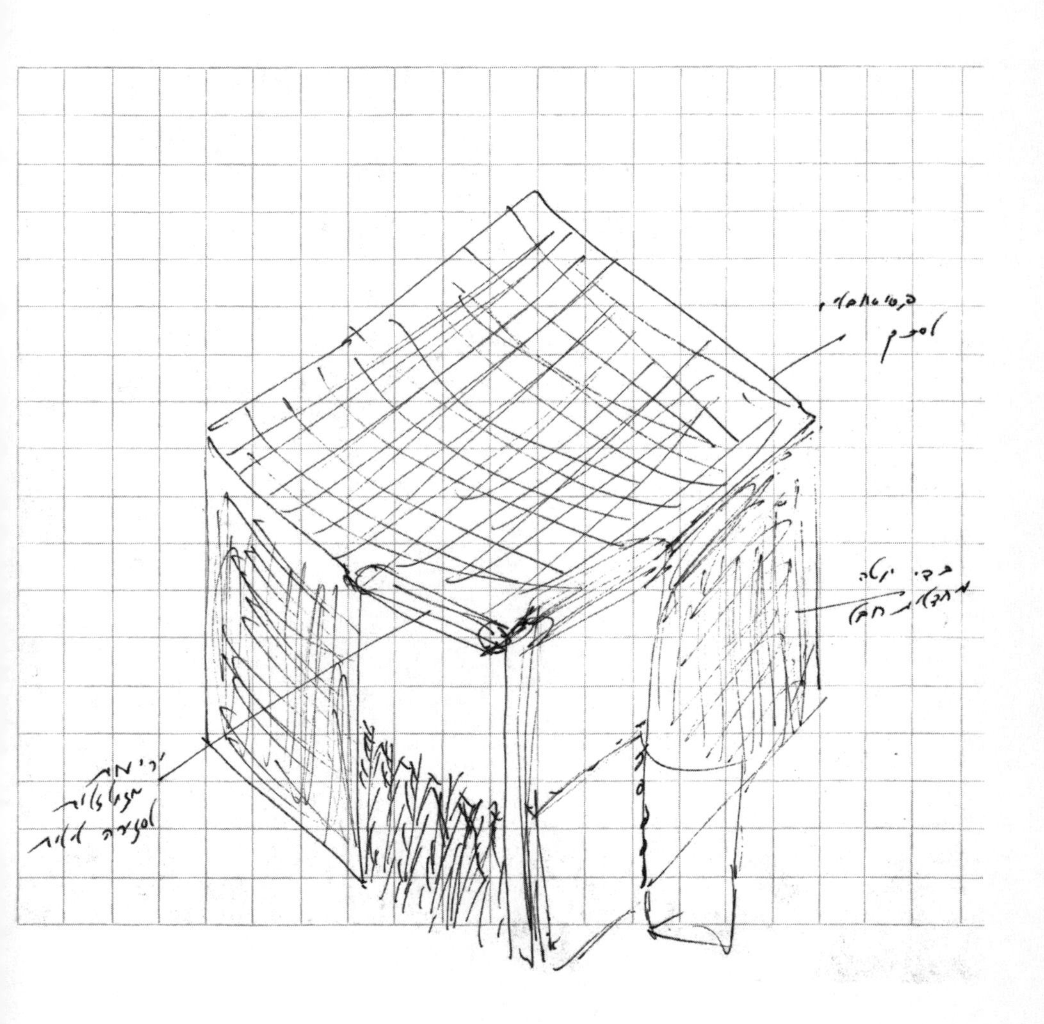

Sukkah

Shapes of Sukkah

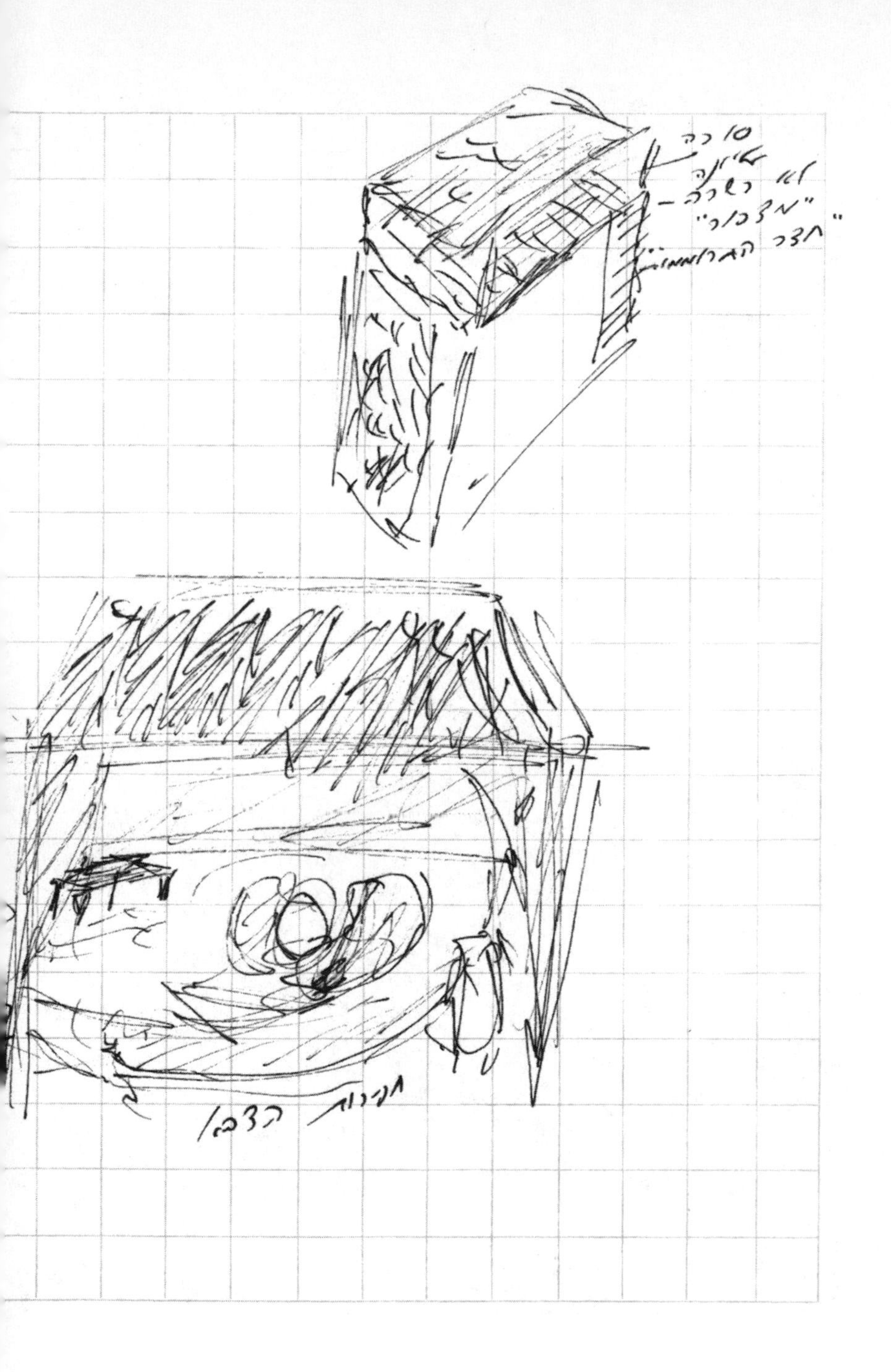
סוכה
עליונה
לא כשרה –
״מזכיר
חדר
מערות הזבל

Silhouette

ACKNOWLEDGMENTS

The writing of *Snapshots* began in a conversation with Jacques Derrida and continued in a conversation with the writings of my late father, Pinchas Govrin, and the formative stories of my beloved cousins Abraham Argov and Dikla Baidatz. Lindsay and David Shapiro built the architectural conversation, which led to a seminar at the Cooper Union School of Architecture, inspired by the spirit of John Hejduk. There, I developed the ideas of Ilana Tsuriel of Sukkah and Sabbatical Year and later in lectures at Kolot, Le Collège International de Philosophie, Rutgers University, and listening to the Jerusalem Seminar in Architecture, presided by Béatrice de Rothschild Rosenburg. Together with my students at the School of Visual Theater in Jerusalem, I experienced the joint creativity of Israelis and Palestinians, with faith that "the show must go on." I first went out to the landscape with Shalva Segal to make snapshots in words, and then I went out with my daughter, Rachel Schlomit Brezis, to photograph. Written and verbal exchanges with my friends and colleagues Aharon Appelfeld, Don DeLillo, Shlomith Rimmon-Kenan, David Rosenberg, Omar Yussuf, Amalia and Ron Margolin, Haviva Pedaya, and Peter Cole were a constant source of inspiration. My profound gratitude to Nili Mirski, the dedicated Hebrew-language editor of the novel; Julie Grau, who believed; Judith Graves Miller, who read; Sean McDonald, who sensitively edited all aspects of the English-language edition of the book; and Meighan Cavanaugh, for the elegant design. To my literary agent, Deborah Harris, for representing me and for our friendship, and Barbara

Harshav, who once again found the perfect American voice for my writing. Haim Brezis, my husband and companion, and our two daughters, Rachel Shlomit and Mirika, were with me on the way and in all ways.

The writing of *Snapshots* has crossed the events of history, which writes us all, and ended in the middle of two wars. The worse the situation has become, the more water—at least in words—has flowed in the aqueduct of Ilana Tsuriel's plan for a Monument to Peace in Jerusalem.

July 1993–December 2001